More Genie Problems

Can the Hero Billionaire Hold off Judgment Day?

by
Doctor MC, Mad Scientist
doctor_m_c@hotmail.com

Ὑπό Τῷ Ἥλιῷ

HYPO TO HELIO BOOKS
Houston

Paperback ISBN: 978-1-938293-34-4
Ebook ISBN: 978-1-938293-35-1

Front-cover render art by: Commotion22.

I wish to thank alpha-readers Debi Ennis-Binder and Commotion22 for their insightful comments.

Contact Doctor MC, Mad Scientist at: doctor_m_c AT hotmail DOT com

BISAC Subject Headings:
Fic002000—Fiction > Action & Adventure
Fic009010—Fiction > Fantasy > Contemporary
Fic009100—Fiction > Fantasy > Action & Adventure
Fic027030—Fiction > Romance > Fantasy
Rel000000—Religion > General

HYPO TO HELIO BOOKS, 2427 Clearbrook Dr., Missouri City, TX, 77489-6061

Prologue
Solomon Sets the Rules

(*MARVIN HARPER'S NOTE:* Things that happened to me are told in first person—"I did this," "I said this." Things that happened to people other than me are written in third person—"He did this," "She said this"—told with the knowledge of a mind-reading angel. Reader, I hope you don't find this confusing.)

Early morning
June 19, 632 B.C.
Inside Fatima's lamp

Seventeen hours and 22 minute had passed since Fatima of the Green Tribe of *Djinn* had been commanded to enter a brass lamp. No matter how hard she tried, she could not leave the lamp.

When Fatima made herself be solid but tiny, she could see light coming in through the spout of the lamp. So this meant that she could fly out, if she made herself small enough, right?

No. Every time she tried to fly out of the spout, she slammed into an invisible wall at the end. Maybe Kharmesh of the Blue Tribe could punch through *his* wall by muscle force, but Fatima had to use magic.

The problem was, magic was not working. Not one bit.

Fatima was pissed. She was now as magic-helpless as a wormfood (human); and Fatima was trapped in this stupid lamp, even though she had done nothing—

"BOUND *DJINN*, COME FORTH," Fatima heard the angel command.

That was when Fatima's problem turned into its opposite. Fatima did *not* want to talk to the wormfood king who had imprisoned her, nor did Fatima want to talk to the angel who, for whatever reason, was doing the wormfood king's bidding. But Fatima was unable to stop herself from green-smoking, and could not stop her green-smoke self from leaving her lamp and then de-smoking.

****

Seconds later
Royal bedchamber
In the palace of Solomon, King Of Israel

Five brass lamps, one unstoppered brass bottle, and Solomon's ruby ring were set on the floor. At the angel's command, Solomon watched smoke billow out of those seven Vessels—blue smoke, green smoke, pink, and brown.

The smoke reshaped itself into seven colored smoke-columns, which pulled in and reshaped themselves to become two *djinn* of the Blue Tribe, two *djinn* of the Green Tribe, two *djinn* of the Pink Tribe, and one *djinni* of the Brown Tribe.

The Pink Tribe female (Jerngert) looked nervous; the Brown Tribe male looked calm; and the other two female *djinn* and the other three male *djinn* were giving Solomon death-glares.

The five angry *djinn* were not quiet, either. Solomon heard many insults, and sometimes it was hard to keep a calm face. But the king smiled, amused, whenever he was called *wormfood*. Yes, he would die someday—so what?

The angel had been standing behind Solomon as he sat on his portable throne; the angel had said nothing as Solomon had been berated. Now the angel spoke: "SOLOMON, WISEST OF HUMANS, SHALL DECREE THE RULES OF YOUR SERVICE, AND HEAVEN WILL GIVE FORCE TO THOSE RULES. SHOW RESPECT TO

THIS HUMAN, FOR HE IS GRANTED AUTHORITY TO MAKE YOUR SERVICE BE EASY OR HARSH."

That quickly shut up the insulters!

The Green Tribe female, Fatima, said timidly, "Pardon me, human king, but I was the last *djinni* to be put into a brass lamp or brass bottle. So what is the Turd Tribe person doing here?" She flicked a finger to momentarily point toward the Brown Tribe male.

Before Solomon could answer, the Brown Tribe male did. He stood straight and said, "I am Roshradzam of the Brown Tribe, and we are as worthy as any other Tribe of *djinn*, though our powers be less."

This assertion was greeted with snorts and rolled eyes from the other bound *djinn*.

Roshradzam continued, "Why am I here? Because Hakeezib, Chief of the Blue Tribe of *Djinn*, threatened to water-swap the favorite concubine of Chief Thointorgos unless Brown Tribe sent a *djinni* to kill the human king. I was sent; I was unsuccessful."

"Because Brown Tribe beings are puny weaklings!" said Kharmesh of the Blue Tribe with a laugh. Kharmesh was the tallest *and* the most muscular *djinni* in the room.

Solomon smiled at the seven bound *djinn*. "I have a friend in high places"—Solomon gestured toward the angel—"who tipped me off that an assassin was coming. But since I didn't have any more brass Vessels and time was short, I had to put Roshradzam into my hollowed-out ruby ring. Sorry, Roshradzam, no disrespect intended."

Fatima looked shocked that Solomon had apologized to Roshradzam, when the human king had nothing to fear from the captured Brown Tribe *djinni*.

Solomon thought, *What, djinn have never heard of kindness, grace, and mercy toward a defeated opponent?*

****

The main reason that Roshradzam had not succeeded at his assassination was because Solomon had not been in bed at the time. Solomon had stayed awake till late the previous night, again and again rewriting the rules that the bound *djinn* would be compelled to obey.

Now there was no more reason to delay the bad news. Solomon reached inside his sash, pulled out the small scroll, and unrolled it.

Solomon read the rules to the seven bound *djinn*. The angel had nothing to say afterward; the bound *djinn* had much to say afterward. Yet Solomon did not waver.

Still, the bound *djinn* accepted the rules better than Solomon had expected. Jerngert, the Pink Tribe female, pointed out to the others that, while the master's nonmagical commands must be obeyed, each genie was free to ignore the master's orders and requests that the genie perform magic. Jerngert said, "This is a mercy that I wasn't expecting from the human king."

To which Fatima, Jerngert's friend in Green Tribe, added, "In addition, if a human tries to harm my master, I'm allowed to punish that human as I choose. I intend to choose some *creative* ways." Fatima's smile was scary.

****

Then Solomon had a thought. He looked at Roshradzam and asked (in Arabic), "Can you speak any other language besides Arabic?"

Roshradzam shook his head.

"Can you learn new languages quickly, like they can?" Solomon gestured to mean the other six genies.

Roshradzam's head-shake was emphatic.

Kharmesh and Sumera insulted Roshradzam; Solomon stopped listening.

Solomon looked at the angel. "Roshradzam has a problem with becoming a genie, and we need to fix it."

****

A minute later

Solomon looked at the bound *djinn* and asked, "So now that I've spoken the rules and Roshradzam's language problem is fixed, does anyone have questions?"

"I do," spit blue-skinned Sumera. "What do we do when all seven of us are owned by the same *djinni?* I want to puke, thinking about taking orders from Ashnadim or Sigvard." (Chiefs of, respectively, the Green Tribe and the Pink Tribe.)

Solomon smiled at her. "It is impossible for a *djinni* to grasp your Vessel or to rub it, so a free *djinni* cannot be your master. Only a human can."

"*Liar!* You're saying what I want to hear, but *I'll* be the one fetching Ashnadim's slippers."

Fatima said, "You're as stupid as a camel. A *djinni*'s forearms and hands turn to smoke if he touches your Vessel. Kharmesh, Jerngert, and I all saw it happen—go ahead, ask Kharmesh."

Sumera looked at big blue Kharmesh. Kharmesh shrugged.

"*Fine,*" Sumera replied. "So now I need only worry about a *wormfood* owning all seven of us bound *djinn*. My life is improved."

The angel replied, "AFTER THIS HOUR, YOUR VESSELS WILL BE SCATTERED. EVERY HUMAN ALIVE TODAY WILL BE CRUMBLED BONES WHEN NEXT YOU ARE GATHERED TOGETHER."

Sumera crossed her arms. "You think so, White Wings? Before this year is out, some human wizard or sorcerer will have tracked down our Vessels. You scattering the Vessels means only that the human must work harder, and cast more spells. Either sooner or not quite so soon, we seven will have one master."

"NOT SO," replied the angel. "YOUR VESSELS SHALL BE AS NOTHING TO HUMAN MAGIC, *DJINN* MAGIC, AND DEMON MAGIC. ONLY HEAVEN WILL KNOW WHERE A BOUND *DJINNI'S* VESSEL IS. FEAR NOT."

Sumera had no more loud words of reply. But Solomon heard her mutter, "I wouldn't count out demon magic so quickly, angel. Those demons know a thing or two."

****

Of the seven bound *djinn*, Fatima became Solomon's favorite (though he would never tell her this). Fatima was outspoken, like Kharmesh; but like Jerngert, Fatima would *think*. (Or rather, *sometimes* Fatima would think. She had a lot of anti-human prejudice that she refused to question.)

Fatima asked Solomon, "How do we become free *djinn* again? Or are we stuck like this till Judgment Day?"

Solomon turned around to look at the angel. The angel announced, "AS SOLOMON DOTH SPEAK IT, SO SHALL IT BE."

Solomon's father, King David, had warned him that there would be days like this.

Now Solomon thought hard. The others waited silently.

Then Solomon spoke: "You *djinn* will be freed before Judgment Day, I promise you. You all will be freed on the day that all your Tribes prove worthy of your freedom."

The seven bound *djinn* looked puzzled by this prophecy.

Chapter 1
The Lost Election

AUTHOR'S NOTE: Characters Susie (Susan) Cooper and Tim Hanson have appeared in my novels *Names Have Power* and *Three More Wishes*.

****

October 6, 2016 (Thursday night)
Local chapter, Abzug Society

Michelle Landrieu-LeClerc sat on a brown folding chair and hated Marvin Harper for the 7,846th time in six years.

Jane Yancy-Miller was running unopposed for the Treasurer position, so she was chosen to moderate the election for chapter Chairperson.

There had been a time when Michelle had likewise been unopposed when she'd run for Chairperson of the local chapter—but that was before Marvin Harper had become famous as the "hero billionaire."

Now in 2016, when it came to Michelle being re-elected Chairperson, that *man* Marvin Harper had messed things up for her, *again*—

Michelle now had a challenger for the Chairperson seat: Gertrude Price-Weatherby. And Gertrude was running on a platform of "Marvin Harper is not our enemy."

Now Jane walked to the lectern and banged the gavel. "Women, each candidate for Chairperson will speak for two minutes, then we will vote. Ms. Price-Weatherby won the coin-toss and chose to speak last. So Ms. Landrieu-LeClerc, please come forward now."

After taking the lectern, Michelle looked into every face. "I am Mitchell Landrieu-LeClerc, and you know me. I have been active of this chapter of the Abzug Society for fifteen years, since my daughters entered middle school."

As Michelle took a breath, she noticed: *A lot more women here are wearing a lot more makeup than they did in 2010.* Six years ago, no woman in this chapter would have dared wear anything more than muted-color lipstick, like Michelle herself wore.

What does this mean? she wondered.

A worried part of her brain replied, *It means that they're not your minions anymore. You can't count on their votes.*

Michelle shoved down that worry, and went back to speaking:

"I have been tireless in the struggle to give my daughters a world of equality for women. I will not allow any man, no matter how admirable he seems, to take our rights from us. I do not trust Marvin Harper, and you should flee any woman who says we can peacefully coexist with him. Many find him charming, and he is generous with his money, but the fact remains: Marvin Harper is a dedicated, resource-rich, and seductive agent of *Patriarchy.* Good grief, he has a *harem!* He is dangerous to our cause, for as long as he breathes."

Thus Michelle ended her speech; she did not ask for the women of the chapter to vote for her. With head held high, she walked from the lectern to her chair and sat down.

Seconds later, it was Gertrude at the microphone: "*Michelle* here has many times listed Marvin Harper's faults and sins. Let me point out one of his virtues. When one of his harem girls, Kristin Curry, was told that Marvin would pay for all her college expenses, she told him where she wanted to attend: *Smith College.* That's right, the one in Northampton, Massachusetts. And once she got there, you can bet that not one student there, or professor, told Ms.

Curry that she had to bake cookies for the rest of her life and stand by her man."

Gertrude looked into every pair of eyes, though she only glanced into Michelle's. "Ms. Curry now has a degree from Smith, without borrowing one dollar of student loans or flipping one burger. According to *The Sophian*, Harper did not try to talk Ms. Curry into a different school when she asked for very expensive, very feminist Smith College."

Gertrude made eye contact again, then resumed her speech. "Michelle is abrasive. How many women of this chapter has Michelle expelled for failing to uphold feminist purity? Virgilia O'Keefe, Bellina Mott, Rivka Goldheim, and I'm sure I'm forgetting others. Remember when Michelle called Susan Cooper a bimbo and a disgrace, and Susan denounced Michelle as a 'man-hater with anger issues' just before she loudly *quit?* These women whom Michelle kicked out or drove away, where have they gone? Except for Susan Cooper, they all joined Marvin Harper's harem. The LeClerc twins are shacking up with him right now! Though oddly, *they* haven't been drummed out of our chapter."

"Thirty seconds," Ms. Yancy-Miller said.

Gertrude looked into everyone's eyes for the last time. "Marvin Harper has not yet chosen to become our enemy. But *as* our enemy, he would be formidable, perhaps unbeatable. Elect me, and he will never become our enemy. But re-elect Michelle, and war with him is only a matter of time. Why is this bad? A public-relations war with the 'hero billionaire' is something the Abzug Society cannot win, and feminism cannot afford to lose more support."

Seconds later, it was Jane, not Gertrude, at the lectern. Jane banged the gavel and announced, "It's time to vote."

****

Across the city, the next morning (Friday)
At Tim Hanson Ford, off Smith Freeway

Almost every Friday morning, I climbed into my car and drove from my mansion to Tim Hanson Ford.

By no coincidence, Friday mornings were when Tim Hanson Ford had the fewest customers.

At the car dealership, there was a separate small building where the dealer had his office. That building was tiny, since it held only Tim Hanson's office, his receptionist's desk outside his office, a postage-stamp-sized breakroom, and a conference room.

I parked my gold Mustang near the door to this tiny building; seconds later, I was walking in the door.

Even before my eyes adjusted, I heard a mega-cheerful female voice: "Good morning, Mr. Harper! I hope you're having a wonderful, *wonderful* day!"

The speaker was Susie (*née* Susan) Cooper, Tim's receptionist. Her blond hair was fake, her large tits were real, the blue ribbon in her hair was satin, and her big, friendly smile was ever-present.

There was a time, before I met her, when Susie did not smile at all. Furthermore, I am told Susie was very unpleasant to any human male.

The reason that Susie now looked and acted like the ultimate bimbo receptionist was the same reason why I, Marvin Harper the "hero billionaire," spent my Friday mornings hanging out with a car dealer in his office.

Tim Hanson and I were friends because we shared a unique situation: We both had magical mind-control powers, and we tried to do right by the people we mind-controlled. I had been given my powers by a genie wish; Tim had been given mind-control powers as a reward by the Golden God.

In Tim's case, whatever mind-rewriting he did was irreversible. Tim had accidentally reprogrammed Susan, his ultrafeminist receptionist, and bimbo Susie was the result.

Bimbo Susie now was looking at me and smiling. I replied, "I am indeed having a wonderful day, and you're looking great. Will you please let Tim know I'm here?"

"Sure. He's at the Service Garage now, though I don't expect him to be gone long." Susie picked up her desk phone, and spoke briefly with Tim via his smartphone.

After Susie hung up, she theatrically looked left and right, as though checking for eavesdroppers, and said, "The Abzug Society's local chapter had an election last night. *You* were the main campaign issue. And Mitchell—"

"You mean *Michelle*—"

"—Michelle lost the election. She's out, she's only a peon now, too-bad-so-sad."

I laughed. "Feeling a little vindictive, are we?"

Susie smiled, but the smile was cruel. "Six years ago, in front of the *entire group*, she called me a 'bimbo man-pleaser' and 'a disgrace to the cause.' She was seconds away from kicking me out when I quit. But now she's no longer the big cheese here. Do you want to know what *really* delights me?"

"What?"

"Gertrude—she's who won—reminded the members that Michelle's twin daughters aren't living with *her*, they're living with *you!*"

I made a rocking-hand gesture. "Not at the moment. I've sent the twins on an all-expenses-paid trip to France."

Chapter 2
Elvira Finds a Lamp

Late afternoon Friday, local time
In the French countryside

Almira LeClerc was driving a rental car, with her sister Elvira in the passenger seat. The American twins were headed to a family reunion—with French "family" whom they had never met. Fortunately, both sisters were fluent in schoolbook French.

With only the twins in the rental car, they spoke American English—

Almira asked, "Why do you think she did it, Marvin's old aunt Claire? Why she pushed Marvin to give us this trip to France?"

Elvira replied, "Maybe she likes France? After all, *Claire* is a French name. What's really weird is how, once old Claire convinced Marvin to help us take this trip, Marvin needed only one short phone call for our parole officer to go along."

Almira shrugged. "Why is it weird? Marvin Harper deserves to be served, and everyone realizes this." Then she laughed. "Everyone except you, Elvie. Though you've gotten along much better with him and everybody else in the past two years."

Elvira said, "Everybody except *Mother*." The twins laughed.

Elvira added, "I've been trying hard to be a good person these last two years. But I never imagined that I would be rewarded with a trip to, ohmigod, *France!* And we get to use Marvin Harper's credit card while we're doing it."

Almira grinned. "Yeah, we tour France, we meet *arrière grand-père* Armand's relatives, and the 'hero billionaire' pays for everything. Life is good." Then Almira eyed the dark clouds ahead. "Except that we're headed into nasty rain. And these roads are not good."

****

As Almira had predicted, soon rain fell on the French countryside. Minutes later, the rain was *pouring* down.

Just as the rain started to *blast* down, the car passed a construction site. (Which was an odd thing to see, as Mlle. Fontaine had explained in high-school French class.)

The blasting rain slowed the car's speed to a crawl. Looking through the car's windows, even with the wipers going their fastest, was for Elvira like looking through shower-door glass.

Still, she could make out a man at the construction site, who was wearing a white hard hat. Elvira saw him make a throat-slash gesture. Then all the men at the site (including Monsieur Hard-Hat) dashed for their cars.

From the driver's seat, Almira said, "I can't drive in this. We're two kilometers from a village. I'll head there and hope they have an inn for travelers."

Elvira said, "That will make us late to the reunion."

Almira shrugged. "Not if we get rolling tomorrow at dawn."

The village was too small to have an inn. The good news was, the village had a villager who would rent the twins a room for the night. The bad news was, the rain was still blasting; Elvira was soaked to the skin before she'd moved ten feet from the rental car.

****

Once the twins had a room to themselves, Elvira yearned to frolic with her twin sister. But Almira was tired, or so she claimed. Elvira sighed.

****

Early the next morning (Saturday), local time

It was not yet dawn, but the eastern sky was bright when the twins climbed back in their car. To get back to the road on which Almira had been driving when the rain had hit, the rental car now drove past the construction site.

Elvira saw a bright-yellow reflection where she was not expecting it. She yelled, "Almie, stop the car! *Stop, stop!*"

The car screeched to a halt. "What's wrong? What's wrong?" Almie asked, sounding frightened.

"The construction site, there's a big pile of dirt there. I see a teapot sticking out of the dirt."

"You're making us late for a *teapot?*" Almira rolled her eyes. "Besides, teapots mean England, not France. Which is where *we* are."

"It's yellow metal, and it has a handle. It's an antique teapot."

"How do you know it's antique?"

"Remember what Mlle. Fontaine told us in class? In France, they don't tear down a building until they have to. See that burned lumber? See that pile of scorched bricks? *Who knows* how long that house stood before they had to tear it down. That teapot could be *centuries* old!"

"So what? Neither of us drinks tea."

"Jeez, twin, use your brain. It'll be a unique souvenir of our trip to France, not some mass-produced trinket."

Almira's voice got stern. "You want to quote Mlle. Fontaine? She *also* said that the French have crazy laws that we don't have, about old stuff. And we're *parolees*. Marvin wouldn't like me if you and I got arrested for stealing a teapot."

Elvira replied, "Twin, this burned-down house used to belong to someone. He or she could have grabbed the teapot at any time. They didn't."

"But that doesn't mean that *we—*"

"*It's not stealing!* But if we sit here, gabbing about it, the construction crew will come back and I'll lose my chance. Construction guys work from sunrise to sunset, remember?"

"Which means that if you get out of the car, somebody could come along in the next few minutes, and then we both might get arrested."

Elvira rolled her eyes. "I *know* you, Almie. You don't give a shit about the laws of France, only about the laws of Marvin Harper."

"The last time you wanted to do something on your own and I let you, the result was Anna Kay and us getting kidnapped by gangsters."

"No gangsters are near *here*, just French construction guys. Who are headed this way even as we speak."

Almira said, "*Fine.* Go. But if the car gets dirty and we get charged extra, you're paying Marvin back."

As Elvira was slip-sliding on the muddy ground in the pre-dawn light, she muttered, "Jeez, Almie, you were *gutsy* six years ago. Now you're a total scaredy-cat."

****

When Elvira pulled the handled brass thing out of the pile of dirt (which was now a pile of mud), she knew instantly that she was not holding a teapot.

She also knew instantly what the brass lamp *might* be.

But Elvira did not rub it with her hand. She was not even slightly tempted. Not because she wasn't curious, but because the brass lamp was so *yucchy* with all that mud.

Instead of rubbing the mud off the brass lamp with her hand, Elvira walked over to some still-wet grass, and dragged the brass lamp around by its handle till the lamp was clean.

When Elvira returned to the rental car with her prize in hand, she saw Almira staring at her through the glass.

When Elvira opened the car door, Almira blurted, "Holy shit, you found a motherfucking *genie lamp!* Rub it, rub it!"

"No way. The construction crew will be here any minute, remember? I'll rub the lamp later."

"Arrggh!" Almira replied.

****

The twins reached the city of Clermont-Ferrand a little after ten o'clock, and found the family reunion soon after.

But the twins didn't join the reunion, not yet. Elvira suggested that they find a local hotel first. "So while we're talking to all our new aunts and uncles, we don't have to worry about our suitcases being stolen out of the car."

Almira smirked. "Ri-i-ight, you're worried about *suitcases* getting stolen out of the car."

"I don't think it's a genie lamp. It got rubbed clean, and no genie came out."

Yet when the twins brought their suitcases (and the brass lamp) into their hotel room, Elvira made sure to lock the brass lamp inside the emptiest of her suitcases. Elvira told herself that her reason was that the brass lamp was a unique souvenir, and she didn't want to lose it.

"You know," Almira said casually, "you don't need to deprive yourself; it's okay to unlock that suitcase now and to satisfy your curiosity."

Elvira said, "Our relatives know we're here. They expect us to reappear soon at the reunion. I'll rub the lamp later."

"Arrggh!" Almira replied.

****

Much later, hours after dark Saturday, local time

When the twins returned to their hotel room after spending hours at the reunion, they were tipsy.

Almira said, "Here's your chance. Grab the lamp, rub it, and let's find out if there's a genie in there."

"No way," Elvira said. "I'm tired and I'm drunk. That genie would eat me for breakfast. Speaking of breakfast, morning seems like a good time to see what I've got."

"Dammit, twin, I've been wondering all day whether that brass lamp is the real deal. Now I'm gonna have to wonder all *night*, too?"

"Yep," Elvira replied, grinning drunkenly. "Remember, I'm the person who dipped your Barbie in black paint. I can be a bitch sometimes."

"Arrggh!"

****

The next morning (Sunday), local time

After both twins had taken showers, Almira asked, "*Now* are you going to rub the lamp?"

Elvira grinned. "Certainly not. I'm dressed only in a towel. If there *is* a genie in there, he deserves for me to be dressed more respectfully, don't you think?"

"Arrggh!"

But an hour and a half later, Elvira was dressed, her hair and makeup were done, and the twins had eaten breakfast. Elvira had all her suitcases unlocked by then.

With her left hand, Elvira reached into the suitcase that had the lamp in it, and grabbed the brass lamp by its handle. Elvira stood and faced Almira.

Elvira said, "I don't think anything will happen. But here goes."

Elvira rubbed the brass lamp with her right hand.

The brass lamp shook in Elvira's hand like a frantic rat were trapped inside of it. *Then—*

A plug of mud shot out of the spout of the lamp, hitting Almira full in the face.

SPLAT!

Almira ran off to the bathroom then, to wash her face (as Elvira called out laughing apologies).

So Almira did not see lots and lots of blue smoke billow out of the lamp, and Almira was not there with Elvira when the blue smoke turned into a blue woman.

Chapter 3
Sumera Drops a Bomb

AUTHOR'S NOTE: Events referred to in these next two chapters took place in Chapter 28 of *Three More Wishes: Be Kind to Your Genie.*

****

Still Sunday

Elvira saw that the genie's skin was light blue. Her hair, which was pulled up into a bun, was dark blue, as were her eyebrows. Her eyes were not merely blue, but *glowing* blue. She wore Middle Eastern clothing, including harem pants and silk slippers—all of which were blue.

The genie-woman looked at Elvira, sighed deeply, and said, *"Bonjour, Maîtresse. Je suis Sumera, ligoté djinni de la lampe, ici d'accorder trois vœux à vous."*

"Holy shit, you're real!" Elvira said.

The genie frowned. Elvira figured out that Sumera might not know English.

Elvira might have shot her mouth off in French then, and spoken her wishes *bam-bam-bam,* if the genie had not *sighed.* That sigh said to Elvira, *Granting this human's wishes is an unpleasant task, so let's get it over with.* A genie with such an attitude would not help Elvira if Elvira worded her wishes poorly.

So instead of wishing, Elvira said, *"Plus tard, mes vœux."* Later, my wishes. *"Parlez-vous anglais?"*

"No, Mistress," Sumera replied in French.

"Holy shit, a real genie!" Almira exclaimed in English.

Sumera turned around. Wet-faced Almira was standing by the bathroom door, staring back at Sumera.

When Sumera turned to face Elvira again, Elvira said in French, "She is Almira, my twin. Almira LeClerc. I am Elvira LeClerc. Can you tell us apart?"

It was a simple question; Elvira expected a simple answer.

****

To Elvira's question, Sumera replied, "It's easy to tell you two apart. You each have a spellmark, and your spellmarks are different."

Elvira said, "What do you mean? What is a 'spellmark'?"

"Someone has cast a spell on each of you—"

"*WHAT?*" Almira and Elvira said together.

"—and all I know is that the spells have different sources. Your sister's spell came from a *djinni*; while *your* spell, Mistress, came from a being who is not a *djinni*."

"What are the spells on us?" Almira demanded.

Elvira said, "Who cast spells on us? Find out, find out!"

"*No*," said Sumera. "That is a magical request, and I may refuse to obey a magical request. Now if you were to *wish* for answers to your questions—"

Almira glared at the blue genie. "You're just trying to get Elvie to use up a wish."

Elvira said to Sumera, "You can refuse a magical request? What *can't* you refuse?"

Sumera clenched her fists and gritted her teeth, and her body shook, rather than answer the question.

But soon Sumera said, "I cannot refuse nonmagical requests. And unless you ask a question that can be answered only by me using magic, I must answer any question you ask with the truth."

"Except the questions we *really* want answered," Elvira said. "Quite a loophole you've got, Sumera."

"Yes, you're a big help, blue genie," Almira said, disgusted. "You tell me a genie cast a spell on me, and won't tell me more. Trouble is, I've never met a genie before."

That's when Elvira thought of something. "Almie, I know who the genie is."

"Who? *Who?* Tell me!"

"Actually, I *don't* know. But I have a *really* strong gut feeling."

"*Twin!* Say his name. *Now.*"

"It's—"

FOOM. Green light flashed, and now there was a fourth female in the hotel room.

"*Fatima?*" Almira blurted.

"*Fatima,*" Sumera sneered.

Fatima, who was casually dressed all in green, gave blue genie Sumera only a glance. Then Fatima's eyes locked on Elvira's brass lamp.

Fatima looked up from Elvira's hand to Elvira's face. "Oh, *shit,*" Fatima said.

Chapter 4
The Hotel Room Gets Crowded

Still Sunday

Sumera said something to Fatima in a foreign language. To Elvira, Sumera's words sounded insulting.

Fatima said to Sumera, "I do not have the time for your stupidity"—speaking in sixteenth-century French.

"You really are a genie?" Almira asked Fatima in English.

"*Shit*," Fatima said.

Elvira asked in English, "What are you doing here?"

Fatima replied, "Entertainment—I came here to watch Sumera be forced to grant wishes. But now I have to work."

Fatima reached into a pocket of her green-denim jeans and pulled out her smartphone.

Elvira saw that Sumera was frowning. Fatima noticed this too. Instead of Fatima making her phone call, she asked Elvira, "Does Sumera understand English?"

It was Almira who answered: "No, because Sumera is too lazy to learn, I'm sure. She's already informed Elvie she doesn't have to obey magical requests."

Fatima rolled her eyes. In sixteenth-century French, she advised Elvira, "Order Sumera to memory-read you. She may not refuse to do that."

Elvira commanded Sumera thus, not sure what she was ordering. Sumera glared at Fatima, then reached out a blue hand to touch Elvira's forehead.

Then life for Elvira turned weird.

****

When Elvira finished reliving her entire life at high speed, she discovered that Marvin Harper was standing next to Fatima in the hotel room.

Marvin was yawning, his hair was mussed, and the buttonholes of his shirt were mismatched with the buttons.

The sunlight through the windows seemed to Elvira to be the same as before. "How long was I out?" she asked.

"Five minutes, maybe more," Almira said. "I was scared shitless, till Marvin told me he's gone through the same process lots of times."

"So *you* are the famous Marvin Harper, master of Fatima," Sumera said in sarcastic English. She dropped a curtsy. "I am *so* pleased to meet you at last."

Elvira put her fists on her hips then. "Now that we're all *here* and we're all *acquainted* and we all *speak English*, would *someone*—Sumera, Fatima, Marvin, I don't give a rat's ass who—tell me, WHEN AND WHERE AND HOW AND WHY MY TWIN SISTER AND I GOT SPELLMARKS ON US, AND WHAT THE SPELLS DO."

"Jeez," said Marvin, rubbing his face with one hand, "and I have to answer this on four hours' sleep."

Then Marvin looked each twin in the eye. "*Why* is simple: Because you two were out of control. *When* and *where* is even simpler: the party."

There was no need for Marvin to specify *which* party. May 15, 2010, the LeClerc twins had been arrested for drug possession, at the costume party to which Marvin had been invited and which the twins had party-crashed.

Now Marvin said, "But the *how* and the *what* of you two getting spells put on you, those take some explaining."

Chapter 5
Fanzelle

Meanwhile, back in the USA (Sunday)

The local time was several hours past midnight, and Michelle Landrieu-LeClerc was deeply asleep. But though she was sleeping, *no way* was she resting as she dreamed—

Michelle is standing on a featureless plain—no buildings, no hills, no lakes, no grass or trees. In front of Michelle are thousands of men.

She sees a man with gray hair and trimmed gray moustache, a pressed black-pinstripe suit, and gold cufflinks. She sees a man in his twenties with three days' growth of beard, a dirty wife-beater t-shirt, and a can of beer. Michelle sees young men, middle-aged men and old men; men rich and poor; men who are black and white and yellow and brown.

This is the Patriarchy, and every man in the Patriarchy is grinning triumphantly at Michelle.

At the front of the penis-horde are two men who are not content to grin at her; they are pointing at Michelle and laughing.

One of the two men is tall, muscular Marvin Harper. He says, "I'm not the enemy of the Abzug Society, but I am your enemy, Michelle. I've corrupted your daughters, and I've bamboozled your local chapter into voting you out. Sucks to be you, 'Mitchell.' "

The other man mocking Michelle is her ex-husband Dennis. Dennis LeClerc looks the same as the day Michelle Landrieu met him, right down to his chocolate-brown mullet and mustache, and his tight blue Hawaiian shirt. Dennis now says, "Karma is a bitch, <u>bitch</u>. You shut me out of my daughters' lives, and yesterday you lost the thing most important to you: head harpy of the local chapter of man-haters."

Michelle answers, "You lost your rights as a father when you cheated on me and I caught you."

"That isn't your call to make, Michelle. I'm the twins' father; they <u>need</u> me in their lives. Who knows what trouble they've gotten into, with me not there?"

Michelle says nothing. She has never told Dennis that his daughters were arrested, tried, convicted, and thrown into prison. Why tell him now? Michelle has done the right thing by not telling Dennis, but he would not understand.

"<u>Enough!</u>" a woman's voice says. Dennis, Marvin, and the rest of the Patriarchy become statue-still. The woman's voice continues, "I'm tired of hearing these <u>men</u> prattle on—aren't you, Michelle?"

All the men vanish except for frozen Dennis and frozen Marvin. Where the horde of men was standing, now stands a sexy young woman who is facing Michelle.

The woman has the figure of a porn star, the red skin of a sunburn victim, bright-red shaped eyebrows, and waist-length pink hair. Her clothes *are a gray-leather, halter-top bra; a chain-mail loincloth; and black-leather, porn-actress high-heeled pumps with spikes. Her heavy makeup says <u>I'm easier than a two-piece jigsaw puzzle.</u>*

Michelle thinks, <u>This woman looks completely slutty. Dennis would love her.</u>

The woman walks up next to Michelle's frozen ex-husband, looks at him, and says, "Michelle, you first realized that <u>all men are beasts</u> when you caught Dennis and that bimbo. You are absolutely right: No man deserves any kindness from you."

The woman taps Dennis on his shoulder; he vanishes. Then the red woman walks up to unmoving Marvin Harper.

"Marvin Harper, you <u>man</u> you," the woman sighs. "You have humiliated Michelle here, after all she's done for women's equality. You should be taken down a peg. Or three. Or thirty."

Michelle replies, "Good luck, honey. Marvin Harper is the 'hero billionaire,' remember? When you trash-talk him in public, nobody believes you. When you sue him, his <u>turncoat lawyer</u> Victoria Allblue gets the lawsuit dropped."

The woman turns to face Michelle, putting hands on shapely hips. "Do you want vengeance on Marvin Harper? I can get you vengeance. I am Fanzelle, and I promise what nobody else can."

"Oh, yeah? How?" Michelle says skeptically.

Fanzelle shakes her head. "I can't answer well enough in a dream. Wake up, summon me, and I'll explain everything."

" 'Summon me'? What does that mean?"

"I'm a succubus. I seduce men, then claim their souls during sex. But this job was forced on me by lower-downs, and <u>to Heaven</u> with all those male demons I work for!"

"Hold on, they <u>make</u> you fuck men? Even when you don't want to? That's <u>sex slavery!</u>"

"Exactly. So summon me, Michelle, and I'll explain how <u>you</u> can get vengeance on Marvin Harper, and how <u>I</u> can get promoted out of being ordered to gratify men's base desires."

"Not so fast," Michelle says reluctantly. "I'm going to lose my soul if I do this, won't I? I'll get eternal punishment in hellfire?"

Fanzelle looks left and right, checking for eavesdroppers, then she murmurs, "Not if we word the pact right."

In a normal-volume voice, Fanzelle says, "I've said all I can say in this dream. Wake up and summon me if you want vengeance on Marvin Harper."

"How do I summon you?" Michelle asks.

****

As soon as Michelle woke up, she rushed into Elvira's old bedroom and headed straight for her closet. On a shelf, Michelle found a box of playground chalk.

There were only two pieces of chalk in the box. Two pieces were more than enough.

Next, Michelle threw on her clothes and drove to a (fortunately nearby) 24-hours Wal-Mart. Michelle bought a box of red birthday candles and a disposable lighter.

When Michelle returned from her shopping trip, she left her car parked in the driveway, instead of again parking her car in the garage.

****

Barely twenty minutes after Michelle had awakened from her dream, she stood in her garage next to a chalk pentagram. At the five corners of the pentagram, five little red candles burned. *Happy birthday, Marvin Harper*, Michelle thought. She smiled eagerly.

Michelle took a knife in her right hand and sliced into her left forearm. She let blood run down her arm to drip off her elbow, then—making sure she did not step on the chalk lines—she leaned forward so that the dripping blood splattered on the concrete floor inside the pentagram.

Michelle promptly stepped away from the pentagram, again making sure she did not step on the chalk lines.

Michelle spoke solemnly: "Harken, Demon Fanzelle, I summon thee. Appear thou afore me, here and now, bound in place and deed by the pentagram."

Above the middle of the pentagram, the air got darker, becoming black smoke. The black smoke began to swirl, faster and faster. When the black smoke was an enclosed tornado, the black became red. The red tornado stopped its spinning. The red smoke diffused to the boundaries of the pentagram, then the red smoke pulled itself in.

Within the pentagram stood Fanzelle. Just as in the dream, Fanzelle had huge breasts, red skin, bright-red eyebrows, and pink hair; Fanzelle was dressed exactly the same as in Michelle's dream.

But within the pentagram, Fanzelle had more to her appearance. Namely, a red, barbed tail; pointed ears; glowing-red-iris eyes; horns coming out of her forehead; and huge bat-wings coming out of her shoulder blades.

Fanzelle looked at Michelle and said formally, "O mortal named Michelle Joan Landrieu-LeClerc, I the demon Fanzelle do come to you as summoned."

Then Fanzelle grinned at Michelle and added, "You ready to mess with Marvin Harper?"

Chapter 6
Three Wishes and a Pact

One second later (still Sunday)
In the garage of Michelle Landrieu-LeClerc

Michelle said to Fanzelle who was trapped in the pentagram, "You are definitely a succubus. If my ex-husband were here, he'd fuck you in a heartbeat." Michelle laughed. "Then I'd watch the pig die."

Fanzelle purred, "Oh, I don't soul-suck only men who cheat, I soul-suck lesbians too. I've soul-sucked *many* lesbians, trust me."

Michelle shrugged. "Since I'm not a lesbian, that doesn't matter to me."

Fanzelle said, "Not a lesbian, *really?* Have you forgotten Salina?"

Fanzelle shape-shifted, and Michelle gasped.

Michelle would never forget Salina McBride; so Michelle would never forget how Salina had been dressed when they had met in college. Salina had had long, straight, blond hair; blue eyes; pale skin; and huge boobs. The day that Michelle had met Salina, Salina had covered her huge boobs with a Day-Glo, turquoise, V-neck t-shirt, with a denim vest covering the t-shirt. Below the waist, Salina had worn tight blue-jeans and blue sneakers.

Michelle was stunned because Fanzelle now looked in every way identical to Salina of thirty-odd years ago.

Fanzelle said (in Salina's voice), "When Salina kissed you, you kissed back. She pursued you and seduced you into lesbian sex, but your third time together was initiated by *you*, Michelle. You and Salina made love nine times."

Michelle said, "Okay, fine, I *misstated*, and you caught me out. But eventually I broke off the sapphic stuff with Salina, and I never had sex with another woman."

"But you ended your affair with Salina," duplicate-Salina said, "because you were scared of being publicly labeled a lesbian. Admit it: Part of you has always missed the love and passion you had with her."

"Yes, yes, I was a timid scaredy-cat then. I dumped her, rather than be out-and-proud with her. This has always shamed me. So later on, when I became a feminist, I was damned-sure *not timid at all* about it!"

"You became a feminist fifteen years ago," duplicate-Salina said, "soon after you found in your bathroom trash can a cocktail napkin with a phone number written on it. Want to know who wrote that number? Fiona."

Fanzelle now shape-shifted to look like a red-haired, green-eyed, freckled hussy in her twenties with a 2001 hairstyle. Fanzelle was wearing a green cocktail dress and was smirking at Michelle, exactly as Michelle had always imagined Dennis's unknown phone-number-writer doing.

Duplicate-Fiona said, "You became a feminist not because you were angry at all men, but because you were angry at Dennis. Who never called Fiona, by the way."

Michelle glared at the demoness. "Is there a point to this?"

Fanzelle shifted back to her red-skinned, bat-winged shape. "You mortals can successfully lie to each other and lie to yourselves. But remember, we demons of Hell *always* know the truth."

"*Fine.* So how about we get down to horse-trading," Michelle said. "But first, what did you mean that I could make a deal with you without losing my soul?"

"You're worried. Calm down, Michelle, I'm on *your* side. I want to be able to stick it to all the demons I work for and laugh in their faces. 'Ha ha, Michelle Landrieu-LeClerc got away!' "

"You still haven't explained anything. Talk!"

****

Meanwhile, in the twins' hotel room
Late morning Sunday, local time
Clermont-Ferrand, France

Marvin, with help from Fatima, had just finished explaining exactly how Almira and Elvira had each been given a spellmark. Sumera had listened, but had not said a word (except for calling Fatima "ridiculously generous").

Elvira would have convinced herself that Marvin's tale was a bald-faced lie, except that—

1) In six years, Elvira had never known Marvin to lie; and

2) Marvin's tale explained lots of weird things that had happened in the last six years, such as Elvira's burning, unsisterly cravings for her twin.

Now Elvira said to Marvin, "So Tim Hanson the car dealer, along with you—you two control minds."

"Yes," Marvin said.

"Six years ago, Tim Hanson whammied me, and you whammied Almira."

"Yes."

Elvira said, "What a chump I've been, admiring you these last two years." She filled her voice with contempt: "You're disgusting."

Marvin glared. "*I'm* disgusting? You two were all ready to frame an innocent woman for drug possession, when all she'd done wrong was to tell you to leave her party. *Which*, I remind you, you two had crashed. You both would have destroyed her life, and neither of you was bothered by that! Tim Hanson and I stopped your evil plan."

Fatima glared at Elvira. "Marvin didn't *wish* for mind-control powers, I *gave* them to him, because he is good enough not to misuse them. You would have been a *better woman*, Elvira, and this planet would have been a *better place*, if Marvin had 'whammied' you as well as your twin!"

Elvira looked at her twin. "What do *you* think?"

Almira shook her head. "I don't know *what* to think. I know I should slap his face, and yet I want to kneel in front of him and suck his cock."

"Jeez, Almie, that last part is the genie-magic talking."

Almira shrugged. "But I still want to do it."

Elvira said, "This is fucked up."

Elvira spun around to face her genie. "For my first wish, I wish that Almira be free of all of Marvin's mind-control, I be free of all of Tim Hanson's mind-control, and neither Marvin nor Fatima nor Tim Hanson can mind-control Almie or me in the future."

****

Meanwhile, in Michelle's garage

Fanzelle said to Michelle, "Here's the problem: I can't just give you what you ask, as a freebie. Hell's rules say we have to make a pact, 'I'll do blah-blah-blah in return for your soul.' You with me?"

"Yeah." Michelle wrung her hands nervously. She thought, *I can always say "No deal," then nothing bad happens to me.*

"Now, you wouldn't make the deal, if you're smart at all, where as soon as I fulfill my part of the pact, I immediately kill you and take your soul. Right?"

"You would *do* that to me?"

"Only if the big bosses downstairs ordered me to. Which couldn't happen unless our pact allowed this. What I'm trying to explain to you is how to make sure that the pact *won't* let my bosses do jack shit. Remember, I'm on *your* side."

"Okay, fine, go on."

"So to have any hope of hooking you, Hell lets me make the grab-your-soul part be conditional. 'Demon X will give John Smith one million dollars; and in return, Demon X will collect John Smith's soul after ten years or when John Smith visits the Eiffel Tower, whichever happens first.' "

Michelle smiled. "Great. Let's make the condition be 'When Michelle walks on the moon.' "

"Sorry, Satan reviews all pacts, and he won't allow one where the soul-condition is obviously impossible."

"So what's left?" Michelle asked. She was scared now, but trying not to show it. "What's your big idea?"

"We make the soul-condition be impossible, but not *obviously* so. The pact passes Satan's review."

"So what's your idea?" Michelle asked. "You've figured one out, right?" Michelle's heart was pounding.

Fanzelle grinned. "Marvin Harper, the 'hero billionaire,' fucks his wife *and* he fucks his housekeeper—"

"*What?* That is harassment!"

"—*and* he fucks the thirty-three young women in his harem. If you watch TV, you know how *devoted* his *haremées* are to him."

"It's disgusting—they really should have more pride. But *what is your idea?*"

"I collect your soul when one of his harem girls turns him down for sex."

"Right, like that would ever happen, those sluts!" Then Michelle frowned. "Wait, it *could* happen. One of them could get really bad cramps. Or an actual headache!"

"This happens now. What happens next is that the girl offers to blow him. But I'm on your side—how about we make the condition be *two* harem girls turning Marvin down for sex in one night?"

Michelle said, "*Two* girls? Why not write-in Harper getting turned down *three* times in one night?"

"I don't think Satan would okay that."

"Okay, okay, that's fine. Especially if Marvin won't be propositioning his harem for too much longer."

Fanzelle asked innocently, "Oh? Why is that?"

"Because, demoness, you are going to *kill* Marvin Harper very soon."

****

In the twins' hotel room

Elvira had just made her first wish: that she and Almira be free of magical mind-control and that they could not be whammied in the future.

Now Sumera turned both her palms up. A ball of blue lightning appeared over each hand. Sumera shoved one blue-lightning ball toward Almira and the other blue-lightning ball toward Elvira.

As soon as Sumera released the two blue-lightning balls, she turned to Fatima. Sumera's grin was sassy.

Elvira saw her twin's lightning-ball disappear into her body, while Elvira saw (but did not feel) her own blue-lightning ball vanish into her own chest.

Instantly Elvira stopped being horny for her twin sister.

"One wish made, one wish granted," Sumera said. Sumera was looking toward (and grinning at) Marvin and Fatima as she said those words.

Now Elvira looked over at Almira. Elvira could not tell what Almie was thinking—the last time *this* had happened, they had both been in kindergarten.

Before Elvira could ask Almira what she was thinking, Elvira was herself asked by Marvin, "Did Sumera explain the rules to you?"

Elvira snapped, "Shut up, Harper. I don't need to know any stinking rules."

"Yes, you do. One of the rules is that all three wishes have to be wished the same day. So now you have until midnight, or your other two wishes are gone for good."

Fatima nodded.

"Is he right?" Elvira asked Sumera.

"Yes, that's a rule."

"*Why didn't you tell me?*"

Sumera grinned cruelly. "Because you didn't ask."

Almira had been staring off into space; now her eyes focused on Marvin. "Did what just happened to Elvie and me ever happen before? Has one of your *haremées* ever become unbrainwashed?"

Marvin said, "Yes. Virgilia."

"*What?*" Elvira said. "Virgilia O'Keefe? I've seen how she touches you and smiles at you. Plus, she's been president of the Harper Foundation for two years now, she's raking in the bucks, but she still shares a bedroom at your mansion. Admit it: She's another brainwashed sex-slave of yours."

Marvin replied, "Virgilia has her reasons for living with us. One of her reasons is that she loves me."

Elvira made a rude noise. "I don't believe it."

Almira said, "*I* do. I find this *easy* to believe."

Elvira snapped, "Tell me how, twin. What he's saying, it's bullshit."

Almira's eyes narrowed. "Do you know, *twin*, that your nonstop anger, suspicion, and insults are a royal pain in the ass for everyone else? *Shut up and listen!*"

Elvira was so shocked by Almira's outburst, she did indeed shut up.

Almira said, "Until your wish cleared my mind, I would have become a ten-cent whore for Marvin if he had asked. I would have made porn films for him. I would have slit Mother's throat if he'd asked me to; I would have slit *your* throat if he'd asked me to. And if Marvin had smiled at me afterward and said, 'You did good,' I'd have been *glad* I'd slit whomever's throat."

"Whoa," Marvin said.

Almira continued, "And with all this eagerness to please him, how has he used me? I fuck and suck him, scrub pots sometimes, and clip newspapers—and the last one, he pays me for. Not to mention, whenever my name comes to the top of the Sex Schedule, he always gives me more orgasms than I give him."

Elvira said, "Dammit, Almie, none of that matters! You and I, we're entitled to not have sex with a man unless we freely consent!"

"You mean, just like we're *entitled* to attend a party we weren't invited to, and so we're *entitled* to plant drugs if the hostess tries to throw us out? *That* kind of 'entitled'?"

"They're not the same thing," Elvira said sullenly.

"They *are*, Elvie. Do you think Marvin would have abracadabra'd me if we'd been good girls when we were told to leave the party? *We brought this on ourselves.*"

"But Almie, he still shouldn't have—"

"No, Elvie, *we* shouldn't have. But we did. Then *he* did."

Elvira wanted to scream. "Why are you being such a goody-two-shoes now, Almie? Why are you taking *his* side? Six years ago, you were just as . . ."

"Evil?" smiling Fatima suggested.

Elvira glared at Fatima, then said to her twin sister, "Six years ago, you thought like I did."

"That was before I lived these last two years in the mansion as a goody-two-shoes. I liked everyone there, they liked me, I fit in, and I was *happy*. I miss that life—already—and *so fucking what* if I was mind-controlled at the time? The person I was at the party, six years ago, I don't want to be her again."

Marvin rubbed his face with his hand. "Elvira, I'm sleepy, and I want to go back to my comfy bed in the USA. Would you *please* argue with Almira some other time? Right now, would you *please* make your other two wishes?"

Elvira stood straight. "I was not put on Earth to do whatever *a man* wants me to do."

Almira murmured, "Jeez, Elvie, you sound like Mother."

****

In Michelle's garage

White light flashed in the garage, and Fanzelle the succubus saw an angel appear where Michelle could theoretically see the angel. But Michelle did not react.

The angel looked at Fanzelle and said, "FALLEN ANGEL WHO CALLS HERSELF FANZELLE, YOU SHALL NOT CONTRACT TO KILL MARVIN STEVEN HARPER."

The angel's voice was loud to Fanzelle's ears, but Michelle did not react to the angel's voice.

Fanzelle did not know what to think. Only a few times in thousands of years had Fanzelle heard of an angel interfering with the wording of an unholy pact. How did Marvin Harper rate an angel butting in?

Fanzelle shrugged and said to Michelle, "Sorry, I can't agree to killing Marvin Harper."

"*Why?* He cheats on his wife, and you're a succubus. You could kill him anytime, without needing to make a pact with me."

Fanzelle glanced over at the angel. The angel was silent and its face was expressionless—no help there.

Fanzelle shrugged again. "I can't kill Marvin Harper, and that's that. What else can I do for you?"

Michelle grinned cruelly. "Make him poor and make him not be a hero, and make the whole world *forget* he ever was a hero."

"YOU MAY MAKE MARVIN STEVEN HARPER POORER, BUT YOU MAY NOT RUIN HIM, said the angel.

Fanzelle thought, *That angel is becoming a true killjoy.*

Fanzelle sighed. She said to Michelle, "Genies granting wishes can change people's memories, but we demons can't, I'm sorry. But making Marvin Harper be not a hero, I can do that. Also, I can make him lose most of his money."

"*Nuh-uh*," Michelle said. "I don't want him to lose *most* of his money, I want him to lose *all* of his money. I want him to be forced to sell off his mansion. I want to see him sleeping under an overpass."

Fanzelle glanced over at the angel. The angel shook its head.

Fanzelle looked at Michelle. "Sorry, that's the best I can do. Do we have a deal? I make Marvin Harper be not a hero, I make him be not a billionaire, and in return, I get your soul on the day that two of Marvin Harper's harem girls turn him down for sex."

Michelle shrugged. "I suppose," she said.

****

One second later

Michelle continued, "But I must say, I'm disappointed. 'Killing Harper is not allowed. Bankrupting him is not allowed.' Next time I talk to the priest, I'll have to tell him, 'Satan is a 97-pound weakling.' Besides—"

As Fanzelle magicked-up a human-skin printed pact and a cactus-needle pen, she started to say, "I'm sorry, Michelle, but this is the best—"

Michelle said, "Besides all the rigmarole involved in a summoning. I'm going to be summoning you *a lot*, because I'll want updates often."

Fanzelle was worried now. Heaven was interfering in the negotiation of Fanzelle's pact about Marvin Harper— would Heaven also interfere in Fanzelle carrying out the pact? If the pact could not be fulfilled and so Michelle's soul could not be collected, Fanzelle would not get a *pro*motion. Rather, Satan would *de*mote Fanzelle to becoming succubus for winos.

Both Fanzelle and Michelle were quiet for the next few seconds, except for Michelle's hisses of pain. But then Michelle finished signing the pact in her own blood. Michelle stood up and pushed the pact across the chalk-lines boundary of the pentagram and into Fanzelle's hand.

With a flash of white light, the angel vanished. Again, Michelle did not react.

An instant later, a idea popped into Fanzelle's head. An idea so fiendishly clever, she *knew* that she was a shoo-in for promotion *at the least*. And if she, Fanzelle, could give Satan the thing he had been wanting for *six thousand years*, who knew *what* titles she might reach!

Now Fanzelle looked left and right, as though checking for eavesdroppers, then she looked over her shoulder for good measure. "Michelle, you know I'm on your side, right? There is a quick and easy *magical* way to make a pentagram, *but you can't tell anyone else!* You interested?"

"Yes, yes, tell me!"

Fanzelle pointed to a different part of the garage floor. "When you're ready to draw a pentagram, stand facing where you want the pentagram to be, and say, '*Pentagrammonub enkephalodub*.' Try it now."

Fanzelle had to repeat the phrase three times before Michelle could say it perfectly. The result was that a fully-loaded second pentagram appeared on the garage floor—a pentagram with yardstick-straight chalk lines and five tall, red, tapering lit candles.

When grinning Michelle looked at Fanzelle, the demoness said, "To summon me, you need only say, 'I summon you, Fanzelle.' When you want for the pentagram to go away, say, *'Pentagrammonub enkephalodub evanokuk.'* "

Saying that phrase correctly took Michelle only two tries.

After Michelle had removed the second pentagram, she asked, "Why is this a big secret?"

Fanzelle looked Michelle in the eyes and replied, "Every time a mortal summons a demon, it messes up Hell's work schedules. Hell doesn't like any trick to make summoning demons be easier."

"Well, too bad for those *men* demons," Michelle said, grinning at Fanzelle. "Now I know the trick, sister, and I'm going to use it, thanks to you!"

****

A few seconds later

Michelle had dismissed Fanzelle from summons, and Fanzelle was back in Hell.

A few minutes after that, Fanzelle was reporting directly to Satan—

—who laughed at the end of Fanzelle's report. "Really, *'Pentagrammonub enkephalodub'*? And the stupid mortal has *no* idea what it means? Great job, Fanzelle!"

Fanzelle grinned. "I convinced her to trust me, the fool."

****

In the twins' hotel room

Elvira had ordered Sumera to tell her the wishing-rules. When Sumera quit talking, Elvira said to her, "For my second wish, I wish that Almira and I would be identically beautiful enough to each catch a rich husband."

"Whoa, *this* ought to be interesting," Marvin remarked. Elvira saw Fatima roll her eyes.

Sumera again made her two blue-lightning balls, she again shoved a blue-lightning ball at each twin, and each blue-lightning ball again hit its target.

Sumera said with a grin, "One wish made, one wish granted."

Elvira and Almira pointed at each other at the same time; each said, "She looks the same as before."

Sumera's laugh was scornful. "Because you each *already* look good enough to catch a rich husband. *Provided* that you each act nicer to men than you have in the past."

"I can't argue with that," Marvin remarked, while Elvira glared at her genie.

"So *that's* how it's going to be, huh?" Elvira muttered.

Elvira turned to Marvin and Fatima. "When I wish for a million dollars, how should I word it so Blue Bitch here can't pull a trick?"

"Small, unmarked bills," suggested Almira. "Because you're a *parolee*."

"Legal tender," Marvin suggested. "So she can't hit you with Monopoly money."

"U.S. currency," Fatima suggested. "So she can't hit you with Jamaica dollars instead."

Sumera yelled something angry at Fatima in their foreign language. Fatima replied in the same language, giving Sumera an *eat shit, dearie* smile all the while.

Elvira made her wish then—and discovered that Sumera had one more trick to play.

Sumera magicked a million U.S. dollars in cash (in small, unmarked bills)—all on top of Elvira's hotel bed. Elvira thought, *How am I going to keep the hotel maids from either stealing the cash or phoning the local police, and how am I going to get this back to the USA without getting arrested at the airport?*

With a smirk, Sumera said, "One wish made, one wish granted."

Elvira said, "You are a bitch, Sumera."

Fortunately for Elvira, Marvin then made a magical request that Fatima transport the cash to a "big enough" cardboard box in his mansion's attic. Fatima gave Elvira a long stare, and Elvira was expecting Fatima to refuse; but then Fatima vanished the cash.

This started another round of Fatima and Sumera arguing again in foreign language.

Meanwhile, Elvira was walking over to her twin sister. "I've made my three wishes; now it's *your* turn. But watch out, Sumera is one tricky bitch."

Almira backed away from the lamp. "My mind's still confused. I'll make my wishes later. You hold on to the lamp until then."

"Jeez, Almie, how am I going to get a *genie lamp* through Customs?"

Fatima said, "Give it to Marvin. He'll hold on to it till Almira asks for it."

Elvira said, "Ri-i-ight. Like he'll just *hand it over* when she asks."

Almira said, "Jeez, twin, your always-on suspiciousness gets old."

Then Almira smiled at Marvin. "*I* trust him."

Fatima snapped, "Listen up, Elvira—want to know why he will indeed 'just hand it over when she asks'? You twins remember the genie Kharmesh from two years ago? Same skin color as Sumera here, same shitty attitude? Master here wound up being also Kharmesh's master till Master got rid of the lamp. Listen up: Master *never made a wish!*"

Elvira stared at Marvin. Almira stared at Marvin. Even Sumera stared.

A minute later, Sumera was back in her lamp, Sumera's lamp was in Marvin's hand, then Marvin and Fatima vanished from the twins' hotel room in a flash of green light. *FOOM.*

Elvira looked at Almira. Almira looked at Elvira. "Whoa," they said at the same time.

Chapter 7
Not-Great Sex

Still Sunday

One second, I was in a hotel room in France, with the curtains glowing from sunlight. Then my ears popped. The next second, Fatima and I were standing in her bedroom at the mansion, inside a green-smoke Silence Box.

Fatima deleted the Silence Box; now I could see her entire bedroom clearly. Beyond her bedroom window, I saw only blackness. As I was no longer seeing sunlight, my sleepiness instantly doubled.

"Talk to you later," I mumbled to Fatima. "Thanks for bringing me into this."

I still had Sumera's brass lamp in my left hand. I walked from Fatima's bedroom to my bedroom. In my dark bedroom, I could hear Anna Kay—she was not snoring, but she was clearly asleep.

I slid Sumera's lamp under my side of the bed as a temporary hiding place, then I climbed into bed.

"What did Fatima want you for?" Anna Kay asked in a sleepy voice.

I weighed my options, then answered, "Can I tell you in the morning?"

Instead of answering, Anna Kay wriggled backward till we were spooned together. I draped my arm around her waist in the darkness, and I fell asleep.

****

Hours later (after dawn)

My master bedroom has windows in three walls. When I woke up, the bedroom was brightly lit. But it was not sunlight that woke me up. Rather, I awoke to Anna Kay's eager mouth on my cock, and—

Why am I smelling this?

—the smell of burned sulfur. I decided that Anna Kay had lit a match in order to light a scented candle. I started to wonder why I smelled the match, but not the candle, when Anna Kay giggled and then deepthroated me.

I promptly forgot all about the sulfur smell.

"Suck me hard," I ordered, "then I want to fuck you."

Anna Kay stopped delighting me for long enough to reply, "I obey, my husband."

To the left of the bed was a loveseat. From that loveseat came a young woman's voice: "Ooh, it's always *so sexy* when Anna Kay submits to you, Marvin sir."

The speaker was *haremée* Tiffni Daniels, whom the Sex Schedule had ordered to give me my Morning Blowjob. But evidently my wife had pulled rank about whose mouth slurped me this morning.

I said to Tiffni, "I'm glad you came here to suck me off, per the Schedule. This pleases me." Tiffni beamed. "But it seems I'm going to be making love to my wife this morning, then I have husband-and-wife stuff to discuss with her. So give me a kiss, Tiffni, then run along."

Tiffni slid off the loveseat, sashayed two steps to the king-sized bed, then bent down to kiss me. Tiffni was wearing tight-fitting black lingerie; very high, black-patent heels; and fire-engine-red lipstick. I said what I was thinking: "Tiffni, you look hot."

Right after that, Tiffni kissed me, making sure to slip me lots of tongue. Reader, have you ever been passionately kissed by one woman while another woman was deepthroating you? I recommend it.

When I broke the kiss, Tiffni kissed my forehead, then sashayed to the bedroom door. Tiffni shot me a come-hither look over her shoulder, then walked out of the room.

****

Maybe two seconds after Tiffni had shut the bedroom door, a floating green lightball appeared by the door. The lightball spoke, sounding like Ensign Chekov of "Star Trek": "Good morning, Kiptin. I trust you slept werry well?"

I replied to the lightball, "Start breakfast without us. It'll be a while before we're downstairs, hint-hint."

"That's *fantastic*," the lightball replied in Arnold Schwarzenegger's voice. Then the lightball vanished.

Six months ago, SJ-1 had figured out how to synthesize *any* voice on her half-magical laptop. Taking this as a challenge, Fatima had cooked up a spell to synthesize voices magically. I had first learned of this when one morning, the bodyless voice of Scott Weinger (as Aladdin) had spoken by the bed to say, "Princess Jasmine, breakfast is ready downstairs." (Reader, have I mentioned that Fatima *loves* that 1992 Disney cartoon?)

****

One second later

I spoke to Anna Kay like I were a barbarian king: "Now that you've made my dick big and hard, I intend to fuck you. Slide up here."

"I obey, my husband," Anna Kay said, her face and voice as submissive as a slave-girl in the king's harem. She took her mouth off my cock, climbed up the bed, then rolled over onto her back. "Take me."

The eagerness in her eyes was no surprise—fucking Anna Kay was always indescribable pleasure for both of us. As a result of one of Fatima's wish-grants, my erect cock was the perfect length and girth for Anna Kay's pussy.

Anyway, now Anna Kay was completely naked except for light-blue silk panties. I reached for the sides of her panties; she lifted her ass off the bed in order to make removal easier. No surprise, the pussy-part of her panties was wet. When the panties had passed her toes, I tossed Anna Kay's panties onto the carpet, then I looked her naked body up and down.

"You are the hottest woman in the state, maybe even the USA, and I am going to fuck you now," I growled.

Anna Kay replied, "*You* are the hottest *man* on the planet, and I will *enjoy* being fucked by you." With that, her arms rose up to embrace me.

I used both my hands to spread her knees. I lined up the head of my cock, then I pushed into her pussy as I kissed her.

Her sugar-walls stroked my cock—*nice*. They were tight and wet and hot—just the way I liked them.

When I broke the kiss, I said, "You feel wonderful, Anna Kay."

Anna Kay's voice was puzzled. "You feel . . . different. Did you not enjoy my blowjob?"

****

One second later

I had no idea what Anna Kay meant by that. I knew it was nothing insulting, because Anna Kay was *never* insulting or mean.

In any case, my attention quickly returned to the fucking. My pleasure was building.

It seemed that Anna Kay's pleasure was building too. She was kissing me like the end of the world was nigh, and thrusting her hips like she'd swallowed a barrelful of horniness-potion.

****

Ten minutes in, I was computing the cube root of 99 in my head, in order to take the edge off my excitement, and yet *Anna Kay had not climaxed even once.*

"Everything okay?" I asked.

"I love you, my husband," my wife replied, and pulled my head down for a kiss.

****

Fifteen minutes in, I was imagining being ripped apart by zombies, in order to hold off my first climax.

Anna Kay was murmuring, "So close, I'm so close."

****

Sixteen minutes after I started fucking Anna Kay, she arched her back. "Yes, finally! Give it to me, oh yes!"

Even as I was shoving deep into Anna Kay's pussy and spurting hard, I was thinking, *She's not screaming. Always when Anna Kay climaxes with me, she screams.*

****

One minute later

What with Anna Kay and me being together for six years, all the postcoital kissy-huggy affection between us took only a minute. Now I slid out of bed, stood up, and walked to the bathroom doorway.

Anna Kay gasped. "Marvin—you're *shorter!*"

"*What?*"

"Always your hair brushes against the top of the doorframe. But now it doesn't."

I said, "That's impossible, Anna Kay."

"I swear, it's true. Stand in the doorway and look in the bathroom mirror. You're not as tall."

I turned to face the bathroom mirror. *What the fuck?* Indeed, I was now two inches shorter.

But the mirror told me something else, something just as bad.

For the past six years, when I had walked through this doorway, my giant triceps had made my shoulders almost as wide as the doorway. But now I saw a slightly larger gap between my shoulders and the doorframe; my shoulders weren't as bulked-up as they had been.

I flexed my biceps. They too were a little smaller.

I need to talk to Fatima!

****

After both Anna Kay and I had showered and dressed, and Anna Kay was putting on her makeup, she asked, "So why did Fatima drag you away in the middle of the night? She seemed worried."

I answered, "Yesterday in France, Elvira found a genie lamp—"

"Jeez, *really?*"

"Elvira made her three wishes, then gave me the lamp to hold onto till Almira gets ready to wish."

Anna Kay paused, then asked nervously, "What did she wish for?"

I repeated Elvira's wishes, as best I could remember them.

Anna Kay looked unhappy. "You're *sure* those were her wishes?"

"If you need the exact wording, Fatima has a perfect memory." Then I asked, "Babe, why are you so interested in Elvira's wishes?"

Anna Kay bit her lip. "I'm wondering why you're shorter, and how much further it will go."

I did not say anything, but now I was even more worried than Anna Kay was. I did *not* want to become 5′2″ and puny again!

Chapter 8
In the Attic

Still Sunday

Right after that unpleasant conversation, Anna Kay and I walked downstairs and into the monster kitchen. The women eating breakfast smiled (knowingly) at us, and greeted us by name. Alarmingly, nobody noticed that I had shrunk two inches—not even Fatima.

It was odd that nobody noticed my shrinkage, because so many people were in the monster kitchen right then.

Including my wife and me, thirty-seven people lived in the mansion full-time—and that was with the guest bedroom being empty almost all the time. Two of the thirty-seven residents were vacationing in France at the moment, so that left thirty-five. But when I walked into the monster kitchen, I saw roughly fifty faces smiling at me.

The extra faces at breakfast belonged to former *haremées*. They were no longer living at the mansion, and they were no longer enthralled to me, but any former *haremée* was welcome to have breakfast or dinner at the mansion, anytime (provided she gave Fatima twenty-four hours' notice). So many former *haremées* took me up on my offer, I had needed to buy two more tables with chairs.

When Anna Kay and I walked into the monster kitchen, Virgilia O'Keefe was saying, ". . . reading the story of 'Aladdin and the Magic Lamp' on my computer. Anyone else read it?"

"Virgie reads a lot," Sherry Benson told the crowd. Sherry was no longer living at the mansion, and I had paid to have her implants removed, but she came to the mansion for breakfast several times a week.

"No, I haven't read the Aladdin story," Fatima said from the stove. Fatima's face showed amusement. "I figure my Blu-Ray of *Disney's Aladdin* is all I need."

"I read the story six years ago," SJ-1 replied in her usual fake-robotic voice. "It is available online."

"I wish it weren't just a story," sighed current *harémée* Tabitha Donaldson. "I'd *love* to own a genie lamp."

Most of the room spoke agreement with Tabitha. SJ-1's face showed no expression (nothing new there), but Anna Kay, Virgilia, and I were working hard to not grin at the irony. Fatima, however, frowned briefly.

By now, Anna Kay and I had taken our places at the head table, and Barbara Drysdale—one of the *harémées* listed on the Kitchen Schedule—was setting plates down in front of us.

I smiled at Barbara and said "Thank you." She beamed.

I called over to Virgilia (who was sitting several tables away), "So how was it for you, reading 'Aladdin and the Magic Lamp' as an adult?"

"Well, *of course* I thought about what I would do if I had my own genie lamp—"

Virgilia was being ironic now. She had in fact owned Fatima's lamp for three minutes, six years ago, and had made two wishes with it. (Virgilia had declined her third wish; Fatima always treated Virgilia respectfully after that.)

"—but going back to *Disney's Aladdin*, the original story also has Aladdin become the master of the Genie of the Ring. The cartoon doesn't mention the Genie of the Ring at all."

By now, Fatima had taken her seat at the head table, immediately to my left. She said, "The Genie of the Ring didn't go into the cartoon because Disney figured out he wasn't really a genie. All he could do was move Ala ad-Din from Point A to Point B; a *true* genie grants wishes." Fatima's voice was thick with scorn.

Sherry said to Fatima, "I'm, like, *soo* confused. I thought you said you hadn't read the story. How do you know all this stuff about the other genie?"

Whoops.

Thinking about what Fatima had just said, I realized that there must be a seventh bound *djinni* out there, one whom Fatima had never mentioned: the Genie of the Ring.

But in the meantime, I had to divert everyone's attention away from Fatima's opinions about genies. So I replied, "I've discussed the Disney movie with Fatima lots of times. I probably mentioned something about the Genie of the Ring."

Everyone nodded.

I continued, "I think having a magic ring like in the story would be fun. I'd never again get stuck in traffic, and I could eat authentic Italian food in Sorrento whenever I wanted to."

This started the *haremées* and former *haremées* on a lively discussion about what each woman would do if she could instantly travel anywhere. Clothes-shopping on Rodeo Drive in Beverly Hills turned out to be a popular imaginary use for the Genie of the Ring.

Meanwhile, Fatima squeezed my arm; she realized what I had done.

****

Thirty minutes later

Breakfast had ended, and I had told Fatima that I needed to "borrow" her in the attic. Almost everyone overhearing probably presumed that I was working Fatima in her role as housekeeper for the mansion.

Now I was standing in the second-floor hallway, in front of the door to the attic, with a black plastic trash bag in my hand. Nobody walking by could guess this, but in the trash bag was Sumera's brass lamp.

Fatima walked up the foyer stairway to the second floor. She walked across the asparagus-green Oriental rug that covered the second-floor hallway floor, and she joined me at the attic door. I opened the door, motioned her up the stairs, followed her just past the door, then I locked the attic door from the inside. Neither of us spoke until we were both up in the attic.

"Where did you *foom* Elvira's cash to?" I asked Fatima.

"Warren's toy box," she replied.

"Ah. Good choice."

We walked over to a huge cardboard box that I had hand-labeled at the top, "Warren Harper's toys (1930s)." Uncle Warren had been born in 1925.

I opened up the big cardboard box. Sure enough, inside on top were many, many twenty-, fifty-, and hundred-dollar bills. I took Sumera's lamp out of the black trash bag and set the lamp aside. But before I started to stuff the cash into the now-empty trash bag, I turned to Fatima.

I asked her, "Can a wish-grant run down after a while? Like a battery or an alarm clock?"

"No," said confused-looking Fatima. Her tone of voice asked, *Where are you going with this?*

I asked, "Does anything look different with me? Admittedly, the light in the attic"—one bare-bulb light fixture every twenty feet—"isn't that great."

Fatima looked me up and down, then replied, "Your pants are too long, Master."

I let the trash bag fall to the board walkway of the attic, then I used both hands to pull my shirt off. "I'm two inches shorter, and my biceps and triceps are smaller."

My genie stared. "They are. But that's *impossible!*"

"So you don't know how this happened, or how much further it will go?"

Fatima looked stunned. "*No,* Master. I've never seen anything like this before, and I can't begin to guess why it happened to you."

"Could I become 5'2" again?"

"I'm sorry, Master, but I don't know."

I nodded toward Sumera's lamp. "Could *she* have done this?"

"As much as I can't stand the bitch, I don't see how."

"*Fuck,*" I said, then I pulled my shirt back on. "Let's get back to work."

Reader, I messed up then. I had known for years that *djinn* magic was real and angelic magic was real, but I did not think through what I knew. Alas, Fatima was as just as unclever as I was, up there in my attic.

****

Seconds later

I began stuffing cash money into the trash bag. As Fatima watched me work, she asked, "What are you going to do with the money?"

I replied, "Deposit it in the bank, as soon as Elvira comes home."

Then I changed the subject: "So is there a real Ring and a real Genie of the Ring, just like there is a real Aladdin's Lamp somewhere in West Virginia?"

Fatima said, "The Ring is real, and a person is in the Ring. But he is of the Brown Tribe. He is neither a true *djinni* nor a true genie. He doesn't count."

"I see," I replied, unwilling to argue with Fatima's long-held prejudices. "If he's not a *djinni,* what is he?"

"A human, almost. Turd Tribe people look like humans, and they have barely more magic than humans."

"I see," I repeated.

A few minutes later, all the cash was removed from the cardboard box. It turned out that a million dollars in cash filled a 39-gallon trash bag about a third of the way full.

Only one task was left: Hiding Sumera's lamp.

Now I began to remove Warren's childhood collectibles from the big cardboard box—

• Various wooden and painted-sheet-metal toys: a police car, a regular car, a firetruck, a dump truck, and a propeller-driven airplane. They all had a Thirties look to them.

• A leather baseball mitt, sized for a boy's hand.

• Two issues of *Detective Comics*, issues number 2 and 26 (neither issue had Batman in it).

• A very old and worn-out Monopoly game.

• A Valentine's Day card with 1930s art and Art Deco lettering; it was signed "Millie Davis, XXX" in red ink.

When I had removed all these things from the cardboard box, only one thing was left, at the bottom of the box: an olive-drab Army footlocker with "HARPER W G" stenciled in faded white letters on the lid. I lifted the footlocker out of the cardboard box that contained it.

Fatima said, "Smart. Nobody will see that footlocker accidentally, since it's inside a bigger box; and anybody who bothers to go through the big box will figure that the footlocker holds only more of Warren's old junk."

"That's the idea," I said, as I was pulling the padlock key from my pocket and inserting it into the shiny padlock. I unlocked the padlock and opened the footlocker's lid.

Inside the footlocker were two old photo albums and an old brass oil lamp.

Fatima's old brass oil lamp.

I asked Fatima, "Do you need to go into your lamp for anything?"

The bound *djinn* had a magical instant-messaging system, but Fatima could use it only when she was in her lamp. Normally, a genie spent over a century at a time in his or her Vessel, and only a few minutes outside the Vessel; but Fatima had last been in her lamp—and then, it was for ten minutes, and at her request—in 2014.

Now Fatima smiled at me. "No, Master, I'm good. But thank you for the offer."

I picked up Sumera's lamp in my left hand, and slapped the brass body with my right hand. As Sumera's lamp shook in my hand, I glanced over at Fatima. "I need to talk to Sumera now. Stick around?"

Fatima's grin was bloodthirsty. "And watch Sumera have to take orders from you? *No way* would I miss this."

****

Half a minute later

Sumera asked me, "Master, are you ready to wish now?"

Fatima spoke before I could: "What, not even a *hint* to your master that there are rules for making wishes?"

Sumera shot a *Whose side are you on?* glare at Fatima; I had to work to keep my face straight. Sumera said, "I'm sure Master already knows *all* the rules. Especially the rule I can't say yet."

I said, "It doesn't matter that yes, I know the rules, because I won't be wishing today."

Sumera looked shocked. Back in the twins' hotel room, I had rubbed Sumera's lamp only to transfer Sumera's ownership; I had declined to make wishes then as well.

Sumera now said, "You have twice summoned me from my Vessel, but you do not make wishes with me." She glared at Fatima. "Has someone told you I am not up to the task? I am as magically skilled as any other bound *djinni*."

"*More* skilled, if rumors are true," Fatima remarked.

Sumera glared at Fatima; then Sumera looked at me and nervously bit her lip.

Twenty-six hundred years ago, the *Djinn* War had almost been fought because a Green Tribe *djinni* had spread the rumor that Sumera of the Blue Tribe had learned magic spells from demons. Sumera had denied the charge, and Blue Tribe had demanded that the Green Tribe rumormonger be handed over for punishment for this "slander." Green Tribe's reply to the demand had been "Fuck off," followed by less polite language. It had taken King Solomon and an angel to prevent the *Djinn* War—the magical equivalent of nuclear war.

But now, if I asked Sumera about those demon-spells she had maybe-learned, she would be compelled to answer truthfully, and Fatima would hear every word. *Of course* Sumera acted nervous!

I said, "Sumera, I won't ask you about that rumor. That's a promise. The subject is not relevant to me."

Fatima said, "C'mon, Master. It takes only five seconds for you to ask her the question."

I said, "Fatima? Drop it." Fatima frowned; Sumera grinned.

Then I looked at Sumera. "But I called you out of your lamp for two reasons. The first is to ask you whether you have cast any spells on me—"

"*What?*"

"—either at Elvira's request or by your own choice."

"I have not worked magic on you a single time, never." Sumera glared at Fatima. "These allegations are *false.*"

Fatima growled, "Don't lie to Master, you Blue Tribe bitch. Today Master is shorter and his muscles are smaller; admit you caused this!"

"Again Green Tribe slanders me!" Sumera yelled at Fatima. "You're a bound *djinni* too, so you *know* I cannot bespell a human without my master's request, and I cannot lie to my master."

Fatima shot back: "Those rules are true for *most* bound *djinn*. But if *anyone* could find a way around the rules, it would be *you*, Sumera!"

I held up a hand. "Sumera? Fatima? If Sumera says she didn't bespell me, I believe her."

"You're too trusting," Fatima muttered.

****

One second later

While still looking at Sumera, I said, "I also called you out of your lamp to give you a choice. I can let you stay out of your lamp, subject to the same restrictions as Fatima—"

"Which are?"

"Tell her, Fatima."

What followed was a short conversation in Arabic.

Sumera said, "Sounds good. *Too* good. What's the catch?"

I replied, "The first restriction is, you would have to look human. No blue skin, no blue hair. Your eyes may still be blue, but not *glowing* blue. Blue lipstick is okay."

"But would make you look freaky," Fatima said.

Sumera sighed. "Looking human, I guess I can live with that."

I said, "Number two, you would live here at the mansion. The bad news is, while Fatima's role at the mansion is housekeeper, you would be one more *haremée*."

"*What?* Take orders from Green Girl? *No way!*"

Fatima demanded, "Will I have to share my room with her? All the other rooms are full up—two girls."

"Hey, I just realized," said Sumera to me, "not only would I have to take orders from Fatima, I would have to *fuck* you too."

"*That* part is a perk, Blue Girl," said Fatima. "Master has forgotten more about pleasing a woman-*djinni*'s body than all the males of Blue Tribe have ever known."

I said, "To answer Sumera's question, she would stay in the guest bedroom downstairs."

Sumera smirked at Fatima. "*You* have a bedroom to *your*self, *I'll* have a bedroom to *my*self. Master is making me your equal."

Fatima smirked back. "Except I can assign you to clean toilets and you'd have to do it."

Sumera frowned.

I frowned too. "Fatima, since I can't trust you not to fuck Sumera over, I'm going to lay down a rule: You may not assign Sumera to Toilet Duty or Scullery Duty without my permission. Permission you don't have right now."

Sumera grinned triumphantly at Fatima, then said to me, "Master, I accept your generous offer. It is much more than I could expect from *some* beings I could mention."

We made plans then. Tomorrow at noon, I would drive to the local Greyhound station and pick up "out-of-town arrival" Sumera. With those plans made, I now said to Sumera, "You've memory-read Elvira, so you know how a *haremée* acts. I expect you not to cause problems for other girls here, or for me. If you do, I'll 'put you back on the bus,' got me?"

"Sure, whatever."

"I promise to never send you back into your lamp, but you upsetting my household is the one exception to my promise. Just so you understand."

Sumera stared at me in shock and whispered, "You would promise me *that?*"

Fatima smirked. "She won't last a week."

Sumera said, "Camelshit, Green Girl. If *you* can pass for human, and make nice with humans, I can do it standing on my head."

I sighed.

FOOM. Sumera left for Baghdad without even a *Thank you.*

Reader, again I messed up. Things I should have thought of, and questions I should have asked, I didn't.

****

I locked Sumera's lamp in the footlocker (right next to Fatima's lamp), I put the footlocker back in the cardboard box, I put back Uncle Warren's stuff on top of the footlocker, then I closed up the cardboard box.

As I walked down the attic stairs carrying a million dollars of cash in a black trash bag, I said to Fatima, "You know the magic smartphone you carry? Sumera will need one too."

I carried a smartphone. As did Anna Kay, all of the *haremées*, and SJ-1. Fatima also carried a smartphone; hers had a green plastic case and a "GT Technologies" logo. Fatima's smartphone was magical: It worked when the nearest tower was far away, its battery never ran down, and it was on no carrier's billing plan.

Best of all, whenever I called Fatima or Fatima called me, the USA cellular-phone network was convinced that my phone was turned off. It was impossible for any third party to tap our phone call.

"D'Oh!" I said on the attic stairs. I added, "Sumera's phone needs to be blue."

"Does it have to?" Fatima pleaded. "I don't *do* blue."

"Master has spoken," I replied in a pretentious voice, as I unlocked the attic door.

A minute later, a trash bag that held a million dollars in cash was parked in my walk-in closet.

****

That evening
At a supermarket across town

Kelly Brown was twenty-four, the same age as Marvin Harper. In fact, Kelly had graduated from the same high school, on the same day, as Marvin Harper.

Kelly was genetically blessed: she had boobs that other women were convinced were implants (but were not), and puffy lips that other women were convinced had received collagen injections (but had not). The only thing fake about Kelly's body at twenty-four was that her hair's blond color came from a salon.

Kelly at twenty-four also was prosperous. Last year she had bought a yellow Mustang convertible from Tim Hanson Ford, and she had paid cash for the car. Her fat bank account came from being Marvin Harper's stockbroker at Value Trade. She was able to say truthfully that she had boosted the hero billionaire's net worth from thirty-two billion to eighty-six billion. This achievement netted Kelly many other clients and many other commissions.

How had Kelly become a stock-trading genius? Marvin had paid for four years of her college education at Gorshin University; but more than that, he had let her spend her undergraduate years poring over the stock-trading records of his great-uncle Warren. Warren Harper had been a stock-trading *genius:* Somehow he had known, right down to the day, when to buy stock and when to sell stock.

After Kelly had spent five years rummaging through Warren Harper's file cabinets, she had started to see trends, she had started to see patterns. She had spotted three NASDAQ "sleepers" *before* their stock prices exploded.

So now at twenty-four, Kelly Brown owned expensive clothes and wore them well, she owned an expensive car, she almost owned her own house (she could pay off the mortgage tomorrow if she chose), and other stockbrokers spoke of her in awe.

Not too shabby for the woman who had been the joke of her middle school and her high school!

Q: Is Kelly Brown a whore?

A: No. A whore requires payment before fucking you, your brother, and the landscaper.

Q: What happened when Kelly Brown's mom sent her to the grocery store?

A: Kelly Brown came home with bananas, cucumbers, and sausages. Each smelled like fish.

But Kelly, back in her mega-slut days, had not bothered with good boys, only bad boys. And Marvin Harper, straight-A student, had been the goodest of good boys at Plato Smith High School.

But near the end of their senior year, Marvin had gone from zero to sixty: He had begun to gather a no-shit *harem*, of students *and* teachers. Days had passed, but Marvin had never asked Kelly to become one of his harem girls.

Girls jealous of Kelly's looks, and even some old "boyfriends," had told her, "Marvin won't ask you to be one of his girls because he doesn't want skanks."

Kelly had forced the issue: She had sashayed up to Marvin and had asked to join his harem.

Marvin had not insulted her when he had given his answer. He had been polite, and he had bent over backwards to spare her feelings.

That had made his rejection sting all the more. Worse, he had rejected her in the high school, before first period, so kids who had been walking by had overheard Marvin's "No, Kelly."

In that moment, slut Kelly had hit rock bottom.

Less than a half-hour later, Kelly had briefly returned home, to change into less sexy clothes. While she had been at home, she had looked up Sexaholics Anonymous in the phone book, and had called them. That evening, Kelly had attended her first SA meeting.

Kelly had been celibate for all of the six years since. Which was even more of an achievement considering all the time that Kelly spent around Marvin Harper—Kelly was convinced that Marvin now was the sexiest man in the whole USA!

Not all the time that she spent with him was business-related. Marvin invited Kelly to have dinner at the mansion once a week—even though she had never been a *haremée*.

But six days out of seven, Kelly had to provide her own dinner. Now she was in the Produce section of her local supermarket, buying the ingredients for a chef's salad.

A can of Swedish ham was in her handbasket, as were three avocados, a bundle of green onions, and a head of lettuce. Kelly was picking up a cucumber when a woman's voice purred, "Cucumbers are useful for *all sorts of* things, don't you agree?"

Kelly recognized the woman's tone of voice; she had spoken that way herself, back in the day.

So Kelly was not surprised when she looked over and noted that the other woman looked like a slut. The other woman was young like herself, had big boobs, and was wearing a skirt so short and platform heels so high, they were totally inappropriate for a grocery store. With short, black, spiky hair, the other woman looked especially trashy.

Kelly snapped at the woman, "Cucumbers are *very* useful. For making salad. And cucumber facials."

The slut smiled. "*Other stuff* makes good facials too. We both know this."

"You are vulgar."

The slut replied, "And *you* are Kelly Brown. So drop the prim-and-proper act, honey. Your place or mine?"

Kelly stood straight. "If you know who I am, you know I was never really into girls—"

"*Pfft.*"

"—and you know I gave up that life six years ago."

The slut stepped closer. "But don't you miss it, Kelly honey? Don't you miss wave after wave of screaming cums? You could have that again, tonight—I *know* how to make a woman feel right."

"*Of course* I miss it. But I have a good life now, and I'd *lose it all* if I went back to Kelly the Slut."

Then Kelly walked past the spiky-haired slut. "Excuse me, 'honey,' but you're blocking the cherry tomatoes."

The slut said other things to Kelly then, but Kelly did not listen, Kelly did not reply, and soon Kelly was standing in a checkout line.

****

Fanzelle frowned. It had been a long time since she had propositioned someone and had been turned down. And by Kelly Brown, no less!

Okay, back to the drawing board. Which meant that Fanzelle would have to cook up a new look and a new line of gab to hit Kelly with.

But sooner or later, Fanzelle *would* seduce Kelly Brown—and not only because seducing a celibate person was so *fun!*

Chapter 9
Three LeClercs are Informed

Morning, a day and a half later (Tuesday)

Fatima and I met the LeClerc twins at the airport. Almira's first words to me were "Marvin, you're *shorter!*"

"Tell me about it," I grumped. In three days, I had shrunk six inches, and my muscles were not so big and defined as before. Oh, I was still tall and strong, but no longer did I get stared at by strangers.

"How did this happen?" Elvira asked.

I looked Elvira straight in the eyes and said, "I was hoping *you* could tell me."

Elvira's eyes narrowed. "Whatever is happening to you, Sumera and I had nothing to do with it."

Almira said, "She's telling the truth."

Elvira said to me, "I'm pissed you would even *think* such a thing about me."

Fatima said, "Yeah, sure, you're a choirgirl."

****

As soon as all four of us were in my car, I said, "Almira, I've got Sumera's lamp hidden away, but whenever you're ready to make your wishes, I'll fetch it for you."

In my rear-view mirror, I saw Almira smack her sister's stomach with the back of her hand. "I *told* you I could trust him, Elvie."

Elvira muttered something.

Almira said to me, "I'm not ready to wish yet. So hold on to the lamp for a while longer."

"And stay *stuck* in your sucky life a while longer, Almie," Elvira commented.

Then Elvira's mirror-reflection looked me in the eyes. "What about my million in cash, where is it at?"

I said, "I can get hold of the money whenever you want to go to the bank. But you should know that when you deposit the money, the bank has to report anything over ten thousand to the tax man. And when the nice man from the IRS asks you how you got hold of a million dollars in cash, how are you going to answer?"

"*Shit!*" Elvira said.

Almira said, "Everyone will think she robbed you, Marvin. Elvie will get arrested again."

I said, "Fortunately, Elvira, I've been thinking about this. I've figured out a way to keep your reputation good and keep you out of the Graybar Hilton."

Elvira said skeptically, "You would *do* that for me? Keep me out of jail after all the shit I've given you?"

****

As soon as the twins and Fatima and I were back in the mansion, I made a point of taking the twins to the monster kitchen. There I introduced the twins to "my newest *haremée*, Sumera Hatfield."

We walked in on Rivka Goldheim teaching Sumera how to make Omaha Salad for fifty people. Needless to say, with Rivka standing right there, the conversation between the twins and Sumera was *awkward*.

(Part of that awkwardness was because Michelle LeClerc had kicked Rivka out of the Abzug Society a year ago, and Rivka still was angry about that. Now at the mansion, Rivka was always quick to call out Elvira on any of her shit.)

Haremée-Sumera had the same brown skin and black hair as Fatima, but Sumera had blue eyes, not green. *Haremée*-Sumera was wearing blue sneakers, comfortable blue jeans, a blue ribbon in her black ponytail, and a blue-text/blue-background "I'm full of surprises!" t-shirt.

From time to time as we were talking, Rivka looked me up and down with a worried expression. Not only were Anna Kay, Fatima, and I worried about why I was losing height and muscle, but now my *haremées* were worried too.

After Fatima and I and the twins left the kitchen, Elvira said to me, "You don't have *enough* women fucking you? You couldn't leave Sumera in her lamp, you had to make her be another fuckbunny?"

Fatima said, "Spoken like a human who's never spent *centuries* stuck in her Vessel. Sumera would fuck Master *ten times a day* if it meant she would stay out of her lamp."

"Especially since she'd enjoy it all ten times," Almira said.

Elvira glared at her twin.

****

Almira and Elvira did not go to work at the Harper Foundation that day, because they were jet-lagged. So the twins did not get a chance to talk to Virgilia O'Keefe until that evening.

By then, the twins' body clocks were saying it was after midnight, and the girls were struggling to stay awake. As tired as they were, I expected the twins to defer their conversation with Virgilia till tomorrow.

Not so. After dinner, the twins and Virgilia withdrew to the gazebo by the swimming pool. Almira and Elvira each walked out with a can of hypercaffeinated cola in her hand.

****

Minutes later

Virgilia was saying to the twins, ". . . no longer Warren's sex slave. When he died, my cravings *stopped.*"

"All of a sudden?" Almira asked.

"Like flipping a switch. The same thing happened to Sherry. Anyway, three days after Warren died, Sherry and I were here at the mansion for what we figured would be our last time, to pack our things. God, I *couldn't wait* to put that part of my life behind me!"

"I'll bet," said Almira.

"Uh-huh, being a man's sex slave is disgusting." Elvira agreed.

Virgilia continued, "Then the mansion's new heir introduced himself, a virgin eighteen-year-old. I shook his hand, because it wasn't *his* fault his uncle was a dickhead, right? Anyway, I shook his hand and *click.*"

" 'Click'?" asked Elvira.

"Even as I was thinking, 'He's wonderful, he deserves to be served, I need for him to like me'—"

"*That* sounds familiar," said Almira.

"—part of me was thinking, 'Fuck, here I go again.' "

"So what happened next?" Almira asked.

Virgilia laughed. "What *happened?* We three went to bed, and Marvin lost his virginity."

Elvira said, "But you were his sex slaves by then. He *used* you for his own sexual gratification."

Virgilia sighed. "You are truly Michelle's child sometimes, Elvira. Marvin wasn't a brute that day, he was a virgin—alone with two willing strippers. *Of course* he had sex with us."

Elvira said, "I just think that a man should respect women *all the time*, is all."

Virgilia laughed. "By 'respect women,' you mean 'bow to their every dictate without challenge.' You know what you call a man who unfailingly 'respects women'?"

" 'Liberated.' "

"No, sooner or later he's called 'Cuckold.' "

Almira said, "No more arguing! Skip ahead to the part where you became not Marvin's sex slave."

Virgilia said, "This was the night that Paula Sarin was trying to magically kill Marvin, which was about two weeks after Warren died. Paula Sarin was Fatima's genie-master at the time. Well, I stole Fatima's lamp away from the bitch. My first wish was to be free from all magical mind control. I've had a clear mind ever since."

"And then?" asked Almira.

"Not much to tell," Virgilia said. "Within seconds, I realized that there was a long list of things that I had been willing to do for Marvin as his 'touch-slave,' and the *only* things he had ever asked me to do was to fuck and suck him. Oh, and to clean the pool."

Almira said, "Uh-huh, same here."

Elvira said, "That doesn't seem like much of a reason to devote your life to someone—that they could have acted like a prick around you but they didn't."

Virgilia said, "How do I explain this to you, princess? Warren made my life *miserable* for two years because of the power he held over me. Five minutes after he met me, on April 12, 2008, he had me giving him a blowjob in the parking lot of the Nimfo Club, he held the car door open, your mother caught me in the act, and *that's* how I got kicked out of Abzug Society! Then later on, after Warren had made me get implants and collagen injections and bleached-blond hair, he sent me back to the Nimfo Club, the site of my greatest humiliation, *to apply for a job as a stripper!* I tell you, when he was first dead, in May of 2010,

I fantasized about dragging him out of the mortuary and running him over with my car, again and again!"

"And Marvin wasn't *at all* like that?" Elvira asked. "Not even a little?"

"Marvin had just as much power over me, until my wish, but he never made me do anything that now I'm ashamed of. Not to mention, Marvin *didn't ask* for sex-slave powers, Fatima *gave them* to him, which makes a *huge* difference in my mind."

Almira sighed. "I've been telling you the same shit, Elvie, but you won't listen to me. Marvin is a good man."

Elvira could not disagree with Almie without sounding like a broken record; and she did not want to agree. So Elvira said nothing.

Elvira thought, *If Mother were here and she heard Almie say "Marvin is a good man," she'd burst a blood vessel. Then she'd disown my twin.*

****

Meanwhile, in Michelle Landrieu-LeClerc's garage

Alone in the garage, Michelle spoke in a clear voice: "*Pentagrammonub enkephalodub.*"

On the concrete garage floor, a chalk pentagram appeared with five lit candles at the outer corners.

Michelle said, "I summon you, Fanzelle."

This time, no Hollywood CGI tricks happened. One instant, the pentagram was empty; the next instant, Fanzelle the succubus stood inside the pentagram.

Michelle was bursting with excitement now. In an excited voice, she said to the demoness, "What's happening? What have you done to Marvin? How messed-up is his life now?"

Fanzelle replied archly, "You realize that it's been a little over three days since we made our pact, right? Don't expect *miracles* from me."

"You're stuck here in my garage till you tell me what I want to know."

Fanzelle rolled her eyes. "Very well. Marvin is six inches shorter, and less muscular. Every day, his body will get worse, until he's 5′2″ and puny-muscled."

"What about his money? Is he poorer?"

"Not yet. I've tried to seduce his stockbroker, but no luck so far."

Michelle made a raspberry. "You expect me to believe this, *looking* like you do? What, is the man *gay?*"

"Marvin's stockbroker is not a man, it's a woman, and she's determined to not have sex of any kind."

"But you can bring her down, right? Eventually?"

Fanzelle replied, "Eventually I'll get her naked in bed with me, I'm sure of that." Indeed, Fanzelle looked and sounded utterly confident.

Michelle said, "Very well. I dismiss you, Fanzelle. Begone."

Unlike her arrival in the pentagram, Fanzelle departed from the pentagram in a puff of red smoke.

Seconds later, Michelle had magically vaporized the pentagram and candles, and was walking toward the door to the laundry room.

****

An instant after Fanzelle had vanished, she reappeared—not in Hell, but inside an empty barn thirty-eight miles away.

Fanzelle laughed, loud and long, but no humans heard her.

Fanzelle gloated. "For the first time since 4004 B.C., a summoner trusts her demon—aren't *I* the clever one! And isn't Michelle the stupid one? If she'd spent even one hour on Google, she'd know that *pentagrammonub enkephalodub* means *imaginary pentagram*. She summoned me without the protection of a pentagram—at any time, I could have stepped across the 'pentagram' and ripped her heart out of her chest. Lucky for her, I have *bigger* ambitions than one foolish woman's soul."

Fanzelle wiped the grin off her face. "Now to work."

She held out her hand; with a puff of smoke and the smell of brimstone, a piece of paper appeared in her hand. On the paper was a list of demon names.

Fanzelle held the list in front of her and said, "I summon you, Bilewine."

There was a puff of smoke, and a demon Fanzelle did not know well, appeared in front of her. Bilewine appeared with an evil smile; clearly he was looking forward to torturing and killing his summoner. Bilewine's smile vanished when he saw that his summoner was not human.

Fanzelle said, "You are free to do work on Earth for Satan, Prince of Darkness. Begin your work."

Bilewine nodded at Fanzelle, then vanished in a puff of smoke.

"I summon you, Murder. I summon you, Scaly."

A tall demon and a short demoness appeared before Fanzelle, standing side by side.

Fanzelle gave the same orders to Murder and Scaly. They vanished together.

Fanzelle was inhumanly tireless, not stopping till she had summoned all 735 of the other demons of Hell.

Chapter 10
Kelly Falls Off the Wagon

The next morning (Wednesday)

My height was now 6'0". *Sigh*. Eight inches shorter.

After a deep sleep, the twins were no longer jet-lagged (for the most part). After breakfast, they dressed to go to work at the Harper Foundation. But rather than go to work in Elvira's car (the twins took turns driving to work), today Almira and Elvira rode with me in one of my seven cars.

In the car: Almira and Elvira, myself, and a trash bag containing a little over a million dollars in cash.

The twins wanted to come in with me and actually watch me make the cash deposit; but I reminded them that their faces would be videorecorded, and this was not smart. So while pouting, the women stayed in the car.

It was the bank manager who handled my million-dollar deposit. (Actually, I'd added some cash from my safe, so the official deposit was one-million-sixteen dollars.) I told the bank manager that this bagful of cash was "poker winnings." Thanks to my magic pheromones, he completely believed me.

He felt obliged to inform me that the bank was required by law to report this deposit to the Internal Revenue Service. I shrugged. I did not inform him that SJ-1 would block the IRS from ever receiving the message.

When I returned to the car, a half-hour later—the bank counted that cash three times—the twins were eager to see the deposit slip.

Elvira said, "And when the coast is clear, you'll write me a check for a million dollars? That's still the plan?"

I rolled my eyes. "Yes, Elvira, that's still the plan."

Almira said, "Dear sister, I don't hear you saying 'Thank you.' Marvin won't mind if you say it, hint-hint."

As we were pulling into the Harper Foundation parking lot, a green lightball appeared in the car. Greta Garbo's voice asked, "Anything special for dessert tonight?"

Before I could answer, Almira said, "*Ooh*, chocolate éclairs, Marvin, *please?*"

I shrugged. "Sure, why not?"

"Very well, chocolate éclairs for dessert," Greta Garbo's voice said. The lightning-ball vanished.

****

Meanwhile, elsewhere in the city

Kelly Brown was having an awful day.

Wellness Labs (NYSE symbol: WLLB) was an up-and-coming pharmaceutical company. Three days ago, the company had been hit by a rumor that their best-selling heart medication, Coronarix, was dangerously unsafe. Even worse, so the rumor said, Wellness Labs had known that Coronarix was dangerous, and the drug had been given FDA approval only after Wellness Labs had submitted altered reports.

Today's *Wall Street Journal* was reporting that not only were the rumors true, but the rumors had been started by Wellness Labs's corporate officers, who had sold short all of their Wellness Labs stock. As a result, the Food and Drug Administration and the Securities Exchange Commission now were both investigating Wellness Labs.

Last week, Wellness Labs stock had been selling at 87 dollars a share, and had been climbing. Now WLLB stock was selling at 19 and was dropping fast.

For the past year, Kelly had been pushing Wellness Labs stock to all her Value Trade clients as a "sure growth" stock. And now, at least one client was angry about this—

"It's my own fault," the man was saying, "for thinking that one of Marvin Harper's former harem girls knows anything about stocks."

What? Kelly thought, *You've crossed over the line, buddy!* Aloud, she said, "Mr. Binder, I assure you that I have never slept with Marvin Harper, or even dated him."

"Don't try to flimflam me, Ms. Brown. You were in the Society pages three months ago, attending Harper's 'Dance to End World Hunger.' I must say, you were *not* dressed like a stockbroker that night!"

Kelly had been wearing a gown that had been tight and scarlet, and that had shown off her boobs. Eunice, Kelly's sponsor at Sexaholics Anonymous, had tried to talk Kelly out of wearing so racy a dress.

Now Kelly replied, "Mr. Binder, I've made seventeen recommendations of stock to my clients as 'sure growth' stocks, and I was right about thirteen of them. Last week, I was right about Wellness Labs too."

"Dumb luck, Ms. Brown. You're what, twenty-five—"

"Twenty-four. *Ahem*, I'm twenty-four."

"—and stockbrokers *twice* your age don't have such a good batting average with little-known stocks. Besides which, *those older guys* haven't slept with Marvin Harper!"

Kelly wanted to scream. "Mr. Binder, I say again: Marvin Harper and I are *friends*. No hanky-panky."

"Sure, not *now*. Ms. Brown, please close out my account with you, effective immediately."

Kelly sighed. "As you wish, Mr. Binder."

As Kelly was closing out Donald Binder's account, her desk phone rang. It turned out that she was being summoned to her boss's office.

She knew she was in trouble when her boss's first words to her were "Shut the door."

Her boss's next words to her were, "It has been alleged that you are sleeping with Marvin Harper. Who, besides being a married man, is our biggest client."

Five minutes later, Kelly still had her job (though she now was on probation). The first thing that Kelly did when she was back at her desk was to phone her Sexaholics Anonymous sponsor, Eunice—

"Eunice, I am under *killer* stress, and it's either go to an SA meeting tonight, or else fuck an entire sports team. Meet me there? . . . Even if nobody is there but me, you, and the Group Leader, I'm going!"

****

That evening

Kelly's luck continued to be shitty. Wellness Labs stock had closed for the day at 13-1/8; Kelly was *stressed*.

The local Sexaholics Anonymous chapter met in the basement of an Episcopal church. As Kelly was stepping out of her car in the parking lot, she discovered she had a text-message waiting for her—

My car making awful noises. I can't get to meeting. Stay strong today, girlfriend.

Kelly sighed.

Seconds later, Kelly walked into the meeting room and glanced around. She saw ten folding-metal chairs set out, but only seven people (including herself) were in the room. Kelly recognized everybody except for a redhead who was sweetening her coffee.

The redhead was sex on (high-heel-booted) legs.

Kelly sat down in a gray chair, and the redhead immediately sat down next to her. "Hi, I'm Zelle," the redhead said, smiling at Kelly.

"*Zelle*, short for *Gazelle?*" Kelly asked.

"Something like that," Zelle said, still smiling at Kelly.

"I'm Kelly," Kelly said, and shook hands with the newcomer.

"Kelly *what?* What's your last name?"

"You must be new here. *That* is one of the questions you never ask. Another thing you don't ever say is who in the group is hot."

"Shit, Kelly, I'm glad you told me. Because I was just about to say how hot *you* are. It isn't often I meet someone with boobs as big as mine."

"Thank you," Kelly said, blushing, "but that isn't appropriate to say here."

"I gotcha, I gotcha," Zelle replied. "So I won't say anything about how *lickable* you look."

"Just so you know," Kelly said, "I'm straight." But Kelly said it with a smile.

The meeting started. Zelle, as the first-timer, was asked to speak first. She said she was a lesbian, and she had been told about the SA group by "a friend of a friend," but "I'm not a sexaholic, so I don't need to be here." Kelly made herself not roll her eyes at Zelle's last comment, but others in the group were not so polite.

Then it was Kelly's turn, since she was attending an SA meeting out of her normal schedule. Kelly talked in generalities about her run-in with her client and her boss, "and they both accused me of sleeping with Marvin Harper, who's my client." Kelly finished with "I feel like driving to the truck stop and fucking every man I find!"

"Don't do that," said the Group Leader. "Stay strong today."

"Why *not* fuck everybody at the truck stop?" asked Zelle. "Or better yet, go over to Marvin Harper's house and then fuck him silly. *Ha*, it's not like he turns down pussy!"

The Group Leader said, "Zelle, this is not a good idea. It would not be good for Kelly."

"*Besides*," Kelly said bitterly, "I asked to join his harem six years ago, and he turned me down flat. To him, I'll always be a skank!"

Zelle put a hand on Kelly's arm. "You poor thing. For what it's worth, *I* don't think you're a skank."

****

After the end of the meeting

Zelle said to Kelly, "Let's grab some Starbucks. I'm buying."

Kelly laughed, then said, "I think you're trying to seduce me."

"Is it working? Meanwhile, yes or no to the coffee?"

Kelly said, "Sure, I'll drink coffee with you. But booze is out."

"Too bad, because I know this great little place—"

"Let me guess: Either no men there at all, or no man there will bother me."

"Wow, Kelly, you're psychic."

****

A half-hour later
Parking lot, Starbucks Coffee no. 9,385,639

Kelly pounded her fist on the steering wheel. "It makes me so *mad!* I haven't fucked Marvin Harper—hell, for the past six years, I haven't fucked *anybody!* And yet I catch just as much shit today as when I was the school slut."

To Kelly's right, Zelle turned as much as the car's front seat would let her; Zelle looked Kelly in the eyes. "Sweetie, if you're going to get the shit, you should get the glory too."

Zelle put her hand on the back of Kelly's head, and pulled Kelly forward into a kiss.

Kelly let herself be kissed, even as she was mumbling words of protest.

The second time Zelle kissed Kelly, Kelly kissed back.

When Kelly broke the kiss, she said, "All the times I've had sex with a girl, she was some guy's girlfriend. The lesbian stuff never did much for me. I'm probably wasting your time."

Zelle did not reply; instead, she kissed Kelly a third time.

****

An hour and a half later

Kelly and Zelle were in Kelly's bedroom, and Kelly's brain was melted.

As straight as Kelly had once believed she was, she had never had *so many* orgasms, or such *intense* orgasms, as what Zelle's hands and mouth had given her tonight. Zelle was heaven-sent!

But now it was time for payback. Kelly eagerly took up the task of licking a clitoris for the first time in six years.

****

Ten minutes later

Kelly Brown had now both received from Fanzelle, and had given to Fanzelle, lesbian attention. Now the Protocol permitted Fanzelle to soul-suck Kelly Brown dead.

But Fanzelle had other plans for Kelly.

Now Fanzelle grabbed the back of Kelly's head with one hand, and stroked Kelly's forehead with her other hand. Kelly's eyelids slammed shut.

Fanzelle said, "Listen to my voice, Kelly. You hear only my voice. . ."

Kelly mumbled, "I hear only your voice. . ."

"You must obey my voice. . ."

"I must obey your voice. . ."

Fanzelle said, "Kelly Brown, when you get to work tomorrow, this is what you shall do . . ."

****

The next morning (Thursday)

At work, Kelly Brown felt jittery; her whole body felt like she was waiting for something. Her nervousness did not go away until the New York Stock Exchange opened. Within minutes, Kelly sold every share of stock that Marvin Harper owned—for a penny a share.

When Kelly realized what she had done, she logged off her computer, fled the building without telling anyone where she was going, then drove straight to the truck stop.

Chapter 11
Kelly Dies, I Get Short

An hour later (Thursday)

This morning I had discovered that I was only 5'10" tall, and that I could bench-press less than half of the weight that I could lift a week ago. And now *this?*

I was in the middle of the most shocking and surreal phone call I had ever received. *Kelly Brown had sold over eighty billion dollars' worth of my stock for pennies!* Okay, fine, Value Trade would electronically transfer thirty-seven million dollars and change to me—but compared to eighty-something billion dollars, this was pennies!

"Let me assure you, Mr. Harper," the man on the phone was saying, "Value Trade will give full cooperation to law enforcement when you press charges against Ms. Brown."

"Mmm," I grunted in response. I was not calm enough to say more.

"For what it's worth, Ms. Brown has been fired."

"I see," I replied, not trusting myself to say more.

The call ended soon after. And I'll bet it took all of the self-control that Kelly's boss had, *not* to end the call with *Please don't sue Value Trade! Please don't sue me!*

The *only* good news out of the phone call? Value Trade was waiving the stockbroker commission. Nice of them.

I tried calling Kelly's smartphone. It went to voicemail. I called her a second time; I got voicemail a second time.

"*Fuck!*" I yelled in the nearly-empty computer room. Across the room, SJ-1 looked up from her laptop, startled.

"SJ-1, please fetch Fatima," I said. "Faster than light. And bring Sumera too."

SJ-1 ran from the room.

I already knew that neither Fatima nor Sumera could explain why I was shrinking; but I was pretty sure that Fatima and SJ-1 could get me some answers to *Kelly, why did you do this to me?*

And who knows, maybe Sumera could be useful too.

****

Two minutes later

The computer-room door was shut, and four people were in the computer room: SJ-1, both of my genies, and myself. Fatima was working her scrying ball.

Fatima announced, "Kelly is at the truck stop where State Highway 36 crosses Smith Freeway, north of the city."

"What's she doing at a *truck stop?*" I asked, completely puzzled. "Please show me."

Fatima sighed. "Master, you're *not* going to like it."

Fatima created a green-lightning ball, which floated up and stopped just below the ceiling. Then the green-lightning ball shot a continuous bolt of green lightning to Fatima's scrying ball.

The wall between the computer room and the foyer disappeared, to be replaced with asphalt and semi-trailer trucks. Fatima had created the illusion of us standing in the truck stop's huge parking lot.

Two eighteen-wheeler rigs were parked side by side, five feet apart, seemingly on either side of me. Kneeling down between them was Kelly, seemingly five feet in front of me. She was sucking off a man in a "Peterbilt" cap, while giving a second man a handjob, while her other hand had disappeared up her pinstripe-wool skirt.

Several men were standing nearby and were watching all this; they made no effort to interfere.

The matching pinstripe top to the skirt was lying on the pavement, a few feet away from Kelly.

Kelly's black "professional woman" pumps were scuffed. Her red-satin blouse was unbuttoned enough to show off a red bra. That blouse had cumstains on it, and there was semen in Kelly's hair and on her chin.

"Suck him good, slut," an onlooker-man said.

The man whom Kelly was sucking off said, "You can't beat a free blowjob from a big-tittied slut."

"*What is wrong with you, Kelly?*" I yelled. "Have you gone *crazy?*"

But Kelly was not really kneeling a few feet away from me, so she did not hear my question. Not to mention, she acted so focused on the blowjob that even if she had heard, she might not have stopped what she was doing in order to answer me.

Fatima said sadly, "She didn't stay strong today. It's amazing she lasted six years."

I said, "But why all the crazy stuff? What possesses her to sell off my stock and then suck off truck drivers?"

" 'Possesses'?" said Sumera.

Fatima said sadly, "Master, I can't answer your questions. But I *can* tell you she's doing all this freely; I see no spellmark on her."

"*Pfft,*" Sumera said. "You *sure* about that, Green Girl?"

Sumera turned toward me and said, "Master, I'd like to try something. Is this okay?"

I nodded, then a marble-sized blue-light ball flew from Sumera's hands to the floating green-lightning ball. The green ball absorbed the blue ball, then the illusion changed.

At first I thought that the only change was that the three-dimensional color illusion was now shades of gray. But then I saw something red on Kelly's forehead.

On gray-Kelly's gray forehead was a red pentagram, in the middle of which was a red goat-head. Just to the right of the pentagram-and-goat-head was a stylized red *f18*.

"What am I seeing?" I asked. But I suspected I already knew.

Sumera said, "She has a hidden demonic spellmark. The demon being Fanzelle, FoulArse, Friendless, FaceBurnt, . . ." Sumera recited a long list of *F*-names.

Sumera shot Fatima a triumphant smile. Then Sumera summoned her scrying ball.

A few seconds later, Sumera announced, "That woman has been marked by Fanzelle, a succubus."

Right then a nasty thought hit me. I remembered that *brimstone* was the old-fashioned word for *sulfur*, and sulfur was what made matches light. I asked my two bound *djinn*, "Do *I* have a hidden demonic spellmark?"

Fatima shook her head. "I can't answer that."

Sumera grinned. "*I* can." She shot a blue-light ball straight for my face. It rose slightly as it got closer, and hit me in the forehead.

For one second, I felt a burning sensation.

Fatima, while staring at my forehead, gasped.

I sighed. "My life gets more and more interesting."

****

One second later

Gray-and-red Kelly Brown was still performing her live-action porno at the all-gray truck stop. Then a woman's voice called out, "Kelly? Kelly Brown? Where are you?"

Kelly pulled her mouth off the guy's dick. "*Zelle?*"

The man she had been sucking, said, "Don't stop!"

A woman-creature walked into the illusion. Instead of being gray like everyone else, she was solid red—and she had giant bat-wings, a devil-tail, and horns. The demoness said, "Stand up, Kelly, we're leaving now."

Kelly stood up, rushed to the demoness, and kissed her with passion. "Zelle, I *really* messed up today and I *need* you to make love to me. I promise I'll make it good for you."

I yelled, "Kelly, why are you kissing that demoness? Get away from her!"

Fatima said, "Kelly is now sexually addicted to the succubus. And will stay like this till she dies."

"Which is probably five minutes from now," Sumera said. "Fanzelle doesn't need Kelly around anymore."

"Five minutes from now?" I said. "*Over my dead body!*" My fists were clenched. "Fatima, I request you please *foom* us over to the truck stop. *Now.*"

"Master," Sumera said, "if you and Fatima plan to fight a demon, even a succubus, you need *me* there too. But I warn you: We won't be enough."

"Is this true?" I asked Fatima. "We need Sumera there too?"

Fatima looked down at the carpet. "Yes."

At the gray truck stop meanwhile, red Fanzelle was leading gray-and-red Kelly toward a gray car with an open driver-door.

"Kill the illusion and let's go!" I said.

My ears popped.

An instant later, I stood outside at the full-color truck stop. Kelly and a sexy woman were walking five feet in front of me; they were almost at the demoness's car.

I took off running.

****

Nearby, male voices yelled, "Motherfuck, where'd *they* come from?"

As I ran toward Kelly, I passed the demoness, who now looked like a porn-actress redhead wearing lots of tight black leather. I caught a glimpse of a surprised expression on the demoness's face.

I threw my arms around Kelly, Firstly, to carry her away from the demoness; secondly, to make her my touch-slave. Since May of 2010, I had avoided kissing, shaking hands with, and hugging Kelly Brown, so to prevent making her my touch-slave; but now I needed her to be obedient.

Such was my plan—but my plan got derailed.

In my arms, Kelly struggled fiercely. "Who the fuck are *you?* Let go of me!" Kelly had cock-breath.

I found that lifting Kelly off the ground was hard now, because of my reduced height and strength; and carrying Kelly was impossible while she struggled.

Meanwhile, I was replying, "Calm down. I'm Marvin! Marvin Harper."

Struggling Kelly said, "No, you're not—Marvin is tall and strong. Zelle, call the police!"

"No need," Fanzelle replied scornfully.

I felt something slim and muscular wrap around my ankle, then my ankle was yanked back. Both Kelly and I crashed onto asphalt. *Oof!*

A man's voice said, "What the fuck is going on? Should we call the police?"

Another man said, "No way am I letting any kind of cop near my swindle sheets."

I heard a sizzling sound that moved through the air, as Fatima demanded, "Let go of him!"

Fanzelle laughed. "Really, dearie, hitting a *demon of Hell* with a *fireball?* For shame, sweetie, all I did was to trip him with my tail."

Then Fanzelle purred, "Hello, Sumera. HatesBeauty says *nice things* about you."

An instant later, someone else hit the asphalt with a *thump*. "Ow!" Fanzelle said.

Fanzelle yelled, "An *repulsion spell*, Sumera? *This* is how you repay Hell's hospitality?"

In reply, Sumera yelled something angry in Arabic.

Meanwhile, Kelly had taken advantage of my getting tripped. She broke my grip and jumped to her feet.

Kelly's running footsteps took her straight toward the demoness. "Zelle, what's *happening?* Why is Marvin's housekeeper throwing things at you?"

I felt the tail unwrap from my ankle. I yelled, "Hold your fire, don't hurt Kelly!" even as I was rushing to stand.

Once I was standing, I was only inches away from both Fanzelle, who herself was standing again; and Kelly, whom Fanzelle was hugging. I brought my fist back, intending to punch the porn-actress redhead in the face—

Lightning-fast, one of Fanzelle's hands left Kelly's back to grab me by the jaw. I was yanked up in the air.

"Fuck, that redhead is *strong!*" a man's voice said.

Meanwhile, from somewhere by Fanzelle's knee, a red fireball shot toward Fatima's face. Right afterward, a second red fireball flew from Fanzelle's knee toward Sumera's face.

Sumera tried to duck. Wide-eyed Fatima didn't. Sumera's fireball curved to follow her.

Both bound *djinn* were hit in the face; both bound *djinn* screamed.

Fanzelle laughed. "Hellfire, it *hurt*, ain't that right, bitches?"

Meanwhile, I tried hammering on Fanzelle's wrist, then I went back to my earlier plan of punching Fanzelle in the face. Hammering did no good, and she dodged my punches.

"Zelle, how are you *doing* all this?" Kelly asked.

"You *really* want to know, Kelly?" the porn-actress redhead asked in an ominous voice.

Then the redhead's hair turned pink, and her skin and eyebrows turned red. Bat-wings, horns, and a tail all appeared. Fanzelle still was dressed in tight black leather.

"Damnation!" a man's voice said.

Kelly struggled to get away from the demoness, but could not break free of Fanzelle's one-armed grip.

Fanzelle looked over at me. "I'm forbidden to kill you. But why should I wait four more days to make you a scrawny shorty?"

I felt my body change.

"*Whoa,*" said a male voice, "poor dude's getting *short!*"

"*Nooo!*" yelled Fatima. She started throwing green fireballs at Fanzelle, one after another—

But those fireballs hit an invisible shield, two feet from Fanzelle's body. Fanzelle's pink hair was not even mussed.

Sumera added her own blue fireballs to Fatima's green. But Sumera had no more success at injuring Fanzelle than Fatima was having.

I did not need a mirror to know what Fanzelle had just done to me. The demoness, and even Kelly, were now bigger than me; I was 5'2" again.

Meanwhile, Kelly was saying, "You put a spell on me, *that's* why I sold Marvin's stocks for nothing?"

Fanzelle said, "Yes, sweetie. You've been useful as well as fun, but now I don't need you anymore. KISS ME."

"Yes, Zelle," Kelly said in a robotic voice. She kissed the demoness.

"Master!" Fatima yelled, while she was still trying to fireball-hit the demoness. "Fanzelle is soul-sucking Kelly— try to stop her!"

I tried, I surely did. I could not manage to even inconvenience Fanzelle.

I was still trying to hurt Fanzelle, all while I was still being held aloft, when the demoness let go of me.

I stumbled as I hit the ground, even as—

—Fanzelle resumed her "porn-actress redhead" look, even as—

—Kelly Brown slumped to the ground.

"She's dead, Master," Fatima said.

The porn-actress redhead stepped over Kelly Brown's body as if Kelly were a sack of potatoes, then slid behind the wheel of her car. The porn-actress redhead looked at me and said, "Kelly will be in Hell within the hour—dying unshriven for mortal sins will do that to you. Goodbye, 'hero billionaire.' "

Laughing Fanzelle shut her car door before driving away.

I heard sirens then—police cars racing north on Smith Freeway. Fatima said, "Master, we need to *go!*"

I took a deep breath with my puny, shorty body, then I looked up at the faces of my two genies. "Yes, let's go."

My ears popped.

****

One second later

Fatima, Sumera, and I were back in the computer room at the mansion.

Now what do I do with my life? I thought. I was strongly tempted to wallow in self-pity.

SJ-1 stared down at me. Now she was as many inches taller than me as I had been taller than her, five days ago.

I looked up at my two genies and said "Thank you for your help. Thank you for fighting for me."

Sumera shrugged. "I did it because I was compelled to."

Fatima snapped, "That's your *only* reason?"

Sumera shrugged. "Maybe also because you're the nicest master I've ever had."

I said to Sumera, "I try. Now please find my wife and ask her to come in here." I glanced at the clock. "Anna Kay's probably in the exercise room."

Sumera nodded and left.

Fatima looked at SJ-1 and said, "I need to talk to Master in private."

SJ-1 walked out of the computer room and shut the door.

As soon as we were alone, Fatima asked, "Master, pardon me for asking this, but have you cheated on Anna Kay without her knowing? Is it possible that you've fucked the succubus?"

"*No.* I fuck only women in the mansion. I stopped 'auditioning' women to be *haremées* five years ago."

Fatima sighed. "Then the only other way Fanzelle would be allowed to spellmark you is if she made a pact with a mortal about you."

"Who hates me that much? I have no clue."

The computer-room door opened, and Anna Kay walked in. "Why is SJ-1—*Marvin?*"

I turned to face my wife, so that she could see me in my puny, 5′2″ glory. I said to her, "Turns out my shrinking was because of demon magic. Today Fanzelle the demoness decided to not drag things out."

Anna Kay looked at me, for what seemed like years. She *did* not speak; I *could* not speak. It occurred to me, *I might be served with divorce papers in a week.*

Then Anna Kay hurried forward and wrapped her arms around me. "I'm here for you," she said.

I sighed with relief.

Anna Kay murmured into my hair, "Tell me what you are thinking, my husband."

"What am I thinking?" I paused. I made a choice then, *not* to wallow in self-pity. "Even with this *shit*, I have a great life."

Then I said, while not speaking to anyone in particular, "God, please somebody tell me who put out a demon-hit on me, and why."

White light flashed in the computer room, and a white-winged, silver-eyed angel appeared. "MARVIN STEVEN HARPER, YOUR PRAYER IS ANSWERED."

Chapter 12
Another Angel, Another Genie

One second later (Thursday)

I said to SJ-1, "Please go fetch Sumera again. Don't mention the angel when anyone else might overhear."

SJ-1 hurried to the door.

Fatima, glaring at me, said, "*Must we* bring Sumera in on this?"

SJ-1 stopped with her hand on the doorknob. She watched Fatima and me; SJ-1 gave the angel and Anna Kay each only a glance.

I replied, "The angel could have appeared when I was on the toilet, and talked to me alone. Instead, the angel appeared in front of me when a powerful bound *djinni*— that's you—could hear the angel's words. Sumera is also a powerful bound *djinni*; she deserves to hear the angel's words for herself, not hear selected quotes afterward."

Fatima turned to SJ-1 and snapped, "Hurry and find her. Hurry back."

After the door shut, Fatima resumed glaring at me. "When you made your wishes six years ago, I gave you *more* than you asked for. In six years, I have turned down *only one* of your magical requests. I have given you the best sex I could, and I have given sex to you often. I have often praised you to the rest of Green Tribe. Then the blue-skinned bitch shows up, and you treat her *better* than you treat me!"

I made my voice sound calm: "How have I treated Sumera better than you?"

"When you first brought her out of the lamp, you told her she had to pretend to be a *harémée*. But as housekeeper, I make up the work assignments for the *harémées*. Except for Sumera—you expressly interfered with me assigning her!"

"If I hadn't interfered, I'm sure you would have split toilet-scrubbing duty between Elvira and Sumera. Tell me if I'm wrong."

Fatima frowned but said nothing.

Again I made my voice sound calm: "Is there any *other* way that you feel I'm showing favoritism to Sumera?"

Fatima snapped, "Yes, this whole incident with Kelly at the truck stop, and Fanzelle the demoness. You basically made Sumera the *lead djinni* and I got made the *sidekick*."

"It quickly became obvious to me that Sumera knows more than you about demons. And about demon magic. Make of this what you will."

Fatima muttered, "Aleser was *right* about the bitch. But he got stuck in a lamp for supposedly causing trouble."

I caught the reference. Twenty-six hundred years ago, Aleser of Green Tribe saying that Sumera of Blue Tribe had learned magic from demons had been the cause of the almost-fought *Djinn* War. Six *djinn* had been shoved into brass Vessels in order to prevent that war.

Now Fatima glared at the silent angel in the computer room. "Aleser got *shafted* by Solomon and his pet angel."

The angel stayed silent.

SJ-1 entered through the door then, with Sumera right behind her. Sumera glanced at the angel, then said to me, "What *is* it with you, Master? I've been out of my lamp *four days*, and already I've seen a demon and an angel."

I laughed. "Welcome to *my* world."

Then I turned to the angel. "What is your message for me?"

****

One minute later

The angel had told me who had made the pact, and had told me everything in the pact (except for what was required to send Michelle to Hell).

I said, "*Michelle*, huh? If there's *anybody* I know who would make a pact with a demon in order to mess with me, it would be her."

Sumera nodded. "I've read Elvira's memories of her mother. Michelle is disgusting, even for a wormfood."

I asked the angel, "Any chance I can persuade you to undo all this? Rip up the pact?"

"NO. IT IS HEAVEN'S POLICY NEVER TO INTERFERE WITH A DEMON PACT, ONCE MADE."

Fatima looked at the angel. "Why are you here then? 'Michelle LeClerc is who made the deal' is too *un*important a news item to send an angel to tell it to Master."

The angel looked at me. "MARVIN STEVEN HARPER, READ THE WORLD NEWS FOR A WEEK AND YOU WILL FIGURE OUT WHY. TWO DAYS AGO, THE DEMON CALLED FANZELLE UNLEASHED ALL THE DEMONS OF HELL."

I said, "*All* the demons? *How?*"

"THE DEMON CALLED FANZELLE IS FREE TO REMAIN ON EARTH, AND SHE HAS SUMMONED ALL THE OTHER DEMONS WITHOUT HER DRAWING A PENTAGRAM. THESE OTHER DEMONS, SUMMONED WITHOUT BINDING, ALSO ARE FREE TO REMAIN ON EARTH. A FEW DEMONS HAVE RETURNED TO HELL, IN ORDER TO TORTURE DAMNED SOULS; BUT EXCEPT FOR THOSE FEW, HELL IS EMPTY."

"*Whoa,*" I said. "And this has never happened before?"

"NEVER."

The angel explained—

Michelle completely trusted her demon, which had never happened before. Fanzelle had taught trusting Michelle a spell to conjure up a pentagram; in truth, the pentagram was illusionary, and so Michelle was unprotected against demon attack. But Fanzelle had not immediately killed her defenseless summoner, which likewise had never happened before.

Before, when a demon immediately killed his unprotected summoner, afterward the demon ravaged the Earth until two angels came and sent the demon to Hell. "The Protocol" allowed the angels to punish this demon in this way.

But the demoness Fanzelle not only had spared her summoner, she herself had harmed no mortal on Earth—

I yelled, "Say *what?* Fanzelle killed Kelly Brown in cold blood. The three of us saw it happen. Spank her demon-ass right now!"

"KELLY MARIE BROWN COMMITTED HOMOSEXUAL SIN AND WAS UNSHRIVEN. BY THE PROTOCOL, THE DEMON CALLED FANZELLE WAS ALLOWED TO KILL HER."

I said, "The Protocol is fucked up."

The angel then said something mysterious: "THE PROTOCOL IS NOT WRONG, THE PROTOCOL *SEEMS* WRONG. THERE IS A DIFFERENCE."

Nobody in the computer room replied to that.

The angel finished its lecture with: "THE PROTOCOL DOES NOT MENTION A FREE DEMON SUMMONING OTHER DEMONS. AS A RESULT, THE DEMON CALLED FANZELLE HAS DONE NOTHING SO THAT THE PROTOCOL ALLOWS HER TO BE CAST DOWN."

I figured out the rest: "You angels are overworked now, catching demons by the truckload and sending them to

Hell. Then as soon as you cast a demon down, Fanzelle summons him back up, but you can't touch Fanzelle."

"YES. IT IS A PROBLEM."

"A problem that, for some reason, you want *me* to know about."

"YES."

I was quiet for several seconds, while the angel looked at me with silver eyes and an expressionless face. When I spoke again, it was not to say *Why me?* Or *It looks like I'm being handed a lot of responsibility.* Instead, I said to the angel—

"While I've got you here, let me ask you a silly question: Is the Genie of the Ring real, or just a character in a story?"

****

One second later

Fatima slapped her forehead with her palm.

Sumera muttered something.

SJ-1 and the angel each stayed expressionless.

The angel replied, "THE GENIE OF THE RING IS REAL. ROSHRADZAM IS ALSO THE BOUND *DJINNI* TO GO THE LONGEST TIME SINCE HE LAST LEFT HIS VESSEL: 332 SOLAR YEARS."

"That's awful!" I said. "Why so long?"

"HIS VESSEL, A RUBY RING, IS IN A CREVICE IN A STONE FLOOR. ONLY A HUMAN WITH A GOOD LIGHT AND LONG, SLIM TONGS COULD CLAIM THE RING."

I said, "Stuck in there for 332 years? That's cruel to the genie—"

"So what?" said Sumera. "He's Turd Tribe. No big deal."

I looked at the angel, put my hand out, and said, "I ask for the Ring."

Reader, it is not often that someone catches an angel by surprise.

"NO. IT IS GOD'S PLAN THAT A VESSEL BE FOUND ACCIDENTALLY, BE GIVEN BY THE PREVIOUS MASTER TO THE NEXT MASTER, OR BE SEIZED BY THE NEXT MASTER FROM THE PREVIOUS MASTER. A HUMAN MAY NOT PETITION HEAVEN FOR A VESSEL AND ITS BOUND *DJINNI*."

I said, "With all due respect, God's plan has a stick up its ass."

Fatima slapped her forehead with her palm again.

I continued, "I own a garageful of automobiles and a jet airplane, all of which I have current licenses for. Even after what Kelly Brown did to me, I have money enough to fuel my cars and airplane. I can go *anywhere on the planet* with what I've already got."

I did not add that if I needed *magical* transportation, I could request this of Fatima, and she would probably take me wherever I wanted to go. As annoyed as Fatima was at me right now, I was not about to even *hint* that I maybe was taking her request-grants for granted.

I continued, "I'm not asking for the Ring so I can scam Heaven into granting me wishes. The Genie of the Ring can't grant wishes, and Sumera owes me three wishes which I haven't spoken yet. Give me the Ring so I can rub it and free this guy Roshradzam."

Fatima remarked to Sumera, "Our master is the most compassionate being I have ever met."

Sumera sniffed. "Compassion for a Turd Tribe human is wasted."

I had been holding out my hand all this time, my palm up. The angel spoke no reply, but now white light flashed, and a man's ruby ring pressed down on my palm.

"Thank you," I said to the angel.

I slipped the ring onto my right hand. I noted that a hole had been drilled into the center of the ruby. When I looked down into the hole, I saw something brown and shifting, like a miniature brown-smoke cloud.

I swiped my fingertip across the ruby.

The ring vibrated on my finger, quickly and forcefully like a jackhammer. I heard a high-pitched squeal, while brown smoke poured out of the hole in the ruby—lots and lots of brown smoke.

The angel said, "YOU IN THIS ROOM HAVE BEEN TOLD A SPECIAL REVELATION. USE THE KNOWLEDGE WISELY." With a flash of white light, the angel vanished.

****

Thirty seconds later

The Genie of the Ring had Arab features and he wore brown Middle Eastern clothing. His skin was brown, and his hair and beard were brown. His eyes were brown, and did *not* glow. Most of his legs were missing; his hips and upper body "stood" on a cloud of brown smoke.

Oddly, the Genie of the Ruby Ring was himself wearing a man's ruby ring. It even seemed to have a hole drilled into the center of the stone, like mine did.

Roshradzam bowed deeply to me. (Neither Fatima, Kharmesh, nor Sumera, in their respective first times being summoned by me, had even bothered with a head-nod.)

Roshradzam spoke in ritual tones, in what I guessed was Arabic; of his words, I understood only the words *Roshradzam* and *djinni*.

I was taking a breath, to ask Fatima to translate Roshradzam's words, when the Genie of the Ring's ring translated for me. His ring spoke in Roshradzam's voice, but the ring spoke English—

"Greetings, O Master. I am Roshradzam, bound *djinni* of the Ring. I shall instantly take you anywhere that you want to go."

I said, "I am named Marvin Harper. This is my wife, Anna Kay Harper."

Right afterward, I heard Roshradzam's ring speak in Arabic with my voice.

Roshradzam had appeared with his back to Fatima and Sumera. I said, "Look behind you. I believe you know Fatima and Sumera?"

For sure, he did.

For the next minute, all three bound *djinn* yelled Arabic to each other—with Roshradzam's ring translating every trash-talk word. Fatima called Roshradzam a "Mud-Smoke" and a "*Djinni*-Wannabee," while Sumera called him an "Almost-Wormfood"; Roshradzam returned the favor by calling Sumera "Demons' Whore."

Myself, I just stood there and tried not to smile. In the room with me were three beings who were each thousands of years old, and they were acting like children!

After a minute of letting the three of them insult each other, I ordered them to be quiet. Then I told them what would happen to my newest genie.

****

Roshradzam would go back in the ring for now. In the meantime, I would buy clothes for him online and pay big bucks for "get it here yesterday" delivery speed. I would rent a small RV, which I then would park in the monster garage, and this would be Roshradzam's "home." Roshradzam would be known to the *haremées* as my groundskeeper. Once his clothes had been delivered to the mansion and his RV delivered, Fatima and I would leave the mansion and use the "bus station" trick again; after that, Roshradzam would be out of my Ring nonstop.

After I told the bound *djinn* this, I looked sidelong at Fatima. "While I can afford to get Roshradzam clothes at breakneck speed through Walmart.com, it would be faster for me if you would please magick him some clothes now."

Fatima rolled her eyes, and mumbled under her breath, but created good-fitting workclothes for Roshradzam. He bowed to Fatima and thanked her in Arabic. Then I hugged Fatima and thanked her in English; Roshradzam and Sumera looked surprised when I did this.

I told Roshradzam that he would have to take off his magic translator-ring, except when he was alone with me or alone with Anna Kay, because I did not dare risk the questions that would come up if a *haremée* would "overhear" his ring. I apologized to him because my order meant that for most of the day, the only people he could talk to were Fatima or Sumera. I also apologized to Roshradzam that the only way I could think of to keep him out of his Vessel was to make him a groundskeeper—a servant role.

This is when Sumera said to Roshradzam (as translated by his ring), "Don't gripe. *You* don't have to fuck Master."

****

Ten minutes later

Roshradzam was back in my Ring, Fatima and Sumera had left the computer room and had returned to their work, and I had ordered a used mini-RV to be delivered to the mansion. Now it was time for me to read the news, as the angel had requested.

I sat in the now-too-big computer chair and surfed news sites. Anna Kay stood behind me and rubbed my shoulders. Neither of us spoke.

Reading the news, what I noticed immediately was how dramatic the crime stories were—

In Chicago, a female middle-school teacher demanded of a male student whether yesterday he had keyed her car and had let the air out of all four tires. He admitted the misdeeds in class. "With a smirk," according to witnesses. She pulled a gun out of her teacher-desk drawer and shot at him. Before she killed him, she wounded two other students; she acted unconcerned. Just before she herself was taken down by police bullets, in front of her school, she yelled "Evil is good!"

In Minnesota, a mosque was vandalized; in Paris, France, a synagogue was vandalized; in New South Wales, Australia, a Roman Catholic church was vandalized. In each case, small property inside the building was destroyed and fires were set. "Evil is good!" (or its language-equivalent) was spray-painted on each holy building's inside walls.

Canada was buzzing with a rumor that Prime Minister Pierre Lefevre and opposition MP Stanley Boswick had traded punches during a contentious private meeting.

In Boston, Massachusetts, a Catholic bishop preached that it was past time that Protestants be brought back to the One True Church, "by force when necessary."

In Biloxi, Mississippi, a gang of youths fatally beat up a homeless woman and stole her purse. "Police estimated that the purse contained ten dollars or less." Someone wrote on the dead woman's forehead, "Evil is good."

Chapter 13
Six More Busy Hours

Lunchtime (Thursday)

In the last six years, I had faced down pimps with knives who wanted to stab me to death. In the last six years, I had faced down pimps with pistols who wanted to shoot me dead.

I had faced down Paula Sarin, who had a pistol in her hand and Fatima at her command.

I had faced down Hakeezib, Chief of the Blue Tribe of *Djinn*, who had a circle of Blue Tribe *djinn* working together to make me die of old age, decades early.

Because of all these experiences, I like to think of myself as brave.

Reader, it took all the bravery I could gather, in order to walk out of the computer room at lunchtime and to walk toward the monster kitchen.

Why? Because at breakfast, I had been 5'10". Now I was only 5'2", and could do only three push-ups. Fear of powerlessness, fear of scorn, pressed down on me like a millstone. But I made myself leave the computer room, my place of safety.

Anna Kay was again taller than me, even if she had been barefoot; but now wearing fuck-me heels, she towered over me. During the walk from the computer room, she asked, "Why did the angel ask you to read the news?"

I replied, "No clue. Maybe so I can pray better-informed prayers? All those demons are really messing up the world."

Soon we were at the door to the monster kitchen. Anna Kay said, "I love you and I am with you, my husband."

I thought, *But the last time I was 5'2", you didn't look twice at me.*

****

One second later

I pushed the monster-kitchen door open, walked through, looked back as I held the door open for Anna Kay—

I heard young women's gasps.

—and let go of the door as I turned to face everyone else in the room. This was the moment I had been dreading.

It could have been worse. It was lunchtime, and former *haremées* ate only breakfast and supper with us, never lunch. Of my thirty-three *haremées* (not counting Sumera), some were in classes at lunchtime; and some *haremées* were working at the Harper Foundation or were working at jobs they enjoyed.

The bottom line: Not counting Anna Kay, the two genies, and SJ-1, eleven young women were staring at me.

Eleven was bad enough.

I said, "Kitchen helpers, serve the food and then everyone take your seats. I have things to tell you."

Two minutes later, I stood up from my seat at the head of the head table. "I don't expect to get shorter; that's the good news. The bad news is, I don't expect to get any bigger. I will have more to say tonight at supper."

Rivka Goldheim asked, "Will you at least tell us *how* you got to be this way, Marvin sir?"

I replied, "I'll answer that tonight."

Rivka said, "You still deserve to be served, Marvin sir. But I can't lie, I'm really weirded out by seeing you as a shorty with all those *wonderful* muscles gone."

The other *haremées* spoke similarly: *We still want to serve you, but ewww.*

I thought, *For whatever reason, Fanzelle left me with my slave-touch, magic pheromones, and my harem. Now my women all think I'm short, puny, and pathetic, but they'll still obey me. My glass is half-full.*

****

During the afternoon

I did not go in to work (the Harper Foundation). Instead, I spent the afternoon on my computer, pushing Google to answer one question—

With so many demons running around and causing shit, had anyone noticed this, or had anyone other than me been told the truth by an angel?

I spent all afternoon on this. I used every search-term trick I could think of; I even pressed SJ-1 into service, searching on her computer while I searched on mine.

We found nothing.

By 5:28 that evening, I could not avoid the truth: Earth had a big-time problem, but the only humans who knew about the problem were SJ-1, Anna Kay, and I.

SJ-1 and I Googled away till 5:28, when Virgilia O'Keefe walked through the back door of the mansion. Virgilia was wide-eyed at my puny, short body when I met her at the back door and I asked her to join me in the computer room. Two minutes later, history repeated itself at the back door when I met and then diverted the twins.

****

5:30 p.m.
The computer room at the mansion

My wife Anna Kay, my two bound *djinn* Fatima and Sumera, SJ-1, Virgilia O'Keefe, Almira and Elvira LeClerc, and I were all packed into the computer room.

In short, everyone at the mansion who knew I was a genie-master was in one room and the door was shut.

I took the floor, looked the twins in the eye, and said, "For the last five days, I've become shorter and I've been losing my big muscles. Nobody knew why, including the genies. But now I know the reason: *Your mother* made a pact with the demoness Fanzelle to make me be neither a hero nor a billionaire anymore. Oh, by the way, eighty *billion* dollars of my wealth disappeared between yesterday and today."

"*Lies!*" Elvira shouted. "You're *lying* about Mother!"

Almira sighed, then said, "Elvie, let's hear him out."

I said, "Not much to tell." Then I told of this morning's events at the truck stop. ". . .Then an angel appeared and told us what I've just told you."

Elvira crossed her arms. "An *angel*," she said. "You expect me to believe this? You expect me to buy what this quote-unquote angel says?"

Virgilia's voice dripped scorn: "Of course not, *Mitchell Junior*. A *penis-person* is telling you this, so obviously it's a 100 percent lie. Even though you see the man in question is a foot and a half shorter, and you know for a fact that *genies* are real—only people with ovaries tell the truth. Jeez, truly you are Michelle's daughter."

Elvira snapped, "You hate Mother just because she kicked you out of the Abzug Society."

Virgilia laughed. "Yep, one blowjob was all your mother needed to pass judgment. But she didn't treat you two better—when she found out you had each slept with Marvin, she stopped visiting you at the prison."

Almira shrugged. "The woman's got a point."

Sumera said, "The demoness is real, wormfood—she blasted me in the face with a fireball. The angel is real, too—I heard it speak. It amazes me that after all the misery that your mother created in your life, now you talk like her." Sumera laughed scornfully. "But what else can a *djinni* expect of a wormfood?"

Elvira said, "Mother loves Almie and me; but sometimes she doesn't show it well."

Fatima said, "Any person who makes a pact with a demon is *not* a good person." Fatima gave Sumera a hard glance before Fatima turned hard, unsympathetic eyes back to Elvira.

Almira said, "The genie's got a point."

Elvira said, "*What?* Twin, *if* Mother made a pact with a demon, I'm sure she had a good reason."

"*Pfft,*" Almira said. "Our mother, 'good'? Elvie, I've always wondered if Mother was telling the truth about passing our address on to Dad."

Almira turned to explain to the rest of us: "When Elvie and I went to prison, we were way too embarrassed to write Dad and say, 'We're convicts now, we're both in the women's prison, here's our address.' But Mother—before she stopped visiting us—promised me that she would pass my prison address on to Dad—"

Elvira said, "Mother promised me the same thing."

Almira continued, "But Dad never visited us in prison and he never wrote to us. Once when I mentioned this to Mother, she said, "I did my part, but clearly your father doesn't want to act like your father. Men are like that.' "

I said to Almira, "And you think maybe Michelle broke her promise, then lied to you about it?"

Almira said, "There's no *maybe* about it. Once Mother quit loving Dad, she didn't want either of us loving him."

Elvira said, "He cheated on Mother. *Of course* he would do other things than writing us and visiting us."

I looked at Fatima and Sumera. "I'm making a request to you. Will one of you please answer this question?"

Sumera said archly, "I don't do magical requests, Master."

Fatima said, "Master, you're too generous to people who shit on you. I'll do this so *Almira* can sleep better. Elvira, you can go piss up a rope."

Fatima summoned her scrying ball, searched it, then vanished it. Then Fatima waved her hands.

FOOM. A handsome man in his forties appeared in the computer room. Oddly, everything about him—his hair, skin, and clothing—was green.

The green man rushed forward, to wrap a green arm around each LeClerc woman and hug her to him. "Twins, are you okay?"

Elvira said, "The green man *grabbed* me!"

"Why is Dad green?" Almira asked Fatima.

****

One second later

Fatima answered, "This is not Dennis LeClerc. This is *the magical clone of* Dennis LeClerc, who must answer any question truthfully."

"*Any* question?" said Elvira.

Almira asked, "Dad, why did you ask if we're okay? Don't we *look* okay?"

Green-Dennis said, "You look great, but I asked if you're okay because you two disappeared off the radar six years ago, Michelle didn't tell me *shit*, and Google turned up nothing."

Elvira asked, "Mother never told you we were in prison?"

"*No!*" Green-Dennis said. "When were you in prison?"

The twins exchanged a look. "Oh, shit," said Almira.

Elvira looked at Fatima. "*Any* question, you said?" Then Elvira crossed her arms and looked at Green-Dennis. "Why did you cheat on Mother?"

Green-Dennis was magically compelled to tell the truth, the entire truth, and the truth without shading. He told the twins about Michelle sexually starving him, about coworker Alicia's husband dying in an auto accident, and the conversation that changed everything, seven months later—

****

In August of 2009, Alicia Vanderveer and Dennis LeClerc were in RegalCo's Engineering breakroom, waiting for the coffeemaker to fill.

New widow Alicia said, "God, I miss Gregor." Then she looked at Dennis. "You remind me of him."

Dennis laughed. "Why, because it's been seven months since Gregor had sex?"

Alicia looked at Dennis in shock.

"I'm joking," Dennis said hurriedly.

Alicia paused to stare at Dennis's face, then said, "But not completely joking. Your wife is blind, because you have much to offer a woman."

Dennis stared at Alicia.

Four months later, it was the evening of the Engineering Department's mid-December Christmas party. Michelle refused to go with Dennis: "I will not stifle my personhood for an evening in order to boost your status in the patriarchy at RegalCo."

So Dennis went to the Christmas party alone, while Michelle went to an Abzug Society Christmas party.

Alicia also attended the Engineering-Department Christmas party. Two hours in, Dennis and Alicia walked into the host's back yard for a "smoke break" (though neither of them smoked). By then, Alicia had drunk several glasses of wine, and she was *relaxed.*

Moonlight revealed that a tree in the back yard had honest-to-god mistletoe hanging from several branches. Dennis and Alicia kissed—and kissed, and kissed.

When they broke the kiss, Alicia said to Dennis in a throaty voice, "Reach in my skirt. Go ahead, I want you to know I *want* you. Reach in my panties."

Even as cold as it was outside, it turned out that Alicia's pussy now was slicker than Michelle's pussy had *ever* been—even when Dennis and Michelle had been dating.

As Dennis finger-fucked Alicia in the darkness, she clung to him tightly and murmured, "Michelle is an idiot. I want to milk your dick with my pussy till you see stars."

****

Now Almira asked, "So did you fuck Alicia that night?"

Green-Dennis replied, "No. Too many people would have seen us leave together, including both our bosses."

Elvira asked, "So when and how did you two hook up?"

"Two weeks later, I invited Michelle to the RegalCo New Year's Eve party. Michelle replied, 'No way, I'll catch Trophy-Wife Cooties if I go.' This was good, Michelle not going with me, because there *wasn't* a RegalCo New Year's Eve party—except at Alicia's house. When the Ball dropped at midnight, *my* balls were dropping too."

Almira asked, "How did Mother catch you with Alicia?"

"Alicia wanted to see my house. Then Alicia wanted to see my bedroom. Then Alicia got playful. Then the Abzug Society meeting broke up early. Michelle walked into the bedroom and I was leaning against the footboard, getting my dick sucked by buck-naked Alicia. What *really* put the icing on the cake was two hours later, when Michelle discovered Alicia's pink panties shoved under her pillow."

I thought, *For Michelle, one pair of found panties would be <u>more</u> than enough to make her run straight to divorce court.*

Almira said, "But you guys went to counseling, right?"

Green-Dennis shrugged. "Michelle's attitude was, I owed her a thousand apologies, she owed me none, and even setting aside Alicia fucking me, I was stifling Michelle with my 'patriarchy' expectations. We went to counseling *once*; Michelle hired her lawyer the next day."

Elvira asked, "So what happened with Alicia?"

Green-Dennis blinked. "Your mother never told you? Alicia and I *married* in 2010. You have a half-brother, Jean-Luc, in kindergarten now, and Yvonne is in pre-K."

Elvira looked at Fatima and pleaded, "Can you please send him"—Elvira gestured at Green-Dennis—"back where he came from? I don't want to know any more."

****

One second later

Fatima *foomed* Green-Dennis gone.

I said to Fatima and Sumera, "Before we got caught up in the drama with the twins and their father, we were talking about the demon invasion. So far as I know, you two are the only *djinn* who know about it. Fatima, please inform Green Tribe and Pink Tribe what the demons are up to; Sumera, please inform Blue Tribe."

Fatima fired off two green-light balls, and Sumera fired off one blue-light ball, which all flew diagonally into the floor and vanished.

That done, the eight of us walked from the computer room to the monster kitchen. It was suppertime.

During the walk, Elvira never said a word. She and Almira held hands.

Meanwhile, I was saying to Anna Kay and Virgilia, "I wonder why Heaven has not told any preacher about the demon invasion. You'd think *somebody* would be preaching about this."

Virgilia shrugged.

Just before we eight reached the door to the monster kitchen, Almira pulled her sister over to me. Elvira, while staring at the floor, said, "Making a clone of Dad and letting us ask him questions—thanks, Marvin."

I blinked. I was not expecting a thank-you from Elvira.

By now we were at the door to the monster kitchen. Over forty young women were on the other side of that door, and many of them were in for the shock of their lives as soon as they saw me—

And that was *before* I told them the facts.

****

Ten minutes later
The monster kitchen in the mansion

"A *demoness* did this to you," former touch-slave Bellina Mott said to me. My former English teacher's tone of voice said I must be either lying or crazy.

I replied, "The demoness's name is Fanzelle. She is the same demoness who killed Kelly Brown."

"By killing her with a kiss," Bellina said, still sounding skeptical.

FOOF. A red puff of smoke appeared by the deep-fat fryers, then Fanzelle stood there in all her succubusness— horns, bat-wings, devil-tail, pink hair, reddish skin, fuck-me red high heels, tight red dress, and porn-star tits.

Fanzelle walked toward Bellina with a sashay that screamed *I'm fuckable.* "Honey," Fanzelle said, "you hung around my client Michelle too long. Just because Marvin is male *and* a thief, *doesn't* mean he's a liar. "

I stood up. "I am not a thief."

Fanzelle laughed. "Maybe we should ask Almira what *she* thinks. You have a toy that belongs to Almira, and you haven't offered to give it back to her."

By *toy*, Fanzelle meant *Sumera's lamp*.

Sumera said scornfully, "You're trying to rile people up. Has Almira asked for her *toy* back?"

"No," Almira and I said at the same time.

Sumera said, "Then Marvin hasn't stolen Almira's *toy*. Like I said, demoness, you're trying to stir up trouble."

I looked at the succubus and said, "Why are you here, Fanzelle? What do you want?"

By now, Fanzelle was standing behind Bellina's chair, with Fanzelle's hands resting on Bellina's shoulders; Bellina looked worried. Fanzelle said, "What do I want? To see the hordes of Hell battle the hosts of Heaven and *win*. But why am I here? To tell you guys a few awkward truths."

Virgilia said, " 'Truths'? Demons of Hell are *liars*."

Fanzelle laughed, as she walked over to where Sherry Benson was sitting. "But when *mortals* lie, sometimes the nastiest thing a demon can do is to tell the truth. Virgilia, you think Sherry here is a bimbo. But whenever she's asked you, 'Virgie, am I stupid?', you've always said, 'No, Sherry, you're smart—in your own way.' "

Fanzelle patted Sherry on her shoulder. "But Sherry, the truth is that Virgilia thinks you're a moron, and has thought so for eight years."

I looked around. Both Virgilia and Sherry were sniffling, and were avoiding looking at each other.

Fanzelle now lifted her chin and raised her voice, to address the whole room. "What Marvin told you a few minutes ago, before I so *rudely* interrupted, is the truth. I got Kelly Brown to make Marvin's stocks disappear, then I killed her. I made Marvin as he is now, 5'2" and puny.

Heaven allowed me to do these things because I made a pact with the mother of those *lovely* twins over there. In fact, eventually Michelle will die untimely when I collect her soul; Michelle's unwitting killers are in this room."

Everyone turned to look at the twins. Elvira said, "Yeah, there have been times I've wanted to kill Mother, but I never did. And I won't now. Bat-Wings Girl is full of shit."

Fanzelle continued, "Ladies, Marvin told you truth, a few minutes ago, but he didn't tell you *the whole* truth. You see, Marvin has a *big* secret."

Oh shit, she's going to bust me as a genie-master! And there isn't a thing I can do to stop her.

Fanzelle continued, "A privileged few already know his secret. His wife, his housekeeper, and his housekeeper's little sex-pet all know his secret. Virgilia knows it, but she's never shared it with Sherry. The twins know it. New girl Sumera Hatfield, who has been in the mansion only four days, knows his secret. This should *gall* you other ladies, that this *newcomer* knows the secret and *you* don't."

Clearly Fanzelle was trying to sow dissension among the former *harémées* in the room, all of whom were (mostly) free of my enthrallment.

Former *harémée* Bellina Mott bit on the hook: "So what is Marvin's secret?" she asked.

The succubus shook her head. "Nuh-uh. It's more fun for me when you guess wrong."

Sherry Benson stood up. "I don't know Marvin's secret, and yeah, I'm like dumb, but I know *this:* Marvin is *kind.* He's kind to strangers, and he's kind to people he knows. If he hasn't told me his secret, I'm *sure* he has a good reason. So stick it in your ear, devil-lady!"

As Sherry sat down, everyone else except for Fanzelle clapped loudly. Fanzelle frowned.

Fatima stood up. "I agree, Master is kind. He showed me a great kindness on the day we met. Don't ask me for details, because it relates to his secret."

Fanzelle pasted on a smile now, as good as any socialite's, and sashayed across the room to me. She said, "You are not the *only* being with a secret, kind Marvin. The angel that you talked to, this morning? It kept a *huge* secret from you."

I shrugged. "Nothing in the contract says Heaven has to tell me diddly-squat."

Fanzelle said condescendingly, "Your faith in Heaven is touching. What the angel *didn't* tell you directly affects you—but who am I to say that your trust is misplaced?"

I snorted. "Our dinner is getting cold, while I have to listen to religious advice from one of *Hell's whores.*"

Fanzelle's face was no longer sexy when it became enraged. Pointing a finger at me, she yelled, "You're trying to stop Hell from succeeding, Marvin Harper, but you are no more than a *mouse* to us! You told Fatima and Sumera to contact their . . . *families*, but those *families* will not prevail against Hell, either! When Hell prevails, Marvin Harper, I will *personally* make sure you *suffer!*"

I shrugged. "You aren't telling me what you're planning—speaking of secrets—but I'm not worried. The last time you demons tried to cause big trouble, you lost the war and got kicked out of Heaven. You demons try shit again, you'll get slapped down again."

"Ah, but you're forgetting something," Fanzelle said to me. I did *not* like her smile.

"And what might I be forgetting?"

"If the demons would fight the angels in 2016, now there are *seven billion human shields* we can grab."

Fanzelle looked at Fatima, then Fanzelle turned to look at Sumera. "Some friendly advice: Keep your families out of this. Even if they worked together—ha, ha, and ha—your families couldn't beat Hell."

FOOF. Fanzelle vanished in red smoke.

Chapter 14
Heaven Has a Problem

Still Thursday

Dinner was silent. Twice I caught Bellina Mott giving me a long look. *I'll bet she's wondering what my "secret" is.*

The good news was, The silence made it easier for me to think.

During dessert, I said, "Fatima? Sumera? I would like to talk to you in the computer room after dinner. About your *families*."

"Yes, Master," replied Fatima.

"Sure, whatever," Sumera said. "Marvin, sir."

I sighed.

Five minutes later, when I stood up from the table, Almira also stood up. "Marvin, can I talk to you a second about my *toy?*"

Almira hurried over and murmured in my ear, "Right now you need Sumera *lots* more than I do. You get Fatima and Sumera to kick that devil-lady's ass, okay? *Then* I'll ask for the lamp back."

I thought, *How can Almira and Elvira look so much alike, yet be so different?*

****

Ten minutes later
The computer room at the mansion

In the computer room, with the door shut, were my two genies, SJ-1, Anna Kay, and I.

I said to Fatima, "I want to read for myself the Protocol between Heaven and Hell. I request you make me a copy, translated into English."

Fatima shook her head. "I'm sorry, Master, but I cannot. That document is hidden away by heavenly magic, which is more powerful than what any *djinni* has."

"Any *djinni* but one," Sumera said. "I can't find Heaven's copy either, but I can copy Hell's copy."

I turned to Sumera. "Then I request you make this for me: a copy of the Protocol, transl—"

"I said that I *could* make it, not that I *would*. That's a magical request, et cetera, yada-yada. Now if you *wished* for a copy of the Protocol in English, I would help you out."

Fatima said, "R-i-ight, but then Marvin would have to make his other two wishes by midnight, or else he'd lose them forever."

Sumera shrugged. "Not my problem."

Fatima said, "It seems to me that if you refuse to help Master when he *really* needs your help, that you should lose the *privilege* of spending time out of the lamp, *hm?*"

Sumera gave Fatima a smug smile. "Master is kind. You said it yourself."

Fatima said, "That was six years ago. Now he has Elvira giving him shit and Fanzelle giving him shit—why does he need *you* giving him shit too?"

Sumera looked at me—nervously, I thought. "Master, you made a promise to me that you would not send me into my lamp."

I replied, "This is true, I did promise this—as long as you didn't rile up the *haremées*. That's the good news."

Fatima and Sumera grinned at each other. Then Sumera snarled, "Why are *you* smiling? Master just said he won't send me back into my lamp."

Grinning Fatima said, "Because I've learned that when Master tells you 'the good news,' *next* he's going to smack you with the bad news—and the bad news always is *bad.*"

I said, "Fatima, whoever has bathroom-cleaning duty, take her off of it. You have my permission to transfer Sumera to bathroom duty, beginning tomorrow."

Sumera gave me a smart-aleck grin. "Not a problem, I'll—"

I said to Sumera, "The bad news is, You must *scrub* all twenty-two toilets in the mansion. You must wipe down all twenty bathtubs and showers, and all twenty-two bathroom mirrors in the mansion. You must do all these things every day, and I forbid you to use magic."

"Hey, wait a minute!"

I continued, "Each day, you may pause from your work for lunch and dinner. But till either Fatima or I say that your bathroom-cleaning work for the day is finished, you may not enter the ballroom, the pool room, the electronics playroom, the library, the swimming-pool area, or the upstairs lounge; nor may you magically leave the mansion."

"*What?* That's a low blow!"

Reader, up till now, both Fatima and Sumera went into their rooms at 10 p.m., shut and locked their doors, then *foomed* away to visit their respective Tribes. My new rules meant that Sumera could no longer take nightly visits to Blue Tribe for granted.

Sumera said, "You *know* that if I can't *foom* away from here till Fatima signs off on my work, she'll never sign off."

I shrugged. "Quote, not my problem, unquote."

Then I said, "But tonight is still under the old schedule. So the good news is, Unless Fatima has scheduled you to wash dishes, you have tonight free."

Fatima's smile was vampiric. "Enjoy it while you have it, Blue Girl."

****

Three hours and some minutes later: 10:03 p.m. The computer room at the mansion

Fatima had already "gone to bed" when I heard a quiet knock on the computer-room door. My visitor turned out to be Sumera; she was holding papers in her hand.

I said, "I figured you'd have *foomed* off to Baghdad by now."

Sumera said, "I waited till Green Girl *foomed* off to Cairo." Sumera waved the pages she held. "Everything is in English, just like you requested."

The Protocol that Sumera was holding was about twenty pages long.

Sumera eyed me. "Do I still have to scrub all the toilets and do all that other stuff *by hand* tomorrow?"

"Yes."

"*Why?*"

I gestured at the printed pages in her hand. "Because it seems to me that scrubbing toilets is the only way I can get your attention."

Sumera pouted, but handed me the Protocol.

Instead of gloating that I had bent Sumera to my will, I picked up the Protocol to read it. I expected Sumera to *foom* out of the computer room then.

Light flashed, but it was white, not blue.

When I looked up, an angel was standing between Sumera and me; the angel's hand was out. "HUMANS ARE NOT MEANT TO READ THIS."

****

One second later

I stared at the angel. "So what Fanzelle said is *true?* You're keeping a secret from me?"

"SOME TRUTHS MAY NOT BE REVEALED TO ANY HUMAN, BEFORE THE PROPER TIME."

Sumera said, "The angel doesn't want you to read the next-to-last page. Which talks about what happens after the demons fight a second war against Heaven."

I flipped to the next-to-last page. Sumera pointed to two paragraphs near the bottom.

The angel said, "YOU ARE NOT A PARTY TO THIS AGREEMENT. YOU HAVE NO NEED TO READ IT."

White light flashed, and the Protocol disappeared from my hands.

Sumera muttered, "Have I mentioned I *hate* angels?" An instant later, blue light flashed, and I held another Protocol in my hands—

Which promptly vanished in a flash of white light.

Sumera looked at the angel. "I have a perfect memory. If you keep vanishing written copies, I'll *tell* him, word for word, everything the Protocol says."

"BOUND *DJINNI* SUMERA, YOU ARE INTERFERING WITH THE WORKS OF HEAVEN."

"Do I care? Heaven has *fucked* with my freedom for 2,648 solar years!"

Blue light flashed, and another copy of the Protocol appeared in my hands.

I looked at the angel and at Sumera. "*Enough!* You two, grow up!"

Then I asked Sumera, "What is the angel hiding?"

Sumera replied, "Most of the stuff here in the Protocol is what demons can and cannot do since they lost the war against Heaven. For instance, how a human summons a demon with a pentagram is spelled out in Amendment One of the Protocol. But on the next-to-last page—"

"Hold on," I said, "demons are evil. They're not going to follow pages of rules!"

"Except that lots of what is written here is 'spoken by the power of God.'"

"I don't know what that means."

"Listen, the rules that Solomon laid down for us bound *djinn* are 'spoken by the power of God.' I *cannot* disobey the rules Solomon laid down for us; in the same way, the demons *cannot* disobey what is in the Protocol. Elvira whines because of all those rules she had to learn in Sunday school? She's lucky: None of those rules were spoken by the power of God, so she's free to break them."

"HUMANS ARE LEFT FREE TO DO EVIL SO THAT THEY CAN CHOOSE TO DO GOOD. CHOOSING THE GOOD IS THE MOST PRECIOUS THING IN CREATION."

"Even more than gold?" I quipped.

I said to Sumera, "Okay, now I understand 'spoken by the power of God.' On the next-to-last page . . .?"

"On the next-to-last page, the Protocol talks about if the demons wage a second war against Heaven. If the *demons* win, the Protocol gets thrown out, so all the rules in the Protocol that protect humans get thrown out. Meaning, any demon can do any nasty thing to any human—kill you instantly, torture you for a hundred years, whatever the demon wants."

"Earth would be like Hell."

"But if *Heaven* wins, then God immediately calls for Judgment Day: *Djinn*, humans, and demons all get Judged. After the mass Judgments, every human and every *djinni* goes straight to eternal reward or eternal torment. Since Hell doesn't bother demons, they're erased instead."

I turned to the angel. "What exactly is considered 'war' between Heaven and Hell? Is angels catching demons and sending them down to Hell considered 'war'? Has the 'war' already begun?"

"THE WAR HAS NOT STARTED. IT IS WAR WHEN THE FALLEN ANGELS ENTER HEAVEN OR WHEN THEY ATTACK ANGELS WHO SERVE GOD."

"Then why did Fanzelle bring all the demons up to Earth? The demons still aren't in Heaven, so what do they gain by coming to Earth?"

'THE FALLEN ANGELS CANNOT ENTER HEAVEN FROM HELL. HOWEVER, THEY CAN ENTER HEAVEN FROM EARTH."

I shook my head. "I'm missing something. What makes the demons think they'll win this time, when they didn't win last time?"

"THE FALLEN ANGELS ARE LURING HUMANS TO EVIL. WHEN A HUMAN BECOMES EVIL ENOUGH, HE BECOMES THE WILLING MINION OF A FALLEN ANGEL. HUMAN MINIONS WILL ENTER HEAVEN TO FIGHT GOD'S ANGELS, AND HEAVEN HESITATES TO KILL HUMAN MINIONS."

"Who can kill a demon? As in 'He's gone forever'?"

"OUR GOD, OR A REGIONAL GOD."

"Why did you try to stop me from learning all this?"

"YOU ARE ONE HUMAN. REMARKABLY, YOU CAN COMMAND THREE BOUND *DJINN* IN SOME THINGS. BUT SUMERA HERE OBEYS YOU UNWILLINGLY, AND ALL THREE BOUND *DJINN* HAVE THE LIMITATIONS OF *DJINN*. YOU AND YOUR *DJINN* CANNOT DEFEAT HELL. HEAVEN WANTED TO SPARE YOU WORRY ABOUT PROBLEMS YOU CAN DO NOTHING ABOUT."

With that, the angel vanished in white light.

I picked up the Protocol, and pointed to Sumera with a corner of its pages. "You getting me this and you pushing back against the angel both helped me a lot. Thank you very much, O Sumera of the Blue Tribe of *Djinn*."

Sumera looked surprised, just before—

FOOM. Sumera vanished in a flash of blue light.

As I began to read the Protocol in the now-empty computer room, I said, "Angel, you think there's no way I can stop this upcoming war between Heaven and Hell. But I will find *something* I can do."

Chapter 15
Recruiting War Gods

Next morning, before breakfast (Friday)
At the mansion

Virgilia O'Keefe was the CEO of my charity organization, the Harper Foundation. She also was one of the few humans who knew all my secrets. She also still lived at the mansion.

Seconds ago, I had shanghaied Virgilia and my wife, and had herded them into the computer room.

Now I looked up at them and said, "Beginning today, I am taking a leave of absence from the Harper Foundation. I'm needed for something else."

Anna Kay looked puzzled, but Virgilia said, "I certainly understand why you don't want to be seen in public." Virgilia was tactful enough to not mention that now I was a shorty with zero muscles.

I shook my head. "Vanity isn't my reason. Last night I got another visit from an angel. Fanzelle wants to jump-start another war between Heaven and Hell; no matter the result, life will be bad for humans."

Anna Kay asked, "So what will you be doing now, that is more important than the Harper Foundation?"

"The angel mentioned something, and it's given me an idea how to fight all the demons. After breakfast, I'll try out my idea."

Anna Kay asked, "Is it dangerous?"

I said, "Honey, the good news is, I'll have three bound *djinn* with me." I did not say the bad news out loud.

But Sumera did: "Four of us are going to be fighting demons, who outnumber us, and who *way* outmagick us."

I tried to act optimistic. "True, but I've thought up a workaround for that. Virgilia, has Fatima ever told you that the Greek and Roman gods really exist?"

****

After breakfast
Back in the computer room

Three human women, three bound *djinn*, and I stood in the computer room, behind a closed door.

My *djinn* and I had held a short planning session; now it was time to carry out my plan.

Anna Kay knew the plan, and now she was looking at me with worry. I could not read Virgilia's expression. SJ-1's face showed nothing, as usual.

Meanwhile, Sumera was back to her blue skin color; and all three of my bound *djinn* were again wearing their Middle Eastern clothing. Roshradzam was wearing his magic-translator ruby ring on his right hand.

When Sumera muttered something in Arabic, Roshradzam's magic ring dutifully translated it: "Why do we have to bring the Turd Tribe boy along?"

"For exactly this reason," I said, gesturing toward Roshradzam's ring. His ring was now speaking Arabic with my voice. "Unless you or Fatima can speak Latin, Old Norse, Japanese, *and* Hawaiian, I need Roshradzam."

Fatima and Sumera each shook her head.

I continued, "Also, Roshradzam can *foom* us to a place without knowing exactly where that place is."

Roshradzam bowed to me and said something florid in Arabic; it translated to, "I am grateful for the opportunity to serve you with all I have, Master."

"Suck-up," Sumera muttered in English.

Now I turned to look up at Anna Kay's face. "If I have not returned in a week, I will not come back ever, and these three genies will be stuck in their Vessels. If I am not back in a week, take Virgilia up into the attic. She knows what to look for."

I did not mention that if I were not alive in a week, my three genies might not be alive either.

Now Virgilia looked stunned. Anna Kay cried. I did *not* cry, but it was a close thing.

I hugged and kissed my wife and hugged Virgilia, while Fatima hugged SJ-1. Once all the hugs ended, I walked over to my three bound *djinn*. "Let's do this," I said.

Roshradzam touched my forehead with his brown left hand. My ears popped.

****

An instant later
Honolulu, Hawaii (sort of)

The local time, I knew, was a little after 3:30 in the morning. I saw stars and the moon. In front of me and the *djinn* stood a carved statue of Ku, the Hawaiian war god. The carved statue was huge, almost as tall as I had been until recently.

Every direction I looked, I saw an almost-invisible white haze. But this was not fog, because fog does not glow with its own light in the darkness.

Fatima evidently figured out why I was confused. She explained, "We are in Honolulu, but not in the earthly plane. The spiritual plane has an ever-present glowing mist, which is what you're seeing."

I asked, "Is Ku here?"

"Not nearby," Roshradzam replied. "If he were nearby, my ring would be translating our words into his tongue."

"I'm going to try to summon him now," I announced.

Since I had no idea how to pray a Hawaiian-language prayer of *Hey Ku, please come talk to me*, I stuck with clapping my hands while chanting, "Ku! Ku! Ku! Ku!"

I did this for maybe fifteen seconds when a strong man stepped out of the huge wooden carving.

The man glared at me and yelled. Roshradzam's ring translated his words to "Why do you mock me, puny outlander, by calling to me?"

Ku looked like a strong, tattooed, brown-skinned man who was wearing a white loincloth (inside of which, his penis bulged with erection). He wore a cape that had bright-red bird feathers sewn onto it, and a tall hat that was covered with bright-yellow bird feathers. Ku was shirtless, pantsless, and barefoot. His spear had a spearhead that looked like black glass—*wicked-sharp* black glass.

The huge wooden statue looked fierce. Ku himself looked even fiercer—his teeth were like needles.

I said, "I called to you because the people of Hawaii need your help. They just don't know it yet."

I explained to Ku about the war between Heaven and Hell that the demons wanted to start. ". . . I'm sure that Heaven will win, but then every human alive will face Judgment Day. This includes every man, woman, and child in Hawaii."

Ku grinned, showing his needle-teeth. "How much do you want my help, human? Normally for me to help one side or the other in a war, I require a human sacrifice. *You* are the only human here, puny man."

I said, "You haven't even said whether you'll fight yet. Are you one of those beings who can't make up his mind? If so, you're not worth my time."

He said, "Sure, I'll fight the demons. So now it's time for your sacrifice." He waved his spear at me.

Fatima gasped, and Sumera muttered something.

Their reason? It had been explained to me, before we left, that even a regional god like Ku could be killed by only the God of Heaven; whereas a regional god could kill demons, and one demon was much more powerful than one *djinni*. What this meant: Ku could easily kill any bound *djinni*, who was compelled to defend me to the death.

Meanwhile, Ku had just demanded that I sacrifice myself? I said to him, "Do you have *poi* for brains? If I die, who's going to lead this thing?"

Ku sneered, "Let me think. Should it be *you?* Smaller than even the women *djinn*, and you're human besides?"

I laughed. "Should it be *you* then? You didn't know there was a problem till I told you! *I* have a plan; what's *your* plan? Maybe it's to walk around impressing the demons with your erection?" I laughed again. "Some of those incubus-demons have cocks twice as big as yours!"

Ku took a step toward me, as he swung his spear around from pointing at the stars to pointing at me. "You anger me, puny man. Prostrate yourself *now*, beg for forgiveness, and I might yet you live."

I said, "That is the *stupidest* thing I could do."

FOOM. Fatima appeared in front of me and slightly to my right. She growled, "War god, to kill my master you must first kill me."

FOOM. Roshradzam appeared in front of me and slightly to my left. He did not speak; instead, he made a beckoning gesture to Ku: *Bring it.*

Sumera said, "You're stupid, Fatima! He's a *god*. If he slices you with that sharp spear, you *die*. Don't fight till you have to."

Fatima replied, "I've always suspected you Blues were cowards."

I said calmly, "Thank you, Fatima and Roshradzam, but this is my fight."

Ku looked at me like I were a cube-shaped coconut. "You are not afraid of me."

"No," I said.

Ku went silent then. Nobody else spoke either.

After a time, Ku asked me, "If I go with you, I'll get to kill tens of demons?"

I replied, "Hundreds of demons."

Ku said, "I will set aside requiring you to be sacrificed; you should feel special."

I said, "I already do." Then I said, "I am named Marvin."

Ku walked up to me and slapped me on the shoulder (*hard!*) "What do we do next, War-Leader Ma'vin?"

I looked around at my bound *djinn*; they all were looking back at me with expressions of *How did you manage that trick?* I said, "Next stop: Japan."

****

Two hours later (5 p.m. CEST)
Late afternoon Friday, local time
Rural Norway (spiritual plane)

Fortunately for me, war gods Hachiman, Mars, and Odin were not interested in giving my *djinn* or me a hard time. All I had to say was "You get to slay demons by the hundreds" or "The demons want to treat humans dishonorably" and each war god signed on.

By now, my companions looked like guests at a costume party. The three *djinn* wore Middle Eastern clothing; Ku looked like a Hawaiian war chief; Mars looked like a clean-shaven Roman general; Hachiman looked like a *daimyo* (Japanese nobleman) general; and Odin looked like a gray-haired, bearded warrior wearing brown-leather clothing and a blue wool cape. Odin had a glowing pale-blue right eye; his left eye was gouged out.

At the moment, Odin was trying to convince Tyr to join our cause, after I had made my own pitch to Tyr. Tyr looked like Odin (leather clothing, glowing light-blue eyes, a beard), except for two differences—

Odin had gray hair and a gray beard; Tyr had blond hair and a blond beard; and—

Tyr's right arm was missing its hand.

Both Roshradzam and I were standing close to the two Norse gods; Fatima gave Roshradzam a *Stay there!* gesture, then pulled me beyond the range of the translator-ring.

Fatima said, "I have no idea why the Norse have two war gods, but why do *we* need both of them? Why do we need a one-handed god *and* a one-eyed god?"

I said, "Odin has a bit of a split personality: When he's calm, he writes poetry, but in battle, he turns into a berserker. I need Tyr to talk Odin down, once this is over. Also, Tyr is big on honor—that's how he lost his hand—and demons *offend* him because they are dishonorable."

About that time, Odin and Tyr slapped each other on the shoulder, then Tyr walked over to me and slapped me on the shoulder. Tyr spoke words I could not understand, but he spoke them with grave sincerity.

****

A minute later

"Marvin son of Steven needs a worthy weapon," said Odin. "As do the *djinn*."

Odin held his left hand out with palm up. He murmured words; then glowing runes appeared to the right, to the left, and above his outstretched hand. When the runes disappeared, a bronze sword laid across his palm. Odin gave the sword to me.

I thanked Odin, but I'm sure my face showed disappointment. The bronze sword's point was not all that sharp, the edges were not especially sharp, and the "flat" surfaces were not perfectly flat. The sword looked like it had been made in a high-school shop class.

Odin said, "The sword is more than it seems, Marvin son of Steven. It is a god's sword; it is *instant death* to any demon."

Then to my surprise, Odin repeated his trick. When the glowing runes disappeared and a bronze sword again laid across Odin's palm, he handed this second sword to Fatima. Odin told her, "Green *djinni*, Ku tells me you are brave and loyal. I honor you with a worthy gift."

With similar words, Odin gifted a third bronze sword to Roshradzam.

None of the war gods badmouthed Sumera as a coward; but Odin gave Sumera only a bronze dagger.

Up till now, Odin had been holding a spear casually with his right hand, treating the spear as a walking staff. But now Odin grasped the shaft of the spear with both hands, as he looked at me.

"Are we about to fight?" Tyr asked. He slapped his left hand against his thigh; instantly he was holding an iron war axe of fearsome size. "I am ready," Tyr said to me.

I looked around. All five war gods, all three *djinn*, and I held weapons. I said, "Let's go hunt demons."

Roshradzam touched my forehead with his weaponless hand. My ears popped.

Reader, sometimes I am not as smart as I think I am.

Chapter 16
War Gods v. Demons

An instant later (Friday)

My ears popped, and I was no longer standing in long shadows in late-afternoon Norway. Instead, my eyes burned for a few seconds as I stood under bright lights.

When my eyes adjusted, I saw that I was outside, standing on a large green field in the middle of a stadium. Painted lines on the ground, and a soccer goal at each end of the field, told me what kind of stadium this was. A man in a suit was standing in the exact middle of the field, standing at a podium; he was silently giving a speech to a large crowd. People in the crowd were silently cheering and were waving preprinted signs in French—I figured out I was at a political rally.

But the man and the crowd were not quite where the war gods, the *djinn*, and I were. The speechmaker was in the earthly plane, whereas my team and I were in the spiritual plane—

As was a green-skinned demon, who was talking in the speechmaker's ear.

With a roar, the five gods ran toward the demon. The demon turned to look at us; he seemed surprised.

Ku was the least weighed down by armor of the five war gods; he got to the demon a step ahead of Tyr.

Whish! The spearhead of Ku's spear moved quickly sideways, a black blur, and the demon's head fell from his shoulders. Then the demon's head and the headless body both caught fire.

In the earthly plane, the speechmaker paused and began to stammer. Some in the crowd silently yelled jeers.

In the spiritual plane, Ku thumped his chest and yelled, "I am the mighty god Ku! I have killed again!"

After this was translated into five different languages, Mars muttered, "Whatever."

****

Soon after
Sort of in a Moslem country

My ears popped, then I stood in the spiritual-plane version of a large tent. The earthly-plane version of the tent was filled with Moslem men, and a paper sign that was covered with large Arabic script was pinned to one of the tent walls.

Fatima pointed to the writing and said, "They're Moslem extremists, everyone."

I pointed to a bullet-holed American flag and a bullet-holed French flag that were pinned to tent walls. I said, "That explains the flags."

Meanwhile, a bearded guy up front was silently yelling and was waving a picture in each hand. One picture was the American flag; the other picture was of a bunch of white-winged angels. "Oh, *shit!*" Fatima said.

But before Fatima could explain herself, the war gods had taken off for the demon who was speaking into the rabble-rouser's ear. The war gods ran *through* the humans as if the humans were illusions.

That is, *four* war gods rushed forward—Ku had somehow tripped and fallen hard. Just before the other four war gods reached the demon, Hachiman grabbed Mars's wrist from behind and jerked back hard, which sent Mars flying backward.

The rabble-rouser Moslem and the demon who was speaking to him were both above the crowd, so I clearly saw what happened next. While the demon watched the war gods scuffle, he turned one hand palm-up, and a paper appeared there. I could not tell from the distance I was at, but it seemed to me that this paper began filling up with black writing. Then the paper vanished in black smoke.

Right after, Odin thrust his spear into the demon's heart. The demon burned up, but his message had gone out.

Sumera pumped a fist. "Two demons down, 734 to go. This is *fun!*"

I asked Fatima, "What was the 'Oh, *shit*' for?"

She replied, "Because of what the 'teacher' was saying. 'The angels of Heaven now believe what America teaches. The heavenly angels have become enemies of truth, and we must fight them.' "

I said, "The problem is fixed. We killed the demon."

Fatima said, "The problem is *not* fixed. The men here have heard those words."

****

Soon after
The spiritual plane, near a third demon
Idaho, USA

We arrived in what looked like a survivalist military compound; at least the earthly-plane part looked this way.

Instead of finding *one* demon in the spiritual plane there, we found *three* demons.

This was either a good thing for us or a bad thing for us. (To the war gods, this was better than cake and ice cream.) While I was trying to decide whether the situation was good or bad—

FOOF. In a puff of black smoke, a fourth demon arrived.

FOOF. In a puff of red smoke, Fanzelle joined the party. The war gods and the demons were now evenly matched.

****

One second later

I yelled out, "DON'T ATTACK YET! LET'S FIGURE OUT WHAT THEY'RE UP TO."

Fanzelle actually looked offended when she asked me, "What are you *doing?*"

I grinned at her. "These war gods never signed the Protocol. They're allowed to kill you."

I was hearing mutterings from the war gods (they were here to *fight*, and I was being no fun at all); but now I also heard talking in a foreign language between Fanzelle and the other demons. But oddly, Roshradzam's translator-ring stayed silent.

I asked Roshradzam about this, but it was Sumera who explained: "The language of demons is the same as the language of angels, and clearly *Heaven*"—Sumera made the word sound like an insult—"doesn't want us lesser beings to know what angels say to each other."

"That's a big problem," I said. "Now we can't eavesdrop on the demons."

Mars said to me, "We need to attack *them* before *they* attack—"

FOOF. A frog-eyed demon disappeared from where he had been standing (by Fanzelle), and reappeared an instant later, two feet in front of me. During that instant, Frog-Eyed Demon somehow had grabbed a steel sword, the flat blade of which he was now laying against my neck.

"*Excretum,*" Mars said.

The frog-eyed demon said to me in English, "You cannot harm me, mortal. Drop your weapon, and you have my oath I will not harm you."

I did not tell Frog-Eyes that I had read the Protocol, and I *knew* that he would not harm me. He was not allowed to give me even a shaving nick with his sword.

FOO-F-FOOF. Three other ugly demons who had been jawboning with Fanzelle, disappeared in puffs of smoke. Each instantly reappeared, holding a sharp, steely sword, in front of a *djinni.* The demon in front of Roshradzam said, "*Djinn* aren't protected by the Protocol, Turd Tribe boy."

I said to Frog-Eyes, "Mr. Demon, I think—"

I plunged my god-magicked bronze sword into his abdomen, angling the blade up so that I stabbed his lungs. I twisted the blade, just before yanking the blade out of the demon's body.

The demon gasped, then caught fire even as he and his sword dropped to the ground.

Meanwhile, Fatima, Sumera, and Roshradzam had pulled the same trick with their own god-magicked weapons. Scratch four demons.

"—you're lying to me." I pointed my sword at Fanzelle, who now was the only surviving demon, as if to say *You want a piece of this?*

Odin yelled, "*Let's get her!*"

FOOF. In a puff of red smoke, a squid-headed, loin-clothed man, who was holding a black-glass knife, appeared by Fanzelle. At first I thought he was just another demon.

****

One second later

With a primal scream, Odin ran up to the newcomer and plunged his spear through Squid-Head's chest. Squid-Head screamed, but then used his free hand to pull the spear out of his chest and to thrust Odin's spear aside.

Squid-Head moved forward—*quickly* for a being who had just received a fatal injury. Squid-Head slashed with his knife across Odin's neck, and then Odin dropped to his knees, with arterial blood spurting from his neck—

But only for a few seconds, before the spurting stopped. Odin was, after all, a god. Still, Odin remained on his knees, in no hurry to stand up.

Meanwhile, Squid-Head and Ku were yelling at each other. Their words sounded like insults.

I asked Ku, "You know him?"

Ku answered, "He is Kanaloa. He has no good in him."

But while Roshradzam's ring was translating my question and Ku's reply, Fanzelle was speaking to Kanaloa in what I was guessing was Hawaiian. Fanzelle pointed me out to Kanaloa (whose chest by now showed no injury).

Kanaloa ran toward me—or tried to. The five war gods formed a defensive line—Odin by now was back on his feet.

Fanzelle smiled over at me and grinned. "Kanaloa didn't sign the Protocol either." *Oh, shit.*

Then Kanaloa came up against the five war gods.

What followed was *ten minutes* of stabbing, slicing, screaming, and staggering. I learned that god-blood smelled like human blood. No god suggested stopping.

Twice I saw Hachiman slice off some body part of Kanaloa's—then the severed body part jumped off the ground, flew to where it had been cut off from, and reattached itself.

Meanwhile, my three bound *djinn* had formed a second defensive line in front of me, each genie holding a magicked bronze weapon at the ready. I had to yell the question in order to be heard over the racket: "How do we end this? These gods will fight *forever!*"

Fatima yelled back, "Don't worry, I have a plan." She gestured with her free hand—

FOOM. Green light flashed. Where Kanaloa had stood, there was a seven-foot-tall, four-foot-diameter column of seawater, which immediately fell to the ground.

("*Kill the slut-demon!*" Hachiman yelled. Five bleeding war gods staggered toward Fanzelle.)

Fanzelle laughed scornfully at Fatima. "You *water-swapped* him? Stupid Fatima, he's a *god!* Water pressure won't crush him, and you can't drown him."

Fatima laughed right back. "Shows what *you* know, Demon Slut."

(*FOOF.* When the pack of war gods got close to Fanzelle, the succubus disappeared in red smoke, instantly to reappear thirty feet away. The injured war gods changed the direction of their attack.)

Fatima taunted the succubus: "In a few minutes, Kanaloa will swim to the surface. But he is an ocean away from Hawaii, and nobody he meets can speak his language, so he will have no idea how to get home. He will be away from home for a *long* time."

Mars called over to Fatima, "If one of Kanaloa's mortal followers prays to his idol, or prays at one of his shrines or temples, he can be summoned home."

(The succubus let the war gods close in on her a second time. Then she *foofed* herself fifty feet away.)

Fatima said, "In *that* case. . ." Green fireballs flew from Fatima's free hand, diagonally into the ground.

Fatima said, "Ten minutes from now, every idol of Kanaloa in Hawaii will have gone kablooey. Then Kanaloa can't be prayed home."

Fanzelle laughed. "Fatima dear, aren't *you* the clever one!"

An instant later—

FOO-F-F-FOO-FOOF. Five war gods were replaced with five (briefly standing) columns of water.

Fanzelle turned a hand up, a piece of paper appeared on her hand, black writing appeared on the paper, then the paper burned up on Fanzelle's hand. Fanzelle taunted us:

"Five minutes from now, it will be impossible to pray to any of your war-god friends. Usa Shrine in Japan? It's a beautiful building, but its minutes are numbered."

"You're forgetting something, succubus," Roshradzam said, as he slowly pulled his sword-arm back.

"*Don't!*" I ordered. I figured that Roshradzam was planning to *foom* close to Fanzelle, then to stab her with his god-made sword. But what I was *sure* would happen was that Fanzelle would kill Roshradzam instead.

Instead, Roshradzam froze statue-still.

Fanzelle smiled at me. "Don't worry, I won't hurt your brave brown genie. The bad news is—"

Our bronze weapons were replaced with small columns of seawater.

"—you all are now defenseless."

Ten seconds passed, enough for Fanzelle to make her point. Then Roshradzam unfroze.

Fanzelle still was smiling at me. "Marvin Harper, you killed my fellow demons today. Do you own a little dog?"

"*What?* No!"

"Too bad. I know a movie quote that would fit perfectly."

FOOF. Fanzelle vanished in a puff of red smoke.

****

Minutes later

Fatima and Sumera tried every trick they could think of, to track down the five war gods so we could reassemble the team and then kill more demons.

But nothing they tried, worked. Apparently, just as genie Vessels are immune to locator spells and angels are immune to locator spells, so regional gods are immune.

After five minutes of fruitless spellcasting, I told Fatima and Sumera to stop. I told Roshradzam to *foom* us home.

My ears popped, then my three genies and I were back in the computer room at the mansion.

Five minutes later, Fatima and I were telling Anna Kay and SJ-1 about our adventures. My smartphone rang.

It was my bank calling. My banker acted just short of rude to me.

Soon I found out why: *Millions* of dollars had just been electronically transferred from my bank account to a bank in Nigeria. My banker presumed that this had happened because I had foolishly given out my bank-account number.

I *did* tell the banker that I had not divulged anything to anyone. I *did not* wail *How did this happen to me?*

(Mainly because I knew *exactly* how this had happened to me: *Fanzelle* had happened to me.)

I now asked the banker, *almost* calmly, "How much money is left in my account?"

The Nigerians didn't take *everything*, I was told; I had 322 thousand dollars left in the account.

Which meant than one year from now, Anna Kay and I would be broke. Unless I soon closed down the Harper Foundation and sold off the mansion.

This meant that I soon would have to release all my *haremées*.

I was short, puny, now almost-broke, and soon to be forced into unending monogamy—Reader, Fanzelle had *really* messed with me!

Chapter 17
Venus Consoles Me

Ten minutes later (Friday)
The computer room at the mansion

Fatima and I were telling our tales to Anna Kay, with Roshradzam occasionally adding a comment. Sumera was in the room, but she stayed silent with her arms crossed. SJ-1 was likewise silent, but this was usual for her.

I was stumped by what had just happened. I thought I had cooked up a great plan—so how did Fanzelle get the better of me?

I also was worrying about my finances. Not only for myself—I wanted to keep my employees at the Harper Foundation drawing a paycheck; but more than this, the Harper Foundation helped out many unlucky people. The Harper Foundation's future clients would lose hope if we were forced to shut our doors.

Anna Kay must have picked up on my feelings, because she walked up to me and, while not saying a word, began to rub my back.

That's when there was a flash of lavender light, and a beautiful, black-haired woman appeared. With her tied-up hair and her gown-like dress, she looked Roman.

And speaking of "Roman"—

The newcomer looked at me and, in a sexy voice, asked, "*Numquid Marvinus nomine?*" Which Roshradzam's ring translated as *Are you named Marvinus?*

I replied, "Yes, except my name is Marvin, not Marvinus."

Roshradzam's ring had barely begun to translate when the newcomer's appearance changed: Now she was blond-haired, blue-eyed, sharp-cheekboned, muscle-toned, and—don't be surprised, Reader—big-breasted. (She still was dressed like a Roman senator's trophy wife.) This world-class hottie sashayed toward me as she said in English, "I am *so* glad to meet you, mortal Marvin. Mars speaks well of you. I am the goddess Venus."

FOOM. Fatima now was standing in front of me, confronting the newcomer. "*You* can't be Venus," Fatima growled. "Mars spoke only Latin."

Maybe-Venus stopped her walk as she laughed with amusement. "To love someone, you have to be able to talk to them, yes? Whereas Mars says it works better when you fight a man if you can't understand his taunts. So while Mars refuses to learn other tongues, the Goddess of Love has learned hundreds."

Maybe-Venus looked at Sumera. "Test me, *djinni* Sumera. Discover for yourself that I am no demon."

Sumera gestured, blue light flashed, and a floating blue eyeball appeared in front of her hands.

The blue eyeball was the size of a grapefruit. Its cornea was light blue; its iris was glowing-blue. It floated across the room to maybe-Venus, stopping only inches away. Maybe-Venus made no attempt to deflect the blue eyeball; instead, she struck a model's pose.

The blue eyeball moved up to the top of the newcomer's hair, then moved down to where half of the blue eyeball disappeared into the floor, then floated up to the height where it had started (chest height). The blue eyeball did not move for five seconds, then it zoomed sideways to the east. The blue eyeball faded out before it hit the wall.

Sumera announced, "She is not a demon, an angel, or a *djinni*."

Venus looked over at Roshradzam, and spoke sexy words in Arabic. I did not know what she was saying, but Roshradzam stood straight and smiled. Venus's words made Roshradzam preen, but they also made Sumera roll her eyes. The translator-ring stayed silent.

I asked Venus, "Why are you here?"

Venus faced me as she answered, "You are trying to prevent the God of Heaven from holding Judgment Day, by preventing the Second Heaven-Hell War. All we regional gods will lose our worshippers if the God of Heaven holds Judgment Day, so we Roman gods favor your goal."

"Okay, so?"

"I came here because Mars told Mercurius that you were clever in seeking out war gods, and you were brave in leading the war gods against demons."

Now Venus resumed her sashay, her voice a purr. "Marvin, I am always *very impressed* with mortals who are clever and brave."

By now, Venus was alongside Fatima. Venus said to Fatima, "You protect him because you love him. I approve, *djinni* Fatima. I promise you I will not harm Marvin, beyond some happy exhaustion."

Seconds later, Venus was standing in front of me, stroking my chest. I asked her, "So Mars is okay now? Mercury rescued him?"

Venus made a shrug look sexy. "As of a few minutes ago, Mars was bobbing in the Peaceful Ocean, west of La Serena, Chile. I'm not sure Mercurius could carry another god back to Roma; but in any case, Mars refused the rescue. Mars floated in the water and told his tale to Mercurius, who has a perfect memory for words. Then Mercurius told Mars how to return to Roma, before Mercurius himself returned to Roma and repeated Mars's tale to us other gods. That's when I decided I would *reward* the mortal who got Mars put in the ocean."

I said, "When you tell it that way, I would expect you to be angry at me."

Venus laughed. "Not at all. Mars won't be so arrogant when he returns—that's a good thing. As for you, Marvin, how could you know how *tricky* a demon can be? Don't feel disappointed in yourself, or sad."

In a phone-sex-operator voice, Venus added, "I'm here to do *everything I can* to make you happy, not sad."

Then Venus looked over her shoulder and, in a bedroom voice, spoke (ring-untranslated) Arabic to Roshradzam. The Genie of the Ring sucked in a breath.

Venus turned back to me, and resumed stroking my chest. "For all your sexual adventures, you have not experienced many orgies, have you?"

I said, "Only two or three, and those were six years ago."

Venus smiled. "I *love* orgies. I should—I invented them. I came here to give you another one."

So saying, Venus turned her back on me, and walked straight and quickly across the room to SJ-1.

****

Seconds later

SJ-1—the former Sheila Heather Johansson—watched Venus walk up to her, and it seemed to me that the fake-fembot's normally unreadable face looked *panicky*. Then Venus ran the fingertips of her left hand across SJ-1's forehead, and SJ-1's silver-painted face went blank again.

Venus said to SJ-1, "You love your mistress Fatima, and you know that your mistress loves Marvin. But this puzzles you, because you think all men are boring. Tsk, Sheila, I can't have *that!*"

Then Venus said to SJ-1, "LOVE MARVIN TODAY."

Instantly, SJ-1 went from staring at Venus to staring at me. She gasped, her lips parted, then she rushed across the room to me.

SJ-1 dropped to her knees in front of me, seized my left hand in both of hers, and said, "I *love* you, Marvin. I'll do anything to make you happy. *Anything!*"

I said, "Um, Venus? If we change her personality, I'd be breaking a solemn promise to Sheila."

As Venus was walking across the room, she called over to me, "Relax. I set her adoration to stop at midnight."

Now Venus was walking toward Sumera, who began to back away—until Venus commanded, "STAND THERE."

Once Venus was close, she swiped her fingertips across Sumera's forehead. Meanwhile, as I watched Sumera and Venus, SJ-1 was kissing my hand over and over.

(Reader, once you looked past SJ-1's silver skin-paint and her tight-fitting, cowled, silver catsuit, SJ-1 was a babe. She was tall, slim, busty, and had a cover-model's face. So can you understand why SJ-1 kissing my hand, over and over, was giving me a boner?)

While SJ-1 was kissing my hand, Venus was saying to Sumera, "Of you three *djinn* who are bound to Marvin, you are the most powerful, while Roshradzam is the least powerful. For this, you scorn him. Yet earlier, he was twice brave, willing to fight the war god Ku and the demon Fanzelle to the death. But you? *You* were a coward until your Binding compelled you to fight for your master. It is *you*, Sumera of Blue Tribe, who deserves scorn."

Then Venus commanded something in Arabic.

Right after, Sumera rushed to Roshradzam and, as best I can guess, pledged her undying love to him. In any case, now Sumera was touching Roshradzam, rubbing against him, and shooting him long looks, while she spoke Arabic to him in a pleading voice.

****

Five minutes later
The master bedroom at the mansion

While Venus had given magical "LOVE HIM!" commands to SJ-1 and Sumera, Venus had pulled no such trick on Anna Kay and Fatima. As Venus had explained to me, "These two *glow* with their love for you."

Now the entire group was in the master bedroom: one love-goddess, three bound *djinn*, a human female who pretended to be a fembot, and Anna Kay and I.

The master bedroom had enough empty floor space (even after my monster-sized bed, the recliner, the dresser, and the loveseat) that a twin-sized bed could be added to the room. This was exactly what Venus did: she magicked up a twin bed, on which Roshradzam and Sumera would soon scream and thrash.

But at the moment, Sumera and Roshradzam were standing by the twin bed, as Sumera spoke Arabic words. Roshradzam's ring did not translate Sumera's words, but Fatima's murmur in my ear did—

"Sumera is calling Roshradzam *darling*," Fatima told me with laughter in her voice.

Foom. Now Sumera's clothing vanished; she stood naked and blue-skinned in front of Roshradzam. While biting her lip from nervousness, she asked him a question.

Roshradzam shook his head, and pointed a thumb at me. Sheila/SJ-1 was undressing me then; a moment later, Sumera stepped forward and began to manually undress Roshradzam. Sumera's Arabic endearments continued.

****

One second later

Venus asked me, "Do you think Sheila looks prettier *with* or *without* silver skin-paint?"

I replied, "Without, but—"

Before I could say something nonjudgmental and tolerant, SJ-1's silver skin-paint vanished in a flash of lavender light.

Now that Sheila's face had ordinary skin color (but incredible beauty), I noticed that she had pale-green eyes. In six years, I had never noticed SJ-1's eyes before.

By now, naked Roshradzam was fucking naked Sumera, who was clutching his back and thrusting upward. Anna Kay nodded in their direction and said to me, "We're falling behind. Which one of us four do you want to fuck first?"

I smirked and said to my wife, "I dunno—you're all *dressed.*"

Venus suggested that my four lovers for tonight— Venus, Anna Kay, Fatima, and Sheila—line up side by side and do stripteases. I replied that this was a great idea.

Sheila was not skilled at striptease—she did little more than to take her clothes off. On the other hand, Venus, Anna Kay, and Fatima could each be star headliners at the Nimfo Club.

I truly could not decide whom to fuck first—but then Anna Kay said, "Do Venus first. I know you're curious."

And this, Reader, was how I soon wound up naked in bed with the also-naked Roman Goddess of Love.

****

Now I was naked—Sheila had undressed me—and I was standing by the monster bed. Naked Venus sashayed up to me. She stroked my cock with both hands, while she muttered words. *Is she casting a spell?*

After this, she asked me a question in Latin. She did not wait for an answer or a translation; instead, she slid down our half of the monster bed and put my cock in her mouth.

I was still hard from the four-woman striptease, so of course those first seconds of mouth-on-dick would have felt good. But Venus's blowjob felt *wonderful*, even from the start. My dick felt, three seconds into her blowjob, like the best cocksucker in the world had already been entertaining me for an hour.

In response to Venus's magical mouth, my hard cock became the hardest that it has *ever* been.

Only seconds passed before she had my dick at the point of exploding; I knew that I was going to see stars before my eyes—

Venus took her mouth off my cock *right before the glory*, then she grinned at me. My cock was red and twitching. *DON'T STOP!* I thought.

Still grinning at me, Venus began whispering Latin words. I don't know the language, but soon I figured out that she was making a countdown.

After fifteen seconds of my cock being twitchy and frustrated, Venus slid her lips back onto my cock. *Thank you!* She began to energetically deepthroat me.

Immediately the nerve endings in my cock went supernova.

As my brain melted and my knees buckled, I looked around. Sheila was kneeling at the foot of the monster bed, facing me and jilling herself with two fingers. Anna Kay and Fatima were kneeling on Anna Kay's side of the monster bed; the two buxom beauties were fingering each other as they kissed. Roshradzam was grunting in time with his thrusts, as he fucked moaning Sumera on the twin bed.

****

A minute after I had exploded in Venus's mouth, now I was only barely panting, and my dick was feeling happy. Venus took her lips off my cock (she had sucked me to softness), then she shimmied up the bed till we were face to face. "I enjoyed sucking you off, mortal Marvin," Venus said. "Would you like to fuck me now?"

I brought a hand up to feel her large tits. Her nipples, pressing against my chest, felt like two pushing fingertips. I said, "No way will I pass up a chance to fuck a goddess."

Venus gave me a fake pout. "But I made you all soft. I need to fix that." So saying, she slid down the bed again.

Venus needed only thirty seconds to suck me to titanium hardness for the second time. Then she broke the "kiss" and shimmied up the bed again.

I'm *sure* Venus used magic on my dick. I had *never* recovered this quickly, not even when I had been an eighteen-year-old virgin in bed with two strippers.

Venus lay down on her back, her head on the pillow. When I moved between her legs, she wrapped her arms around my neck. "Take me, hero."

I *did* take her—my way. I moved between her widespread legs and I started sucking on Venus's perfect nipples. Erect, they were an inch long. I licked them and sucked them; Venus groaned and arched her back.

Then both of Venus's hands grabbed my hips. I quickly used my clever brain to figure out that Venus wanted me to fuck her.

I obliged her. Once I pushed my cockhead between her labia, I discovered that Venus's vagina was very wet. This surprised me, because I had done little foreplay.

I pushed my cock in slowly, and Venus sucked air in through her teeth. When I bottomed out, I pulled my cock out slowly—

Or rather, that was the plan. Venus thrust her hips up, overtaking my cock. She said, "Please go fast! Fuck me fast, fuck me hard! Use me!"

So I did—I rutted like an animal with the Goddess of Love. After only a few minutes, I was ready to spurt again— not only was Venus's pussy wet, but her walls were squeezing my cock.

As much fun as I was having, Venus was having more. Barely a minute after I had first pushed my cock into her pussy, Venus was thrusting her hips, squeezing my back with her arms, and either making a high-pitched keening sound or else yelling Latin words.

Venus and I fucked for only fifteen minutes, by the bedside clock; but in those fifteen minutes, I shot my sperm twice into her pussy; and Venus came four times, I think.

When I collapsed onto my back on the bed, Venus rolled on top of me, grabbed my head with both hands, and kissed me like she meant it. After the kiss, she said, "Fucking a hero gets me *so hot.*"

I sighed. "I'm not a hero, Venus. My plan *failed.*"

"But you will come up with a new plan and you will try again, yes?"

I nodded. "Too much is at stake. I can't quit now."

Venus kissed me tenderly on the lips, then said, "You are brave and clever, and you do not quit. You *are* a hero, mortal Marvin."

Venus's mouth and pussy had made my cock feel good. But now Venus's *words* made my *heart* feel just as good.

I looked around the room. Fatima was on the other side of the monster bed, on her elbows and spread knees; Fatima's pussy lips were being licked by Anna Kay, who was lying on the bed on her back, underneath Fatima. One of Anna Kay's hands was fingering her own clit; her other hand was up above, caressing Fatima's right boob. Sheila still was fingering herself; Sheila's flushed face was looking at me with a pleading expression. Over on the twin bed, Roshradzam was lying back and Sumera was blowing him.

****

One second later

Venus sat up, then crawled across the monster bed to where Anna Kay and Fatima were frolicking. I beckoned Sheila to join me on my part of the bed. She hurried over.

Sheila looked deep into my eyes and said, "I love you. I want to give you my body."

This *had to be* by Venus's magic. My slave-touch and magic pheromones had never worked on Sheila, and Fatima had told me that Sheila had never liked guys much. During the last six years, Sheila had always been distant with me, and not only because she was living out her lesbian-sex-slave-fembot fantasy.

Okay, so Venus had said that Sheila's infatuation with me would end at midnight. No mention had been made whether SJ-1 would remember our lovemaking tomorrow, but the smart thing for me was to presume that SJ-1 would remember everything.

I decided right then that I would do nothing to embarrass Sheila/SJ-1 when her infatuation wore off.

So deciding, now I pushed Sheila's shoulders down on the bed. I kissed her soft lips, then I moved down her body.

For several minutes, I licked her big boobs, and my lips and tongue played with her erect nipples. "Ooh, I *like* that," Sheila said.

I liked that, too. Her boobs were big and firm, and her boob-skin was soft.

After several minutes of boob-licking, my body resumed moving downward. Sheila said, "No, beloved, *I* should be licking *you*."

I lifted my head a little bit. "Ssh," I replied. "Enjoy." Soon after, my face was between Sheila's knees.

Having just kissed down Sheila's body from her boobs and her stomach, now I kissed up her inner thighs from her knees, alternating left and right.

"You're making me wait," Sheila said. "You're so bad."

But eventually my face was within tonguing distance of Sheila's pussy lips.

Sheila's smell was strong. She was oozing pussy-juice, which was running down her thighs and wetting the sheets.

"*Mmm*," I said as I licked her clean (for the moment). Sheila writhed and groaned.

"That'sss nicccce," Sheila said.

I put my left hand on top of Sheila's right hip, which meant my left thumb was perfectly placed to cause Sheila delight. My thumb followed the plan: While my tongue was finding places to lick, my thumb was sliding in and out of Sheila's pussy.

Soon I was tonguing Sheila's clit. She seemed to like that—"Mmmore," she moaned, while rocking her hips.

I obliged her, replacing my shorter thumb in her pussy with my longer left index finger. In and out my finger went, in and out, while I licked Sheila's clit and Sheila thrashed.

Elsewhere on the bed, Fatima was gasping out Arabic words. My clever brain figured out: Fatima was having fun being pleasured by Venus and Anna Kay.

Sheila brought my attention back to her when she said, "I love you. You are too good to me. Let me do you back."

"Ssh," I said, then went back to making Sheila's hips roll and her mouth gasp.

Then Sheila's climax hit. Her hips thrust off the bed, she screamed, and her hands grabbed my hair *hard*. She shoved her mound against my tongue, and her pussy was squeezing my finger.

Meanwhile, Venus was eating out Anna Kay and was fingering Fatima. Anna Kay screamed, "Oh yes, oh *yesss!*"

****

A minute later

I had slid up the bed and now was fucking Sheila, as she licked her own pussy juices off my face. Sheila was no longer gasping from the oral orgasm I had given her.

Now one of her arms was wrapped around my back, while her other arm's hand played with my hair. As for my own hands, they were holding Sheila's ass cheeks.

I fucked her. She was wet and she was tight, so every inch of my cock was lovingly stroked and squeezed. Her pussy around my dick was as hot as a summer afternoon. Sheila's passion for me was magically caused; but from now until midnight, she was one world-class fuck.

"I love you, darling Marvin," Sheila said. "You make me feel *soo good*, but *I* should be making *you* feel good."

Instead of replying, I kissed her.

About a minute later, while I was pistoning Sheila, she started gasping. Her hands switched their work from holding onto my upper body to grabbing my ass. She yanked my hips against hers.

I speeded up my pace; Sheila liked that.

"Oh Marvin, yes, oh baby, oh here it—here it *comes, yesss. . .*"

Sheila orgasmed, and her thrusting, frantic hips and clenching pussy sent me over the cliff.

As I *bellowed*, and I *slammed* my hips against Sheila's still-bucking hips, and I *spurted* into Sheila's pussy—

And as red, green, blue, yellow, and white fireworks exploded in my brain—

I heard Anna Kay yell, "Venus! Fatima! *Give it* to me!"

Millions of my little tadpoles promptly found themselves in Sheila's dark cave. They each knew what to do next: Go find Sheila's basketball and be the first (and only) to dribble it. I had mixed feelings about one of them achieving its goal, but I hoped they had fun—after all, each of those little guys was half of me.

When I was no longer spurting semen, I rolled off of Sheila. Both our chests were wet, because we had worked up a sweat. She slid toward the side of the bed to give me room to lie on my back. I pulled Sheila on top of me, and we kissed. The kissing was tricky at first, because we both were still panting.

Meanwhile on the twin bed, Roshradzam was lying on his back and smiling. He was feeling-up two dark-blue erect nipples as Sumera lifted herself up and slid down his dick.

****

One minute later

Venus and Sheila were lying down on the other side of the monster bed; from their positioning, they were about to do sixty-nine.

Meanwhile, Anna Kay and Fatima had left the other side of the monster bed and now were standing by my side of the bed. Anna Kay and Fatima were holding hands.

"I love your genie," Anna Kay said to me.

"I love your wife," Fatima told me.

Together, they said, "And we *both* love *you*."

Anna Kay had a foil-wrapped condom in her free hand. Then she did the trick that she had learned from Georgia, an ex-prostitute who had joined the harem in 2013—

Anna Kay tore open the foil, took out the rolled-up condom, and put it in her mouth. Then she deepthroated me. In the process, she unrolled the condom onto my dick. Listen, Reader, putting on a rubber never felt so *good!*

Anna Kay took several minutes to slide her lips up and down my cock, to make sure the condom was properly placed. By then, my dick was hard and pointing up.

After Anna Kay had lifted her lips off my cock and was again standing by Fatima, Anna Kay said, "Tell us what you want to do now, my husband."

I said, "I'm up for some doggy style, Wife." I climbed off the bed.

Anna Kay got on the monster bed and moved herself around till her knees were at the foot of my side of the bed, and her feet were spread apart.

Anna Kay asked, "Where do you want Fatima?"

I said, "Fatima, please lay your head on that pillow. Wife, *you* lay your head—or your face, rather—on *Fatima*."

Anna Kay looked at Fatima and said in a husky voice, "I *like* that idea. But Fatima might be bored now by me licking her labia."

Fatima climbed onto the bed, knee-walked to Anna Kay, and kissed her on the lips. Then Fatima lay back on the bed. "I'm *never* bored with *you*, Anna Kay Harper."

With that, Anna Kay bent over at the waist, put her elbows on the bed between Fatima's legs, and brought her face just below Fatima's hips. I walked over to stand on the carpet right behind Anna Kay's muscular and shapely ass, I grabbed Anna Kay's narrow waist, and I slid my condom'd cock into her pussy.

"*Mmm*," Anna Kay said, while Fatima gasped.

I said, "I love you, Anna Kay, and I plan to make you feel good." Then I fucked her.

Anna Kay was wet—*Because of my hard cock? Because of Fatima's earlier pussy-licking? Because of Venus's magic? Who cares?*—and so fucking Anna Kay doggy-style was fun.

It occurred to me that I was being quick to recover my hard-ons today, and my cock was not sore even slightly. I wondered if Venus had caused all that.

"Ooh, fuck your wife!" Fatima now gasped out. "That's it, Master, fuck your loving wife! You are a good master, and you deserve to come hard and come often!"

Anna Kay lifted her face off Fatima's slot to speak over her shoulder: "Lucky for you, my husband, I *enjoy* making you come hard and come often."

Then Anna Kay resumed her licking; Fatima moaned.

****

Minutes later

In-out, in-out, in-out. My cock felt happy, hard, and tingly.

I grunted, then said, "I'm going to come hard in just a few minutes. I love fucking your pussy, Anna Kay."

Fatima said, "Ooh, I feel Anna Kay's boobs slap my legs every time you slam your cock into her pussy. *Soo* sexy."

"It's a *wet* pussy I'm slamming, Fatima," I said. "Anna Kay is *wet* for me."

Anna Kay didn't say anything, but one hand briefly lifted up in a thumb-up gesture.

Fatima gasped. Then she said, "Oh, Anna Kay, for a woman who never licked women before she got married, you lick me *very* well!"

Again, one of Anna Kay's hands briefly came up in a thumb-up gesture.

No sooner had Anna Kay's two hands and one mouth resumed pleasuring Fatima, but Anna Kay lifted her face up again. Anna Kay arched her back as she said, "Your cock is getting *bigger* now, my husband—I can feel it."

I replied, "I'm about to come, Anna Kay. Your silky pussy is bringing me to the cliff!"

Then I was thrusting and shoving and spurting. Maybe I screamed, or maybe I was silent—I don't remember. All I remember for sure was that my dick felt *great*.

Fatima groaned then, and both her hands buried themselves in Anna Kay's hair. Fatima gasped out, "Watching Master come in his wife's pussy gets me *so hot!*"

Anna Kay lifted her face off Fatima—right then Anna Kay *needed* to lift her face, because now she was panting and gasping. She thrust her pussy back against my cock several times, as she arched her back; then her body went absolutely still—

Except for Anna Kay's clenching pussy and gasping, orgasmic screams.

"*Mmm*," Fatima moaned.

Over on the twin bed, Roshradzam and Sumera had resumed plain-vanilla missionary sex. *Wow, he's really slamming her*, I thought. But judging by Sumera's gasps and moans, she was enjoying the energetic fucking.

****

A half-hour later

I had climaxed in Anna Kay twice more—which had required me to change out my condom twice more. (Anna Kay loved sex but did not want to get pregnant.)

Now my shrinking cock was out of Anna Kay's pussy, and I had decided that it was time for me to fuck Fatima.

That still left the minor but icky problem of getting rid of the cum-filled condom that was still on my dick.

Green light flashed, then my dick was naked and clean. Anna Kay commented, "A genie is useful for *all sorts of* things." Anna Kay kissed Fatima.

As for the sex, Fatima did not need to move at all; she remained lying on her back, with her head of the pillow. I knee-walked over to Fatima on the bed and was about to fuck her when Anna Kay said, "Just a moment, my husband. I want to make you rock-hard for Fatima."

Anna Kay put her arms around my knees, pulled me to the edge of the bed, and sucked me superbly.

Reader, Anna Kay looks for *any* excuse to suck my cock. It's reason number 243 why I am lucky to be married to her.

Eventually Anna Kay moved my cock away from her mouth. Seconds later, my erect cock was inside Fatima, and she and I were fucking.

I said, "I love you, Fatima, and I plan to make you feel good."

Anna Kay lay down on the edge of the bed, next to Fatima and me as we cavorted. Anna Kay slid one arm under Fatima's neck, as Anna Kay wrapped her other arm over my back.

The entire time that Fatima and I were fucking, writhing, thrashing, thrusting, and moaning (and also kissing and hugging), Anna Kay was next to us both. What was Anna Kay doing during this time? She was kissing and caressing, first one of us and then the other.

Anna Kay stroked my hair.

Anna Kay caressed Fatima's side-boob.

Anna Kay kissed me.

Anna Kay kissed Fatima.

Anna Kay stroked my face, then she stroked Fatima's face.

What the three of us were doing was, in its way, very romantic.

****

Half an hour later

Fatima had climaxed twice while I had been fucking her, then I had spurted in her pussy. Now our hips were motionless while Fatima, Anna Kay, and I were enjoying a three-way make-out session.

"Goodbye, Sheila," I heard Venus say. "I enjoyed you." Then Venus rolled out of the other side of the monster bed and stood up. *Flash*—now Venus was dressed again.

While my wife, my genie, and I climbed out of bed, Venus walked over to where Roshradzam and Sumera were still(!) fucking. Venus tapped Sumera on the shoulder (I guess because Sumera was the partner on top at that time). Venus said, "Pardon me, but I need to leave now, and I need to take my twin bed with me."

"Sure, not a problem," Sumera said. She stepped off the bed, said something in Arabic to Roshradzam, and he rolled off the twin bed.

The twin bed vanished in a flash of lavender light.

Venus had only briefly said goodbye to Sheila, but now Venus gave Anna Kay and Fatima lavish, praising goodbyes, as if those two were rock stars.

Then my turn came. Venus gave me a long, hot kiss; then she gushed, "Marvin Harper, besides being clever and brave, you are good-hearted, you are kind, you are generous with your money, you *inspire* people, people *admire* you—"

In the middle of this, Fatima started to giggle. When I shot Fatima a *What's going on?* look, she said, "Wow, Venus, you love-whammied Sumera *hard!*"

Venus turned to look, and smiled. I turned to look, and stared—

Naked Roshradzam and naked Sumera did not have a bed for sex anymore? Not a problem—Roshradzam was standing where the twin bed had been, and Sumera was on her knees in front of him. Sumera eagerly deepthroated Roshradzam as her light-blue hands squeezed his brown ass cheeks.

Chapter 18
Elsewhere in My City

Meanwhile (Friday)
In the Newspaper Room of the Harper Foundation

In a big room, Elvira LeClerc, Almira LeClerc, and eighteen other young women each sat at a small table, each skimming an out-of-town newspaper.

The towns and cities that were represented by these newspapers ranged in size from New York City, NY to Indianola, Mississippi.

Each young woman had on her table, besides the newspaper that she was reading through, an Inbox, a stapler, a pen, and a sharp pair of scissors.

Each young woman in the room was looking for a newspaper story of someone who needed a gift of Marvin Harper's money. If the reader found someone worthy, the reader would cut out the newspaper article and would write on the clipping the newspaper's date, the town or city, and the reader's name.

Now Elvira heard a young woman's voice: "Hey, ladies, I have more sad stories for you."

The speaker turned out to be Josie the mail-room clerk. Josie was pushing into the reading-room a rolling cart that was stacked with newspapers; this was Josie's second trip to the reading-room this hour.

Josie was the mail-room clerk by day, and a *haremée* at the mansion by night. Josie was typical in this way—*every* employee of the Harper Foundation, from CEO Virgilia O'Keefe down to the mail-room clerk, was a *haremée* or former *haremée*. Almira was a *haremée*; Elvira was technically a *haremée* too.

Lizzie Lou Forrester, while stopping to stretch, said, "The more newspapers Josie brings, the more people Marvin can help. It feels *so good* to know that in my own little way, I'm helping Marvin to help people. Y'all agree?"

Nineteen female voices agreed with Lizzie Lou's words; *even Almira smiled and agreed.* Only Elvira was silent.

Part of Elvira's silence was from shock. *Why is Almie agreeing with this "Go Marvin!" speech? Almie isn't mind-controlled anymore, right?*

Naturally blond Gustava Svedberg of Minnesota, who was another reader-slash-*haremée*, said, "I'm proud that Marvin wants to help everybody. But it's enough for me that Marvin told me to come here and do this. After all, Marvin deserves to be served."

"*By me and by other people*," nineteen female voices chorused. Only the LeClerc twins did not speak this line.

Elvira felt relief. For a second, Elvira had worried that Marvin had again mind-whammied Almie.

Lizzie Lou said, "It is so sad, y'all, that Marvin is shorter than all of us now." Even Elvira agreed to that. "But Marvin still deserves to be served," Lizzie Lou added. As before, everyone but the twins agreed.

Meanwhile, in one corner of the room were thirty-one thirty-gallon trashcans, labeled from *1* to *31*. Today was the fourteenth day of the month, so while people were talking, Josie dumped all the newspapers on her cart into the *14* trashcan.

"Hey Josie," Almira called out, "I forgot to ask earlier. How did your GED test come out?"

"I passed my last two sections!" Josie said, grinning. "I'm supposed to get something official in two weeks."

"That's great, congratulations," Almira said. All the readers agreed, except for Elvira.

Elvira was not only silent now, she was staring at her twin sister in puzzlement. Six years ago, Almira would have *sneered* at any girl who had dropped out of high school, instead of congratulating the girl for fixing her mistake.

Gustava asked Josie, "So when you get your GED, what will you do next? Get a job at the mall? Or at Nimfo Club?" Josie had a pretty face and a stacked chest; now she could get a job anywhere where good looks and a high-school education were job requirements.

Josie blushed. "Actually, um, I was hoping I could work *here*. Reading. It's ten cents an hour more than the mail room. Besides, What—"

Almost everyone in the room—even Almira—chorused, "*What We Do Is Important.*" That phrase was stapled to the corkboard in every breakroom in the building. Again Elvira was silent.

Elvira looked at Josie and made her voice sound casual: "I'm sure Almie will be promoted out of here soon. So stick around if you want her table."

Elvira *knew* that Almira was staring at her now, but Elvira did not turn her head to confirm it.

Elvira knew that *she* would not be promoted out of the reading room, *ever*; there was too much bad blood between Marvin and her. But until Sumera's first wish-grant had unspelled the twins' minds, as long as Almira had worked in the reading room with Elvira, Elvira had caused no problems at work.

But now, Elvira was no longer obedient to her twin sister's commands; add to this that now Almira got along *great* with Marvin, Fatima, and the other *haremées* and former *haremées*, while Elvira was a misfit at the mansion. Put all this together and the result was obvious: Soon Elvira would be left behind.

Elvira felt intense sadness then. *My twin is not my <u>twin</u> anymore—now she's just my sister who looks like me.*

Josie, with her newspaper-delivery task done, now pushed her cart toward the door. Almost everyone called out goodbyes to Josie—again, Almie was one of the goodbye-ers, while Elvira was not.

In another corner of the room were two giant rubber trashcans on rollers. Each trashcan had the Recycle symbol painted on it, and each trashcan was partly filled with discarded, cut-up newspapers. Five minutes after Josie had left, Almira stood up, walked over to drop her old newspaper in the nearer Recycle trashcan, walked over to the *12* trashcan, and took out an unread newspaper.

But instead of then walking back to her own table, Almira detoured to Elvira's table. Almira leaned down and murmured in Elvira's ear, "My advice, Elvie? Make friends. Be friendly. We're not queens of the universe anymore, we're parolees. Besides, Josie is nice, once you take the time to know her, *hm?*"

Elvira did not reply to what Almira said. Instead, Elvira said, "Tonight, let's google Dad's phone number and call him up. Let's talk to Real-Dad, not some green guy. It's time, Almie."

Almira grinned down at Elvira. "That's a *great* idea! It'll be scary, talking to Dad after six years—will he be angry at us? But it'll be good too, getting close to Dad again."

Elvira gave Almira a weak smile, and did not say what she was thinking. *My relationship with Mother is ruined, and my relationship with my twin is not close anymore. I need a family connection with <u>somebody</u>.*

****

Meanwhile, across town in Michelle's garage

"I summon you, Fanzelle," Michelle Landrieu-LeClerc said.

FOOF. In red smoke, Fanzelle appeared inside the illusionary pentagram.

Michelle said, "I notice Harper isn't in the news anymore. No 'Batman' stories, no public appearances."

Fanzelle laughed. "He's 5′2″ now, and can do only three pushups—his days of beating up criminals are *over*. And since he's embarrassed at being five-two and puny, he's avoiding being seen by mortals."

Fanzelle did not mention that Marvin Harper had made himself *very* visible to demons and war gods. Harper's group had killed six demons. Now Satan was angry with Marvin Harper, sure, but mostly Satan was pissed at Fanzelle. Well, Michelle did not need to know any of that.

Now Fanzelle added, "But I have good news. I arranged with a demon in Nigeria to siphon off most of the money in Marvin Harper's bank accounts. Now Harper has less than a million dollars in the bank."

Michelle glared. "Grab the rest of it, Fanzelle! Ruin him!"

Fanzelle shook her head. "Can't. Long story. But what you don't realize is, Harper spends money like firemen spend water. A year from now, Marvin Harper will have to make hard choices."

"*How* hard?"

"Whether to close down the Harper Foundation, or to send all his harem girls away and to sell the mansion." To this truth, Fanzelle now added a lie: "This is assuming that Harper's ex-cheerleader wife doesn't file for divorce and clean him out sooner."

Michelle said, "Just from pictures I've seen of Anna Whatzername, I can tell she's a gold-digger whore. She'll dump Marvin Harper soon, and then I'll laugh my ass off."

Then Michelle pressed, "No other news about Harper to report?"

"Nothing worth mentioning," Fanzelle said with fake casualness. Fanzelle's shrug was fake too. After Marvin

Harper's group had killed six demons and Satan had held Fanzelle *personally* responsible (joy, oh joy), Fanzelle wanted to avoid telling Michelle how Harper had tried to act the hero again. Besides, Harper's plan of using war gods to kill demons had been thwarted, so his recent activity *did not deserve* mentioning.

Chapter 19
Bad Guys 1

In the master bedroom at the mansion (Friday)

The next-to-last thing that Venus did before she left us was to make lavender light flash around Sheila's head. Sheila's expression changed to shock.

The last thing that Venus did before she left us was to make Sheila's entire body flash lavender. An instant later, Sheila's silver skin-paint, silver catsuit, and silver cowl all were back—Sheila was SJ-1 again.

With that, Venus disappeared in yet another flash of lavender light.

SJ-1 stared at me for several seconds, shook herself, then tore her gaze away from me to look at Fatima. SJ-1 said, "Um, Mistress, may I—may this unit be excused? This unit has, um, work to do in the computer room."

Fatima replied, "Yes, SJ-1, you may be excused."

In six years, I had never seen SJ-1 move quickly, except when ordered to. But now, SJ-1 ran for the bedroom door.

But with her hand on the doorknob, SJ-1 stopped and looked at me. "I would have done *anything* for you, but you treated me like a queen. I thank you—I mean, this unit thanks you—this unit means, this unit thanks you."

I smiled at the pretend-fembot. "You're welcome, SJ-1."

SJ-1 hurried out of the room.

****

Suppertime
The monster kitchen at the mansion

Fanzelle had dropped in uninvited during dinner last night; at dinner tonight, I noticed that not as many former *haremées* were eating with us. Why? I wondered whether former *haremées*, who were only barely mind-controlled, did not want to spent time with short and puny Marvin Harper now, or whether they were scared of Fanzelle barging in again and causing shit.

That kind of thinking was depressing, so I shifted my thoughts to the roast beef I was eating, which was tasty.

What a day, I thought. *Recruiting war gods, fighting demons, and having an orgy with the Goddess of Love. No wonder I'm starving!*

At the head table, Anna Kay sat to my right, Fatima sat to my left, and SJ-1 sat to Fatima's left. SJ-1 never quite met my eye during the meal; but I do not think anyone but Anna Kay, Fatima, and I noticed.

Virgilia O'Keefe walked into the monster kitchen then, ten minutes after food had been served. She walked over to where I was sitting, and said, "Want to know what I heard on the news, driving home? President Obama got in a fistfight with Mitch McConnell"—the Senate Majority Leader—"and Paul Ryan," the Speaker for the House.

I said, "*What? Are you sure?*"

"Sure am. Fox News is saying Obama started the fight, but CNN says the Republicans threw the first punches."

"That's *insane*," I said.

I worried. The worldwide corruption and evil that Fanzelle and the other demons were trying to spread, had now reached into the White House.

Tiffni Daniels, who had been randomly selected to sit at the Head Table tonight, said, "The news lately has gotten *really weird.* Lot more bombings and hostage stuff than there used to be, even a month ago."

Virgilia looked at me. "Also on the news, a school in Bolivia and a school in Denmark have children being held hostage by gunmen. Some guy in North Carolina is preaching that evil people have a right to be evil, and that churches are 'oppressing' these poor evil people. I agree with Tiffni: lately the news is strange and disturbing."

I looked at Fatima, and mouthed the word *Demons*. She nodded.

****

Hours later (after midnight, Saturday morning) Master bedroom at the mansion

FOOM. I was completely asleep, but the sound of a teleporting *djinni* halfway-woke me.

I woke up completely when a finger tapped my shoulder. Fatima said, "Master, please wake up!"

I opened my eyes and reached for the bedside lamp. When the light came on, Anna Kay grunted, and rolled away from the light.

I saw that Fatima was wearing her Middle Eastern clothes instead of her American clothes. She did this only when she was greeting a new master, or when she was *foom*ing off to Cairo to hang out with Green Tribe.

I shook my sleepy head. "Why aren't you in Cairo?"

"Six men have climbed over the fence. They're trying to break into the mansion."

Behind me, Anna Kay gasped.

I was wide awake now. "*Can* they break in?" All the ground-floor windows were covered with iron bars.

Fatima said, "They have a six-foot-long boltcutter and a stepladder. They'll be through the window in five minutes."

I jumped out of bed, and was walking to the recliner, on which my pants were folded, when Anna Kay said, "Marvin, you're going out to fight them?"

I replied, "If I call the cops, they'll show up too late. So yes, it's invaders versus me."

"And me," Fatima said.

Anna Kay said, "But Marvin, you—you aren't Captain America anymore. You're a *short* guy now."

I winced, then replied, "But thirty-five women in the mansion, *including you*, are trusting me to keep them safe tonight. I have to *try*, Anna Kay, I don't want you hurt."

I turned to Fatima. "Sumera is in Baghdad. If I summon her back here, will she protect the women if the bad guys get in?"

"*Ha.* She won't lift a finger, except to protect *you*."

I said, "Roshradzam will fight, but there is little he can do beyond throwing punches."

The bad guys are making progress with the window while Fatima and I are talking. But hey, no pressure.

Meanwhile, Fatima was saying, "Roshradzam could wrap his arms around a bad guy and *foom* the both of them far away from here. But that would reveal your secret."

"*Fuck*," I said. "So Sumera is out, and Roshradzam is out."

Then I got a thought. "Do any of the six men have a DOFD"—Date of Fated Death—"really soon?"

Fatima summoned her scrying ball and worked it. She did not take long, but iron bars were being cut-through while she was doing her research. But hey, no pressure.

Fatima vanished her scrying ball and said, "Bradley Grant's DOFD is today."

I had pulled on my pants by then, but now I pulled them off and dropped them back on the recliner. I said, "A magical request, Fatima: Please dress us both like security guards. Give me a working Taser, and give yourself a 9-millimeter semiautomatic pistol."

Fatima's smile was vampiric. "I've never killed a wormfood by shooting him. It'll be fun."

Green light flashed, and now Fatima and I were dressed as guards. The uniforms were sea-green, and each shirtsleeve sported a "GT Security" patch. We each had a shoulder-mounted radio. We each wore a wide black-leather belt that had a weapons holster attached to it.

Anna Kay said, "Hold on, why is *Fatima* wearing the gun instead of you?"

I replied calmly, "I'll explain later."

"How do you know there's gonna *be* a 'later'? You're almost defenseless!"

I gave Anna Kay a reassuring smile (I hoped). "I'll come back—most likely, without a scratch. *That* isn't what I'm worried about." I did not add *I'm not worried about me, I'm worried about you women in the mansion.*

Meanwhile, I was tapping my "radio," and wondering why Fatima had given us each a radio. Fatima said, "Remember my ventriloquism trick? Don't be surprised when your radio talks to you. Are you ready?"

I said to Fatima, "Out there: We'll play it as Good Cop, Bad Cop. Change that: Sane Cop, *Crazy* Cop. I'll be Batman and you're Joker. Now, what's the situation?"

Fatima summoned her scrying ball again, worked it for two seconds, then vanished it. "They're—"

Fatima drew her pistol with surprising speed. "—almost in."

I was surprised to see that Fatima's pistol had a silencer on it.

I drew my Taser, then I asked Fatima, "Can you put us on the lawn behind the bad guys without making a *foom* sound or a green flash?"

My simple request stumped Fatima; meanwhile, the clock was ticking. "Yes," Fatima said after a time.

Anna Kay said, "Marvin, be—"

My ears popped.

****

An instant later

Four men were holding onto the iron-bar mesh that covered one dark window. Two other men were working the giant boltcutter that was about to cut the one intact iron bar at the top of that window.

One of the invaders said, "Thirty-odd bitches in there, and a lot of them have big tits—I can't wait."

"Unless 'Batman' shows up. Marvin Harper," another man said. He sounds worried.

"If Harper shows up, he'll get his ass kicked. It's six against one, " one of the boltcutter-men replied.

"Evil is good!" a fourth man said. "Rape gets me hard!"

SNIP—the last iron bar was cut. The four men who were holding on to the now-severed iron-bar mesh threw it on the grass.

This is when the intruders noticed Guard-Fatima and Guard-me. They froze—probably because Fatima and I were each holding weapons.

"Gentlemen, step away from the window," I said calmly.

Fatima pushed the button on her radio with her left hand, while her right hand was aiming her pistol at the men. "Window Eight is now cut through," Fatima said.

Both Fatima's radio and my radio sounded with a male voice saying, "I copy. Police are on their way. Mr. Harper has been informed."

The intruders shared nervous looks.

One of the men stuck his chin out and said to Fatima, "You can't have a silencer on your pistol. That's illegal."

"Illegal? Really?" Fatima replied, in a bored, lady-cop voice. "Marvin Harper is a billionaire. I'm not worried about going to prison."

Fatima added, "I'm not worried even about six counts of Murder in the First."

I said, "So how about you men grab your big boltcutter and your stepladder, and get gone, *hm?*"

One of the men said, "Six of us, two of you."

Fatima shrugged. "Two of us armed, six of you unarmed."

One of the guys who was holding the boltcutter, let it fall sideways. The giant boltcutter hit the now-unprotected window glass; the shatter-sound was *loud*. The window-breaker said, "It's time for us to have some fun and grab us some poontang hostages. Brad?"

The man who had talked about illegal silencers suddenly had a pistol in his hand—a pistol with its own silencer. My brain had barely realized *He's pointing his gun at Fatima!* when—

Thyoo! I heard, coming from in front—

Thyoo!—this came from my left. Bradley Grant dropped to the ground.

I took three quick steps forward, and tasered the nearest of the other five men. Over his screams of agony, my "radio" sounded again with that male voice: "Code Double-Zero. I say again, Code Double-Zero."

"Oh, goody," Fatima said. Nobody could miss the *glee* in her voice. She took a two-handed grip on her silencered pistol, and pointed her pistol at the four men still standing.

I said, "Guys, Guard Delaverte is now weapons-free, with a Get out of Jail Free card. Still want to stick around?"

The five living men fled then, taking their stepladder and their boltcutter with them. Marines they weren't: They carried away their stunned buddy, but left dead Bradley lying on the grass, next to the cut-away iron-bar mesh.

****

One minute later

When Fatima and I walked back into the mansion, our security-guard costumes were gone. I was wearing pants, flip-flops, and no shirt; bunny-slippered Fatima was wearing a "Disney's Aladdin" nightshirt, with a light-green bathrobe covering it. We both were weaponless.

As Fatima and I were climbing the stairs, Barbara Drysdale peeked at us around the corner from the upstairs hallway. "I heard a noise," she said. "Broken glass. It woke me up. I heard men outside. I was *scared*, Marvin sir."

When I reached the top of the stairs, I hugged Barbara. "It was just some teenage boys acting goofy. Fatima and I got them to leave. Who knew Fatima could talk tough?"

Across the upstairs hallway from the stairs was the Upstairs Lounge. Sitting in the lounge, with every table-lamp turned on, was nervous Anna Kay and four nervous *haremées*. They all relaxed when they saw that Fatima and I were unhurt.

I talked the *haremées* into going back to bed, then Fatima, Anna Kay, and I walked back to our own bedrooms. Anna Kay murmured, "Were they truly rowdy teen boys, or something more?"

"Six evil human men," Fatima murmured back. "I wanted to kill *all* of them, not just one."

Anna Kay choked. "Someone is *dead?* Where's his body at? Do we need to call Victoria Allblue in case you're arrested, Marvin?"

"Relax," I said. "I don't expect the police, Fatima used a silencer, and the guy now is swimming in lava in Mount Kilauea—along with his blood, hair, fibers, and epithelials."

Fatima murmured to Anna Kay, "If the cops come, their technicians will work hard for nothing."

"And the window?" Anna Kay asked. "The bars?"

I looked at Fatima, who made strange gestures. She said, "The bars are fixed: they're uncut and back on the window. But since Barbara heard glass breaking, I had to leave the window busted. Is that okay, Master?"

I nodded.

Anna Kay asked, "The other bad guys, what do you think they're doing after they left?"

I shrugged. "I don't care, so long as they don't come back here."

****

An hour later at night

I had fallen back asleep when a knocking on the master-bedroom door woke me up.

Anna Kay gasped. She did not wait for me to turn on my bedside light; she immediately turned hers on.

I walked to the bedroom door and opened it. Lizzie Lou Forrester said, "Y'all, there are lots of police cars at the house next door. And ambulances. *Lots* of ambulances."

I pulled on pants, shirt, and shoes. I ran down the stairs, out the front door, down the front driveway, and through the front gate. There I saw that the mansion to my right was lit up like a rock concert. I heard the same dispatcher's voice coming from the cabs of four police cars.

I knew things were bad when I noticed that four ambulances were parked in front of my neighbor's house; in all four cases, the ambulance crews were leaning against their vehicles instead of rushing into that mansion.

The next thing I noticed were two crime-scene vans that were parked across the street from my neighbor.

Right after that, I noticed yellow crime-scene tape across my neighbor's front door.

****

The next morning

My neighbor's mansion was shown on the local morning news, on all four stations. Everyone who lived there—Todd Williams, his wife Marie who had disapproved of my lifestyle, and the two teenage Williams boys—had been killed violently.

I felt sick with guilt.

****

Minutes later, before breakfast

Gustava Svedberg grabbed my hand as Anna Kay and I were walking into the monster kitchen. Gustava declared, "Marvin sir, you have a problem."

"I do?"

I was instantly worried. That the five evil men were trying to break into the mansion again. Or else that more *haremées* had figured out that Fatima was more than my housekeeper. Or else—

Gustava replied, "I saw Sumera Hatfield kissing your new groundskeeper."

I had to concentrate to not show my relief. "Okay, Gustava, I'll talk to those two, find out what the deal is."

Gustava's face was as disapproving as Michelle Landrieu-LeClerc's face at a strip show. "Sumera was *really* kissing him. 'Get a room' kissing him. If you're not her first choice, she should leave."

"Okay, I'll *definitely* talk to them."

****

After breakfast, I ordered "haremée" Sumera and "groundskeeper" Roshradzam to follow me into the deep-sink room. Since both Sumera and Roshradzam were bound to me, they obeyed.

Once the three of us were in the deep-sink room and the door was shut, I ordered Roshradzam to take his translator-ring out of his pocket and to put it on.

I informed my lovebird-genies that Gustava had seen them necking like teenagers. Then I ordered, "If anyone who does not know my secret is around, then you two will do *no* PDA," public displays of affection. "I forbid any part of your body to be closer than one foot's distance from the other one's body, when someone who does not know my secret can see you two together. Sumera, you are not to walk into Roshradzam's RV at any time; Roshradzam, you are not to walk into Sumera's room at any time."

Sumera glared at me; Roshradzam nodded.

Sumera said, "But PDA right now is okay with you? Because no ignorant human can see us right now?"

"Yes, except—"

Sumera's hand grabbed the back of Roshradzam's head. She pulled his head down and gave him a red-hot kiss.

"*Ahem*," I said.

Roshradzam pulled Sumera's hand off his head and broke the kiss.

I said, "*As* I was saying. Each of you has assigned work here at the mansion. As long as your work is done well enough, and not done late, and you don't cause gossip, you two can act like rabbits the rest of the time."

"Great," Sumera said. "Glad to hear it." With that, Sumera dropped to her knees in front of Roshradzam, then unzipped his pants.

"*Ahem*," I said. Roshradzam grabbed Sumera's shoulders and pulled up. Sumera scowled as she stood.

I said, "Edited to add: When I, your master, are talking to both of you, I allow no PDA and no sex. Doesn't matter who else is around, or if nobody else is around."

While Roshradzam was zipping his fly, Sumera glared at me. "You're just envious of the love we share!"

Roshradzam gave me a crooked smile.

****

Half an hour after breakfast

I was in the computer room, talking with Fatima and SJ-1, when a bright-eyed, grinning Rivka Goldheim appeared at the open doorway. "Come watch the TV— they've caught the men who killed the Williamses!"

Fatima, SJ-1, and I rushed into the Electronics Playroom. We were just in time to see on TV, gray vapor come out of the broken window of a house. The reporter on the scene told us that we were seeing tear gas.

Seconds later, the TV showed the house's front door opening. Five miserable men stumbled out.

After the TV had clearly shown the five men's faces, I looked over at Fatima. Fatima, who has a perfect memory, caught my look and nodded.

The five bad guys had been arrested; the danger to my wife and my *haremées* was over.

****

Two hours later

Fatima walked into the computer room to tell me, "A police detective wants to talk to you."

Before I walked out of the computer room, Fatima, without me asking, wrapped me in an illusion of being 6'8" and hyper-muscular. Then Fatima apologized: "Fanzelle's demonic magic on you is strong enough that my illusion is going to fade after twelve minutes."

I shrugged. Hopefully, that would be enough.

Detective Ennis was standing just inside my mansion's front door. When I talked to him, he clearly did not believe a word he had heard from the five suspects, and so clearly intended only bare effort at following procedure.

The five bad guys had told the police during interrogation that they had had a sixth associate, Bradley Grant, and that he had been shot last night on my property by a lady security guard. Supposedly this lady security guard had boasted she could get away with murder.

When the detective told me all this, I laughed. "I have only two employees: my groundskeeper Roshradzam; and Fatima here, my housekeeper. The only time I hire security guards is for the annual Christmas party in the ballroom." Yesterday's date was over two months before Christmas.

Fatima asked Detective Ennis, "What security-guard company did they say the two guards worked for? Something-something Security?"

Detective Ennis pulled a notebook from his pocket, flipped through it, then said, "GT Security. Their uniforms were green."

Fatima said, "I'm the person who hires security for the Christmas parties, and that name doesn't sound familiar. Let me check something." Fatima ran off.

While Fatima was supposedly checking something, I led Detective Ennis outside. He looked around.

Ennis was walking around the grass, looking for bloodstains—*good luck with that*—when Fatima rushed out the front door with the local phonebook. Fatima said, "Detective, I was right: There is no 'GT Security' listed."

Ennis shrugged. "The perps also said that they had completely cut through all the bars on one window, and were about to climb inside the house. But all your windows have all their bars undamaged."

Ennis wrote a brief note in his notebook, then put the notebook back in his pocket. "Mr. Harper, I'm sorry to have bothered you. You're our city's best citizen; the idea that *you* would abet murder is just silly. But I had to check. I see no evidence of murder, I see no body, and I see no evidence of an attempted B&E beyond one broken window—*behind* intact iron bars."

Fatima asked innocently, "So why are they saying this about Mas—about Mr. Harper?"

"Scumbags like that? They had a falling out, they killed their buddy, and one of them noticed your house is next door to the Williams's house. They'd name John Wilkes Booth as the killer if they thought I'd buy it. Anyway, I'm done here."

Ennis shook my hand. I said, "Let's just be friends." He got into his unmarked police car and drove away.

As Fatima and I walked into the mansion, I remarked, "The bad guys are arrested, and neither of us is going to prison. A happy ending all around."

Reader, you would think that I would have learned by now, *never* to say *My problems are over.*

Chapter 20
Bad Guys 2

At breakfast, the next day (Sunday)
The monster kitchen at the mansion

Everyone had taken their seats—except for the kitchen helpers, who were setting out food—when the door to the monster kitchen was pushed in. "Good morning, ladies!" called out Gennifer Ashton, as her high heels *click-clack*ed across the kitchen floor. "I'm back."

****

When I had met Gennifer Ashton in 2010, she had been a TV reporter for CBS Channel Ten; also a blond babe in her early twenties. These days, Gennifer was a former *haremée* and my publicist—as well as being a busty blond babe in her late twenties.

More than this, the reason that I was internationally known as the "hero billionaire" was because of Gennifer. Six years ago, while I had been dressed as Captain America for a costume party, I had rescued two little kids from a house on fire. Gennifer and a cameraman had filmed me, and the video of "Captain America" using a stairs-bannister to rescue the children had gone viral. (Later that day, another TV station had revealed that I, "Captain America," had inherited billions from my great-uncle. I have been a celebrity ever since.)

Five years ago, I had hired Gennifer as my publicist. Her job was to send out a ton of press releases about me—mostly by email, but sometimes by fax. Right after I had hired Gennifer, I had installed a fax machine in the computer room, with its own dedicated phone line. I had given Gennifer the then-minor job of buying paper and toner for the fax machine whenever it needed it.

Four years ago, construction had finished on the Harper Foundation building, and so Gennifer had been given her own office with its own fax machine and email. Faxes for her had still come to my home fax machine—but only one or two a week.

Gennifer and I had agreed on a simple rule then: Whenever she was in my house—such as when, as a former *haremée*, she was eating breakfast or dinner in the monster kitchen—she would go to the computer room and would collect the faxes there.

A year and a half ago, my home fax number had been posted on the internet. I immediately had become swamped with faxes. The messages were hard-luck stories—people who bypassed the Harper Foundation's procedures and directly asked me for help. After a week of this, I had told Gennifer that, after she collected the faxes, to pass them to Virgilia for the Harper Foundation to evaluate.

I do not know whether Virgilia funded most of the fax-requests that Gennifer handed her, rejected most of them, or if Virgilia trashed every fax-request unread. What I *do* know was that for the last 1-1/2 years, Gennifer had been buying paper and toner regularly instead of rarely.

****

Now I called out to Gennifer, "Ah, another world traveler returns! Did you enjoy your vacation?" Just as I had paid for the LeClerc twins to vacation in France, I had paid for Gennifer to enjoy a week at a spa in California. Gennifer had a deeper tan now than a week ago.

Gennifer replied, while she was facing Virgilia instead of looking at me, "I had a *marvelous* time! Thanks for buying me that spa trip."

As Gennifer hurried across the kitchen floor, she was wearing a tight green skirt-suit, with matching green heels; she looked both professional and *hot*. At the moment, Gennifer was carrying a sheaf of papers to Virgilia (who also was dressed professional and hot). Gennifer said to Virgilia, "Here you go, a week's worth of please-help-me faxes. The last few are hard to read; the fax machine is almost out of toner."

I called out, "I've had a busy week. I truly didn't think about the fax machine."

Gennifer turned away from Virgilia, with hands on hips and a smile on her face. "C'mon, Marvin sir, how busy—?"

Gennifer gasped. She blurted, "Who are *you?* Where's Mr. Harper?"

I replied, "Don't you recognize my voice, Gennifer? My face? My eternal five o'clock shadow?"

Anna Kay took my hand in hers. "This is my husband," Anna Kay told Gennifer. "Believe it."

Anna Kay and I told Gennifer that Fanzelle—"an evil, nasty demon bitch," according to Anna Kay— had made me this way. Gennifer looked skeptical, until several dozen women agreed that Fanzelle was real, and had even appeared here in the monster kitchen.

Then I said to Gennifer, "Do you remember Kelly Brown? She was never a *harem\u00e9e*, but she has been coming here for the last six years. *I* got off easy: Fanzelle made me a short weakling, but she *killed* Kelly."

Nobody, including Gennifer, had much to say at breakfast after I said this.

****

An hour after breakfast, Sunday morning

Barbara Drysdale, Glory-Anne Blake, and Concepci\u00f3n Alvarez asked me for my credit card and for the keys to my royal-blue Expedition SUV. Their intent was to drive to Target to do grocery-shopping. Gennifer would ride with them; her own plan was to walk next door to Bizniss Value, to buy toner for the fax machine, then to enter Target and to hang out with the three young *haremées*.

I figured that after those four worked their plans, they would return in an hour.

Just before I handed my credit card to Gennifer, I looked at the four women and said, "Besides buying food at Target, why don't you each buy yourself a hundred dollars' worth of clothes?"

The four young women *squealed* and kissed me.

As the SUV drove away, I thought, *Women and their clothes-shopping! Now I won't see those four for <u>hours!</u>*

****

Hours later
Elsewhere in my city

They were sixteen Free People: fourteen Free Men and two Free Women. They each had three things in common—

The first thing that the sixteen Free People had in common: each of them was headed for a particular Target store, or was already in that store.

Their second commonality was that each of them was carrying a gun—in a pocket, hidden under a jacket, or carried in a purse. Each Free Man also carried a knife.

The third thing that each of the sixteen had in common was that each had a Freedom Spirit advising him or her.

The very first advice from a Freedom Spirit? "Have fun. Do what you want." The second advice from a Freedom Spirit was always "Forget what you learned in Sunday School. Those rules are no fun, and they *stop* you from doing what you want." The third advice from a Freedom Spirit was always "Hate the Killjoys."

Killjoys were the exact opposite of Freedom Spirits. Killjoys said, "Follow *all* the Sunday School rules, *all* the time, even when they're not fun and they're not what you want to do."

Killjoys were worthy of Free People's hate for their killjoy-ness alone—but also they should be hated because they looked ridiculous. Killjoys had big, white wings; and what man or woman with any pride would take orders from a creature that was *half-bird?*

The fourth thing that a Freedom Spirit advised a newly Free Person was always "Evil is good. Evil makes you free."

So now the sixteen Free People were headed to a particular Target store to have evil fun. The sixteen were doing this on a Sunday afternoon, right after churches had let out—

One of the rules that the Killjoys were hardcore about was "Remember the Sabbath day, and keep it holy." What the Free People were about to do in the Target store on a Sunday afternoon would send the Killjoys into *conniptions.*

****

The Free People entered the Target store as individuals, never together, beginning at 12:45 in the afternoon. Some of them entered the Target store at the north end, where DVDs and televisions were sold; some entered the store at the south end, by Starbucks and the produce section.

The first two Free Men to arrive, rushed to the jewelry section at Target and lurked. They did this for a half-hour, to draw the attention of Store Security and to draw attention *away* from the other Free People.

At 1:15, the two Free Men in the jewelry section left there. They strolled through an unoccupied checkout line to the front of the store.

Also at 1:15, twelve other Free Men each strolled up to the front of the Target store. Oddly, while the front of the store was where the Men's Restroom was, none of the Free Men ducked into the restroom.

Rather than the restroom, it was a different room at the front of the store that fourteen Free Men ducked into: the security-cameras room.

Meanwhile, one of the Free Women had strolled through a south-side exit door, while the other Free Woman had exited through a north-side door. Each woman, as soon as she left the store, walked twenty feet to an entrance door and re-entered the store. One foot inside the entrance doors, each woman flipped the switch between the two pairs of entrance doors, to turn off the motion detectors for all four doors. This would not stop someone outside from coming in, but moving the doors aside manually would be tricky.

This done, each Free Woman took up station in front of the shopping carts that were between the Entrance and Exit doors; then each Free Woman opened up her purse and drew out a pistol.

Target Store Security did not react to two women "shoppers" drawing weapons. The reason was simple: By then, the two Target men in the security-cameras room were dying of multiple gunshot wounds.

****

1:15 p.m.
Elsewhere in the Target store

Glory-Anne was modeling an orange-and-brown skirt that she had just tried on; Barbara, Concepción, and Gennifer were offering comments.

B-BANG-B-B-BANG-BANG!

"What was *that?*" Concepción asked.

Gennifer's former television-reporter job sometimes had been far from glamorous. So now she recognized the loud sounds instantly—

"Those are *gunshots!*"

Glory-Anne said, "I'm grabbing my purse, then let's get out of here!" She dashed toward the changing booths.

****

One minute later

Gennifer and the *haremées* were not allowed to leave the store. A woman with a gun had already killed three shoppers for trying to leave.

Gennifer and the *haremées* were hurrying toward the other set of doors, to see if they could escape the store that way, when they were spotted by a gang of men. The men ran toward them. The men *reeked* of evil.

Gennifer could not run fast, what with her tight green skirt-suit and her green high heels, and the younger women chose not to leave her. Gennifer partly solved the problem by pulling off her shoes and tossing one shoe to Concepción for use as a warhammer. Still, Gennifer's tight skirt slowed her down, and soon Gennifer, Glory-Anne, Concepción, and Barbara were surrounded by evil men, all holding guns.

An evil man said to Gennifer, "I recognize you. You used to be on TV."

Another man said, "You bet your ass 'on TV.' She works for Marvin Harper." He sneered: "The 'hero billionaire.' "

Gennifer had never been more scared in her life. She had no hope of charming her way out of this. She could *die* today—hell, she could die in the next ten minutes. Her rape was a sure thing. But she saw one way out—and since she worked for the man whom she had once watched walk out of a burning house, Gennifer would now act brave too.

Gennifer tossed the shoe she was holding to Glory-Anne; then Gennifer slowly opened her purse and reached a hand in.

A pot-bellied evil man said, "If you're reaching for a gun, you won't live long enough to shoot it."

Gennifer slowly pulled her smartphone out of her purse.

The potbellied man pointed his gun at Gennifer.

Another evil man said, "Let the bitch call the police. My Freedom Spirit says the police won't bother us."

Gennifer said, "The police aren't whom I'm calling."

A few seconds later, Gennifer was saying into her phone, "Marvin, we're in the Target. A gang of terrorists has taken over the store. They're killing people."

A man walked up to Gennifer, leaned close to her phone, and said, "Hey, Marvin Harper, we're not terrorists, we're just evil. And we don't just kill—in a moment, we'll start *raping* too, *hm?*"

✳✳✳✳

Sunday afternoon, 1:17 p.m.
Upstairs Lounge at the mansion

I was sitting on a comfortable love-seat and was shooting the breeze with ten young women who also were hanging out in the Upstairs Lounge. My smartphone rang.

After I heard what Gennifer told me, and after I heard what the interrupting scumbag had to say, I ran out of the Upstairs Lounge, down the stairs, and through the mansion till I found Fatima.

Two minutes after my smartphone rang with Gennifer's call, Fatima and I were in the computer room. I did not make much of a plan beyond *Rescue my women.*

I nodded to Fatima. My ears popped.

****

Meanwhile, at the Target store

All of the non-evil males in the store, whether shoppers or store employees, had been shot down like rats. "Ugly" women had likewise been killed. Twenty people had been shot in less than a minute.

The remaining women and girls, all pretty, were herded into an aisle by Target's grocery section, then the evil men surrounded them. The men each disappeared from the circle briefly, in order to steal food and beer.

A man strong enough to snap Gennifer in two, said, "None of you are dummies—you know what's about to happen. But I'm gonna make you an offer: Come up here and kiss me, and nothing will happen to you. We won't even unbutton a button."

An older woman said, "Do we look stupid? Kiss you and nothing will happen—*suuure.*"

A shaved-bald man with a tattoo where his hair should be, said to the captive women, "All of us will keep this promise, I swear. Of course, there is something we're not telling you." He grinned.

Silence. No woman argued, but no woman volunteered.

The bald-and-tattooed man stepped in front of Gennifer, "You're one of Marvin Harper's bitches, Busty Blonde in Green. You gonna kiss my friend there?"

"No," Gennifer stated firmly.

The bald-and-tattooed man did a martial-arts leg-sweep; now Gennifer was sitting on her butt. She gasped in horror when the man dropped to kneel in front of her and he pulled out a knife.

The man said, "My friend warned you, things would happen if you didn't kiss him." So saying, he sliced apart the front of Gennifer's green skirt, put the knife on the floor, grabbed the two new ends of the skirt, ripped the skirt complete apart, then jerked the ruined skirt away from Gennifer's body.

Twenty feet away, the strong man said, "*None* of you bitches want to kiss me? All the men here have knives."

The evil men grinned as they pulled knives out of pockets and waved them around.

A young woman who was wearing a "Gorshin U. Cossacks" t-shirt, and a blond-with-dark-roots teen, both walked over to the strong man.

He said to the college girl, "You gotta make the move, girl. Show me you want this."

Gennifer watched the college girl step forward and, with clear reluctance, kiss the man. Then for a second, she went rigid. Then she threw an arm around his neck and kissed him like she was about to film a porno.

When the college girl broke the kiss, she turned around and looked at Gennifer and the other women. The college girl now wore the same evil expression that the men wore: *I will enjoy watching you suffer*. She laughed, then said, "Evil is good! Free Men, *rape* those other women and *fuck* me! Let's betray my fiancé!"

The teen girl stepped back. "I've changed my mind. I don't want to kiss you."

A man who looked like a truck-driver stepped forward; he was brandishing a knife. "Wrong answer, girly. But if you won't play *his* game, *I'm* going to play with *you*." He brought his knife up and laid the flat of the blade against the teen girl's neck.

✳✳✳✳

Sunday afternoon, 1:19 p.m.
The receiving and storage area of the Target store

My ears popped, then I discovered that Fatima and I were standing in an oblong room with a concrete floor.

Labels on boxes and posted notices to employees made clear that I was in the Target store—though not a part of the store that customers ever saw.

Seconds later, Fatima and I crept quietly out through two swinging doors, into the shopping area between assemble-it-yourself furniture and frozen seafood.

Gennifer and the other women would surely wonder how Fatima and I travelled from the mansion to the Target store almost instantly. Hopefully I would figure out an explanation later; right now, delay was unthinkable.

My women need me! I thought.

Fatima and I had not moved two steps into Target's shopping area when something wrapped around my ankle. I was yanked backward and I fell to the floor. I heard Fanzelle's voice behind us: "No, Green Girl, I won't let you make Marvin Harper a hero."

I rolled onto my back and looked up. Fanzelle looked barely human—no horns, (visible) tail, or giant bat-wings; but her hair, skin, and eyebrows were pink or red. The demoness was standing behind struggling Fatima, with the succubus's pink left hand gripping Fatima's left wrist, and the succubus's right arm wrapped around Fatima's waist.

Fanzelle told my genie, "Stop trying to *foom* away, Green Tribe bitch. If you keep resisting, I'll kill you."

"You're bluffing," I said. "The Protocol forbids demons from killing *djinn*." Fanzelle glared at me.

A big man suddenly appeared behind Fanzelle. No *FOOM*, no *FOOF*, no flash of white light or of colored light—the man simply appeared.

The big man was dressed in SWAT gear and he was holding an assault rifle, which he was pointing at Fanzelle's back. He yelled, *"You, holding the woman! Let her go and turn around with your hands up."*

Fanzelle did not let Fatima go. Instead, Fanzelle spun around, effortlessly carrying my genie with her. When the succubus saw the "policeman," she sounded a raspberry and flicked her right hand. The "cop" vanished—

FOOM.

—but during that instant that the demoness was distracted, Fatima vanished out of her arms in a flash of green light. Fatima reappeared instantly, lying on the floor next to me. Fatima threw an arm across my chest, probably with intent to *foom* me elsewhere—

—but the invisible demon-tail that was still wrapped around my ankle yanked on me again, breaking Fatima's hold on me. Snake-quick, Fanzelle bent down, grabbed my genie by her arm, and yanked her up off the floor.

Fanzelle yelled, "You thought you could trick me with an illusion? Stupid *djinni!*"

Recapturing me one-handed was even easier for Fanzelle than recapturing Fatima had been, because I was now smaller and lighter than Fatima.

Fanzelle was strong enough to drag unwilling Fatima and unwilling me fifty feet away, to the wide aisle between two-liter sodas and sunblock.

A group of a dozen men (and one woman) was standing in a circle, grinning at something in the middle. When Fanzelle got close to the circle while carrying Fatima and me, the circle parted without anyone saying a word.

****

One second later

Inside the circle of men (and woman) were—

• Fanzelle, who was carrying Fatima and me;

• seventeen women and girls; and

• one man with a knife.

The women and girls seemed unharmed, physically. But all were terrified of the men encircling them, and with good reason—

Glory-Anne, Barbara, and Concepción had part of their clothing cut away—Gennifer was even more exposed: naked except for green panties. Every one of the seventeen women had some piece of clothing ripped, or cut away, or missing.

My four women in the circle were staring at me. Glory-Anne and Gennifer both took a breath to say something, but I shook my head slightly. *Don't speak.* They nodded.

Meanwhile, the man with the knife was holding his weapon on a trembling, sobbing fourteen-year-old girl. He said, grinning, "We're gonna have *fun*, won't we, bitch?"

Then the inside of the Target store was filled with brilliant white light; two angels were floating in the air.

****

One second later

"NO, YOU SHALL NOT 'HAVE FUN,' " one angel said to the man who was holding a knife to the teen's throat.

The man's knife vanished in a flash of white light. Then the man's flesh and clothes *melted*. Ten seconds after his knife vanished, the man's naked skeleton was lying face down on the floor, in a hardening pool of brown wax.

Meanwhile, the other angel was commanding, "YOU MEN: CAST AWAY YOUR KNIVES AND GUNS, OR DIE. CAST AWAY YOUR PLANS FOR RAPE, OR DIE."

One man shook his fist at the angels. "You Killjoys, always ruining people's fun. We're going to *take care of you*, one of these days!"

The woman in the circle yelled, "Yeah, *birdbrains*, your days are numbered!"

A different man yelled, "You think you can hide in Heaven? You can't, we'll follow you there!"

Neither angel reacted with even a frown.

Fanzelle called out, "Ditch your weapons, Free Men, or suffer the penalty. We can't fight these Killjoys." Then Fanzelle grinned at the two floating beings. "*Yet.*"

With shaken fists and yelled curses at the "Killjoys," the evil men threw their knives and guns away. Each weapon vanished in white light as soon as it hit the floor.

One evil man's response to seeing this: "Hey, I paid good money for that gun! And ammo ain't cheap either!"

The two angels did not reply. Instead, they vanished.

This was immediately followed by an evil man yelling, "Look over there! Why does Annette get to keep her gun and she's not melted? She's *killed* people, whereas Pete hadn't even gotten in Girly's panties yet. No fair!"

I wondered why the angels killed the would-be rapist but not the two murderous women. I suspected the reason related to Heaven's rules about Date of Fated Death.

Nineteen-year-old Glory-Anne looked at the men who were surrounding her and other women. "I'm sure the cops are coming, plus we have angels on our side too. Let us go, shitheads, or the police will shoot you like *dogs.*"

Nineteen-year-old Concepción added, "The angels, now you are their *sodomitas*. We are not scared of you."

The evil men looked insulted. Fatima giggled.

"*Fuck,*" Fanzelle muttered.

Then she raised her voice: "Free Men, *for right now* we have to do what the Killjoys tell us. But that will change *soon*, believe me. *For right now*, leave the women alone. Except for *this* woman I'm holding."

Oh shit, I thought.

Fanzelle murmured to my genie, barely loud enough for me to overhear, "I'm squelching your *djinni* powers. You can't *foom* away and you can't turn to smoke till I let you. You're about to *hurt*, Green Tribe bitch."

Fanzelle sneered in a loud voice, "These two are Marvin Harper and his . . . *housekeeper*, Fatima. They came here to rescue his women."

A woman in her forties shook her head. "No. Marvin Harper is a giant, and he's more muscular than everybody."

"He *was*, yes," Fanzelle replied. "But I made him what he is now."

Now the evil men were grinning, and the women captives (except for my three current *haremées*) were all gasping. I looked back: Fanzelle looked succubus-y again.

The most shocked-looking of the captives was Gennifer.

Succubus-Fanzelle added, "And how Harper is *now*, is how he's going to *stay*: small, weak, poor, and pathetic."

The captive women were all staring at me. They all—including my four women—sent me looks of pity.

Now Succubus-Fanzelle grinned at the captive women. "Ladies, turning a big, rich man into someone that a fifteen-year-old boy can beat up, is not the only work that Hell is doing. *Fear* the demons of Hell, and *fear* what we will do to your world."

Then Fanzelle said, "Anyway, back to these two, Fatima and shrimpy Marvin Harper. Free Men, you heard the Killjoys—you aren't allowed to rape her, and you aren't allowed to kill her or Harper. But beyond those rules, you're free to do whatever you want with them."

A man with tattoos on his shaved-bald head walked up to me. "My cousin punched his girlfriend at the mall after she disrespected him, then you punched my cousin. Now I'm gonna punch you."

So saying, he then punched me in the eye. *My god!* I cannot describe the agony.

****

When the police showed up, Fanzelle released my genie and me, then she disappeared with a *FOOF*. By then, I had painful ribs, painful kidneys, two black eyes, and a broken nose. Some of my teeth were loose, and I tasted blood.

Fatima was in better shape. Still, while Fatima had been restrained by the succubus, one of the evil men had bitten both of Fatima's breasts hard enough to draw blood and to make her scream.

An ambulance took me to the hospital Emergency Room, with Fatima and Gennifer riding in the ambulance with me.

(An employee of the Target store had donated a flannel, floor-length bathrobe to Gennifer. When we arrived at the Emergency Room, the only clothes that Gennifer wore were that flannel bathrobe, and green panties underneath.)

When I told the emergency-room clerk my name, she clearly thought I was being sarcastic; the clerk's eyes went wide when Gennifer and Fatima confirmed that *Marvin Harper* was indeed my name.

Myself, I did not think too much about how my humiliating secret of the last four days was getting out. Instead, I was enduring the agony that I felt everywhere in my body, and—

—for the first time in six years, I was worrying whether I could pay the medical bill that I was racking up.

Chapter 21
Mars's Officer School

That night, after midnight (Monday morning)
The master bedroom at the mansion

Sleeping was impossible. I tried in vain to find a position where I could be comfortable. During this, my latest failed attempt, I hissed in pain.

Anna Kay murmured in the darkness, "I wish there were something I could do for your pain."

I said, "Thanks, Anna Kay, but I'm sure I would be awake even without the pain."

"Why?"

"Money. I don't have much money left—less than a million—and my emergency-room visit today will cost me a big hunk of that. I'm realizing that I'll have to sell the mansion before the end of next year—I can't afford the property taxes anymore."

"Oh, my," Anna Kay breathed.

"The money we'll get by selling the mansion will carry us forward for a year or two. But sometime in 2018 or 2019, I'll have to close down the Harper Foundation."

I laughed a bitter laugh. "That is, if the world hasn't ended by then."

Anna Kay did not say anything in the darkness; instead, she kissed my hand.

With my other hand, I slapped the mattress in frustration. "Do you remember back in high school, when I suggested I tutor you in trig? You replied, 'I'm sure you can solve every problem in the book!' "

Anna Kay smiled in the darkness. "And almost all of the time I was right."

I smiled for a moment, then I went grim again. "The demons are setting up to make war on Heaven. I've tried to stop them, I've failed every time, and now I'm out of ideas. This is the most important problem of my life, and *I can't solve it!*"

Anna Kay kissed my hand again.

I said, "But at least I've made the war gods aware of the problem—Mars, Odin and Tyr, Ku, and Hachiman, those guys. Maybe I should step aside and hope the regional gods can prevent this war. After all, if Hell fights Heaven, no matter the outcome, the regional gods will lose all their followers, which they *really* don't want."

Anna Kay asked, "So you're giving up on fighting the demons?"

"I *really* don't want to. But I'm out of ideas, babe. The *only* thing that sort-of worked was bringing in the regional gods, so let's give the job to them now. Sheesh, Venus fighting the entire demon horde by herself couldn't do any worse than how I've done."

Lavender light and red light flashed in the darkness of the bedroom. I heard Venus's voice say, "Thank you for that left-handed compliment, Marvin Harper. Do you mind if I turn the lights on?"

I said, "Um, sure, Venus, go ahead."

Both night-table lights and the overhead light came on. Standing by the recliner were Mars and Venus.

****

One second later

Venus was dressed sedately (for her)—she looked like an ancient-Roman courtesan going to the DHV to renew her chariot-driver license. Mars was again dressed like a Roman general.

It seemed rude to stay in bed when two Roman gods had paid me a visit. But I'll bet it took me a full minute to climb out of bed and to stand on two feet; and I was hissing in pain during all of that minute. I walked over to the Roman gods, but it was a slow and painful process.

"You are in pain," Mars remarked (with Venus translating) during my walk. "You are not healed from yesterday's injuries."

"This is true," I answered. By now I was standing in front of Mars and Venus. "Why have you come to visit me?"

Venus translated the question; Mars answered in Latin. Venus said to me, "Mars says that he wants to speak with you but needs a translator. As translators go, I am nicer to look at than Mercurius, he says."

I smiled at Venus. "I won't argue."

Mars spoke again; Venus said to me, "You believe that you cannot win against the demons, but Mars has complete confidence in you."

"*Why?*" I said. "Look at what happened yesterday. Fatima and I took on one demon—*one!* And Fanzelle mopped the floor with both of us. But you're telling me that I can fight 730 demons and *win?* No way."

Mars replied (through Venus), "I will not explain why I am confident in you. But the only way the demons will completely defeat you is if you quit now."

This amazed me. I said, "So you're saying that if I keep fighting the demons, I will win?"

Behind me, Anna Kay said, "Wow."

But Mars was shaking his head. "Right now, you are not ready to win. You were not ready to win yesterday, and so you lost. If you say now *I am out of ideas*, you have learned nothing from your defeat."

I said, "With all due respect, Mars, what you say makes no sense. One demon is more powerful than one *djinni* and a short, puny human. Yesterday there was nothing I—"

Mars pressed me: "You command two genies who can heal you; yet now you are injured and in pain. *Why?* You command three genies, yet yesterday you took only one genie with you on your rescue mission. *Why?*"

I got annoyed. "Why do you ask me these questions? You've fought alongside both Roshradzam and Sumera—"

"Yes. Your point?"

"Roshradzam is brave and loyal—but alas, magically he's a 'one-trick pony.' And Sumera? Sumera is a complete diva; and yesterday I didn't have time to finagle her to cast whatever spell I needed, only to likely be turned down anyway. Whereas Fatima, I can count on."

"Just as *Sumera* can count on *you*," Mars said.

"What does *that* mean?"

Mars ignored my question. "So get Fatima in here, tell her to heal you, and she'll do it. Then you can fight the demons without being distracted by pain."

"No," I said. "My *haremées* would wonder how I recovered so fast."

Mars waved a hand in dismissal. "Just about all your women have seen a succubus appear in your cooking room; yesterday, four of your women saw angels during a shopping trip. If you did somersaults down the stairs today at sunrise, your women would be surprised, but they would not be shocked."

Reluctantly I said, "This is true."

Mars said, "Better yet, why don't we get *both* genies to heal you?" Mars waved a hand, red light flashed, and my three bound *djinn* appeared in my bedroom. All three looked surprised.

Fatima was in her green Middle Eastern clothes; no surprise there. Roshradzam and Sumera were naked; she was on top, humping his hard and slick cock.

Venus walked over and tapped blue-skinned Sumera on the shoulder. Venus said, "Mars wants your attention to be on *him*, dear. Please stand up."

Sumera frowned, then climbed off Roshradzam and stood up—still naked.

Foom. Roshradzam summoned clothing, and hurried to dress. When he was dressed, he stood up.

Sumera was making no attempt to dress herself. I told her, "Get dressed. Sumera."

Blue light flashed; clothes appeared on Sumera's body.

I slapped my hand against my forehead. "Ditch that t-shirt, Sumera. *Permanently.* 'ROSHY'S F*CKTOY' is not a suitable t-shirt for company or for *haremées*."

Sumera pouted but obeyed.

Mars, with Venus translating, looked at Sumera and said, "Your master is injured. He needs your magical healing. Heal him."

"*What?*" Sumera said. "Listen, Mars, I don't take orders from you! You can't—"

Mars said, "True enough." Then he said to me, "*You* order her to heal you."

I said to Mars, " 'Order' her to heal me? You don't understand how the system works." Then I turned to Sumera and asked her to heal me.

With a sneer, Sumera turned me down flat.

Mars asked me, "May I help you with Sumera?"

"Sure," I said, expecting verbal advice.

Red light flashed, and Sumera was wrapped in chains of ice from the neck down. Sumera was cocooned in so many ice-chains that her blue clothes were almost hidden.

Fatima, Roshradzam, and Anna Kay (behind me) all gasped. So did Sumera, but for a different reason.

Mars said to Sumera, "By now you've noticed that I have blocked your ability to *foom* away."

Terrified Sumera nodded.

"You'll freeze to death if I don't remove the ice."

Sumera looked panicky.

"When you heal your master from all his injuries, then I will remove the ice."

Sumera said, "O mighty Mars, to cast a spell like this, I must have my hands and arms free."

Mars glanced over at Fatima, who nodded. Red light flashed, then Sumera's arms were outside of the chains.

Sumera made gestures at me. The pain vanished. I turned around and faced Anna Kay. She gasped as I began removing the bandages and tape that covered my ribs.

Anna Kay looked at Mars and said, "*Thank you* for doing my husband this kindness!"

(It was not until days later that I realized: Neither Anna Kay nor I thought to thank Sumera, who had actually done the healing.)

Meanwhile, Mars released Sumera from her ice-cocoon. Sumera began rubbing herself everywhere.

Mars looked at Anna Kay and said, "Wife of Marvin Harper, you spoke of me doing a 'kindness,' and you meant it as a compliment. I thank you. But kindness is *always* a virtue only when young men's work is plowing the fields, and swords and spears hang rusting on walls."

Now Mars shifted his gaze to me. "But in time of war, kindness to someone who is acting insubordinate to you is a weakness. Do you see what I did? When Sumera disrespectfully refused to obey you, I used my power to compel her to obey."

"And damned near killed me!" Sumera yelled.

Mars shrugged. "No big loss."

I said to Mars, "*You* got Sumera to perform, yes, but I can't put her in ice when she turns diva on me."

Mars replied, "But you *can* order her into her Vessel. And once she's in her Vessel, only *you* can get her out."

Sumera looked at me nervously. "He promised me that I can stay out of my lamp."

Mars asked, "Was this promise made *before* or *after* your master learned about the demons' scheme to start a second Hell-Heaven War?"

"Before," I said.

"Then it's settled," Mars said, shooting me a look.

I replied, "I don't feel right, going back on a promise I made."

Mars said, "Young human, you are in a war situation now. In war, seconds matter. If the captain gives an order but the soldiers discuss and debate instead of moving, the soldiers die. If the captain must politick and persuade before the soldiers move, the soldiers die. If some men choose to fight and some choose not to, all the soldiers die."

"I know all this."

"Unless the captain has established his authority *before* the battle, few men will fight, and insubordination will spread. And then the captain's men will lose, they will die. I've seen this—I do not exaggerate—hundreds of times."

Sumera said, "Master, will you start sending me back into my lamp? You're nicer than that."

I came *thisclose* to saying *I __am__ a nice guy, so relax*. But then I realized that Sumera was trying to *manipulate* me with flattery. I replied sternly, "Threats and punishment are the only things that work with you, Sumera."

She said, "Still, things aren't so bad right now. You can let things go on like before for a while—right, Master?"

It was a bad sign when Venus shook her head before she translated Sumera's words to Mars.

Mars said, "In Naples a few hours ago, believers who came into a church for midnight worship found their priest stabbed to death in front of the altar. On the floor near the priest's body were three naked skeletons that were holding knives. Besides the priest's blood, there was other blood on the floor; that blood was mixed in with big white feathers."

"What does that mean?" Anna Kay asked in a worried voice.

Fatima said, "The demons' minions have begun to attack angels."

"Hoo boy," I said. "Somebody needs to stop those demons from doing worse." I stared at Mars—

—who stared back. "You command three genies, Marvin Harper. *You* do something."

"*No!*" said Anna Kay. "Don't go, you could get hurt *worse* this time!"

I shook my head. "No, Anna Kay, if I *can* do something to fight this evil, I *must* do something. But once again: I have no idea what to do."

Mars asked me, "What would give you ideas what to do?"

I replied, "If I knew more about the problem than what the Protocol tells me. But how do I get an angel to pop into my bedroom and to answer my questions?"

Roshradzam said (through his translator-ring), "Why do you need for an angel to come to you? I've never tried it before, but I'm sure I can *foom* you to Heaven. Heaven has over a thousand angels there—"

"Exactly 1,472," Fatima said.

"—and I'm sure *one* of them would tell you what you want to know."

I sighed. "Roshradzam, I thank you for your suggestion, but I'm not sure even *one* angel would talk to me. Five beings in this room are immortal and magical, whereas I'm only the guy who visited his great-uncle in the hospital one time and was ridiculously rewarded."

Venus glanced at Mars; Mars glanced at Venus. Together, they said, "Atrox Fortuna."

"Huh?" I said.

Venus smiled at me and said, "You underestimate your importance, hero."

Mars looked at Fatima and Sumera and asked them, "Of the thousands of thousands of thousands of humans who have walked the Earth from the beginning, do you know how many have been genie-masters?"

Sumera did not bother to summon her scrying ball; but Fatima did, and had the answer to Mars's question in less than a minute. "Master here is the 147th genie-master. Virgilia O'Keefe was the 148th. Vincent Lavagetto was the 149th. Elvira LeClerc, number 150, is the latest."

"Aren't *you* a lucky human," Sumera sneered at me.

Mars then asked, "How many humans have been the master of two different genies?"

It took Fatima only ten seconds with her scrying ball to answer: "Only Master."

Mars then said, "How many humans have been master of *three* genies? Only one human, Marvin Harper here."

"*Ahem*," I said, blushing, "don't forget Kharmesh. I've been master to *four* bound *djinn*."

"Master to four bound *djinn*," Mars said, "by luck alone, never by a locator spell."

"Locator spells don't work on Vessels," Sumera snapped. "Don't you know that?"

Mars's face got angry. "You look hot, *djinni* Sumera. Perhaps you need some *ice-chains* to cool you down."

Sumera quickly apologized for her disrespect.

Anna Kay said to Mars, "I'm lost, Your Godness. What are you telling my husband?"

"That if he has Roshradzam take him to Heaven, he will not be treated as merely another living-human intruder."

I made a decision: "God Mars and Goddess Venus, as soon as you leave, I will have Roshradzam take me and my other two bound *djinn* to Heaven, and I will get answers to my questions."

"Um, Marvin?" Anna Kay said. "May I suggest that after the gods leave, but before you go to Heaven, you shower and put on clean clothes? I think the angels might not be friendly if you're stinky and you need a shave."

****

Then Mars repeated his earlier puzzling remark—

"Marvin Harper, I am utterly confident that you can defeat the demons. But you must think like—"

"A captain of soldiers," I said.

Mars said, "Perhaps you should start thinking like a general."

"A *general?* When I have only three soldiers to command?"

Mars smiled. "Fortune has brought you four genies. Perhaps Fortune will bring you more soldiers. But you know what they say about Fortune during war, don't you?"

It was Venus who answered: "*Fortuna audaces iuvat*, Fortune helps the bold."

Mars and Venus shared a glance, then they disappeared from my bedroom amid flashes of red and lavender light.

Chapter 22
We Go to Heaven (Alive)

Still Monday

When Sumera had healed me, she had done more than to merely undo my injuries. Now my body felt like it had enjoyed eight hours of great sleep. Yes, the time now was a few hours after midnight, but I saw no reason to delay my planned trip to Heaven.

I showered, as Anna Kay had suggested, then I tried to put on a clean suit that was hanging in my closet. Alas, the suit was cut for my body of five days ago. I had to ask Fatima to make the suit fit me now, and she had to shrink the suit *a lot.*

I ordered my three genies to change into their respective Tribe clothes. Surprisingly, Sumera obeyed me with no argument. Either it was because of Roshradzam's encouragement, or because of something that Fatima said to Sumera—

"Do you like fucking Roshradzam for hours? Do you like visiting Blue Tribe at night? I suggest you obey Master in this. Or do you *like* being stuck in your lamp?"

When I was wearing a blue suit, white shirt, and red tie, and when my genies looked like genies, I kissed sleeping Anna Kay goodbye—

She opened her eyes a little, saw me dressed in a suit, then her eyes flew open. She sat up and asked, "You're *really* planning to visit Heaven?"

"I have to," I said. "I need answers."

"But what if the angels don't like you invading their turf? They could *kill* you!"

"I'll be fine, Anna Kay," I said. I mostly believed it.

Then I nodded to Roshradzam. He touched my forehead for a second.

My ears popped.

****

Heaven was not what I expected. It did not look like a meadow, or a city; it looked like a luxury space station.

The cobblestoned street was wide, with big houses and big lawns on either side of the street. Yes, *this* part was like the Heaven that I expected. But when I looked away at some distance, the ground did not curve *down*, it curved *up*, in every direction. Even more strange, the big houses visible in the distance all were at right angles to the tilted ground that they sat on; to me, the houses seemed to lean toward me. It was not only houses acting freaky: Trees close to me stood straight up, but trees some ways away tilted toward me.

I realized that the four of us were standing on the inside of an immense sphere.

Likewise, some miles above where the four of us were standing was a round ceiling. This ceiling was the blue color of sky, and it glowed like sky, but it curved up in a spherical shape. What was odd, however, was that when I looked straight up, I could see a yellow disk *through* the opaque blue ceiling.

Roshradzam muttered something; his ring translated it as "I've seen many strange things, but *this* is the strangest."

"Where to now, Master?" Fatima asked.

I replied, "No clue. Let's walk along this street till we find someone who can tell us how to call up an angel."

We started walking—and I received another surprise. *The ground rolled beneath my feet,* just as if I were walking on a treadmill. As I walked, trees and curbside flowers moved toward me.

Fatima said, "Correction, Roshradzam: *This* is the strangest thing."

We walked past a vacant lot, the same size as the house-covered lots to either side of it. The vacant lot did not have a house on it; what it *did* have was a sign at curbside that read, "Vacant lot 53-26,183. DANGER—KEEP OUT."

Roshradzam laughed. "It's nice to see that the language of Heaven is Arabic."

I said, "*I* read it as English. But how can a vacant lot have 'danger'?"

Nobody had any idea.

After another five minutes, we walked up to a park. It was much bigger than a vacant lot, and the curbside sign was different: "Park 53-Cerulean."

I got my first glimpse of people of Heaven; I stared at them. The four Heaveners were staring back at us, their faces expressing the same amazement I was feeling.

****

One second later

The Heaveners were three men and a woman, all in their twenties. Only one man out of the four people was wearing a robe, which looked like a robe on an old statue, not like robes I had seen pictured in religious art.

The robe-man's robe, while it was white, was not entirely white—two pale-pink stripes ran parallel to the bottom hem of the robe.

The other three people's clothing was whitish but not white—the white clothing was tinged green, or blue, or pink, or brown. The Oriental woman was wearing a pink-and blue-tinged white kimono, one man was wearing green-tinged white Renaissance clothing, and the third man among the Heaveners was wearing brown-tinged white work boots, blue-tinged white jeans, and a white-and-pale-pale-blue workingman's shirt.

All four Heaveners had faces that shone brightly, as if each person had a little spotlight on his or her face. But I could see no source for any of the spotlights.

The man in the whitened blue jeans was ignoring my genies and was staring only at me. *He looks familiar.*

The Renaissance man asked, "Why are you people wearing your indoor clothes outside?"

The man in the whitened blue jeans asked me, "Are you Claire's great-nephew Marvin?"

I replied, *"Uncle John?"*

****

Several seconds of awkward silence passed—I figured out too late that my group was supposed to begin the introductions. Then Uncle John shrugged and introduced the Heaveners—

"The oldest of us is Saintly Septimus Helvetius Antonus, who died in Roman Gaul in 42 B.C. Next up is Saintly Martinus Hoffmann, who died in Leipzig, Germany in A.D. 1667. Then comes Saintly MATSUKAWA Anako, who died in Osaka, Japan in 1706. Last is me, John Greenwich, the husband of Marvin's great-aunt Claire. I died in 2002."

Martinus Hoffmann the Renaissance man said, "John modestly neglects his own title—he actually is *Saintly* John Greenwich, the same as us."

"What does 'Saintly' mean?" I asked.

Uncle John said, "Anyone whose house is located inside of Level 123 must be addressed as 'Saintly,' because our good deeds supposedly so much outweigh our bad deeds. Inprocessing North should have explained all this to you. Come to think of it, Marvin, how is it that you arrived here without me getting a Pending Death Notice about you? I *know* I put your name on my list after the gift of life you gave Claire."

I replied, "You didn't get a notice because I'm not dead." All four Heaveners gasped. I added, "We're here in Heaven by genie-magic."

Sumera sneered at Uncle John, "Does 'Saintly' mean that you're a goody-two-shoes?"

I thought back to how nicely Uncle John and Aunt Claire had treated me when I had been a young boy. Now I answered Sumera before Uncle John could: "Maybe it means he's kind."

I then introduced the genies to the Heaveners. I told Uncle John that Fatima was the genie who had extended Aunt Claire's life by 120 lunar cycles; Fatima and Uncle John smiled at each other.

After I had made introductions, Septimus asked me, "So Living Marvin Harper, why have you tried so hard to go to Heaven?"

I replied, "I need to talk to angels. *Soon.*"

Uncle John said, "I think I can help with that. Come, my house isn't far away."

****

A minute later

On the walk to Uncle John's house, I asked him, "So if this is Level 53, and you're 'Saintly,' how many levels are there in all? And what are they like?"

Uncle John answered, "Heaven is balls inside balls. God is Level 1 in the center—the yellow disk you see through the ceiling is God's Light. Level 2 is for the angels. Level 3 is for the most saintly of Most Saintly people." Uncle John glanced at my companions and added, "*Djinn* too, I suppose, though I'm pretty sure there is no Most Saintly *djinni* in Level 3 right now."

"Wait," said Sumera, "there are *djinn* in Heaven?"

"If they're good and they've already died, yes," Uncle John replied. "I don't know the count, but it's small."

Fatima said, "Jerngert of Pink Tribe is one of those *djinn* in Heaven; I'm certain of it." Fatima was smiling.

I asked Uncle John, "And the worst parts of Heaven? What are they like?"

"The outermost levels aren't labeled with numbers, they're labeled with colors. The color-levels are where souls go who died in the womb, or died at birth, or died as children under sixteen. Those souls are neither good nor evil. In the color-levels, those souls are given three-room apartments, about a thousand square feet in area."

"That's generous, I suppose," I said.

"Just inside the color-levels is Level 1,779. I'm told it's bigger around as Earth. Billions of souls dwell there, and every soul there gets a one-room apartment, ten feet by ten feet. Level 1,779 is for people who did barely more good in their lives than evil. The basics of food, furniture, or clothing—but no luxuries—are abracadabra'd by the angels, but a soul on Level 1,779 has very little room to store his stuff in."

Sumera asked, "What about *djinn* who did more evil than good? How many levels does Hell have?"

Uncle John shot Sumera a look. "Hell has only *one* level. I hear it's nasty."

****

A minute later, Uncle John was saying, ". . . At Level 521, a soul gets a place of its own. The house is tiny, and the lawn is even tinier, but it's private. Inside of Level 521, the houses and lawns get bigger and better. By the time you get to Level 3, there are only thirty-five mansions in the entire level, not counting vacant lots, and each mansion is *huge*."

"*How* huge?" I asked.

"Listen, three days after I arrived in Heaven, Most Saintly Francis of Assisi invited everyone who'd died the same week as me, to a party at his mansion on Level 3. I'm telling you, his place was bigger than Buckingham Palace."

Whoa. And I thought my mansion was big!

Now we arrived at Uncle John's house, which turned out to be one of the two houses next to the vacant lot. I pointed to the sign and asked, "So how can a vacant lot in Heaven have 'danger'?"

Uncle John answered, "Because sooner or later a newly dead, saintly soul will be awarded this vacant lot. Then *abracadabra*, a house will appear there with the new soul living in the house. But what happens to you if where you stood a second ago, the new house stands now? You die."

I said, "Wait, so souls in Heaven can be killed?"

Fatima said, "Master, remember that even demons and angels can be killed. Only regional gods and God in Heaven *cannot* be killed."

****

Seconds later

Uncle John's lot had a driveway, and that driveway led to a detached garage next to his grand house.

Once Uncle John set foot on the driveway, he started to walk faster, and he was clearly excited.

Uncle John said to me, "There are several perks of being Saintly. In the kitchen, an outline of a hand is painted on the wall. Whenever I put my hand on the wall there— *abracadabra*, an angel shows up. Angels, it turns out, are great for moving furniture. But that's not the *really* great thing about being Saintly."

Uncle John led the genies and me to a side door in the detached garage. Uncle John opened the door—it had no lock—and bowed us inside.

The garage was big enough to hold two cars, but so much space was taken up by workshop equipment that only one car could fit in. The workshop had electric lights and electric outlets. Plugged into one outlet was a Sixties-era portable stereo record-player with two small speakers. I noted a Patsy Cline LP laying on the turntable.

Uncle John said, "Marvin, you're not *looking!* Look at the *car!*"

The car was a turquoise-and-white 1957 Chevy Bel Air. "It looks new," I said.

He laughed. "Check out the odometer."

I slid behind the steering wheel. This 59-year-old car not only looked new, it smelled new, and its odometer read 000034.6. A car key was in the ignition.

Uncle John yanked open the passenger door, rummaged in the glove compartment, then he waved a paper at me. "The car even came with a State of Pennsylvania car title, dated 1957."

"You're excited about having your first car back," I said.

"Not my *first* car," he said. "I bought a disaster on wheels when I was seventeen—"

"Oh, I hear you," I said.

"—and other used cars in my twenties. But *this* I bought new at Bertoletti Chevrolet. Claire chose the turquoise."

Uncle John grinned like a small boy on Christmas morning. "Marvin, being given a big house and a garage was nice when I first went to Heaven. But Heaven didn't *feel* like Heaven till my garage had *this car* in it!"

Sumera said, "Master, I hear yelling outside."

Uncle John's face showed surprise. "Yelling in *Heaven?*"

****

One second later

Sumera, on her own, opened the side door and, while keeping the door open, stepped outside. Now I could make out words in a man's voice—

"SAINTLY JOHN GREENWICH, ARE YOU HERE? ARE YOU ALL RIGHT? DO YOU NEED HELP? WE SUSPECT INTRUDERS. SAINTLY JOHN—"

I thought, *Whoever those guys are, they talk like SWAT police.*

Then one of the voices outside said, "Look, by the garage! A *djinni*, and she's wearing *color-clothes!* The intruders might be holding Saintly Greenwich hostage in the garage."

Things happened quickly then. In the car's rear-view mirror, I saw the garage door, which had no electric garage-door opener, go up by itself. An angel appeared by Sumera in a flash of white light; the angel wrapped his arms around Sumera and carried her into the garage. As soon as the garage door had lifted itself four feet off the ground, four bent-over angels rushed through the garage door.

Uncle John pulled his head out the car and stood up, moving slowly the entire time. He still held the duplicated car title in his right hand. Meanwhile, I opened the driver-side door, stepped out of the Bel Air, and turned around to face the four angels—all slowly.

I put my hands up. A second later, so did Uncle John.

F-FOOM. Fatima and Roshradzam appeared in front of me, facing off against the garage-door angels.

"Can I help you with something, angels?" Uncle John asked. I glanced over—he looked confused, not angry.

****

One second later

Only once in my life had I ever seen two angels together. I had never seen three angels together, but now I was looking at *six* angels—

• the angel who was holding struggling Sumera;

• the four angels who had rushed through the garage door; and

• another angel who was standing about twenty feet outside the now-raised garage door. He had his feet spread in a ready-for-anything stance and was staring into the garage.

The weird thing was, the six angels all had the same white wings, white robes, faces, haircuts, and voices. One angel had a pouch tied around his waist, and that was the *only* difference that I could see.

Meanwhile, Sumera was trying to wriggle out of her angel-captor's grip. I said, "Sumera, stop struggling."

The angel with the pouch was opening up that pouch when another angel growled at us, "Don't any of you make any sudden moves."

In front of me, Fatima's muscles tensed. Roshradzam said something challenging; his ring translated it as "Don't give us a reason."

Uncle John said, "Angels, what is going on?"

The pouch-angel replied, "These are four living beings; thus intruders in Heaven. We tracked them to your lot, and we suspect evil intent."

Fatima jerked her thumb over her shoulder. " 'Evil intent'? Do you know who my master is?"

The pouch-angel replied, "We're about to." He pulled a baseball-sized faceted purple stone from his pouch and held it up. "Hold still," he commanded.

The electric white lights in the garage went out. Then the round jewel glowed the same violet color as a bug-zapper, and was bright enough to light up the entire garage.

Uncle John gasped. "Marvin, your forehead has a number on it."

I looked at him and replied, "So does yours. It's glowing purple. It's on your right hand, too."

I pulled down my hands and looked at my right hand. On the back of my hand glowed a fourteen-digit number.

Sumera was likewise marked on her forehead and right hand—though her number was the letter *D* followed by only five digits.

I leaned forward and asked Fatima and Roshradzam, "Are you guys marked too?"

They were.

Roshradzam said, "Hey, angels! Why do *we* have numbers and you angels don't?"

One of the angels replied, "Because humans and *djinn* have souls, so you face Eternal Judgment when you die. Now shut up, intruder."

Uncle John said, "Don't let the angel scare you. Judgment is less nerve-wracking than traffic court."

Then Uncle John said, "I'm putting my hands down." He then walked around the front of the car to stand by me.

The round jewel still was bathing the garage in violet light, and a fourteen-digit number still was glowing on Uncle John's forehead and right hand. Up close, I noted that appended to Uncle John's number was an up-arrow.

Uncle John put his arm around me. "Angels, this is Marvin Harper. He gave my Claire nine more years of Earthly life, through a genie-wish. You don't need to worry about him."

Meanwhile, one of the garage-door angels had pulled a scroll out of a sleeve of his robe, then had unrolled the scroll. He walked around, eyeing our foreheads, then announced, "The living beings are Roshradzam of Brown Tribe, bound *djinni*; Fatima of Green Tribe, bound *djinni*;

Sumera of Blue Tribe, bound *djinni*; and Marvin Steven Harper, whose Date of Fated Death—"

"—is *not* for a while yet," said Fatima, "and he's clearly not a demon's lackey, so *chill out*, you featherhead drones!"

"Listen to Fatima, featherhead drones," Sumera said.

A few seconds ago, my hands had been above my head; now I put them on my hips. "You call us 'intruders'? You want us gone? Fine. I came here to get answers—give me useful information, and we'll leave."

My challenging tone of voice brought glares from five of the six angels.

The violet light ended and the electric lights came back on in the garage. The pouch-angel, while putting his big purple jewel away, conceded, "The name of Marvin Steven Harper is known in Heaven."

With those words, the other angels quit looking like they were about to slice us all in half with flaming swords.

I pushed my luck: "You at the door, let Sumera go."

As the angel was releasing Sumera (and was being glared at by her), the pouch-angel asked me, "Why are you four here in Heaven?"

****

Seconds later

The pouch-angel had a sort-of name: Thirteen. (His explanation: "Only eleven angels now in Heaven have names. The twelfth angel with a name was Lucifer. Every other angel who's still in Heaven has a number, starting with Thirteen.")

After introducing himself, Thirteen walked out of the garage, stood statue-still for a minute, then walked back into the garage.

Thirteen announced that the decision had been handed down to "Tell the Livings everything." Meaning, we four living beings (but not Uncle John) were to be escorted to Level 2 and were to be briefed.

After Uncle John and I hugged, Uncle John threw his arms around Fatima and hugged her with all he had. "Thanks for what you did for Claire," he told Fatima.

Sumera said, "*Ahem.* Can we get going?"

I looked at Thirteen and the five other angels. "We're ready," I said.

My ears popped.

****

A minute later

Djinn and demons can create illusions. Angels can do better: Using faceted yellow stones, angels can record illusions and can edit them. Thirteen was about to show the genies and me an RI (recorded illusion) titled *Why We Still Fight Demons.* The narration would be in angel-language, which Roshradzam's ring could not translate—

Until Thirteen did some kind of white-flash angel-magic on Roshradzam's ring; afterward, the ring translated angel-language just fine.

The translation did not matter to me. Once the RI showed what would happen if Hell won the Second Hell-Heaven War, I paid attention only to images, not words—

Heaven is a burning ruin. All of the Saintly humans have their throats slit; all of the Most Saintly humans are tortured until they die truly. All angels are gone from Heaven; they have all been erased.

The Manhattan skyline is in ruins. Bat-winged demons shriek gleefully as they fly into the few remaining skyscrapers, toppling them. Debris and dust-covered corpses fill the streets.

Two demons are walking down a German street. People flee screaming from the demons. One demon points to a fleeing child; the boy's head explodes and nearby people scream. The other demon points to a fleeing woman; the woman is instantly cut in half at the waist.

In a Spanish-speaking country, a bishop is trying to rally a crowd of people to attack three laughing demons. One of the demons points at the bishop and says, "Go to Hell!" The bishop vanishes in a puff of black smoke.

In a seaside city, ships at the pier burn and humans run panicked in the street. A man-djinni from Blue Tribe floats in the air, watching and not helping any humans. Now two demons appear on each side of the djinni; an instant later, he is wrapped in chains of purple metal. The demons carry the djinni over the ocean; he struggles then, but it seems he can't foom away from his chains. The demons laugh and carry the trussed-up djinni even higher in the air. Then the demons let the djinni fall. Three seconds pass before the djinni sinks below the surface of the water; he screams all the way down.

In a suburban living room, the head-exploded corpse of a fat man slumps on a couch. One demon swings an infant girl around by her legs, bashing her head against the wall; a pacifier goes flying. The other demon clutches a frightened girl, age eight. Unhurt at the moment are a mother with a beehive hairdo, and her ten-year-old son. The demon who holds the girl orders the mother and son, "Get undressed; then lady, we want to see you fuck your son. Or else this girl dies too!"

Reader, I won't lie to you: That RI shook me up bad. I *needed* it when Fatima squeezed my hand in reassurance. (Sumera, seeing this, said, "Humans die, Master. Deal with it.") But Sumera's *doesn't bother me* attitude disappeared when the RI showed the Blue Tribe *djinni* being killed just for two demons' entertainment. Sumera seized my hand when she saw that; I stroked her hand.

When *Why We Still Fight Demons* ended, I said to Thirteen, "That RI tells only half the story. It didn't say *diddly* about if you angels win the war—then you proceed *immediately* to Judgment Day."

Thirteen nodded and summoned a second faceted yellow stone. He told us, "This RI was made two years ago, and is intended for only angels to see. No angels have seen it yet, nor will they see it till they need to. Feel privileged, living beings."

Then Thirteen rubbed the faceted yellow stone, which began *Angels' Work on Judgment Day*—

In the food court of a shopping mall, people wander in and out, holding shopping bags in their hands. Soft music plays overhead. At tables, people eat, talk on their smartphones, and text. At the different franchised restaurants in the food court, employees serve customers or prepare food. A security guard walks around the food court.

A trumpet-fanfare sounds overhead. The fanfare is not part of the mall's recorded music.

In many flashes of white light, all the humans vanish. Smartphones, purses, shopping bags, and food-trays fall to the floor.

The soft music still plays.

On a grill, a hamburger patty begins to give off black smoke. But nobody is there to stop the meat from burning.

Now the scene shifts to a gigantic room that is completely empty, except for angels and Most Saintly Paul. A sign at the front of the room says "Inprocessing South." White lights flash everywhere in the room, and now the room is filled to bursting with confused humans and confused djinn.

Also appearing in the room: demons. The demons aren't confused, they're furious. But since the demons are each bound up in many, many glowing-white chains, all they can do is to yell and to glare at everyone else.

The room is so big that it has a hundred waiting lines. As it turns out, the people from that food court become the first person in every line. Whether wearing a fast-food uniform, a security-guard uniform, a fashionable dress and heels, or a worn pair of jeans and a Green Lantern t-shirt, the person at the head of each line is ordered to step forward onto a short pedestal. In front of the human on the pedestal, a screen comes to life. Clips from the human's life are shown at inhuman speed; it takes less than a minute to review each human life. Two angels watch each screen.

When each screen goes blank, the two angels consult briefly with Most Saintly Paul, then Most Saintly Paul announces his Judgment. The angels then lead the stunned human through a pearlescent door marked "Judged Beings Only."

In the food court, two of the restaurants are on fire now, but nobody is there to notice. Soft music still plays overhead.

Back at Inprocessing South, in the "Judged Beings Only" room, a well-dressed college girl is angrily demanding that her Judgment be changed. The angel shakes his head, and the girl vanishes in black smoke. Meanwhile, the shift-manager at Perfekt Burger looks stunned while an angel tells him about his new home on Level 336. Just before the shift-manager vanishes in white light, his fast-food uniform transforms into a blue-tinged white two-piece suit and a pale-pale-blue satin tie.

After showing all this, the RI gave instructions how the angels were to process thirty-thousand times as many souls as they normally processed in a day. I tuned that part out.

****

When the RI ended, I looked at my genies and asked, "Does anyone have a question?"

Sumera said. "I do. Is Hakeezib"—the former Chief of the Blue Tribe of *Djinn*—"in Heaven or Hell?"

Fatima snapped, "Master meant questions about *what we just saw*, Blue Girl!"

Sumera laughed. "Master did not say this. Master should be careful how he words things around genies." Then Sumera looked at me and said, "I really want to know where Hakeezib is."

I replied, "I was there when he was frozen to death by an angel. You sure you want that answer, Sumera?"

Thirteen confirmed that Hakeezib was indeed in Hell.

I asked, "What *is* Hell's punishment for an evil *djinni*, anyway? They would laugh off hellfire."

Thirteen told us that one part of Hell is actually arctic-cold, and that is where punished *djinn* go. Not only is freezing painful for *djinn*, but the Djinn Hell is contained inside a giant box made of Chekhovium, so punished *djinn* cannot escape—

"Chekhovium? What is *that?*" I asked.

"Bad news for *djinn*," Fatima replied.

Thirteen answered, "It's a purple metal in its pure state. To mine it, you must dig down twelve hundred miles from Earth's surface, or else mine it by supernatural means. It—"

Sumera interrupted: "Remember that Blue Tribe *djinn* in the movie? His chains were Chekhovium. If you're inside Chekhovium, you can't *foom* out; if you're outside Chekhovium, you can't *foom* in."

"Yes, if you're a *djinni*," Thirteen said to Sumera with a smug smile. "Chekhovium does not stop angels."

"I have a new question," I said. "What are the differences between demons and angels?"

Thirteen said, "Every demon chooses a unique name, and each demon chooses a unique appearance. While we angels are shapeshifters too, we seldom use that ability."

"What about in terms of fighting ability?"

Thirteen laughed. "Demons are evil, so they fight dirty. We angels fight by the rules. But the Protocol limits what nastiness demons can do—be glad of that."

I said, "The most important question: You know that I want for my genies and I to shut down the demons just by ourselves, so that the Second Hell-Heaven War is avoided. What else can you tell me so that we four can achieve this?"

The angel shook his head. "I can tell you nothing, because what you ask is impossible. I've looked up your file, Living Marvin Harper; you and your team have several times battled demons and have been bested almost every time. The only time you four have enjoyed a victory was when you allied with regional gods. But I don't see the regional gods as a path to victory for you."

"Why not?" Fatima, Roshradzam, and I said together.

"Because the regional gods have nothing to lose except their worshippers, so they don't *need* to help you. The regional gods will remain on Earth, unhurt, even if the demons achieve total victory. Which means that the regional gods, when you ask them to join you, might refuse to fight; or they might fight for a while, then quit. You cannot count on them."

Roshradzam said, "This is so unfair. *If* all the regional gods fought the demons, the problem would be over. But no, they will probably just watch and laugh, because those regional gods lose nothing if they refuse to fight."

Then I was rocked by an idea. "But the Tribes of Djinn lose *everything* if they refuse to fight. If the War happens, *djinn* suffer as badly as humans. All the *djinn* will help us to prevent the War!"

Fatima and Roshradzam grinned at me.

But Sumera shook her head.

I refused to let Sumera's pessimism infect me. Now I had a plan!

****

Five minutes later
In the master bedroom at the mansion

Once back home, I had thanked my genies for their help, dismissed them, then had awakened Anna Kay. Now I had plans to make—which I could make better when I was wearing comfortable clothes.

In the process of changing out of my suit, I was walking around the master bedroom. My eyes fell on the recliner, by which Mars and Venus had stood during their visit to me.

Laying on the seat cushion of the recliner was a sheathed dagger. Buckles and leather straps enabled the dagger-sheath to be attached to my arm.

I pulled the dagger out of its sheath. The steel blade, I noted, was five inches long and was stamped "VVLCAN."

A minute later, when I was bare to the waist, I buckled the dagger-sheath to my left forearm, then I pulled on a long-sleeved shirt to cover my new weapon.

Chapter 23
Recruiting Djinn Tribes

A few hours later: Monday morning, 7 a.m.

Anna Kay and I walked hand-in-hand into the monster kitchen. This was eighteen hours after I had received a beating so serious that I had to be taken to the emergency room. And yet now, the next morning—

Gustava Svedberg stared as she walked up to us. "My heavens, you look all healed up, Marvin sir."

Gennifer Ashton walked into the monster kitchen then. She stared at me, then said, "Your bandages and your bruises, they're all gone! *How?*"

"I was magically healed a few hours ago," I said.

"Who did it?" many women asked.

I shook my head. "I'm not saying. Because then the story would get even more complicated."

From across the room, Virgilia looked at Fatima. Fatima gave a small shake of her head: *It wasn't me who healed him.*

Gustava looked at me and purred, "*Of course* you were magically healed. Because you *deserve* to be—you're a *wonderful* man."

Right after this, Roshradzam and *Haremée*-Sumera walked into the monster kitchen—always one foot apart. Except for him holding the door for her, those two displayed no public affection. Roshradzam headed for the head table, since he was supposedly an employee of mine; *Haremée*-Sumera walked toward her seat at a lower table.

Gustava and Gennifer were still standing next to Anna Kay and me when Roshradzam and *Haremée*-Sumera walked past us.

Gustava said loudly, "Sumera Hatfield, you disappoint us all. Marvin Harper is a wonderful man. He's good, he's kind, he's generous, he's giving in bed, and—before the she-devil whammied him—he was the sexiest man in the world. He *deserves* to be served. Why don't you look good for him, like the rest of us do? Wear perfume for him, wear high heels, wear skirts and dresses! But *no*, it's just blue jeans, blue t-shirts, and blue sneakers for you. Won't you at least wear some *pink?*"

Sumera turned and gave Gustava a dismissive look. "Mas—Marvin has never complained to me about the clothes I wear. As for colors, I *don't* do pink and I absolutely *don't do green!*"

As Sumera glared across the room at Fatima, I saw Gustava looking confused. Her expression said, *Who mentioned green?*

****

After breakfast

I said to Gennifer, in her role as my publicist, "I'm sure everyone and his cameraman will want to talk to you about me being a shorty now, and being taken to the ER."

"Yes, I've already been taking calls."

I told her, "I'm not available for interviews. Absolutely not. Because I won't be here."

"Marvin sir, do you realize that if they can't find you *easily*, they'll *hunt* for you? And if they hunt for you, the press coverage will be awful *when* they find you."

I gave Gennifer a crooked smile. "I guarantee you that where I'm going, no camera crew can find me." At Gennifer's puzzled expression, I explained, "It ties in with my being magically healed."

****

Minutes later
The computer room at the mansion

I spoke to my genies, as Anna Kay and SJ-1 listened silently.

First, I unbuttoned my left sleeve and pulled it up, to show my wife and my genies the sheathed dagger on my arm. "The Roman god Vulcan made this dagger," I told the room. "This knife is more than it looks." Fatima's grin was bloodthirsty, while Anna Kay looked puzzled.

As I was rebuttoning my sleeve, I told Fatima, "Appoint someone to take over as housekeeper. You're going to be gone for a while."

Fatima pulled out her magic smartphone and made a call. A minute later, she was putting the phone back into her green-jeans pocket. "I've given the job to Barbara Drysdale. What now?"

"Next step: All three of you change into your genie clothes."

After my genies had changed clothes, I ordered Roshradzam to tell Brown Tribe to please gather up everyone in the Tribe, because Fatima and I had an important message to deliver. My order to Fatima was similar, but she was to herald our coming to Green Tribe, and also to Pink Tribe and Blue Tribe.

Roshradzam obediently *foom*ed over to Brown Tribe headquarters to pass on my message in person. Fatima likewise passed on her three messages by *foom*ing to Tribes' home bases to make personal visits.

Ten minutes after Fatima left, she *foom*ed home—in an angry mood. She looked around and said, "Blue Tribe *djinn* are assholes—everyone knows this, right?"

No surprise, Sumera insulted Fatima in Arabic.

"Where are we going first, Master?" Roshradzam asked.

"Our first stop is, wherever Green Tribe hangs out. Fatima and I will try to persuade Ashnadim"—the Chief of the Green Tribe of *Djinn*—"and Green Tribe to all fight the demons with us."

"Sounds like *such* fun," Sumera said sarcastically. "Tell you what: You two go, then you tell Roshy and me about your adventures when you get back."

I said, "Nope, not the plan. You're both going with us."

"Well then, when I'm standing amid all those Green Tribe losers—no offense, Fatima—I plan to have *fun*."

Uh-oh, I thought. "Tell me what you mean by 'fun.' I'm asking as your master."

Sumera went quiet then. But she was not calm—her fists were clenched, and she was gritting her teeth. Fatima was grinning.

At last Sumera said, "When we all go to visit Green Tribe, I plan to say things to anger Ashnadim, anger Green Tribe, anger Fatima, and anger you, Master. All while I laugh at all of you."

Sumera looked over at Roshradzam. "If we visit Brown Tribe, I intend to be a goody-two-shoes, don't worry."

I said, "Sumera, why am I not surprised that you intend to cause trouble?"

Sumera smirked at me. "What do you intend to do about it?"

Fatima's grin got bigger. "That's the *wrong* thing to say to Master, Blue Girl."

By now, I was grinning, too—like a shark. "Harken, O Sumera: Henceforth you may not speak words except when someone is looking directly at you and asks a question, or when someone addresses you by name and asks a question. Hear and obey my command."

Silence.

Fatima clapped and laughed. "Oh, Sumera, you should see your face. It's fun to see you *so pissed!*"

Indeed, Sumera was furious—silently.

****

Five minutes later

I had said goodbye to Anna Kay. Now it was time for me to talk to four Tribes of *un*bound *djinn*.

This time it would be Fatima, not Roshradzam, *foom*ing us all there. I said, "Please put us down a little ways out. Green Tribe will be less alarmed if they see us walk in, rather than if we appear in their midst."

Silent Sumera rolled her eyes.

My ears popped.

****

An instant later
What looked like Cairo

The four of us were standing on a traffic island in a city with much Arabic writing visible everywhere. A sign gave the local time—a little after 2 p.m.—and the local temperature—in Centigrade.

Reader, it was uncanny how *silent* everything was. Cars, busses, and taxis were whizzing by; some drivers clearly were yelling at other drivers; I saw men and women talking on phones as they walked—and yet this crowded street was monastery-quiet. Except for Fatima—

Fatima said, "We're in Cairo, but in the spiritual-plane version of Cairo. Where Green Tribe meets is right there—at, and yet not at, the Green Oasis Hotel."

Sumera rolled her eyes.

Fatima continued, "One of the reasons I brought us right here, Master, is because of this street. In 1943, during R&R, Private Warren Harper traveled on this street on a tour bus that took him to see the Nile River and the Pyramids. It was a *life-changing* trip for Private Harper."

I explained to Roshradzam, "Private Warren Harper was my great-uncle, and Fatima's previous genie-master."

Sumera pantomimed a yawn.

Fatima said, "Now if you all would please follow me? Ashnadim is expecting us." Fatima looked at silent Sumera and grinned.

Then Fatima stepped off the traffic island—right into the path of a bus.

I gasped. Even knowing that a *djinni* can survive accidents that would kill a human, I still expected the outcome to be messy. But *nothing happened.* I heard no screeching of brakes; I heard no *thump*, to be followed by Fatima's body sent flying. Instead, the bus passed through where Fatima was standing. When the bus had rolled forward, I caught a glimpse of Fatima standing in the street in the same spot as before, her left eyebrow up, her right hand reaching toward me to take my hand—

But then most of Fatima disappeared for an instant, as a car "hit" her.

An instant later, Fatima was back in full view, again unmoved and unharmed.

For whatever reason, Roshradzam and Sumera were still standing on the traffic island; the next person to step into traffic would have to be me. I ignored the voice in my head that said *This is suicide! This is death!* and stepped into the street.

Less than a second later, I was clipped by a taxi—or so my eyes told me. I felt nothing. By the time that my hand took Fatima's still-outstretched hand, I had been harmlessly "run over" twice more.

By the time that Fatima and I walked to the Green Oasis Hotel, still holding hands, Roshradzam and Sumera were right behind us—also holding hands. But we did not enter the hotel's space by walking through a door—instead, Fatima lead us to walk through a wall.

The four of us then walked through the hotel lobby—unnoticed by both hotel employees and guests. We walked through another wall, to emerge into a sunny courtyard.

In the human plane, the only people in the courtyard were a young woman in *hijab*, who was sitting on a bench and was reading an Arabic-language book; and a big man who sat on a bench near her, but with his body angled so he could watch two entrances into the courtyard.

In the spiritual plane, however, the courtyard was thronged with beings in green (and only green) clothing. Green flashes announced the arrival of individual *djinn*.

But by this time, I was a little jaded at seeing *djinn*; enough so that the human bodyguard was more interesting to me. When Roshradzam and I entered the courtyard, the bodyguard should have turned his head, if only for a second, to look at us two young males. He did not look at us. I walked right up to the bodyguard; he did not react. I waved my hand in front of his face; he still did not react.

"Ahem!"

I turned around to look at the source of the sound. Sumera had her hands on her hips; as soon as I made eye contact, she broke this pose to point to Ashnadim. *Let's get on with it!* her gestures meant.

I looked around. Some of the Green Tribe *djinn* were frowning, but Ashnadim was smiling with amusement. Fatima's arms were crossed and she was rolling her eyes. Roshradzam was trying not to smile.

****

Seconds later

There were several ways that the language problem could have been handled. Ashnadim could have been the only being to speak for Green Tribe; he speaks unaccented English. Fatima could have translated my words into Arabic and translated Green Tribe's Arabic words into English, and I would have trusted her translations. Instead, everyone made use of the perfect translations worked by Roshradzam's translator-ring.

Meaning that I would speak in English, which the ring then would translate into Arabic; and Fatima (and everyone else) would speak in Arabic, which then would be translated into English.

Fatima spoke first, then I addressed Green Tribe. It did not help our presentations that while Sumera could not heckle Fatima and me verbally, she kept undermining us with facial expressions of *Oh, really? This is news to me* or *I'm trying not to laugh.*

When Fatima spoke, Green Tribe listened respectfully. But when I addressed Green Tribe, a Green Tribe man-*djinni* interrupted me: "Ashnadim, may I say something?"

Ashnadim said, "Yes, Horabwadz?"

"I think this human is trying to sell us rotten figs."

Ashnadim replied, "I have great confidence in Marvin Harper, Horabwadz. He's good and he's brave. And even if you don't believe *him*, believe *Fatima*. She is our sister."

"Fatima is our *bound* sister. If the human orders Fatima to lie to us, she has to do it."

Silent Sumera clapped her hands once and pointed at Horabwadz. *Bingo, you got it!*

I glared at Sumera, whose face now showed innocent puzzlement—*Why are you angry at me?*

Horabwadz continued, "The human is asking *all* of Green Tribe to fight *all* of Hell's demons—what is the human *not* telling us?"

I heard murmurs among the *djinn*.

I am adaptable. I looked at Fatima and said, "Answer truthfully, O Fatima: Have I given you any orders as to what to say or what not to say in these discussions?"

"No, Master, you have not," Fatima replied.

"So you can speak as you choose, even to say things that you know or suspect that I would dislike you saying?"

"Yes, Master, I am free to speak however I think best," Fatima replied.

The upshot of my asking those two questions was: It was not I who persuaded the rank-and-file Green Tribe *djinn* to fight the demons, it was Fatima. Fatima said pretty much the same things that I said—"The demons are gearing up to make war against Heaven. We need to all stop them *now*, or we all will suffer *later*." But coming from *her* mouth, the words were believed by Green Tribe.

But perhaps I underestimate myself. Horabwadz was the only Green Tribe *djinni* to call me a liar. No *djinni* threw rotten eggs at me, no *djinni* called me *Wormfood*, and Ashnadim, Fatima, and Roshradzam all had flattering things to say about me.

Still, I noted that Fatima was asked many more questions by Green Tribe *djinn* than I was asked.

Afterward, all of the *djinn* of Green Tribe agreed to join my genies and me in our fight against the demons.

Reader, I would love to say that I was pleased by Green Tribe's decision. I was indeed pleased—mostly. But part of me thought, *Of the four Tribes, Green Tribes is the easiest to bring on board.*

****

Our next stop: Budapest and the Pink Tribe of *Djinn*. Five of us walked into Pink Tribe's hangout: my three genies, me, and Ashnadim, the Chief of Green Tribe.

Again I asked Fatima those two questions, so that everyone in Pink Tribe knew that I was not forcing Fatima into some kind of hidden agenda. During this visit, I also asked those same two questions of Roshradzam.

Just like before, Ashnadim, Fatima, and Roshradzam had nice things to say about me; but Sigvard (the Chief of the Pink Tribe of *Djinn*) flattered me as well. As before, the *djinn* of Pink Tribe listened to what I had to say, but Fatima was asked many more questions than I was asked. As before, all of Pink Tribe agreed to fight the demons.

****

Our third stop: Tripoli, Libya, the home of Brown Tribe. We travelers were now six: my three genies, me, Ashnadim of Green Tribe, and Sigvard of Pink Tribe.

I think Thointorgos, the Chief of the Brown Tribe of *Djinn*, was wary of us at first. It did not help that Sumera's contempt for Brown Tribe was obvious at first, even without speech. But Sumera's nonverbal disrespect ended *instantly* when Roshradzam angrily rebuked her.

Sumera did not hold her public scolding by Roshradzam against him. In fact, Sumera afterward acted *so* nice to Roshradzam that I realized that she had discovered a loophole in my "no PDA" rules. As everyone watched Sumera pawing Roshradzam, Ashnadim and Sigvard looked nauseous, and everyone in Brown Tribe (except for Roshradzam) looked confused. Fatima was back to crossing her arms and rolling her eyes.

For Brown Tribe, I made Roshradzam the featured spokes-genie and Fatima the assistant spokes-genie. As before, I was praised for all sorts of things by many different *djinn*, and my two genies were asked many more questions by rank-and-file *djinn* than I was asked. In the end, Brown Tribe agreed to join me and my genies, plus Green Tribe, plus Pink Tribe, in fighting the demons.

So far, recruiting tribes of *djinn* had been almost easy. But now seven of us were headed for Blue Tribe, in the spiritual-plane version of Baghdad. It was entirely possible that my plan to bring the Tribes together as a *djinn* army was about to explode on the launching pad.

****

Before we *foom*ed over to Baghdad and made our "Fight the demons together!" pitch to Blue Tribe, I asked Ashnadim, "What is Meedakhad like?" Two years ago, Meedakhad had become the new Chief of the Blue Tribe of *Djinn*, replacing Hakeezib.

Ashnadim answered, "He's not a jerk dickhead asshole. Which is shocking for Blue Tribe, we all know."

Silent Sumera glared hatred at Ashnadim.

Sigvard said, "I'm convinced Meedakhad is a ringer from a different Tribe, who has painted his skin blue. Who ever heard of a Blue *djinni* who isn't a complete pain in the ass to be around?" Sigvard gave Sumera a *fuck-you* smile.

With those words, we *foom*ed over to Baghdad. *Oh, joy.*

****

Seconds later

The Blues had gathered at the spiritual-plane version of a soccer stadium. As we had done before, we seven *foom*ed to a place a little ways away from Blue Tribe. Once arrived, we seven walked through walls—or in this case, through steel-and-concrete soccer bleachers—to get to where Blue Tribe was gathered together.

Blue Tribe was, by my rough count, about half again as big as Green Tribe, and about twice as big as Pink Tribe. Among all those blue *djinn*, nobody looked friendly.

Fatima and I had just started our pitch when a woman-*djinni* yelled out, "Why isn't Sumera talking?"

A man-*djinni* said, "Yes, Sumera, why aren't you adding color-commentary to what Green Bitch and the wormfood are saying?"

After hours of silence, Sumera spoke: "Because *motherfucking* Master here said that I had to keep quiet!"

I held up a hand to stop Fatima speaking. "Sumera, that's not what I ordered you to do, and you know it. Now, I *order* you to repeat my previous order that kept you silent. Repeat it word for word."

Angrily, Sumera repeated my earlier words.

Meedakhad yelled at me, "How *dare* you? I don't care that you're Sumera's 'master,' she deserves more respect—"

Sigvard glared at Meedakhad. "You got a problem with Marvin Harper's order to Loudmouth? I don't. The only time I can stand Sumera is when she's quiet."

I said, "Fatima, continue what you were saying. Blue Tribe, our message is too important to get sidetracked with petty squabbles."

Fatima talked, then I talked, then Roshradzam talked. But judging by the crossed arms and sneers among the Blue Tribe *djinn*, I was not making converts. We got only a few questions from our audience.

When we stopped talking, Meedakhad said, "One thing you have not even mentioned is, Who is in charge? The answer is obvious: *I* should be in charge, because I am chief of the biggest Tribe of the four."

"Camelshit," Thointorgos said. "Put the human here in charge. He shows leadership."

"I agree," said Ashnadim. "Besides, I will not follow Blue Tribe *ever*, even into a *houri* brothel."

Sigvard said to Meedakhad, "Do you think everyone else has forgotten that Blue Tribe tried to start the *Djinn* War? *Twice?*"

Meedakhad sputtered, "Blue Tribe needed to restore its honor! The slanders against Sumera had to be answered!"

" 'Slanders,' huh?" Sigvard looked at Sumera. "So, Blue Girl, you're itching to talk? What's the truth about you learning spells from demons, *hm?* Get it off your flat chest."

Sumera looked Sigvard up and down contemptuously. "Master said that I *may* answer a question, not that I *must*. I have nothing to say to any of you."

Fatima's smile was vampiric. "But if *Master* asked you that question, Sumera, you would have to answer, and you would have to speak truth."

All faces turned to look at me. Sumera looked panicky. Meedakhad looked tense. Some Blue Tribe faces looked angry; some looked worried. Ashnadim and Thointorgos waited patiently, while Sigvard's face looked eager.

I was very aware that Meedakhad had not yet agreed to join the other Tribes in fighting the demons. If I were a different person, I might be now trying to figure out how to not piss off Blue Tribe, while *also* not angering Green Tribe, Pink Tribe, and Brown Tribe.

But I had never been someone to "work the angles"— and besides, I had made a promise. I looked around and I said, "Eight days ago, I promised my bound *djinni* Sumera that I would never ask her about learning magic from demons. Now I reaffirm that promise."

Roshradzam, along with Sumera and Meedakhad (and many other Blue Tribe *djinn*) looked relieved. Ashnadim looked annoyed, and Sigvard looked angry.

Fatima threw her hands in the air.

She said, "Master, I *know* you understand how *important* this question is to the three Tribes who almost fought that war. How *important* it is to us seven *djinn* who were bound into Vessels, in order to *prevent* that war. *You* can answer this question for all time, Master; *please* do so."

Fatima added, "Besides, Master, surely you doubt Sumera's protestations of innocence as much as I do."

Fatima's last statement made all the Blues angry—but only for a second. They calmed down when they saw that I was not nodding in agreement.

Reader, the fact is: Fatima was right. Sumera knew demon magic and she knew demons; it was obvious. I didn't merely "doubt" Sumera; I was *certain* that Sumera's statement of "I have not studied demon magic" was a flat-out lie. But eight days ago, I had given Sumera a promise, and I take my promises seriously.

Now I replied, "Fatima, you make a good case. Had I not given Sumera that promise, I would now compel her to answer this burning question in front of witnesses. But I *did* make the promise, end of discussion."

Sigvard glared at me. "If I were not a being of honor, we of Pink Tribe would be going our own way right now!"

Meedakhad said to me, "One more question, human: Do you like Sumera? As a being, not as your genie."

"Do I *like* Sumera? No way."

Meedakhad nodded. "Blue Tribe will join the other Tribes in fighting the demons. We will take orders from this human, Marvin Harper. He has honor, and Blue Tribe values honor. I trust him."

Which was all well and good, except that Sigvard still looked pissed at me.

Meanwhile, Sumera was looking at me in shock.

Chapter 24
Cause for Hope

Still Monday

When Meedakhad told me that Blue Tribe would also fight the demons, Ashnadim asked, "So, O Great Human Leader, what happens now?"

I answered, "First, I have to return to my mansion. I need to research things, I need to think about things—but mainly, it's lunchtime now and I'm hungry! I'll be in touch with all of you in a few hours."

****

A minute later

My ears popped, then my genies and I stood in the computer room at the mansion. SJ-1 looked up from her laptop and nodded to Fatima; SJ-1 ignored me.

I said to all three genies, "Change clothes."

Fatima and Sumera changed clothes in the time it took them to turn to smoke and to de-smoke; it took Roshradzam a minute to summon his groundskeeper-clothes and to put them on.

While he was dressing, I told Fatima, "Go to the monster kitchen and take over the lunchtime cooking. But tell your substitute that you might disappear after lunch."

"Yes, Master," Fatima said. She walked out of the computer room.

I said to Roshradzam, "After you're dressed, go to the monster kitchen, take your usual seat at the head table, and wait for me." Soon he too walked out of the computer room.

When I could no longer hear his footsteps, I said to still-silent *Haremée*-Sumera, "Follow me."

A minute later, we were both inside the master bedroom. I immediately took off my suit jacket and laid it on the bed; my jacket was soon followed by my tie. I unfastened the collar button on my dress shirt.

Silent Sumera looked at the big bed, looked back at me, and smirked.

I said, "I am royally pissed at you. You may speak now."

Sumera still was smirking. "So you plan to take out your anger on me by *fucking* me? How human."

I walked across the master bedroom, motioning to Sumera to follow me. I said, "We *need* for the four Tribes to work together to fight the demons. But that came very close to not happening, because of *you* making faces and showing disrespect for everything I said and that Fatima said. Why did you undermine me?"

"*Why?* Because I don't think your great idea will beat the demons. Also because I don't want Blue Tribe getting buddy-buddy with the lesser Tribes. And three, I figured you would not do anything about my dissing you."

I opened the door to my walk-in closet. I told Sumera, "Step in there and turn to face me. I want to show you something." Sumera looked puzzled, but obeyed. I said, "You really thought that you could undermine me in front of all *djinn* and suffer no penalty?"

She tensed. "You promised not to send me back into my lamp."

"Indeed," I echoed, "I promised not to send you back into your lamp." Now my smile was vampiric. "I will keep that promise, word for word, the same way that genies grant wishes, word for word."

Sumera stared at me in horror.

I reached up and grabbed a green-glitter Saint Patrick's Day derby off a shelf of the walk-in closet. While holding the hat, I said, "O Sumera, you are to remain where you are standing; you may not *foom* away. You will remain here motionless, except to breathe, to blink, and to move your eyes; you may not otherwise change your face. You may not speak. You will remain this way till I tell you otherwise."

With those words, I set the green hat on Sumera's head, then I shut the closet door on her.

****

Three minutes later, after I had changed into casual clothes, I walked into the monster kitchen. I walked over to Roshradzam and murmured in his ear, "You won't see Sumera for a while."

Next, I walked over to Fatima and murmured, "You won't see Sumera for a while, and don't go looking for her."

I pulled out my smartphone and looked at the time. I had statue-ized Sumera at 1:36 in the afternoon.

****

I was still holding the smartphone when my phone rang; the caller was Harper Foundation.

I took the call, expecting to hear the voice of Virgilia or Gennifer. Instead I heard, "Hello, Marvin, this is Almira. I'm calling you on break; I'm not goofing off."

I replied, "I know, Almira. I know you don't goof off, even . . . after." I did not add *Even after you were freed from my sex-slavery.* "Anyway, what's up?"

"Could I talk to you this evening? I have a question about something that happened during our trip to France. It's a question about a *souvenir*, actually."

Translation: *I was supposed to get Sumera's lamp after Elvira used it, but I've let you hold on to it. Now I've figured out my wishes and I want the lamp back.*

"Um, sure, Almira," I said. "Not a problem."

After I ended the call, I thought, *I have a big problem. I need Sumera with me to help me fight the demons. But now I can't make plans with Sumera till I get this resolved.*

Then I realized that as the owner of the Harper Foundation, I had options. A minute later, I was on the phone to Almira's boss, saying, "I need to talk with Almira in person at the mansion. Give Almira the rest of the day off, with pay, provided that she drives straight here."

Almira walked into the monster kitchen fifteen minutes later. Elvira walked in right behind Almira; I sighed.

Elvira said, "I'm taking a pay-hit to be with Almie when she talks with you about you-know-what."

Then Almira asked, "Where is Sumera?"

****

Ten minutes later
The computer room at the mansion

I was sitting behind the computer desk, in my comfortable executive chair. SJ-1 was sitting in her chair at her smaller computer desk; Fatima was sitting on a corner of SJ-1's desk. The twins were sitting next to each other on my couch; both twins were facing me. Anna Kay was in the Electronics Playroom, watching a game show.

I had just finished giving the twins an update on what I had been doing with my three genies since—jeez, had it really been only four days ago?

". . . And that's the truth," I said.

Elvira now said skeptically, "You've all gone to Heaven and back."

"We did," said Fatima. "We all met Master's Uncle John." Fatima jerked a thumb toward Roshradzam. "Since you don't believe Master or me, ask *him*. He was there."

"*I* believe Marvin," Almira said.

"Great," I said. "So Almira, you understand why I need to hold on to Sumera's lamp for a little longer?"

"Where *is* Sumera anyway?" Elvira asked.

I said, "She is being punished."

"*Good*," Fatima replied. "Is Sumera stuck in her lamp?"

"No," I said. "I made a promise, and I'm keeping it."

Fatima shrugged. "Then she isn't really suffering."

"Oh, she's suffering," I said, "believe me."

Almira asked, "What is Sumera being punished for?"

I replied, "Being even more of a pain in the ass than usual. Any other questions? I have a war to plan."

"*I* have a question," Elvira said. "Since you might die very soon, where is Paula Sarin?"

Senator Paula Sarin of Alaska, along with her assistant Sheila Johansson, had disappeared under mysterious circumstances in 2010. What only Elvira, Fatima, and I knew was that Elvira and Paula had met at the front door of my mansion, shortly before Paula's disappearance.

Now Almira said, "Jeez, twin, let it go."

"Why?" Elvira replied. "If he's fighting demons, he could be *dead* tomorrow, and Fatima could be in her lamp. Then how could I get my answer?"

I asked Elvira, "What does Paula Sarin have to do with me fighting all the demons of Hell? You know, *what I've been talking about for the past however-many minutes?*"

"Nothing," Elvira replied. "But *you* know and *I* know that Paula Sarin walked into the mansion six years ago, then the news claimed she 'disappeared.' So how about you finally tell me what happened to her, okay?"

I exchanged looks with Fatima, then I looked into Elvira's eyes. "Fine."

I heard a gasp; SJ-1 stared at me in dread. That's when I realized that I had never told SJ-1 the whole story about

Paula Sarin, Sheila Johansson's former employer and former dominant-lesbian lover.

SJ-1 said to Fatima, "Mistress, may this unit walk to the monster kitchen and drink some water?"

Fatima said, "Permission granted." SJ-1 rushed off.

I looked at Elvira and said, "To begin, Paula Sarin was a genie-master, just as I am and you and Virgilia were."

"Paula Sarin was evil," Fatima interjected.

Both twins were staring at me now.

Elvira wanted to know the truth? Boy did I tell her the truth—

I finished with ". . . So Paula Sarin is at Pink Tribe's mercy till sometime in 2020, but Pink Tribe has no mercy. Not toward the murderer of Jerngert of Pink Tribe."

There was complete silence in the room. Roshradzam and the twins all looked shocked. I suppose it's because a ten-year-long torture-session *is* shocking.

"I'm done with questions for now," stunned-looking Elvira said.

Almira stood to leave then; Elvira stood too. They walked to the door, but then Almira turned to look at me. "I forgive you for making me your sex-slave six years ago. Back then, Elvie and I made you do it."

Elvira looked at me coldly. "I *haven't* forgiven you."

Almira sighed. "Elvie, do you want to turn out like Mother?"

I shrugged. "Elvira, at the moment I have *much* bigger problems than whether you forgive me or not."

****

At 6:43, after supper, I entered the master bedroom. I walked over and opened the door of my walk-in closet. In my left hand was a scribbled-on legal pad.

Sumera was still a statue, and still posed just as I had left her; she had the Saint Patrick's Day green derby still on her head.

I said, "Sumera, you may move and speak now."

An instant later, Sumera yanked the green hat off her head and threw it to the floor.

"That's childish, Sumera," I said, laughing. "Now pick up the hat and put it back on the shelf."

As Sumera obeyed my order, she said over her shoulder, "Nobody has come in here except you."

"Because I have a system for hanging up shirts and pants in my closet. So whoever has laundry duty, I tell her to leave my clothes on my bed."

"I expected Fatima to open the door and laugh at me, but she never did."

I shook my head. "I ordered Fatima not to look for you, and I told nobody that you were a statue in my closet."

"*Why?* it's not like I've been nice to you since I got here."

"If I had allowed Fatima to see you statue-fied, I would be acting mean to you. I *despise* meanness."

"So," Sumera said, "why are you here? Did you decide I've been punished enough?"

"No, I'm here to ask you a question. I think you're the only *djinni* who can answer it."

Sumera's smile was cruel. "You know that I could *foom* away before you ask your question. How much is it worth to you for me not to vanish now?"

I smiled back. "Stay here, Sumera, till I let you leave." Now her threat was empty. "Let me flip things around: How much is it worth to *you*"—I grabbed the green-glitter derby and held it up—"to *not* become a hat rack again?"

She glared. "Ask your question, *Master*."

I reshelved the hat, then I read aloud from my legal pad: " 'Why would the demons raise up an army of human minions and take them to Heaven? Wouldn't the angels kill the human invaders as soon as they arrived, like what almost happened to me? What do the demons get out of doing this?' "

Sumera said, "Don't you remember Page Three of the Protocol?" I shook my head. Sumera explained, "The Protocol mentions a spell that the demons may not speak in the presence of an angel. It turns out, that spell will *kill* any angel who hears it."

"Okay, so how does this answer my question?"

"It's a spoken spell. Demons teach the spell to their human minions, and the Protocol doesn't say squat about *humans* speaking that spell to angels."

"Would you please *foom* me that copy of the Protocol that you gave me, so I can read the passage for myself?" I asked with seeming casualness.

Sumera looked at me in silence for three seconds, then said, "Sure, no problem."

Foom. The Protocol appeared in my right hand, already flipped to the third page.

One second later, I was reading, " 'The demons may not speak the spell that begins *Ub angellub jonv* in the presence of any angel of Heaven.' Too bad the Protocol lists only the first three words."

"Why 'Too bad'? I'm sure you don't want to kill angels."

"I figure that if I knew this angel-killer spell, maybe we could tweak the wording to make a demon-killer spell."

Sumera smiled proudly: "Nobody in the four Tribes knows this spell, except for me: *Ub angellub, jonv chentaifeth neenan sib jechgoketh neenan trenkuk.* O angel, bleed through your openings until your true-death."

I beckoned Sumera out into the master bedroom; she looked relieved to leave the walk-in closet.

I asked her, "How could we change that spell into a demon-killer spell?"

"Easy—I change one word: *Ub daimonnub, jonv chentaifeth neenan sib jechgoketh neenan trenkuk.*"

In a corner of the master bedroom stood a potted plant. (Which was odd—I did not recall a potted plant being there before.) After Sumera spoke her spell, the potted plant shape-shifted into a purple-furred gorilla. The gorilla gurgled its scream as blood gushed out of its ears, tear ducts, nostrils, and mouth; blood sprayed out of the gorilla's ass and painted the walls behind it. Then the gorilla burned up and vanished.

Sumera laughed scornfully. "Surprise, Krankentot!"

"Wow, you're *good*," I said.

Sumera blinked at my compliment, then she grinned. "And you have honor, Master."

I asked, "Does your knowledge of extra magic spells include a spell to locate demons?" Locating either demons or angels was normally a power that *djinn* did not have.

Sumera now replied, "No, I don't know of such a spell, but I have an idea that might work."

I opened the bedroom door, and motioned Sumera to walk out into the hallway. As she and I walked down the hallway and headed for the grand staircase, I was grinning.

Fanzelle and her entire infernal plan might be shut down very soon.

Chapter 25
Cause for Despair

Five and a half hours later
Just after midnight, Tuesday morning
The (spiritual-plane version of the) soccer field of the soccer stadium in Monterrey, Nuevo León, Mexico

My three genies, not needing sleep, had been eager to take the fight to the demons. But alas, I had been awake for sixteen hours. So we had delayed the *djinn*'s attack on the demons till I had gotten enough sleep to function. Now after my evening nap, we combatants were meeting at a place where demons would not expect to find us.

My ears popped, then I was looking at a sea of *djinn* faces. Brown Tribe *djinn* were standing on the soccer field, looking at me; *djinn* from the other three Tribes were either looking across the field at me or were looking down at me while they floated in mid-air.

Lighting for this gathering was strictly by blue, green, and pink fireballs that lit up the space in the spiritual plane; in the physical plane, the stadium was black-dark except for five spotlights that were trained on the four corners of the field and its center.

I spoke loudly to the thousands of *djinn*, "Thank you for coming. I'm told that all *djinn* 'know' that a *djinni* locator-spell can locate only another *djinni* or a human; the *djinni*'s locator-spell supposedly fails at locating a demon or an angel. True, so far?"

Djinn on the ground and in the air all nodded; nobody disagreed.

I said, "Sumera has an idea how *djinn* can locate demons. Sumera?"

Sumera looked into faces from every Tribe. "*Ahem.* Just as we *djinn* always 'knew' that we could not locate any demon, we also 'knew' that we could not change any human's Date of Fated Death. Well, one *djinni* still cannot shorten the life of one human. But two solar years ago, thirty *djinn* who worked together to cast a group spell, achieved the 'impossible' . . ."

Roshradzam listened closely, as did other *djinn.* But I saw a lot of Green Tribe and Pink Tribe *djinn* exchanging glances among themselves as Sumera spoke.

As for myself, I was experiencing horrible memory flashbacks. Fatima understood; she took my hand.

****

In 2014, genie-master Vinnie Lavagetto had kidnapped Anna Kay and the LeClerc twins. His plan had been to trick me into flying into a killing rage and trying to kill him. Then, so Lavagetto had planned, his genie Kharmesh would save him from harm, then Kharmesh would kill me.

I and invisible Fatima had foiled Lavagetto's scheme. But my troubles had just begun: at our moment of "success," Hakeezib, the Chief of the Blue Tribe of *Djinn,* had *foom*ed in.

Hakeezib had trussed me up in magical blue bindings, and then thirty Blue Tribe *djinn* had done a magical dance and chant, in a circle around me. The final effect had been to move my Date of Fated Death down to that day by speed-aging me, then Blue Tribe had planned to kill me.

Fatima had been part of Hakeezib's plan too. When Blue Tribe had been killing me slowly, Hakeezib had counted on Fatima being compelled to rescue me but being unable to do so, then Fatima summoning Green Tribe and Pink Tribe for backup.

Hakeezib's goal in 2014 had been to start the *Djinn* War that angelic intervention had prevented millennia ago, with me being the unlucky human to replay the Archduke Franz Ferdinand role.

Hakeezib's scheme had almost worked. At the end, I had become an old man, only minutes away from death. And if a *djinni* could die from massive internal injuries, Fatima had been close to death also.

And now, two years later, Sumera was suggesting that a slight change to the spell that had almost killed me, could be used now to track down a demon. Life is ironic at times.

****

After Sumera spoke, the magical geniuses of Blue, Green, and Pink Tribes talked together. They came up with a spoken spell that the dancer-chanters might use to track down one demon.

Meanwhile, I ordered Sumera, "Write a list of all the demons of Hell whom we have not true-killed. Put the sixty-five nastiest demons at the top."

(Reader, I made a mistake in what I told Sumera. Can you spot my error? I did not see it until too late.)

After the magic-experts from the three Tribes cooked up a spoken spell that dancer-chanters could use to find one demon, that spell was tested, using ten *djinn* each from Blue, Green, and Pink Tribes as dancer-chanters.

Sumera suggested that the dancer-chanters find a demon named HatesBeauty.

Success! Inside the circle of thirty *djinn*, at first an illusionary tiny globe of Earth appeared, rotating, with a red dot showing that HatesBeauty was somewhere in Europe. As time passed, and the dancer-chanters continued their spell, our view slowly zoomed in on the illusionary globe. As time passed, we could see that HatesBeauty was in France, then in Paris, then in a particular building on a certain street in Paris. Finally, the demon was revealed to be in a particular room on the third floor of that building.

It took half an hour from the time that the thirty *djinn* began their dancing and chanting, to the time that we could know for sure where HatesBeauty was.

The *djinn* from all four Tribes cheered at this new magical trick they had discovered. I also was happy, enough to give Sumera a hug (which got me a raised eyebrow from Fatima). But one thought dampened my good mood—

How do you win a war when it takes thirty of your people, thirty minutes to find one enemy target?

****

Forty minutes later

Thirty minutes ago, right after the successful test had ended, everyone in the Blue, Green, and Pink Tribes had formed up into sixty-five circles of thirty *djinn*, and Sumera had given each circle the name of a demon to track.

Now we had the exact locations of sixty-five demons— slightly less than 9 percent of all the demons still alive.

So the only thing left for me to do was to send out sixty-five *djinn* assassins at the same time, each *djinni* speaking Sumera's demon-killer spell.

This was when I started to catch major shit. I was saying to Thointorgos, "Pick sixty-five Brown Tribe *djinn* who can handle stress well—"

"Hold on," said Sigvard, "you're sending in *Turd Tribe* weaklings to kill the demons? *Why?*"

"Because *Brown* Tribe can do this job!" Roshradzam yelled.

Sumera wrapped her slim blue arms around Roshradzam's muscular left arm. "Brown Tribe *djinn* deserve respect, Pinkeye!" she told Sigvard.

Now bunches of *djinn* faces—including *everyone* in Brown Tribe—were turned my way. No pressure.

I said, "Roshradzam is right. Brown Tribe beings cannot cast the magic spell to locate a demon, but this last part they can do. Killing a demon requires only the ability to speak and the ability to *foom*."

"This is camelshit," said Horabwadz of Green Tribe. "The three *real* Tribes do the grunt work, and *Turd Tribe* will get the glory."

"Boo-hoo," said Roshradzam. "Now you know what life for Brown Tribe is like."

Fatima said to me, "Please consider letting the other three Tribes join in the fun."

Thointorgos glared at Fatima. "Fine, so long as 'join in the fun' doesn't become 'take over the attack.' "

I was quiet for several seconds, then I said, "Thointorgos, pick sixty-two Browns. Meedakhad, Ashnadim, and Sigvard, you each pick someone from your Tribe. Have the sixty-five demon-killers gather over there by the goalposts, and Sumera will remind them of the killer-spell."

Fatima said, "Um, Master? *Djinn* have perfect memories—even Brown Tribe *djinn*. Sumera spoke the spell; we remember the spell. No reminder is necessary."

Horabwadz muttered something that I could not quite hear.

Sigvard said, "I already know who the *token* Pink Tribe assassin will be." Sigvard tapped his chest with a finger. I saw Ashnadim and Meedakhad shake their heads.

****

Two minutes later

I did not know any of the chosen Brown Tribe assassins, or the Blue Tribe assassin. Ashnadim's pick for Green Tribe was Horabwadz. *Sigh*. Sigvard had not changed his mind; he was still the designated Pink Tribe demon-assassin.

Soon the assassins were gathered together, and repeated the spell together in a chorus. I said, "When I say 'Go,' you all leave at once. You ready?"

I got sixty-five wolfish grins in reply.

"Three . . . two . . . one . . . zero, *go!*"

FOO-F-FOO-F-FOO-FOOM.

****

One second later

"So how did you rank Fanzelle on your list?" I asked Sumera. "Number-one nastiest? Number two?"

Sumera shrugged. "Number sixty-six. I filled the top sixty-five slots with the real hard cases, then I put Fanzelle at the top of the remaining demons."

I frowned. "I just figured, Sumera, that Fanzelle would be high-ranked without me having to order it."

"Why?" Sumera asked. "Fanzelle is a pain in the ass to *you*; but still, she's just a succubus. A whore with horns."

I almost called Sumera an idiot, but then I decided *What's done is done. We'll nail Fanzelle in Round Two.*

****

Two seconds later

FOOM. A Brown Tribe *djinni* returned, looking disappointed. "Vomitkiss wasn't there. I think he left before I got there."

FOOM-F-FOOM. Other *djinn* began returning soon after, all sporting big grins—

"Bilewine is *gone!*"

"I watched HatesBeauty *die!*"

"Pink Tribe has fulfilled its mission"—naturally, this was Sigvard speaking.

In hardly any time at all, Thointorgos turned to me and said formally, "Sixty-one of sixty-two Brown Tribe assassins have each killed his or her demon. Brown Tribe thanks—"

"Hold on," said Ashnadim. "Marvin, Horabwadz has not returned yet."

I said, "Don't worry, he's probably—"

FOOF. A gargoyle-demon appeared by the crowd of assassin-*djinn.*

FOOF. Then a second demon appeared; *FOOF*—now there were three demons among us.

"You killed Bilewine," a demon said to one Brown Tribe *djinni.* Now *you*"—the demon slashed a clawed hand across the *djinni's* throat, and the *djinni* turned to brown smoke— "will die."

FOO-FOOF. By now a dozen demons had appeared among us, with many more appearing each second.

FOO-F-FOOM. My three genies were now inches away from me, acting as bodyguards. I appreciated the thought, but I did not think they could help me any.

Meanwhile, the demons were slaughtering the Brown Tribe demon-assassins, and had already killed the one Blue Tribe *djinni* who had assassinated a demon. Sigvard fired a pink fireball into the face of a demon, which resulted in Sigvard instantly being bound in purple-metal chains.

"Oh *shit,*" Fatima muttered, "they put him in *Chekhovium.*"

"Why?" I asked.

"They plan to toy with Sigvard in front of everyone," Sumera answered. She sounded sure.

"AVENGE HORABWADZ!" yelled a voice in the crowd of *djinn*-spectators. *FOOM.* A Green Tribe *djinni* appeared behind the demons. *F-FOOM*. Two Pink Tribe *djinn* appeared between Sigvard and the attacking demons.

F-FOO-FOOM. The Green Tribe *djinni* behind the demons was joined by three Blue Tribe *djinn*.

Six *djinn* throats spoke the words "*Ub daimonnub, jonv chen—*"

That's as far as the six newcomer *djinn* got. The Green Tribe avenger got his head torn off his neck by a grinning demon, and the two Pink Tribe defenders were disemboweled. Two of the Blue Tribe *djinn* died those ways; the third Blue Tribe *djinni*'s chest exploded.

Meanwhile, one demon had stepped up to Chekhovium-chained Sigvard and now murmured something in Sigvard's ear. Blood spurted from Sigvard's nose and mouth, and soaked the front and back of his pants—then Sigvard turned into wafting pink smoke. The Chekhovium chains dropped to the soccer-field grass.

Sigvard's four-armed demonic killer turned to us onlookers and chortled. "Normally we aren't allowed to kill *djinn*, but you have given us the loophole—self-defense! *Thanks*, suckers!"

FOO-F-FOO-FOOM. As the demons killed *djinn* demon-assassins, or killed the avengers of *djinn* demon-assassins, those slain *djinn* turned into blue, green, pink, or brown smoke. But the places where these *djinn* had been killed were quickly filled again, with *djinn* of like Tribe. Alas, the demons never allowed the newcomers to completely speak the demon-killer spell before the newcomers were killed in grisly ways.

Then I noticed something surprising: By now there was a mob of demons in the soccer stadium, but they were not attacking the *djinn* onlookers, they were not attacking the Chiefs of the Tribes (except for Sigvard), and they were not attacking me.

Oh, the demons were *growling* at the rest of us, and glaring, and acting dangerous, but they weren't actually bothering us. *It's because of the Protocol*, I realized. *The demons may attack only <u>djinn</u> who attacked them with the demon-killer spell or are attacking them now. The rest of us, the demons must leave alone.*

I yelled as loudly as I could, "STOP FIGHTING! RETREAT! GO HOME!"

Arms wrapped around me. Fatima said, "Roshradzam, Sumera, grab Master! I'm going to lose any pursuers!"

More arms wrapped around me, then my ears popped.

****

An instant later

I was being clutched by my three genies in a city park at night. Above the trees, I could see the lit rectangular windows of skyscrapers.

"Where are we?" I asked.

Fatima said, "A park in Chicago that Warren Harper loved as a boy. Roshradzam, you pick the next place."

My ears popped. Now the four of us were in black darkness. The air was cool and moist.

"Where are we?" I asked. My voice had an echo, as did Roshradzam's translating ring.

Roshradzam replied, "We're in the cave in France where my Vessel laid in a crevice for hundreds of years."

Sumera said, "Oh, Roshy, I'm *soo* glad you're not stuck there anymore."

I said, "Sumera, please take us back to the mansion. But not to a place where an enemy would expect us."

My ears popped again. Again, we were in darkness— until I heard a *click* and lights came on. I discovered we had *foom*ed into the attic.

"That was a good pick, Sumera," I said. Sumera looked surprised, then she smiled. Again Fatima hit me with the raised eyebrow.

Before we left the attic, I ordered my three genies to change into their "secret identity" looks—pajamas, bathrobe, and slippers for each of them, plus brown skin for Sumera. Then the four of us walked down the attic stairs as quietly as we could manage—

—which would not have been quiet at all, except that Fatima enclosed the attic stairs in a green-smoke Silence Box. Usually, moving up or down the attic stairs was like walking on kettle drums.

I was last down the stairs. I had just shut the attic door and had just stepped onto the asparagus-green hallway rug when I heard a man's voice from the Upstairs Lounge—

"You took your sweet time coming home, Marvin Harper. I don't like being kept waiting."

****

An instant later

"Hold on," Fatima said. "Master, there was *nobody*—"

I looked into the Upstairs Lounge. Standing there in all her succubus-y glory was Fanzelle—she was showing her tail and her horns, showing lots of bat-wing, and showing lots of reddish, well-shaped skin. Her black high-heel shoes had steel spikes sticking out from them. Fanzelle was facing me in a porn-star pose. She looked both scary and sexy.

Standing next to Fanzelle was a red-skinned man with black hair, moustache, and goatee; his face had prominent cheekbones. He had horns coming out of his forehead and his ears were pointed. He was wearing a dark-red pinstripe suit, a pink shirt, a red tie, and black shoes with white spats. His arms were crossed, and he was looking at me with an expression I could not read.

I kept my voice calm. "Do you go by Lucifer or Satan these days?"

The Prince of Evil replied haughtily, "I deserve to be called 'Satan,' because this is the name I chose for myself. *He*"—a glance up—"named me 'Lucifer.'"

"Gotcha," I said, "you being called by your Heaven-name is an insult. So I shouldn't call your companion 'Ninety-Nine Hundred Ninety-Nine,' or whatever her angel-number was."

Fanzelle snapped, "Actually, I was 'Twelve Hundred Thirty-Seven.'"

Satan said, "You surprise me, Marvin Harper. Your file says you tend to follow the rules—disgustingly so. But a few minutes ago, you visited Alphonse Park in Chicago after that park closed for the night. *Tsk.*"

Behind me, Sumera said to Fatima, "Way to go, Green Girl! You promised you would make it *hard* for the bad guys to trace us! You screwed up, as usual."

Fatima's voice replied, "Or maybe *you* sent the demons a secret message: 'Here is where we are, and here is where we're going.'"

"Camelshit," Sumera's voice replied. "You think Hell has a claim on me?"

Then Sumera's voice became syrupy-sweet: "Lord of Evil, I was *so saddened* to hear of the untimely passing of HatesBeauty. My *sincere* condolences."

Fatima's voice said flippantly, "I'm sorry *I* can't offer condolences, Satan. Unlike *Blue Girl* here, I have never befriended any demon."

I spoke over my shoulder to Fatima and Sumera: "How about you two turning your minds to protecting me magically, like you're *supposed to be doing*, hm? Save the bickering till later."

When I turned back around, Satan and Fanzelle were grinning at me.

Satan said, "I hear you've been to Heaven. You'll have to tell me about it sometime—Heaven was still under construction when Fanzelle and I . . . left."

I replied, "I'm not telling you *anything*. Considering what your plans are."

Satan laughed. "Actually, I already know *a lot* about Heaven. Back when I was Lucifer, I designed the place. So stonewall me all you want—it won't set my plans back any."

I glared at Satan and Fanzelle. "Why are you two here?"

Satan said, "I'm here to make you an offer—"

"Which I'm *sure* I will agree to," I said sarcastically.

Satan's smile said *I know something you don't know.* He replied, "How would you like to get everything back? Your height, your muscles, and your billions. All you have to do is to stop opposing Hell."

I added, "And oh by the way, my soul is forfeit."

Satan smiled like a used-car salesman. "*No.* No charge. No pact will make claim to your soul when you are Judged."

Fanzelle said nervously, "Lord Satan, if you give everything back to Harper, this breaks my pact with Michelle Joan LeClerc, and I cannot collect her soul."

Satan patted Fanzelle reassuringly on the boob. "Relax, it won't be a problem."

Then Satan smiled at me. "Michelle Joan LeClerc is the latest in a long list of humans who made a pact with Hell, believing that the Soul Collection paragraph in the pact could never be invoked. They all were foolish to think that, and everyone on the list except for LeClerc is now paying for his or her foolishness. You'll be glad to know that with just a little push, I could collect LeClerc's soul tomorrow. Then you and I would be free to make our own agreement.

Which, I remind everyone here, will not require that this human forfeit his soul."

Roshradzam had been quiet all this time. Now he spoke something scornful, which made Satan glare at him.

Roshradzam's ring translated his words as "R-i-ight. As if the *one human* who could have stopped the Second Hell-Heaven War, but *didn't* because he accepted your bribe, will be rewarded with Heaven when he's Judged. Lord Satan, your 'generosity' isn't."

I spoke over my shoulder. "Well said, Roshradzam."

To Satan, I said, "No deal. For the reason that Roshradzam just stated; plus, what you're asking me to do is *wrong*."

Satan smiled at me. "How about I add Fanzelle to the deal?"

"*What?*" Fanzelle said.

I said sarcastically, "R-i-ight, I'm a married man, and let's have sex with a succubus. What could go wrong?"

"I *don't* mean that she suck your life-force out of you!" Satan snapped. "You don't forfeit your soul, you don't die, your DOFD doesn't change—it's a straight fuck or suck, your choice."

"No deal," I said.

I glanced at Fanzelle. She looked relieved.

Now Satan's voice was smarmy. "You *sure* you want to say no? Fanzelle was fucking human males *long* before those two smoke-girls behind you got stuck in lamps. Fanzelle can make your dick *see stars* when she tries hard."

"Still no deal."

Behind me, Fatima said, "Aw, part of me thinks, 'Take the deal, Master.' I would *love* to see you make Fanzelle your bitch!"

Fanzelle glared at Fatima behind me.

Now Satan looked at me with disappointment. "And my file says you're *smart*. Here's my final offer: You, Marvin Harper, are elected president of the United States in 2020. You quit bothering my demons, and you'll become president four years from now. No genie can offer this."

I did not point out that if events unfolded as Satan planned, the USA would not exist in 2020.

Instead, I said, "Nope, not interested."

Satan glared at me. "Remember, I tried to be *nice* about this." Then both Satan and Fanzelle disappeared in a flash of darkness.

****

Five minutes later

Anna Kay was not in our bed in the master bedroom. Instead, I found her asleep on the couch in the computer room. (Similarly, SJ-1 sat asleep in her chair behind her computer desk.)

I was just bending down to shake Anna Kay's shoulder when—

FOOF. Fanzelle appeared, three feet away from the couch. She said to me, "You turned down Satan's deal. Now it's going to cost you. *Big time.*"

"Oh?" I said calmly.

"Do you know how many lawyers give free legal advice to Hell, hoping it will lighten their eventual punishment?"

Fanzelle rolled her eyes at how ridiculous such a hope was.

She continued, "A lawyer in Bogotá found an interesting loophole in the Protocol. Specifically, the part that talks about 'A demon may not kill a human.'"

This time I had to work to keep my voice calm: "Oh, really?"

Fanzelle stepped closer to me, so that her huge tits were mashing against my collarbone. "Short man, here's a warning: The *next* time you try to be a hero, *especially* if you try to be a hero by preventing the Second Hell-Heaven War, you will *die*."

Chapter 26
Mars's Pep Talk

Still Tuesday

Right after Fanzelle *foof*ed away, I woke up Anna Kay and SJ-1. Anna Kay asked me, "How did it go?"

"Not good," I said. "I'll tell you tomorrow."

Anna Kay's eyes searched my face. "It was bad?"

"Many *djinn* died. So yeah."

Anna Kay and I walked up the stairs and walked to the master bedroom. We changed clothes, then she and I went to sleep.

Or rather, I *tried* to go to sleep.

After an hour of staring at the dark ceiling, I thought, *Fuck it.* I walked downstairs and into the library.

Two sides of the library were basically tinted glass, with just enough lumber to hold the ceiling up. The library now was bright enough in the moonlight that I could see the three-foot-diameter globe with the tan-colored oceans. So much moonlight meant that I could walk around the library without turning on any lights.

Which was good, because I really preferred being in the dark right now.

Case in point: I sat down in the recliner in the center of the library, which had a standing lamp only inches away. But I did not turn on the standing lamp.

I did not try to read a book.

Instead, I sat and stared at the moonlit globe and I thought dark thoughts: *Djinn who were alive for thousands of years are true-dead now, because of me.*

All three of my genies are with their Tribes right now—I'm glad I'm not hearing what my genies are being told about me.

Red and lavender light flashed—which was very noticeable in a dark room. The standing lamp and the overhead lights came on by themselves. Standing by the big globe were Mars and Venus.

Venus asked, "How was your—?"

Mars interrupted with Latin. Venus said, "Mars says you lost the battle. Is this right?"

I gave a sour laugh. "He's seen depression before, huh?"

Then I told the gods the story. ". . .I was so confident! I didn't put together any kind of back-up plan, and the *djinn*—Brown Tribe especially—were slaughtered like chickens! I was inept, and *djinn* died for it."

The two gods conferred briefly, then Venus told me, "We both agree that if you had asked, you could have 'borrowed' Mercurius to instantly find all the demons, instead of using that slow spell."

I sighed. "He's a god; I didn't want to presume. Shit, another way I fucked up."

Mars's eyes bored into mine as he spoke Latin, which Venus translated as, "Mars says he is completely confident you will win this war."

"I'm glad *he's* confident, because right now, *I'm* not confident even slightly!"

Mars replied, "As God of War, I don't make one side victorious in their war. Rather, I have an infallible instinct for who will win the war, and I bring out his winning qualities as a general."

I stared. "Your infallible instincts are *sure* I will win this thing? I can't see how."

Mars nodded gravely. "I haven't been wrong since swords were bronze."

While I was wrapping my brain around *that*, Mars spoke again: "Tell me more about the demon-locator dance-chant you used and the spoken demon-kill spell you used. How do they work? Maybe you could improve on them—make them shorter and faster-working."

I wondered, *Why is Mars asking _me_ this? I'm the exact opposite of an expert*. I said as much: "If you really want answers, ask Sumera. I'm just the schoolboy, reciting what was taught to me, but here's what I know . . ."

Soon after, I was saying, ". . . I'm guessing that beings who are magical—*djinn*, demons, angels, and regional gods like you—pull the magic out of themselves to work a magic spell. The advantage: It takes only an instant to work the spell. The disadvantage: A spell works only on a being who is of the same or lesser magic than the spellcaster."

Venus nodded. "Which explains why *djinn* spells normally cannot locate a demon, but Mercurius can locate demons easily—and he can find a regional god who's floating in the Peaceful Ocean."

Venus glanced at Mars, smiling; Mars cleared his throat. Then Mars asked a question: "How do spoken spells work? We gods of Rome have enough power in our magic that we don't need them."

Again I wondered why Mars was asking *me* this question; again I told him as much: "I'm not whom you should ask about this, but here goes. First, most things that a human, or *djinni*, or angel, or regional god can say with his mouth are not spells. If I say, 'Universe, bring me a steak dinner,' nothing happens."

Both Roman gods nodded.

I continued: "Second, once someone has thought up a spoken spell—don't ask *me* how spoken spells are invented; that's *way* above my paygrade—that spoken spell draws its magic power from the universe, not from the speaker. The magic-levels of speaker and victim don't matter—if a parrot spoke a demon-killer spell, it would kill the demon."

Mars laughed. "I would pay denarii to see this!"

I continued, "The best example of a spoken spell having the power that it needs to have, is the spoken ritual that summons a demon. As powerful as a demon is, the demon can't prevent . . ."

I did not realize that I had stopped talking until Venus was looking at me with concern. "Marvin, are you okay?"

I distractedly waved a hand. "I just got an Idea, and I'm thinking it through."

For a while, as Mars and Venus waited quietly, I was muttering to myself. At first I thought I saw a major problem with my Idea; but then I realized that the "problem" was no problem at all, because of the Protocol.

When I looked at Mars and Venus, I was grinning. "I have *a doozy* of an Idea how to beat the demons. And it's an Idea that the demons can't do *jack shit* about!"

I explained my Idea to Mars and Venus. Mars's reaction was, "It indeed sounds like a solid plan."

I rocked my hand and laughed. "Solid, just as soon as I solve a huge *practical* problem."

Seconds later, Mars squeezed my shoulder, then the Roman gods vanished. All three of us were grinning.

But as soon as I was alone in the library, my grin faded. I still had one small problem (besides the blood), which I had not mentioned to Mars and Venus—

My new Idea might well work, but my succubus enemy would make sure I did not live to see our victory.

Chapter 27
My Plan: Demon-Summoning in Bulk

Still Tuesday

After talking with Mars and Venus, I had trudged upstairs and had gone back to bed. My plan had been to sleep late and to eat a leftover breakfast.

Sometime around 3 a.m., I had fallen asleep.

Sometime while I had slept, I had dreamed of an angel telling me, "MAKE HASTE UNTO OUR LADY OF MEEKNESS HOSPITAL."

Like I said, when I had gone back to bed, my plan had been to sleep late. But the demons changed those plans.

****

Seven o'clock that same morning

I was awakened from sleep by the words of a lightball near my head. But the lightball spoke not with the counterfeited voice of an actor or a politician; instead, the lightball spoke in Fatima's own voice—

"Master, SJ-1 is headed to your door with a printout she took from CNN.com. We have a *big* problem."

"Oh, dear," said Anna Kay's sleepy voice beside me.

Seconds later, I was standing by the open bedroom door as I yawned. SJ-1 handed me a printed-out news story: "DOMESTIC-TERROR GROUP ANNOUNCES: SOON WE WILL GO 'HUNTING ANGELS.'"

According to the news story, a spokesman for "The Free People of North America"—which CNN called "a known domestic-terror group"—announced an hour ago that "within hours, we will start hunting angels."

The FBI was working itself into a lather, trying to block a terrorist threat when the FBI had no idea what kind of target was in danger. Apparently, the FBI took the Free People's announcement as some kind of code or euphemism, instead of as the literal truth.

I knew better: White-winged angels were indeed the Free People's targets. I was scared shitless—the Second Hell-Heaven War would start in a few hours!

One thing was clear: I had made plans before I had fallen asleep, figuring that I would have days and weeks to carry out those plans. Instead, now I had only hours— maybe only minutes!

****

I skipped breakfast; instead, I herded my three genies into the computer room. From there, we *foom*ed off to the spiritual-plane version of the Utah salt flats. This was where I met with the four Tribes of *djinn*.

The Pink Tribe of *Djinn* had a new Chief, I learned; his name was Gaerwulf.

I told the Tribes my idea: 667 demon-summonings, all performed in the same place, at the same time. ". . .We're going to need an empty building with floor space enough for 667 pentagrams; we'll need 3,335 candles; also, some magical way of lighting all three-thousand-plus candles—"

"*That* part is easy," said Gaerwulf.

"—and lots of writing chalk. I'll provide you a list of demon names—"

"From whom?" Ashnadim asked, looking suspiciously at Sumera. "Who's the source for this list?"

"The list of names will be reliable," I said. "Maybe an angel is the source."

I handed out to each Chief a copy of the Protocol, each copy highlighted on the last page where the text stated the rules for summoning a demon.

While I was handing out the four stapled copies of the Protocol, a man's voice from Blue Tribe asked, "What about human blood?"

I ignored the question. "Fatima has figured out a neat trick to synthesize voices magically. She'll teach all of you her trick. You *djinn* can invoke all 667 summonings at the same time, and then send all 667 demons to Hell, all at the same time."

"I like your plan, Master," Roshradzam said (via his ring). "One second, all the demons are causing shit, thinking life is fine. The next second, each demon is trapped in a pentagram. One second later, they all are sent back to Hell, and no demon is left on Earth to re-summon the others."

I grinned. "That's the idea."

A woman from Blue Tribe called out, "And the human blood, how will we get it? I don't mind grabbing a wormfood or ten and slitting their throats."

I glared at the blue *djinni* woman. "That is *so* not part of my plan."

In the end, Pink Tribe offered to provide the floor space, by means of an empty warehouse in Bucharest. Brown Tribe offered to buy the 3,335 candles and the blackboard chalk. Green Tribe and Blue Tribe would levitate the chalk to draw the pentagrams and would levitate the candles into place. Pink Tribe would magically light all the candles, once those candles were in place.

The three power Tribes (Blue, Green, and Pink) would split the task of dripping human blood into the 667 pentagrams; and the three power Tribes would split the task of creating 667 synthetic voices to summon 667 demons at once.

This presumed, of course, that human blood was available for the *djinn* to drip onto the floor.

"I plan to *buy* human blood from a local hospital," I told the gathered Tribes. "No human will be hurt, if *I* have anything to say about it!"

"It would be easier to grab some humans and to slit their throats," said the blue woman. "Just saying."

I did not dignify that with a reply.

My genies and I stayed at the salt flats until 8 a.m. Eastern time. During that time, Fatima taught everyone how to do the voice-synthesizer trick.

(Fatima touched a fingertip to a *djinni*'s forehead— *voilà*, the *djinni* instantly learned the spell. I hoped that the teacher-unions would never hear news of this; they'd fret.)

At eight o'clock, my three genies and I *foom*ed back to the mansion.

****

Eight o'clock that morning
The computer room at the mansion

I immediately phoned Our Lady of Meekness Hospital, and asked to speak with the hospital administrator. I wanted my hands on that blood ASAP.

****

8:02 a.m.
Office of the hospital administrator
Our Lady of Meekness Hospital

It had been a full day and one hour since Mother Superior Mary Saddler had been visited by an angel. Mother Mary was still trying to wrap her brain around this, and was still puzzling out the angel's mysterious message, when she walked into her outer office.

Sister Theresa smiled at her. "Marvin Harper has already called here. He wants to meet with you as soon as you can see him."

Mother Mary pulled out her smartphone, checked her scheduling app, and told Sister Theresa, "Call him back and tell him I can meet with him at ten."

As Mother Mary walked into her private office, she recalled the angel's message from yesterday—

"YOU WILL RECEIVE AN UNUSUAL VISITOR SOON. HELP HIM."

—but then Mother Mary decided that this message could not *possibly* refer to Marvin Harper. Goodness, the man kept a *harem!* A sinner like Harper could not possibly be an instrument of God.

****

8:03 a.m.
Computer room at the mansion

I had just answered my ringing smartphone.

"Mr. Harper?" I heard. "This is Sister Theresa. I just spoke to the Holy Mother, and she's agreed to see you at ten this morning."

"*Ten?* Ten is no good! I need to see her *now!*"

Sister Theresa's voice got bureaucratic: "What is your visit in regard to?"

I went silent for a while, as I decided how to answer this question. Should I maybe sound like a religious nut, or should I delay getting the blood by two hours?

Sister Theresa hasn't promised that she'll get me in earlier if I answer her question. I probably will lose, and it's very unlikely I'll gain, if I tell her the truthful answer.

"I can't tell you," I finally replied, "why I want to meet with the Holy Mother."

"Well then," Sister Theresa snapped, "You will have to settle for telling your story to the Holy Mother at ten o'clock. Goodbye."

With nothing else to do but wait to for my meeting at the Catholic hospital, I ate a late breakfast. While I worried.

*****

9:57 a.m.
The computer room at the mansion

I watched as Sumera *foom*ed off three copies of the demon-name list to the chiefs of the three power Tribes.

I asked Sumera, "*This* time, Fanzelle is at the top of the list, right? So she definitely will be Summoned?"

Sumera rolled her eyes, "*Yes*, Master, top of the list. But I still don't think she's dangerous. For a demon."

*****

9:59 a.m. (after a FOOM)
Outer office of the hospital administrator
Our Lady of Meekness Hospital

With me in the waiting room were my housekeeper Fatima (who was on the phone), *Haremée*-Sumera, and my groundskeeper Roshradzam. Roshradzam's translator-ring was in his pocket, not on his finger.

And me? I was wearing a gray two-piece suit, a long-sleeved white dress shirt, a red tie, and shiny black shoes. Plus Vulcan's dagger, hidden up my left sleeve.

Now Fatima put her magic smartphone back in the pocket of her green jeans. "The four Chiefs say everything is ready to go. They need only the human blood."

"I'm working on it," I muttered.

Fatima added, "Also, SJ-1 texted me a link. The FBI tried to arrest the Free People after they promised to 'start hunting angels.' Guess what happened?"

"Tell me."

"*Nothing* happened. All of the FBI's vehicles refused to work. Armored Personnel Carriers, helicopters, surveillance vans—none would start, and none would take a charge."

"The demons whammied all those vehicles," Sumera declared.

"Sure sounds like it," I agreed.

The phone rang on Sister Theresa's desk, Seconds later, Sister Theresa told us, "You may see the Holy Mother now."

****

Seconds later
In Mother Mary Saddler's inner office

I was shaking the mother superior's hand. "Holy Mother, I'm Marvin Harper. Thanks for agreeing to see us." I introduced Fatima, but not Sumera or Roshradzam.

Usually when I shake hands with someone for the first time, I see their expression change as they instantly become my touch-slave—this is when I've learned to blurt out, "Let's just be friends." My first clue that my meeting with Mother Mary would not be a slam-dunk was when I shook her hand: Her skeptical expression did not change.

I sat down then, in the chair that Mother Mary had led me to. My genies did not sit; they stood around my chair like the bodyguards they were acting as.

Meanwhile, Mother Mary was staring at me. "You are truly *the* Marvin Harper? The news stories claim that he somehow was made short and weak."

Mother Mary's tone of voice said *But I myself don't believe such wild tales.*

I said, "That's me. A demon named Fanzelle changed me from big, strong Marvin Harper into a runt." I watched Mother Mary for a reaction.

"Mister . . . Harper, while demons are real, they do not cause much trouble in this day and age. I'm sure that in one year, worldwide, the exorcisms that the Church performs can all be counted on one hand. If you are indeed Marvin Harper, I doubt that a *demon* did this to you."

Sumera said, "*Camelshit*, lady. If you think *that*, you've been reading last month's newspaper. You haven't noticed how much *nastier* the world has become in the last week and a half?"

Meanwhile, I had stood up, pulled my wallet from my pocket, extracted my driver's license, and laid my license on Mother Mary's desk. "The demons have staged a jailbreak, Holy Mother. Over six hundred demons are running loose on Earth now—and this isn't the worst part."

Mother Mary now was scratching at my driver's-license photograph with a fingernail, trying to make the photo come off. *Good luck with that*, since my driver's license was not a fake.

Distracted Mother Mary asked me, "What's worse than six hundred demons running loose among mankind?"

"What the demons are planning to do next," I replied. "Start another war with Heaven."

Mother Mary shot me a disbelieving look.

Fatima walked around the desk and snatched my driver's license out of Mother Mary's hands. Fatima said, "*Stop!* This man has never carried a fake license, *period*."

"How would *you* know?" Mother Mary said. Her voice was scornful: "Are you a mind-reader?"

"Something like that," Fatima replied. She handed my driver's license back to me. "Sumera and I tried to fight off the demoness, and *we were there* when Fanzelle changed Mr. Harper to look like he does now. Or am *I* a liar too?"

Sumera said, "Lady, you have the demon-transformed hero billionaire *himself* sitting in your office. Show him some respect!"

Needless to say, I was startled to hear *Sumera* telling someone else to show me respect.

I was also surprised that Sumera's remark had Mother Mary looking gobsmacked.

Gobsmacked, *and* Mother Mary was murmuring, " 'Unusual visitor' indeed." Then she asked, *meekly*, "What can I do for you, Mr. Harper?"

Trust Sumera to restart a fight when things were calming down: "Hold on. Do you believe us now about the *demon* part, or are you just acting nice to the crazy guy?"

Fatima rebuked Sumera in Arabic.

Mother Mary calmly gazed at Sumera. "Yesterday morning at prayer, I was visited by . . . someone in a white robe. He gave me a message, then disappeared. *Literally* disappeared. So yes, young lady, I believe you now."

"What was the angel's message?" I asked.

"He said, 'You will receive an unusual visitor soon. Help him.' "

"*Whoa*," said Fatima.

"So," Mother Mary repeated, "how can I help you?"

My hand went to my breast pocket and pulled out a folded check. "Officially, this thousand-dollar check is a donation to the hospital. In reality, it's a bribe. I want something from this hospital in return. *In secret.*"

Mother Mary barely glanced at the check. "Now we come to the real reason for your visit."

"I need twenty-one pints of blood. That's about ten liters. All the blood has to be of the same blood-type, and it *can't be traced to me.*"

Mother Mary shook her head. "Even if you pick up those pints of blood at the loading dock, I can't put them into your hands without creating a *huge* paper trail. And when the various clerks see the name 'Marvin Harper' as receiving twenty-one pints of blood, the news will be on Facebook five minutes later."

"*[Arabic word]!*" Fatima said.

Mother Mary said, "And five minutes after the news hits Facebook, police, the sheriff, the state medical board, and the FBI *all* will be pounding on your door. They all will be figuring that you're performing illegal surgeries." Mother Mary looked at me with a raised eyebrow.

"No surgeries," I said. "Nothing medical."

Mother Mary sighed. "It puts me and the hospital in an awkward place if we aid illegal activity. I'm not saying *no*, I'll obey the angel. I just don't want to regret saying *yes*."

Roshradzam asked Sumera a short question in Arabic. Sumera answered in two sentences. Roshradzam was quiet for two seconds, then he said something to Sumera.

Sumera said to Mother Mary, "How about this: You box up the blood, and make up paperwork like you're going to transfer it to another hospital. You store the box of blood in whatever refrigerator you normally keep blood in. We'll make the blood disappear."

"*How?*" Mother Mary asked. "If Security doesn't grab you, you'll still be videotaped walking in and walking around the hospital. Plus the refrigerator for storing blood is on the B2 level—that's two floors below street level—and strangers *will be* noticed."

Sumera's smile was smug. "Security won't see us, cameras won't see us, and employees won't. Then the box of blood will *disappear*. Just like your angel."

Mother Mary still looked skeptical.

I said, "Mother Mary, Sumera is telling the truth. Trust me. In any case, I need this blood *quickly.*"

Mother Mary asked me, "When the blood disappears, you're *sure* that neither of us will get blowback from this?"

"*None.* That box of blood will be like Senator Paula Sarin—nobody will have a clue where it went or how it left."

"May I ask what you plan to do with twenty-one pints of blood? Or am I better off not knowing?"

I looked Mother Mary in the eyes. "Do you know how to summon a demon? You draw a pentagram on the floor with chalk, you put five burning candles at the corners, then you drip human blood onto the pentagram. After this, you chant certain words, and the demon must come."

Mother Mary looked confused. "But surely you don't need twenty-one—"

"I'm not summoning *one* demon, I'm summoning *all of them.* Which requires enough human blood for 667 pentagrams. I figure ten liters of blood is enough."

Mother Mary paused, then said, "Blood coagulates quickly when exposed to air. Plan for this."

"I will. Thanks for the tip."

"How soon do you need the blood?"

"Within minutes," I replied. "And no, I'm not kidding."

Seconds later, Mother Mary was on the telephone to someone in room B2-R3 when—

FOOF.

Fanzelle grabbed the phone receiver out of Mother Mary's hand and slammed the receiver into its cradle. Fanzelle flicked her wrist, and my check burst into flames.

"If you're smart," Fanzelle said to Mother Mary, "you'll stay out of this." Fanzelle was meanwhile swatting aside green and blue fireballs that Fatima and Sumera were shooting at her.

(While Fatima and Sumera were unsuccessfully shooting fireballs at Fanzelle, those two genies also were sending green and blue message-lightballs into the floor, to inform their respective Tribes what was happening.)

Meanwhile, Fanzelle was glaring at me. "I *warned* you not to play the hero. Now you will die."

My ears popped. Then I felt *cold*.

I was outside now, in a purple-metal cage that gave me no shelter from the wind. The air was colder than I ever imagined, and all the ground outside my cage was white with snow and ice.

Chapter 28
Five Freezing Deaths?

Still Tuesday

I was at the North Pole—or at least, someplace *way* too cold. Now I felt like a thousand little pins were being stuck into my face, ears, and hands. This cold *hurt*.

Even as I started to shiver violently, my left hand *zoom*ed across my ruby ring, summoning Roshradzam.

FOOM.

Alas, Roshradzam appeared *outside* my cage, not *inside*. The Chekhovium bars blocked him from appearing next to me. Roshradzam hurried to put his translator-ring on his finger.

Fanzelle said, "You both should know that there is a second Chekhovium cage in the spiritual-plane version of this same spot. So Turd Tribesman, there is *no way* you can get next to Harper and grab him."

Roshradzam did not take Fanzelle's word; he *foom*ed away. But a second later, he *foom*ed back, looking annoyed.

I said to Roshradzam, "Fatima, Sumera, Roshradzam," then I pointed just outside the bars.

Roshradzam nodded and *foom*ed away.

Fanzelle was standing outside the cage, grinning. "That's a good idea, Harper, telling your genies to come here and break you out. I hope they try—cold temperatures are even more dangerous to *djinn* than to humans."

I saved my breath (literally) and did not respond to Fanzelle's taunt, except for a glare.

Already my ears and hands hurt. It hurt to breathe deeply. I noticed my fingernails were blue. I jammed my hands inside my suit jacket, and stuck each hand into the other arm's armpit.

FOOM. My three genies appeared, in flashes of brown, just outside my cage. All three were still wearing their American clothes. My genies stood in a straight line: Roshradzam, then Sumera, then Fatima.

"*Master!*" Fatima yelled. "Don't worry, we'll save you!"

"Camelshit," Sumera said. "Feel that cold? We're all *fucked!* But here goes."

Fatima and Sumera began moving their arms. Fireballs appeared—two blue fireballs and a green fireball. These three fireballs flew straight to where two bars crossed on the cage, and tried to melt the bars.

The bars turned red but did not melt.

Fatima said, "Let's try again." Again, blue and green fireballs flew toward the Chekhovium cage—but this time, they ran into an invisible shield just before the bars.

Fanzelle laughed. "You didn't think I'd make it *easy* for you, did you?"

Fatima said, "Plan B—we need to keep both Master and ourselves warm."

Sumera muttered, "Who died and made *you* Chief of All Tribes?" But Sumera's hands and arms resumed moving.

Sss—now two blue fireballs and a green fireball were orbiting the three bound *djinn*, while a blue and a green fireball orbited me. The fireballs around me were big and hot; I almost felt warm enough.

"Things are too easy," Fanzelle said. "Time to take that Bogotá lawyer's advice."

Now I felt achy everywhere, and the Chekhovium bars in front of me began to blur.

Roshradzam said something; his ring translated it as "*Motherfuck!*"

Sumera said, "Shit, Master is getting *old!*"

Fanzelle said, "Because I'm fucking with his Date of Fated Death."

Peachy. The cold was feeling even colder as I aged.

Fanzelle laughed. "The Protocol forbids me to kill Harper, but lets me put him where the *cold* will kill him. Aren't loopholes wonderful?"

Fatima snapped, "This is all Blue Tribe's fault, Sumera! You guys gave Demon Slut here the idea."

Sumera said, "Shut up and help me give Master more heat."

The green fireball and the blue fireball that were orbiting me, now doubled to two apiece.

Roshradzam spoke; his ring announced, "I can't move my toes."

I looked downward. As best as my old eyes could see, the feet of all three genies were frosty-white—which meant they were frozen solid.

This was trouble. When all parts of a *djinni's* body would freeze solid, the *djinni* would die. I realized that Fanzelle was not only trying to kill me, but she also was trying to kill my genies.

The fireballs orbiting me were not enough to keep me warm in my magically-caused old age. My face hurt, the top of my bare head hurt, and my feet hurt. I tried stomping my feet to get blood circulating in them.

I started to feel lightheaded and confused. I was not shivering anymore—did that mean I was warm? But I did not *feel* warm.

Now my genies were all three white and frosty, halfway between their ankles and knees. This was bad, right? I was having trouble thinking.

Roshradzam shot Sumera a look that nobody else could read, then he put his two hands together in prayer, with his upper arms parallel to the snowy ground. One of the two blue fireballs that orbited the genies, diverted to orbit only Roshradzam's hands and arms.

Sumera said, "I can't keep *all* of you warm, beloved, but I can keep *part* of you warm."

Fanzelle laughed. "You surprise me, Blue Bitch. *This* isn't the part of him I would expect you to keep alive."

Roshradzam said (through his ring), "If only there were something I could do to help Master."

Then Fanzelle's chin came up. "Excuse me, children—evil duty calls." *FOOF.*

Fatima asked me, "Are you okay, Master?"

I replied, "It's cold out here. Didn't your mothers tell you to put on a sweater? I'm sleepy."

For some reason, my three genies looked at each other in alarm.

****

Seconds later

FOOF. Fanzelle returned. Actually, the *FOOF* was in stereo; Mother Mary Saddler appeared in the cage with me.

"Hello, Holy Mother," I said.

She looked at me, now an old man. "Who are *you?* Where *are* we?" Then Mother Mary noticed my genies. "How did *they* get here?"

Fanzelle laughed. "Let me fill everyone in. Marvin, Mary was a *baaad* girl—she called downstairs to tell people to throw bags of blood into a Styrofoam box, even after I *told* her to stay out of all this."

Mother Mary said (even as her teeth were chattering), "I follow the commands of God, not threats by some slut spawn of Hell."

Fanzelle ignored the insult. "Mary, this is Marvin Harper in the cage with you. He *looks* old because I *made* him old—just like right now I'm making *you* old. Both of you will freeze to death soon, because we're on an island in way northern Canada. Mary, the three beings outside the cage are Marvin's genies. Marvin doesn't want other humans knowing his secret, but I don't care what Marvin wants—and besides, you'll be dead minutes from now."

Mary said to me, "Your bodyguards are *genies?*"

Sumera called out, "Partly-frozen genies, at the moment."

Indeed, the frozen-line for each of my genies was around knee-level.

Roshradzam said again, "If only there were something I could do to help Master."

I told my genies, "Mother Mary will freeze without our help. Warm her up with a . . . whatchacallit, like you're doing me." I could not remember the word.

"Forget it," Sumera said, "Are you crazy, thinking I'll agree to *this* magical request? A fireball for nun-lady means one less fireball for the rest of us."

Fatima shook her head sadly. "I also must refuse."

It was hard to think now, but one part of my brain said, *Shit, one more death on my conscience—and a mother superior to boot. This sucks.*

Minutes passed of my genies trying to slow down our certain deaths. The frozen-line for the genies was several inches above their knees when Fatima's magical smartphone rang.

Fatima had difficulty dealing with her phone—her arms and hands did not work right—but she managed to levitate the smartphone out of her green-jeans pocket and into the fireball-warmed hands of Roshradzam.

"Hello?" Roshradzam said (in translation). He listened for three seconds, ended the call—

—and grinned at me. Immediately after, Roshradzam walked over to Fatima—with a stiff-legged walk like Frankenstein's monster—and he stuffed the smartphone back into Fatima's pocket.

Fatima smiled distractedly at Roshradzam; her arms and hands still were moving.

Meanwhile, Roshradzam had gone back to holding his hands in prayer position, with one blue fireball again orbiting his arms and hands.

"If only there were something I could do to help Master," Roshradzam said.

I sagged down then, and let my knees hit the metal floor of the cage. I discovered that wool suit-pants gave very little insulation against the heat-sucking power of sub-freezing Chekhovium.

I uncrossed my arms enough to pull my hands out of my armpits and out of my suit-jacket. This was when I saw something interesting—

Or rather, when I *not-saw* something interesting.

I was cold and sleepy; truly it would be *so easy* to let myself slump down and fall sleep now. Instead, I ordered, "Roshradzam, walk over here."

With his Frankenstein-monster gait, Roshradzam obeyed.

I had a moment of confusion, when I could not remember why I wanted him to come over. When I remembered, kneeling-I tried to thrust my hands and wrists beyond the bars of the cage. I kept missing the spaces between the bars and whacking my hands against the cold metal. That hurt. But finally, on my third or fourth try, I managed to stick both hands out beyond the bars.

I said to Roshradzam, "I have minutes left. Give me comfort."

Roshradzam grabbed my outthrust left hand with his own left hand.

Then I looked past Roshradzam to Fanzelle, "*You*, stay away. Keep your distance while I die."

"The Heaven you say!" Fanzelle replied. The succubus walked right up to the cage, so that she was close to me—and close to Roshradzam.

Just as Fanzelle came close to the cage, a voice boomed behind her. "FALLEN ANGEL TWELVE HUNDRED THIRTY-SEVEN, WHAT YOU DO BREAKS THE SPIRIT OF THE PROTOCOL. RELEASE THESE HUMANS."

Fanzelle whirled around. "Eat shit, angel—"

But the booming voice had come not from an angel, but from a green lightball.

At the same time, all the "green" fireballs that had been orbiting either the genies or me , turned blue.

"Um, Fanzelle?" Roshradzam asked.

Fanzelle spun around. "You've *tri—*"

The dagger-sheath inside my left arm's shirtsleeve was no longer invisible. My Vulcan-made dagger was no longer invisible—that dagger, now held in Roshradzam's right hand, was quite visible.

Thanks to Sumera's warming fireball, Roshradzam's hands and arms were supple. His dagger-hand *zoom*ed past Fanzelle's neck, slashing her throat.

Fanzelle flashed into flame. When the fire ended, less than a second after it started, nothing of Fanzelle was left but drifting smoke.

I said, "Heaven, Thirteen, angels, *somebody*—please save my genies and save Mother Mary!"

****

One second later

White light flashed, and an angel appeared. "BEGONE, THESE PRISONS," he said.

The Chekhovium cage disappeared; Mother Mary and I dropped into the snow.

"COME, ALL OF YOU," the angel said.

My ears popped.

I recognized where the angel took the five of us: the spiritual-plane version of the Utah salt flats.

"BE RESTORED TO WARMTH AND LIFESPAN," the angel commanded. All three *djinn* lost their frost and could move freely. Mother Mary looked to be in her fifties again, and I again felt twenty-four. I stopped feeling cold, confused, and sleepy.

"*What just happened?*" Mother Mary asked me, as Roshradzam handed me back my dagger. I resheathed it.

I replied, "A team effort. The god Mars gave me this knife, made by the god Vulcan. Since a god made this knife, it can kill demons. Sumera made magic blue fireballs. The green fireballs were also Sumera's, to make Fanzelle the succubus think that some fireballs came from Fatima. But Fatima's magic was all going into making my knife be unnoticeable. When I stuck my hands out beyond the bars, a genie could grab my knife. I got Roshradzam to come close to me, I tricked Fanzelle into coming close to both of us, and he sliced Fanzelle's throat. Goodbye succubus."

Fatima said, "*Ahem.* Don't forget the fake angel, Master."

I smiled at Fatima. "Fatima also magicked a fake angel voice behind Fanzelle. While Fanzelle was turning around to yell at the angel, Roshradzam was pulling the knife from the sheath on my arm."

I looked at the angel: "What happens now? Why are we here at the salt flats?"

"NOW WE WAIT."

"Why?" I asked.

Mother Mary gasped. "Don't question an angel!" She dropped to her knees. "Blessed angel, please forgive—"

"WE WAIT BECAUSE WE OF HEAVEN CANNOT HELP WITH THE MASS-SUMMONING IN BUCHAREST THAT THE *DJINN* ATTEMPT. BUT KNOW, MARY SADDLER, THAT YOUR BRAVE ACT HAS THWARTED AN EVIL PLAN OF HELL."

Reader, have you ever seen a Mother Superior *grin?*

Not ten seconds later, Fatima's magic smartphone rang. She was not on the phone for more than a few seconds before she too was grinning. *Success!*

"FREE *DJINN*, COME HERE," the angel said. White light flashed everywhere, and now the six of us were surrounded by all four Tribes. Summoned Ashnadim was still holding a green smartphone in his hand.

What is the angel up to <u>now?</u> I wondered.

Chapter 29
Happily Ever After (With Two Exceptions)

A second later (Tuesday)

The angel said, "A PROMISE MADE TO THE BOUND *DJINN* WILL BE KEPT TODAY. COME OUT, BOUND *DJINN* ALESER, THRIM, AND KHARMESH."

Sumera and Roshradzam started to chatter to each other in Arabic, and their faces looked *hopeful*.

Oddly, Fatima did not look *hopeful*, she looked *thoughtful*.

Mother Mary asked me, "What is happening?"

I answered, "My guess is, six genies are about to be mustered out."

I asked Fatima, "Why are those three not here after the angel called them out?"

She replied, "It takes a bound *djinni* time to smoke-out when he's in his lamp. Twenty-three seconds, in my case."

When about twenty-three seconds had passed after the angel's command, the angel gave another command: "BOUND *DJINN* ALESER, THRIM, AND KHARMESH, COME HERE."

White flashes brought three *djinn*: Kharmesh of Blue Tribe, a male dressed in green, and a male dressed in Barbie-pink and rose-pink Viking clothing.

Kharmesh sent an inquiring look to Sumera, while the male Green Tribe genie shot an inquiring look to Fatima. Both female genies shrugged.

Meanwhile, the angel was saying, "LONG AGO, THE SEVEN BOUND *DJINN* WERE PROMISED, 'YOU ALL

WILL BE FREED ON THE DAY THAT ALL YOUR TRIBES PROVE WORTHY OF YOUR FREEDOM.' TODAY IS THAT DAY, BECAUSE TODAY ALL FOUR TRIBES WORKED TOGETHER AND THWARTED A PLOT OF HELL."

Then the angel said, "SUMERA, ALESER, THRIM, KHARMESH, FATIMA, AND ROSHRADZAM, YOU *DJINN* ARE FREE FROM YOUR BINDINGS."

And the crowd went wild.

****

Five seconds later

Ashnadim was hurrying toward Fatima, arms out, clearly intending to hug her. But then Fatima put both her hands up, palms out, in a *Stay back* gesture.

Ashnadim looked as confused as I felt. What was Fatima up to?

Fatima put two fingers into her mouth and whistled loudly (a trick she might have learned by memory-reading Uncle Warren). The yelling and laughing of the *djinn* instantly changed into surprised silence.

Fatima said, "Angel, I ask to keep my binding. I ask to stay a genie who grants wishes."

"Fatima, are you *crazy?*" asked the Green Tribe male (as translated by Roshradzam's ring).

"Crazy? *No,*" Fatima replied. "Some human masters are shitheads, it's true. But some masters, like Ali the Goat-Herder and Marvin Harper here, are kind and good. Such humans deserve a good life; but sadly, the kind and good humans often are abused and are taken for granted instead of being rewarded. Thus it was with Ali the Goat-Herder; thus it was with Marvin Harper. But each of them came to own my Vessel, and I gave two good humans each the good life he deserved. Good and kind humans of the future deserve reward too."

"*Wow*, Fatima," I murmured.

"YOUR REQUEST IS GRANTED, FATIMA OF THE GREEN TRIBE OF *DJINN*," said the angel. "YOUR BINDING TO THE LAMP IS RESTORED, AND MARVIN STEVEN HARPER IS AGAIN YOUR MASTER."

Now Fatima let Ashnadim hug her, but Ashnadim's expression was sad, not joyous.

The angel was not done with us yet: "MARVIN STEVEN HARPER, STEP FORWARD."

****

Seconds later

I walked toward the angel, as commanded; but Fatima walked next to me.

The angel said, "AS REWARD, YOU ARE GRANTED THREE HEAVENLY REQUESTS. THE ONLY RULES ARE THAT YOU MAY NOT ASK FOR SOMETHING EVIL, OR ASK FOR SOMETHING THAT GOES AGAINST GOD'S PLAN FOR THE WORLD. USE THESE REQUESTS WISELY, FOR THEY SURPASS GENIE WISHES."

"*Shit*," Fatima said.

The angel looked at me expectantly.

****

One second later

But the next to speak was not I, it was Fatima: "So Master can become president? He may request to live a hundred years longer? He can resurrect someone?"

"YES."

"*Whoa*," I said.

Then I said, "My first Request is easy: Give me back what the succubus stole from me: my height, my muscles, and my billions."

"DONE."

I began to grow and to become strong. In 2010 it had taken a week to go from short and puny to very tall and very muscular; but now the process took fifteen seconds. Thankfully, my growth was also painless.

Mother Mary watched my transformation, wide-eyed; I was *very* glad that, just as in 2010, when my body got bigger, my clothes got bigger too. (I would hate to freak out a mother superior with my wardrobe malfunction.)

When I stopped growing, I said to the angel, "I know what my second request is, but I don't want to say it here. How do I make my request later, at the mansion?"

"SIMPLY SAY, 'ANGEL, PLEASE COME.' " Then the angel smiled slightly. "NO PENTAGRAM IS NECESSARY."

With those words, the angel vanished in white light.

****

Meanwhile

The Tribes were acting like it were New Year's Eve and V-J Day combined, and the former genies were the guests of honor. The green-dressed male and the pink-dressed male were *foom*ed away by grinning *djinn* of their respective Tribes. Kharmesh was taken away too, but he insisted on giving me a rib-crushing hug before blue *djinn* *foom*ed him away.

Fatima would have also been taken away by kinsmen, but she smilingly waved off Green Tribe *djinn* in order to remain at my side.

The partying was not only within each Tribe. Everywhere I looked, I saw *djinn* of different-colored clothing talking together. Friendly, not angry. I smiled.

Bashira of Green Tribe *foom*ed up. She hugged Fatima, pulled my head down for a kiss on the cheek, magicked me a silver goblet of fig juice, and *foom*ed away.

Then my view of the two thousand celebrating *djinn* was partly blocked by grinning Roshradzam and grinning Sumera. Her arm was wound around his.

"Sumera and I are getting married," Roshradzam told me (through his translator-ring). "Respected former master, you are invited to the wedding."

Sumera added, "As soon as we figure out *how to hold* the wedding. There has never been an inter-Tribe wedding before ours ."

"I'm sure *I'm* invited," Fatima said sarcastically.

Roshradzam almost spoke, but then he looked at Sumera with a raised eyebrow. Sumera paused a second, then said, "Yes, Fatima, you are invited. Aleser and Thrim are invited too."

While Fatima stared in shock, Sumera pulled her arm free of Roshradzam's. Sumera asked me, "Can you and I talk alone?"

"Sure," I said, "but first, let me be the first to give you two a wedding gift." Handing the silver goblet to Fatima, I pulled off my ruby ring and held it out to Roshradzam. "Roshradzam, I'm glad *you* were guarding my back."

Fatima said, "Master, *your* ring is a Vessel. His hand will turn to smoke—"

I shrugged. "The ring is his, regardless." I dropped my ring onto Roshradzam's palm. Nothing happened—

—except that right afterward, I got my second hard hug of the day.

****

Seconds later

Sumera and I were standing twenty feet away from everyone else.

Sumera said, "No other master has ever made promises to me. Even more surprising, you *kept* your promises. You never asked me whether I had learned magic from demons, and you never ordered me back into my lamp."

I shrugged a no-big-deal shrug.

Sumera said, "I'll never tell *them*"—she waved her arm to mean all four Tribes—"the answer to the demon-question, but I've already told Roshy, and now I'll tell you. The answer is—"

"Yes," we both said at the same time.

I said, "HatesBeauty taught you a lot."

Sumera grinned. "You have *no* idea. Watch *this*."

Sumera mouthed words, while her fingers made gestures; a rectangle appeared in the air. That rectangle was made out of something other than paper.

Sumera caught the document before it fluttered to the ground, and handed it to me.

"Holy shit," I said, seconds later. I was reading the pact between Fanzelle and Michelle Landrieu-LeClerc.

When I was eyeing Michelle's signature—written in dried blood, no shit—I heard a collective gasp. Michelle's pact was snatched out of my hand.

Satan was standing two feet in front of me and glaring at me. "That pact is *my* property."

"This is not your day," I replied. "On top of everything else, you got your file drawer looted."

****

A few minutes later

Fatima *foom*ed Mother Mary and me over to Mother Mary's office at Our Lady of Meekness Hospital.

I said to Mother Mary, "I have a selfish request to make: that you not tell anyone that I'm a genie-master."

"I have to tell my confessor. But I'll *also* tell him that you rescued me from a demon, and I'll be sure to mention seeing an angel. So don't worry, my son."

Mother Mary blessed both Fatima and me, then Fatima *foom*ed us over to the computer room at the mansion.

SJ-1 stared, and Anna Kay shouted and ran to kiss me, when they saw my now-tall, now-muscular self.

****

That evening

Dinner was wild. I was in a wonderful mood, since I was again tall, muscular, and rich. The sexual tension in the monster kitchen was off the charts—Fatima and SJ-1 were the only women *not* acting like they were seconds away from ripping my clothes off.

Anna Kay gave me a blowjob under the table in front of the entire harem; it had been two years since she had last done that.

Of course *Haremée*-Sumera and my groundskeeper were not at dinner. Nobody mentioned their absence.

****

Dinner was a near-orgy, but *after* dinner was the opposite: nearly everyone got sick with a stomach bug.

By nine-thirty, Fatima and I were the only ones in the mansion who had not puked into a toilet.

"I can't explain this food poisoning," unhappy Fatima told me. "Everyone in the kitchen is your touch-slave; it's unthinkable that any of them take shortcuts."

At 10 p.m., a doubly-miserable Rivka Goldheim knocked on the bedroom door. "Marvin sir, the Sex Schedule says I'm supposed to serve you tonight. But I'm sorry, I can't. It's all I can do, not to puke on the green rug right here."

I said polite things to Rivka and sent her back to her bedroom. But inside, a suspicion was forming.

By the Sex Schedule rules, since Rivka was unable to fuck me, I would ask the next woman on the list, who was Tiffni Daniels.

Before I went to talk to Tiffni, I stopped just outside my bedroom door and knocked on Fatima's door. Fatima invited me in.

Once the door was shut, I said, "I have two magical requests for you. The first one is, Please go to the twins' room and try to cure them of this food poisoning."

Fatima looked at me, puzzled. "Not a problem. And the second request?"

I said, "Actually, I suspect your spell will fail, because I think this 'bug' is from Satan. Michelle LeClerc's soul is forfeit when two *haremées* turn me down for sex on the same day. "

Fatima nodded her understanding.

I said, "Rivka said no sex tonight; Tiffni probably will too. So my second request is that if I give you the word by smartphone, please *foom* yourself, me, and the twins to their mother's house. Even if the twins are sick."

Fatima's smile was wolfish. "You want to *see* Michelle board the train to Flamesville?"

I dodged the question, saying instead, "Please call me when you've healed the twins. Or were unable to."

A minute after I walked into my bedroom to wait, I was phoned by Fatima. She said, "You were right. My spell should have the twins doing cartwheels along the hallway; but no, they still look like zombies."

"Stand by," I said. "I'm putting the phone down for a minute or two."

I left my smartphone (not hung up) on my night table. I walked out of my bedroom and down the hallway to Tiffni's room, knocked on her door, and spoke with her briefly. As soon as apologetic Tiffni shut her door, I ran back to my bedroom and scooped up my smartphone.

"*Let's go, let's go, let's go!*" I yelled into the phone.

My ears popped.

****

An instant later

Two miserable twins, Fatima, and I all were in a garage. A car was parked in this garage; but part of a pentagram, with dried blood-drops in the center, could be seen underneath the car.

Almira breathed, "Shit, Elvie, Mother really went and called up that demon-lady."

Fatima had already walked up to the door that led into the house. She gestured briefly; "Door is unlocked." Then Fatima added, "I hear voices: Satan and Michelle."

I said, "Twins, you go in first. Then Fatima; I'm last."

As I was waiting to enter the laundry room, I heard Satan's voice: ". . . *her* part of the pact, and now it's time to fulfill *your* part. A deal is a deal."

I heard Michelle's voice: "Girls, this is *not* a good—Who are *you?*" When I walked into the living room, Michelle growled, "Elvie, call the police!"

I spoke directly to Satan: "You can't take Michelle."

Satan sneered, "*Of course* I can take her! *Haremées* Rivka Goldheim and Tiffni Daniels both turned you down for sex today—"

I said, "Uh-huh, *after* they both came down with food poisoning that magic couldn't cure."

"*Magic?*" Michelle asked Almira. "How does Harper have access to magic?" (Somehow Fatima kept from rolling her eyes.)

Now I noticed Michelle looking up and down my 6'8", muscular body. I *knew* Michelle was wondering, *How did he get big again after Fanzelle whammied him?*

Meanwhile, Satan was saying to me, "It doesn't matter whether the women turned you down for sex by free choice or after a nudge. The pact is fulfilled."

I shook my head. "The pact says that when the condition is met, *Fanzelle* collects Michelle's soul. You're not Fanzelle, so Michelle's soul may not be collected."

Satan waved off my words. "A technicality."

Satan looked at Michelle and said, "Right now, Fanzelle is on assignment—"

"Fanzelle is *dead*," I said to Satan. "*You know* I watched her die."

Satan looked angry now. "Are you trying to barracks-lawyer *me?* There are three signatures on this pact; the third one is mine. I have full authority to take her soul."

"No you don't," I said. "Let me repeat: The terms of the pact are not fulfilled."

"I covered this, mortal. Just because demoness Fanzelle is dead—"

I laughed in Satan's face. "What are Fanzelle's requirements under the pact? To make me become not-rich *and* not a hero, right? *I just stomped on your plans for a Second Hell-Heaven War*—I'm the biggest fucking hero on the planet."

It was fun to watch Satan's face when realization hit. When Satan finally opened his mouth to speak—

—the pact vanished out of his hand in a flash of white light. An angel appeared and said, "THE PACT IS INDEED VOID, LUCIFER CALLED SATAN. BEGONE NOW."

Satan snarled, "I was leaving anyway, Thirteen." Satan disappeared.

Michelle said, "*Thank* you, angel, for saving me."

"YOUR THANKS ARE MISPLACED. IT WAS *MARVIN HARPER* WHO SAVED YOU, BY AN ACT OF KINDNESS AND MERCY THAT YOU DO NOT DESERVE."

Michelle said, "I owe my life to *him?* The Patriarchy incarnate?"

"HEED THIS WARNING: ALREADY YOUR SINS ARE GREAT, MICHELLE JOAN LeCLERC. EVEN WITHOUT THE PACT, YOU WILL BURN IN HELL WHEN YOU DIE, IF YOU DO NOT CHANGE YOUR WAYS."

With those words, the angel Thirteen vanished.

"Nonsense," Michelle said, "I'm no great sinner. Now Elvie, call the police—"

Elvira said, "Mother, I'm *not* in the mood for you. You lied to Dad about us, and you lied to us about Dad. Zip it."

Michelle puffed up. "Elvira Karen LeClerc, how *dare* you—?"

Almira said, "Mother, you're busted, so *shut the fuck up* or I'll puke on you. I've decided I'm moving to Colorado to be with Dad and Alicia, if Elvie will come with me."

Elvira glared at her mother. "In a heartbeat, Almie. I have *no reason* to stay here."

Michelle looked sad then; I almost felt sorry for her.

****

Seconds later

We four walked back out to the garage. Elvira looked at the under-the-car pentagram and shook her head.

Then she looked at me, confused. "You saved Mother's sorry ass from Satan. *Why?*"

I shrugged. "I don't hate your mother, Elvira, and she doesn't deserve to die because she's a fool."

That's when Fatima *foom*ed the four of us to the twins' room at the mansion, then Fatima *foom*ed herself and me to the computer room.

****

One second later

The computer room was empty except for Fatima and me; both SJ-1 and Anna Kay were sick in their rooms.

"Angel, please come," I said in the nearly-empty computer room.

Seconds later, I was telling the angel, "For my second Heavenly Request, I ask you to resurrect Kelly Brown, and also the Williams family next door who all were massacred. I want them all to be not just alive but also healthy, as if they never were killed."

"YOUR COMPASSION DOES YOU CREDIT. BUT GOD'S PLAN CANNOT ALLOW MORE THAN ONE RESURRECTION AMONG THOSE FIVE PEOPLE."

I picked the person I knew best: "Kelly Brown."

White light flashed, and Kelly Brown appeared on the carpet of the computer room. But she was naked, she was curled up into a ball, she was screaming, and she reeked of lit matches.

I dropped down, put a hand on her shoulder and said in a quiet, calm voice, "Kelly? *Kelly!* It's me, Marvin. Everything's okay. You're alive and out of Hell."

Her screaming stopped. She uncurled enough to look at my face.

Then she scrambled to her knees, threw her arms around me, hugged me fiercely, and began sobbing.

The angel asked, "WHAT IS YOUR THIRD HEAVENLY REQUEST?"

"I'll make it later," I replied.

The angel vanished in white light as Fatima and I tried to calm down Kelly Brown, who was sobbing and shaking.

****

The next morning (Wednesday)

Everyone in the mansion had recovered from their stomach flu, so breakfast was back to normal—until Kelly Brown walked in, wearing borrowed clothes of Anna Kay's.

Reader, did you ever hear *an entire room* gasp?

Someone said, "Um, Kelly? We were told you *died*."

Kelly's laugh was a little crazy. "I died, yes. Then I went to Hell. Hell is no fun at all, ladies. Then Marvin Harper got me resurrected. If I weren't again pledged to celibacy, I'd be thanking Marvin by fucking his brains out this entire day. Hell, this entire *week*."

****

After breakfast, Fatima and I walked Almira and Elvira into the computer room. I opened up a drawer of the computer desk, pulled out Sumera's brass lamp, and *almost* handed the lamp to Almira. "Almira, I have bad news and good news. All the genies except Fatima are free, so now this is only a 632 B.C. brass lamp."

Amazingly, usually-bitchy Elvira said nothing.

I handed the lamp to Almira. As I expected, she rubbed the old brass lamp. Nothing happened.

"May I?" Fatima asked.

Almira handed Sumera's lamp to Fatima.

Fatima pretended to look over the brass lamp. She too rubbed the old brass lamp; again no genie came out.

Fatima handed the lamp back, telling Almira, "You could fill this with olive oil and use it like a candle. *Or* you could polish it up and sell it on eBay."

Fatima shot me a quick, ironic smile.

"*Fuck*," Almira said, "after I spent so much time figuring out my wishes."

Elvira said, "Almie, Marvin said he had good news too."

I looked at the ceiling and said, "Angel, please come."

I surprised the twins when I told the angel, "I have one Heavenly Request left. I want to pass it to Almira. Almira loaned me Sumera's lamp because I needed it, but now Almira will never get wishes granted by Sumera."

"AGREED. ALMIRA SHARON LeCLERC, YOU HAVE ONE HEAVENLY REQUEST. USE IT WISELY."

Almira looked overwhelmed. "What are the rules?"

I answered Almira's question. I also told the twins my first two Requests: getting my wealth and my heroic body back, and . . .

"*You* really resurrected Kelly Brown?" Elvira asked.

I shrugged. "I thought she got a raw deal, and I could fix that. So yeah."

Elvira turned to Almira, excited. "You could ask the angel to make you a *billionaire*, like the angel did to Marvin. You could be *rich*."

Almira smiled a small smile. "Don't you remember all the stuff Virgilia told us? Marvin's old uncle was worth billions, but he had nobody who loved him, and so he died sad and lonely. There's only one thing I *really* want, because I would feel like *utter shit* if I didn't have it. "

"What's that, Almie?" Elvira asked.

Almira took her twin's hand. "*You*, Elvie. When I was making up my list of wishes to ask Sumera for, I kept coming back to the truth that no granted wish would make me happy if you *died* on me. Virgilia told me that all I could do to prevent this would be to wish you living for nine years longer. But what if you were going to die *tomorrow?*"

Still holding Elvira's hand, Almira turned to face the angel. "My twin and I are twenty-eight. I Request that we live at least another sixty years longer, we are as healthy as possible for as long as possible, and—*this* is the important part, angel—Elvie and I die on the same day."

"DONE," the angel said. "YOU BOTH WILL DIE ON THE SAME DAY WHEN YOU ARE EIGHTY-NINE. USE THIS KNOWLEDGE WISELY."

The angel vanished.

Elvira threw her arms around her twin. "Almie, I love you, I love you! You gave up a fortune—"

Then Elvira looked at me thoughtfully. "Marvin took the million dollars that I wished for, and deposited all that cash in the bank. He promised to write me a million-dollar check, but he hasn't done it yet."

I laughed. "I've been busy for the last two weeks."

Still hugging her twin, Elvira said, "Almie? You're going to *love* this."

****

The next day (Thursday)
The Community Bank of Colorado Springs
Colorado Springs, Colorado

I was recognized as soon as the twins and I walked into the bank. Call me vain, but it was nice to again hear the whispered comments of "That's the hero billionaire! My gosh, he's *big!*"

I was wearing a suit, and the twins were wearing serious business clothing. For what we were about to do, we needed to all be taken seriously.

We were greeted by a middle-aged man, also in a suit. "Mr. Harper, we are honored to have you visit our bank. I'm Stanley Brewer, bank manager."

We shook hands, and I saw the change in his eyes. Instantly I said, "Let's just be friends." I caught Almira and Elvira sharing a glance.

A minute later, the twins were seated in front of Brewer's desk. I too had been given a chair in front of that desk; but at the moment, I was standing, not sitting.

I reached into the inside pocket of my suit-jacket. "Here's my pilot's license. With picture ID." I laid the pilot's license on Brewer's desk. "And here's my back-East driver's license." I pulled out my wallet, plucked my driver's license from my wallet, and laid my driver's license on Brewer's desk. "Also with picture ID." I sat down.

Brewer looked hopeful, like he *maybe* was holding a winning Powerball ticket. "Are you opening an account with us, Mr. Harper? Have you moved to our city?"

"*I'm* not moving here, but Almira and Elvira are. They just arrived in town." *Brought here in my private jet*, I did not add. "The twins have family here." *Their father, his second wife, and a half-brother and half-sister whom the twins have never met*—I did not mention this either.

I looked into Brewer's eyes. "The reason I'm here in your bank, and the reason I presented documentation, is because of these." I reached inside my suit-jacket and pulled two folded checks from the breast-pocket of my shirt. "The twins wish to open bank accounts."

Each check was made out to one of the twins, each check bore my signature, each check said "GIFT" in big letters on the Memo line, and each check was for a half-million dollars.

As Brewer was staring at the checks, I said, "I came here to tell you: That's my signature. Twice."

Brewer laughed a stunned laugh. "Mr. Harper, your presence here helps a lot."

I smiled. "I figured that without me here, the best that the twins could hope for would be a two-week wait before they could spend this money."

I did not mention that the most likely scenario would be that someone in Colorado would discover that the twins were parolees, and they would get arrested for check forgery—possibly in front of their father and new family. Sure, the situation would be straightened out after a few days—but the twins would spend those days rotting in jail.

But I had averted that problem. Now I sat back and listened as Brewer eagerly discussed check colors and savings plans with the twins.

There was one flag on the play, however. Brewer apologetically told us that all the money in all the twins' accounts would be frozen until each twin could document a local address—"Show me a rental contract, or a closing contract, and I'll release your funds. Sorry, it can't be a hotel or motel."

"Not a problem," I said. I stood up, pulled out my wallet again, and laid my titanium credit card on Brewer's desk. "How much cash can I withdraw with that?"

"Ten thousand dollars" was Brewer's quick answer.

Ten minutes later, the twins and I walked out of the Community Bank. The twins now were each five thousand dollars cash-richer.

Almira said, "I can't believe you *gave* us each five thousand dollars, just because that bank was anal."

Elvira said, "Hell, *I* still can't believe you lawyered Mother out of going to Hell."

Almira and Elvira shared a twin-look that I could not read. Then Almira asked me, "What are your plans now?"

I shrugged. "Get a hotel room, watch TV until seven o'clock, go to the steakhouse and eat dinner with you two and your new family, pay the bill at the steakhouse, go back to the hotel, watch more TV, sleep, eat breakfast, then fly home tomorrow morning."

Almira made a face. "So your plan between now and the steakhouse is to *watch lots of TV?*"

I shrugged. "If the TV gets boring, I'll hit the gym. Every good hotel has one."

Almira shot Elvira another twin-look. Elvira nodded.

Almira stepped forward and stroked my suit-jacket with a hand. She stared into my eyes with her own cobalt-blue eyes. In a smoky voice, Almira asked, "Have you ever fucked *twins?*"

"Have you ever fucked *big-breasted* twins?" Elvira purred, while she squeezed my bicep through my sleeve.

Epilogue
April 17, 2068

Tuesday

The day after I had given Fatima away forever, I woke up with a headache.

It was a little after 5 a.m. My second wife, Virgilia, was snoring. I let her sleep.

I caught myself planning to speak to Fatima during breakfast about a healing spell for my headache. Then I remembered that One, Fatima was not in my life anymore; and Two, the closer I got to my Date of Fated Death, the less Fatima's healing spells had worked. I needed a wheelchair now, despite Fatima's best magical efforts.

Thinking about Fatima made me wonder where she was now. It was night in San Diego, so was Fatima hanging out with Green Tribe in Cairo now? Was she stuck in her lamp for decades to come? I hoped that Juanita Gutierrez was a good master for Fatima.

Then I remembered something, and quit worrying. Fatima and "Sheila J." (the former SJ-1) had spent *months* searching for a suitable next master for Fatima. Juanita was the best of the best; she would be a great master for Fatima.

And I was rock-solid sure that Fatima would be a great genie for Juanita.

Virgilia's snoring stopped. She rolled over to look at me in the dark. She whispered, "Popsicle, are you awake?"

"Yes, I've got a headache. Go back to sleep."

"Tonight I'll make up on my sleep," Virgilia said. "Or maybe I won't."

I heard what Virgilia was *not* saying. I grabbed her hand in the darkness and I kissed it.

"Wanna fool around?" Virgilia asked. Now her voice was playful.

I laughed weakly. " 'Sorry, honey, I have a headache.' How about we go downstairs and find out what kind of cold breakfast we can throw together?"

"You got it, Popsicle."

Considering that Virgilia now needed a walker and I now needed a wheelchair, the formerly simple task of taking a shower and getting dressed was a challenge. Not to mention, my headache was a nuisance. It was after six when Virgilia was ready to roll me out of the bedroom.

As we were opening the bedroom door—at our age, opening the door was a team effort by both of us—I said, " 'Today is the day which the Lord hath made.' So let me tell you I love you, Virgilia."

Virgilia did not reply in words; instead, she squeezed my shoulder.

Once past the door, Virgilia was pushing my wheelchair over the asparagus-green hallway rug. I broke the silence: "Fatima gave me this rug." Then I said, very quietly so that the 2068 *haremées* would not hear, "I *still* can't believe that Fatima gave up her freedom for m—"

That's when my headache went supernova. William Shakespeare himself could not describe my agony.

I was dimly aware of hot liquid flowing out of my nose and flowing over my lips and chin.

Virgilia started yelling then, calling for help. But then her voice began to fade. Meanwhile, the almost-dark hallway now held a glowing mist. That mist then glowed brighter and brighter, even as the voices of Virgilia and several *haremées* got quieter.

At the same moment that the voices around me faded to silence, the mist was glowing so brightly that all I could see was white.

Whiteness everywhere, silence everywhere.

Then the whiteness, the silence, and the agony all stopped, and I found myself in a corridor.

****

A second later

The walls, ceiling, and floor of the corridor were pearlescent. If I had not already known that this was my Date of Fated Death, all that pearl would have clued me in that I had kicked the bucket.

The sudden, white-flash appearance of an angel, a few feet in front of my wheelchair, was another clue.

"It is good to see you again, Marvin Steven Harper," the angel said. Amazingly, this angel was not speaking with the angels' usual booming voice. "I am Thirteen. Come."

I said, "You need to be patient, Thirteen, or you need to push the wheelchair."

"You are not a frail old man anymore. Step out of that wheelchair and walk with me."

Not frail? Sure enough, the skin on the back of my hands was young and smooth. I tried to stand; it was easy.

"What happens now?" I asked Thirteen.

"You are greeted by family, friends, and admirers; then you are Judged."

"Lead on, Thirteen," I said calmly. We walked.

Now Reader, if you were Judged long ago, you might not remember those moments between your death and being Judged. Was I scared? Not at all; I had no fear of being assigned to Hell. But I figured that fifty-six years of fucking both my wife and my harem would cost me lots of points. I expected to be assigned to Heaven's slum.

Thirteen and I walked in silence till we got to the end of the corridor. That's when I saw my "family, friends, and admirers." I was shocked.

****

An instant later

The corridor of pearl led into a room the size of my mansion's ballroom. That room was filled with people dressed in almost-white, all facing me when I entered the room. Every person there looked young.

A throng of people were in front, and a huge crowd of people stood behind them. I recognized *nobody* in the crowd at the back. Two people broke loose from the front throng and ran to me: Anna Kay and Kelly Brown.

Anna Kay had died of cervical cancer when she was sixty-nine, and Kelly had died (for the second time) in a car crash at forty-two. But now both women looked like high-school seniors—wearing their mothers' clothes.

Anna Kay kissed me (and kissed me, and kissed me), as onlookers clapped. When Anna Kay finally stopped the kissing, she looped her arm through mine and said to me, "Talk to Kelly."

Kelly Brown grabbed my hands in both of hers. "After you get Judged, look me up. I'm on Level 1,182, meaning I have a two-room apartment that is 622 square feet. It isn't big, but angels send me chocolate and strawberries whenever I ask."

I replied, "Level 1,182? That sounds about right. I figure that in an hour, I'm going to be your neighbor."

"*Pfft*, like *you* will get a high Level! But still, you want to know the *best* part about my afterlife?"

Anna Kay chuckled. "Brace yourself, Marvin."

I wondered, *Brace for what?* Aloud, I asked, "What's the *best* part, Kelly?"

"Even better than all the chocolate and strawberries I want, I'm *not burning in fire every second of every day!* And I owe *this* to *you!*" Kelly threw her arms around me and hugged me with all her strength.

Then Kelly looped an arm through my free arm, and Kelly and Anna Kay dragged me toward the waiting throng.

In that throng were other people from my life—

• Mother Superior Mary Saddler;

• Jerngert of Pink Tribe, and Nadaar of Green Tribe;

• Aunt Claire and Uncle John;

• Eleven former *haremées*, including Bellina Mott, Janice Wesley, and Sherry Benson;

• My lifelong friend, Tim Hanson; and

• Mom and Dad.

Mother Mary and Jerngert had the seemingly-spotlit faces that marked them as Saintly. Interestingly, Aunt Claire had the spotlight-look, but her glow covered her whole body.

I asked Thirteen, "Why does Aunt Claire look like that? The full-body glow?"

Thirteen answered, "Claire Brigitte Greenwich is one of the Most Saintly. As is King Solomon, who has chosen to stand in the back of the room because he is a stranger to you." Thirteen pointed to a Middle East-looking man who was wearing rich whitish clothing and a gold crown. Sure enough, the crowned man also had a full-body glow.

Thirteen added, "This might interest you: The Saintly man talking with King Solomon"—Thirteen referred to a well-dressed man with Middle Eastern features—"is Saintly Ali bin Bilal. He wants to meet you."

"Ali the Goat-Herder? I want to meet him too."

After this conversation, Thirteen allowed me ten minutes to talk with my family and friends. I got many hugs—even from Mother Mary—and everyone assured me that my Judgment would be a piece of cake.

I did not argue with my welcomers, but inside I was not as optimistic as they. All the religious leaders I had ever heard, agreed that God *hated* sex and He *really* hated orgasms. So how would a man who'd had a thirty-three-women harem for fifty-eight years be Judged?

So Reader, I was just like you. You probably were nervous when you were Judged—I tell you, I *definitely* did not swagger into Inprocessing North.

****

My Judgment was *not* like everyone else's.

It started out the same: I was taken into a wide room that had a sign on the front wall, "Inprocessing North." At the front of the big room were three screens, three short pedestals, six angels, and Most Saintly Peter. At the back of the room were three lines.

I went to the back of the far-left line and waited my turn. I did not have to wait long, because each of those screens needed only a minute to show a human's entire life, and the two film-review angels for each human talked only briefly with Most Saintly Peter—my line moved quickly.

The man right in front of me was sentenced to Hell. He started yelling when Most Saintly Peter announced his Judgment. An angel had to carry the Hell-bound man into the pearl-painted "Judged Beings Only" room; he refused to walk there.

Then it was my turn—and something weird happened: Thirteen talked to one of my two film-review angels and got that angel to white-flash away. Thirteen took his place.

They started to show the film of my life. I noticed that the woman on the middle pedestal was watching my screen instead of her own screen.

One minute after my film started, it finished. Then Thirteen, the other angel, and Most Saintly Peter conferred. Based on what I had seen, I expected only one minute of three-way gabbing before Most Saintly Peter announced his verdict about my Eternal Reward—two minutes at the most.

Five minutes in, I was still being discussed.

The talks had been going on for a while—ten minutes? fifteen?—when a giant angel with a sheathed sword appeared, as did Most Saintly King Solomon. Then the three-way discussion of my Eternal Destiny became a five-way discussion—which lasted for many more minutes.

Reader, I had not worried when I had stepped onto the pedestal, but I was worried now.

But when Most Saintly Peter walked forward to announce his Judgment, he smiled at me. King Solomon also smiled at me. Even Thirteen was smiling (a little).

Level *Three?* I am to be called *Most Saintly* Marvin Harper? This is a joke, right?

THE END

Previous novels and stories by Doctor MC, Mad Scientist:
- **"Captive of the Barbarian King"**
- *Names Have Power: Tim's Magic Voice Makes a Harem*
- *Three More Wishes: Be Kind to Your Genie*
- *The Bimborg: Part Nanobot, All Woman*
- **"The Hypno-Talker of Zlar" (HTOZ1)**
- **"Hypno-Talker's First Download" (HTOZ2)**
- **"Revenge at College" (HTOZ3)**
- **"Nerd Saves Women" (HTOZ4)**
- *The Hypno-Talkers of Zlar Four-in-One*
- *One More Genie*
- *Ye Olde Book of Magic*
- *Bimbo-Midas: His Magic Touch Changes Women*

Find out about Doctor MC's previous novels and stories, and read free sample chapters, at:
http://doctormcmadscientist.wordpress.com/about/

Find out about Doctor MC's upcoming fiction, and read free sample chapters, at:
http://doctormcmadscientist.wordpress.com/

If you liked this story: **Please go to its Amazon page and write a five-star review. Thank you.**

Appendix 1
The "Theology" of *More Genie Problems*

Introduction: A Mental Challenge

One of the things that is a blast about what I do is world-building. In *The Bimborg*, I decided how the Cybes (evil cyborgs from the future) would work if I were designing imperialist cyborgs from scratch. (As opposed to merely slapping on a name-change to evil cyborgs from that space-opera TV show.)

In *Three More Wishes*, I had even more of a blast. That's because I wrote down every trope of a three-wishes genie story, and I tried to invent in-universe explanations for those tropes. Three wishes, instead of one wish? The three wishes are collectively a test. The genie's eagerness to twist the wording of the wish? It turns out that the genie is not in her lamp by choice, she can't leave, she's pissed, and her master is there to take out her anger on. Rubbing the lamp instead of rapping on the lamp with knuckles? It turns out that any two-handed contact with the lamp will work—rubbing, rapping, or slapping.

But where the story took an interesting turn is when I asked myself in 2009, "Why is this powerful genie stuck in the lamp in the first place?" The following conversation with myself took place right after I asked that question—

Doctor MC 1: The usual explanation for why the genie is in the lamp is that a powerful human sorcerer captured the djinni and shoved her into that lamp.

Doctor MC 2: That's [ridiculous]. A sorcerer powerful enough to capture a <u>djinni</u> is powerful enough to give himself whatever the <u>djinni</u> could give him in a coerced wish-grant. No, this <u>djinni</u> was stuck in her lamp by a more powerful being— who ain't human, because no human is more powerful than any <u>djinni</u>.

Doctor MC 1: Who's more powerful than a <u>djinni</u>?

Doctor MC 2: That's easy: God.

Doctor MC 1: Why would God stick a <u>djinni</u> into a lamp?

Doctor MC 2: Hm, God stuck this <u>djinni</u> into a lamp to prevent a nasty war among <u>djinn</u>.

Folks, this explanation fostered two sequels. In *One More Genie*, I wrote an evil *djinni* trying to start the supposedly-prevented *Djinn* War; in *More Genie Problems*, Marvin Harper gets sucked into things of God.

So how do "things of God" work in the universe of Marvin Harper and Fatima?

****

The MOREverse, a.k.a. Fatima's universe

If you dig down into Christian theology and Moslem theology, you find that they are oil and water. But since Christian teachings are what I'm most familiar with, in order for *More Genie Problems* to be written at all, I had to combine Christian teachings and Moslem teachings—which like I said, cannot be combined.

My solution in this book, as with the two previous books, was to skip mentioning religious details. In the entire trilogy, no alternate name for "God" was ever given, except "the God of Heaven." God was not called *Jehovah*, *Yahweh*, or *Allah*. Jesus was never mentioned in the trilogy, and Mohammed was never mentioned. I quoted very few Scripture verses.

Since I was not trying to conform my story to any religion's doctrine—this ain't *Left Behind*, folks—I was free to color outside the lines when it came to gods and religion. In two chapters, I use war gods from four different mythology pantheons; and in one chapter, Marvin has sex with the goddess Venus.

In short: No matter whether you're hardcore Christian or hardcore Moslem, *More Genie Problems* is blasphemous. But I don't apologize for this, because this way, I wrote a better story.

*****

Judgment Day in the MOREverse

First, a definition: a *regional god* is a god from some mythology pantheon.

In the MOREverse—

Humans have souls, and are mortal and magicless. *Djinn* have souls, are immortal (with a few causes of death excepted), and are magical. Angels and demons are immortal, soulless, and very magical.

Humans are Judged when they die. A *djinni* also is Judged when (s)he dies, but this is a rare event. At the end of *One More Genie*, only four *djinn* have died since the beginning of the world.

Good humans and good *djinn* are eternally rewarded in Heaven after being Judged. Evil humans and evil *djinn* are sent to Hell after being Judged.

A human's religion in life has no effect on whether (s)he is assigned to Heaven or Hell, or what level of Heaven (s)he is assigned to. Humans and *djinn* are Judged strictly based on their good deeds and their bad deeds.

On Judgment Day, whenever this happens, living humans and *djinn* will be Judged because they have souls; and demons will be Judged because they rebelled. Angels will not be Judged.

Good humans and good *djinn* will be eternally rewarded in Heaven after being Judged on Judgment Day. Evil humans and evil *djinn* will be sent to Hell after being Judged on Judgment Day. Demons will be erased after being Judged on Judgment Day; they will not be sent to Hell. On Judgment Day, Lucifer/Satan will go straight to Hell without Judgment. Angels will not be rewarded on Judgment Day.

A being who is a human, *djinni*, or demon/angel can be killed by a more powerful being, a regional god, or the God of Heaven. Humans and *djinn* who are killed are Judged when they die (see above). Angels or demons who are killed are erased, because they are soulless. Regional gods and the God of Heaven are truly immortal, *but* (if you remember your mythology) regional gods can be eternally imprisoned.

****

Heaven and Hell in the MOREverse

Bishop James Ussher figured out that God created the world in 4004 B.C. I took a chart estimating world population at various times, and I estimated that the number of humans since 4004 B.C. who lived to adulthood, plus the number of humans who died in childhood, plus the number of humans who died in infancy, plus the number of humans who died as miscarried fetuses, added up to be between a hundred billion and a trillion humans.

As a result, the MOREverse Heaven and Hell are each designed to hold *one trillion* souls, with the ability to expand as needed. The Lake of Fire has about as much surface area as all of Earth's oceans. Heaven, the deep-space spherical space station with artificial reverse-direction gravity, is bigger in diameter than Earth.

****

Fate, Destiny, and genie Vessels in the MOREverse

Every human character has a Date of Fated Death (DOFD). The cause of death and the exact time of death can be changed, but the certainty of death on this day cannot be changed. If a genie-master figured out that he would die in an airplane crash tomorrow and so he did not fly on that airplane, tomorrow he would be killed in a drive-by shooting or someone would drop a piano on his head.

On the other hand, a human cannot be killed before his DOFD. In 2014, Vinnie Lavagetto tried to shoot Marvin dead; Marvin's DOFD was not until 2068, and so Vinnie's gun jammed.

An individual *djinni* normally cannot change a human's DOFD. An angel or demon, a regional god, or the God of Heaven can change a human's DOFD. However, a bound *djinni*, while granting a wish, has the authority to extend a human's DOFD by 120 lunar cycles.

A genie-master, when he is close to his DOFD, is compelled to either give his genie's Vessel to someone that the genie-master trusts; or else the genie-master must hide the Vessel where it *seems* impossible that anyone will ever find it.

Note that in the second case, it cannot *be* impossible that the Vessel ever be found. A genie-master feels a sense of "wrongness" if he considers shoving the Vessel into wet cement, or tossing the Vessel into the ocean.

After months, years, or centuries of a Vessel being hidden, God jiggles events so that the hidden-away Vessel is found. God chooses who the next genie-master is, and chooses when (s)he finds the Vessel, but God's selection-process is inscrutable. To humans, it seems to be entirely by chance whether a nice guy or a rat bastard finds the Vessel.

Other than regarding DOFD, and a few selected humans finding genie Vessels, all human activity is by free will. In short, most of the time, the God of Heaven does not make anybody do anything.

****

If you enjoyed this book

If you enjoy soft-core porn with an admirable male hero, angels, and demons (including succubi), I praise *Natural Consequences* by Elliott Kay.